×25.90
12/18/09

THE REIGN OF GREED

JOSÉ RIZAL

THE REIGN OF GREED

A Complete English Version of
El Filibusterismo from the Spanish of
José Rizal
by
Charles Derbyshire

BIBLIOBAZAAR

THE REIGN OF GREED

TRANSLATOR'S INTRODUCTION

El Filibusterismo, the second of José Rizal's novels of Philippine life, is a story of the last days of the Spanish régime in the Philippines. Under the name of *The Reign of Greed* it is for the first time translated into English. Written some four or five years after *Noli Me Tangere*, the book represents Rizal's more mature judgment on political and social conditions in the islands, and in its graver and less hopeful tone reflects the disappointments and discouragements which he had encountered in his efforts to lead the way to reform. Rizal's dedication to the first edition is of special interest, as the writing of it was one of the grounds of accusation against him when he was condemned to death in 1896. It reads:

"To the memory of the priests, Don Mariano Gomez (85 years old), Don José Burgos (30 years old), and Don Jacinto Zamora (35 years old). Executed in Bagumbayan Field on the 28th of February, 1872.

"The Church, by refusing to degrade you, has placed in doubt the crime that has been imputed to you; the Government, by surrounding your trials with mystery and shadows, causes the belief that there was some error, committed in fatal moments; and all the Philippines, by worshiping your memory and calling you martyrs, in no sense recognizes your culpability. In so far, therefore, as your complicity in the Cavite mutiny is not clearly proved, as you may or may not have been patriots, and as you may or may not have cherished sentiments for justice and for liberty, I have the right to dedicate my work to you as victims of the evil which I undertake to combat. And while we await expectantly upon Spain some day to restore your good name and cease to be answerable for your death, let these pages serve as a tardy wreath of dried leaves over your unknown tombs, and let it be understood that every one who without clear proofs attacks your memory stains his hands in your blood!

J. Rizal."

A brief recapitulation of the story in *Noli Me Tangere* (The Social Cancer) is essential to an understanding of such plot as there is in the present work, which the author called a "continuation" of the first story.

Juan Crisostomo Ibarra is a young Filipino, who, after studying for seven years in Europe, returns to his native land to find that his father, a wealthy landowner, has died in prison as the result of a quarrel with the parish curate, a Franciscan friar named Padre Damaso. Ibarra is engaged to a beautiful and accomplished girl, Maria Clara, the supposed daughter and only child of the rich Don Santiago de los Santos, commonly known as "Capitan Tiago," a typical Filipino cacique, the predominant character fostered by the friar régime.

Ibarra resolves to forego all quarrels and to work for the betterment of his people. To show his good intentions, he seeks to establish, at his own expense, a public school in his native town. He meets with ostensible support from all, especially Padre Damaso's successor, a young and gloomy Franciscan named Padre Salvi, for whom Maria Clara confesses to an instinctive dread.

At the laying of the corner-stone for the new schoolhouse a suspicious accident, apparently aimed at Ibarra's life, occurs, but the festivities proceed until the dinner, where Ibarra is grossly and wantonly insulted over the memory of his father by Fray Damaso. The young man loses control of himself and is about to kill the friar, who is saved by the intervention of Maria Clara.

Ibarra is excommunicated, and Capitan Tiago, through his fear of the friars, is forced to break the engagement and agree to the marriage of Maria Clara with a young and inoffensive Spaniard provided by Padre Damaso. Obedient to her reputed father's command and influenced by her mysterious dread of Padre Salvi, Maria Clara consents to this arrangement, but becomes seriously ill, only to be saved by medicines sent secretly by Ibarra and clandestinely administered by a girl friend.

Ibarra succeeds in having the excommunication removed, but before he can explain matters an uprising against the Civil Guard is secretly brought about through agents of Padre Salvi, and the leadership is ascribed to Ibarra to ruin him. He is warned by a mysterious friend, an outlaw called Elias, whose life he had accidentally saved; but desiring first to see Maria Clara, he refuses to make his escape, and when the outbreak [viii] occurs he is arrested as the instigator of it and thrown into prison in Manila.

On the evening when Capitan Tiago gives a ball in his Manila house to celebrate his supposed daughter's engagement, Ibarra makes his escape from prison and succeeds in seeing Maria Clara alone. He begins to reproach her because it is a letter written to her before he went to Europe which forms the basis of the charge against him, but she clears herself of treachery to him. The letter had been secured from her by false representations and in exchange for two others written by her mother just before her birth, which prove that Padre Damaso is her real father. These letters had been accidentally discovered in the convento by Padre Salvi, who made use of them to intimidate the girl and get possession of Ibarra's letter, from which he forged others to incriminate the young man. She tells him that she will marry the young Spaniard, sacrificing herself thus to save her mother's name and Capitan Tiago's honor and to prevent a public scandal, but that she will always remain true to him.

Ibarra's escape had been effected by Elias, who conveys him in a banka up the Pasig to the Lake, where they are so closely beset by the Civil Guard that Elias leaps into the water and draws the pursuers away from the boat, in which Ibarra lies concealed.

On Christmas Eve, at the tomb of the Ibarras in a gloomy wood, Elias appears, wounded and dying, to find there a boy named Basilio beside the corpse of his mother, a poor woman who had been driven to insanity by her husband's neglect and abuses on the part of the Civil Guard, her younger son having disappeared some time before in the convento, where he was a sacristan. Basilio, who is ignorant of Elias's identity, helps him to build a funeral pyre, on which his corpse and the madwoman's are to be burned.

Upon learning of the reported death of Ibarra in the chase on the Lake, Maria Clara becomes disconsolate and begs her supposed godfather, Fray Damaso, to put her in a nunnery. Unconscious of her knowledge of their true relationship, the friar breaks down and confesses that all the trouble he has stirred up with the Ibarras has been to prevent her from marrying a native, which would condemn her and her children to the oppressed and enslaved class. He finally yields to her entreaties and she enters the nunnery of St. Clara, to which Padre Salvi is soon assigned in a ministerial capacity.

O masters, lords, and rulers in all lands,
Is this the handiwork you give to God,
This monstrous thing distorted and soul-quenched?
How will you ever straighten up this shape-;
Touch it again with immortality;
Give back the upward looking and the light;
Rebuild in it the music and the dream;
Make right the immemorial infamies,
Perfidious wrongs, immedicable woes?

O masters, lords, and rulers in all lands,
How will the future reckon with this man?
How answer his brute question in that hour
When whirlwinds of rebellion shake the world?
How will it be with kingdoms and with kings—
With those who shaped him to the thing he is—
When this dumb terror shall reply to God,
After the silence of the centuries?

Edwin Markham

CONTENTS

ON THE UPPER DECK

Sic itur ad astra.

One morning in December the steamer *Tabo* was laboriously ascending the tortuous course of the Pasig, carrying a large crowd of passengers toward the province of La Laguna. She was a heavily built steamer, almost round, like the *tabú* from which she derived her name, quite dirty in spite of her pretensions to whiteness, majestic and grave from her leisurely motion. Altogether, she was held in great affection in that region, perhaps from her Tagalog name, or from the fact that she bore the characteristic impress of things in the country, representing something like a triumph over progress, a steamer that was not a steamer at all, an organism, stolid, imperfect yet unimpeachable, which, when it wished to pose as being rankly progressive, proudly contented itself with putting on a fresh coat of paint. Indeed, the happy steamer was genuinely Filipino! If a person were only reasonably considerate, she might even have been taken for the Ship of State, constructed, as she had been, under the inspection of *Reverendos* and *Ilustrísimos* . . .

Bathed in the sunlight of a morning that made the waters of the river sparkle and the breezes rustle in the bending bamboo on its banks, there she goes with her white silhouette throwing out great clouds of smoke—the Ship of State, so the joke runs, also has the vice of smoking! The whistle shrieks at every moment, hoarse and commanding like a tyrant who would rule by shouting, so that no one on board can hear his own thoughts. She menaces everything she meets: now she looks as though she would grind to bits the *salambaw*, insecure fishing apparatus which in their movements resemble skeletons of giants saluting an antediluvian tortoise; now she speeds straight toward the clumps of bamboo or against the amphibian structures, *karihan*, or wayside lunch-stands, which, amid *gumamelas* and other flowers, look like indecisive bathers who with their feet already in the water cannot bring themselves to make the final plunge; at times, following a sort of channel marked out in the river by tree-trunks, she moves along with a satisfied air, except when a sudden shock disturbs the passengers and throws them off their balance, all the result of a collision with a sand-bar which no one dreamed was there.

Moreover, if the comparison with the Ship of State is not yet complete, note the arrangement of the passengers. On the lower deck appear brown faces and black heads, types of Indians,' Chinese, and mestizos, wedged in between bales of merchandise and boxes, while there on the upper deck, beneath an awning that protects them from the sun, are seated in comfortable chairs a few passengers dressed in the fashion of Europeans, friars, and government clerks, each with his *puro* cigar, and gazing at the landscape apparently without heeding the efforts of the captain and the sailors to overcome the obstacles in the river.

The captain was a man of kindly aspect, well along in years, an old sailor who in his youth had plunged into far vaster seas, but who now in his age had to exercise much greater attention, care, and vigilance to avoid dangers of a trivial character. And they were the same for each day: the same sand-bars, the same hulk of unwieldy steamer wedged into the same curves, like a corpulent dame in a jammed throng. So, at each moment, the good man had to stop, to back up, to go forward at half speed, sending—now to port, now to starboard—the five sailors equipped with long bamboo poles to give force to the turn the rudder had suggested. He was like a veteran who, after leading men through hazardous campaigns, had in his age become the tutor of a capricious, disobedient, and lazy boy.

Doña Victorina, the only lady seated in the European group, could say whether the *Tabo* was not lazy, disobedient, and capricious—Doña Victorina, who, nervous as ever, was hurling invectives against the cascos, bankas, rafts of coconuts, the Indians paddling about, and even the washerwomen and bathers, who fretted her with their mirth and chatter. Yes, the *Tabo* would move along very well if there were no Indians in the river, no Indians in the country, yes, if there were not a single Indian in the world— regardless of the fact that the helmsmen were Indians, the sailors

Indians, Indians the engineers, Indians ninety-nine per cent, of the passengers, and she herself also an Indian if the rouge were scratched off and her pretentious gown removed. That morning Doña Victorina was more irritated than usual because the members of the group took very little notice of her, reason for which was not lacking; for just consider—there could be found three friars, convinced that the world would move backwards the very day they should take a single step to the right; an indefatigable Don Custodio who was sleeping peacefully, satisfied with his projects; a prolific writer like Ben-Zayb (anagram of Ibañez), who believed that the people of Manila thought because he, Ben-Zayb, was a thinker; a canon like Padre Irene, who added luster to the clergy with his rubicund face, carefully shaven, from which towered a beautiful Jewish nose, and his silken cassock of neat cut and small buttons; and a wealthy jeweler like Simoun, who was reputed to be the adviser and inspirer of all the acts of his Excellency, the Captain-General— just consider the presence there of these pillars *sine quibus non* of the country, seated there in agreeable discourse, showing little sympathy for a renegade Filipina who dyed her hair red! Now wasn't this enough to exhaust the patience of a female Job—a sobriquet Doña Victorina always applied to herself when put out with any one!

The ill-humor of the señora increased every time the captain shouted "Port," "Starboard" to the sailors, who then hastily seized their poles and thrust them against the banks, thus with the strength of their legs and shoulders preventing the steamer from shoving its hull ashore at that particular point. Seen under these circumstances the Ship of State might be said to have been converted from a tortoise into a crab every time any danger threatened.

"But, captain, why don't your stupid steersmen go in that direction?" asked the lady with great indignation.

"Because it's very shallow in the other, señora," answered the captain, deliberately, slowly winking one eye, a little habit which he had cultivated as if to say to his words on their way out, "Slowly, slowly!"

"Half speed! Botheration, half speed!" protested Doña Victorina disdainfully. "Why not full?"

"Because we should then be traveling over those ricefields, señora," replied the imperturbable captain, pursing his lips to indicate the cultivated fields and indulging in two circumspect winks.

This Doña Victorina was well known in the country for her caprices and extravagances. She was often seen in society, where she was tolerated whenever she appeared in the company of her niece, Paulita Gomez, a very beautiful and wealthy orphan, to whom she was a kind of guardian. At a rather advanced age she had married a poor wretch named Don Tiburcio de Espadaña, and at the time we now see her, carried upon herself fifteen years of wedded life, false frizzes, and a half-European costume—for her whole ambition had been to Europeanize herself, with the result that from the ill-omened day of her wedding she had gradually, thanks to her criminal attempts, succeeded in so transforming herself that at the present time Quatrefages and Virchow together could not have told where to classify her among the known races.

Her husband, who had borne all her impositions with the resignation of a fakir through so many years of married life, at last on one luckless day had had his bad half-hour and administered to her a superb whack with his crutch. The surprise of Madam Job at such an inconsistency of character made her insensible to the immediate effects, and only after she had recovered from her astonishment and her husband had fled did she take notice of the pain, then remaining in bed for several days, to the great delight of Paulita, who was very fond of joking and laughing at her aunt. As for her husband, horrified at the impiety of what appeared to him to be a terrific parricide, he took to flight, pursued by the matrimonial furies (two curs and a parrot), with all the speed his lameness permitted, climbed into the first carriage he encountered, jumped into the first banka he saw on the river, and, a Philippine Ulysses, began to wander from town to town, from province to province, from island to island, pursued and persecuted by his bespectacled Calypso, who bored every one that had the misfortune to travel in her company. She had received a report of his being in the province of La Laguna, concealed in one of the towns, so thither she was bound to seduce him back with her dyed frizzes.

Her fellow travelers had taken measures of defense by keeping up among themselves a lively conversation on any topic whatsoever. At that moment the windings and turnings of the river led them to talk about straightening the channel and, as a matter of course, about the port works. Ben-Zayb, the journalist with the countenance of a friar, was disputing with a young friar who in turn had the countenance of an artilleryman. Both were shouting, gesticulating, waving their arms, spreading out their hands, stamping their feet, talking of levels, fish-corrals, the San Mateo River,² of cascos, of Indians, and so on, to the great satisfaction of their listeners and the undisguised disgust of an elderly Franciscan, remarkably thin and withered, and a handsome Dominican about whose lips flitted constantly a scornful smile.

The thin Franciscan, understanding the Dominican's smile, decided to intervene and stop the argument. He was undoubtedly respected, for with a wave of his hand he cut short the speech of both at the moment when the friar-artilleryman was talking about experience and the journalist-friar about scientists.

"Scientists, Ben-Zayb—do you know what they are?" asked the Franciscan in a hollow voice, scarcely stirring in his seat and making only a faint gesture with his skinny hand. "Here you have in the province a bridge, constructed by a brother of ours, which was not completed because the scientists, relying on their theories, condemned it as weak and scarcely safe—yet look, it is the bridge that has withstood all the floods and earthquakes!"³

"That's it, *puñales,* that very thing, that was exactly what I was going to say!" exclaimed the friar-artilleryman, thumping his fists down on the arms of his bamboo chair. "That's it, that bridge and the scientists! That was just what I was going to mention, Padre Salvi—*puñales!*"

Ben-Zayb remained silent, half smiling, either out of respect or because he really did not know what to reply, and yet his was the only thinking head in the Philippines! Padre Irene nodded his approval as he rubbed his long nose.

Padre Salvi, the thin and withered cleric, appeared to be satisfied with such submissiveness and went on in the midst of the silence: "But this does not mean that you may not be as near right as Padre Camorra" (the friar-artilleryman). "The trouble is in the lake—"

"The fact is there isn't a single decent lake in this country," interrupted Doña Victorina, highly indignant, and getting ready for a return to the assault upon the citadel.

The besieged gazed at one another in terror, but with the promptitude of a general, the jeweler Simoun rushed in to the rescue. "The remedy is very simple," he said in a strange accent, a mixture of English and South American. "And I really don't understand why it hasn't occurred to somebody."

All turned to give him careful attention, even the Dominican. The jeweler was a tall, meager, nervous man, very dark, dressed in the English fashion and wearing a pith helmet. Remarkable about him was his long white hair contrasted with a sparse black beard, indicating a mestizo origin. To avoid the glare of the sun he wore constantly a pair of enormous blue goggles, which completely hid his eyes and a portion of his cheeks, thus giving him the aspect of a blind or weak-sighted person. He was standing with his legs apart as if to maintain his balance, with his hands thrust into the pockets of his coat.

"The remedy is very simple," he repeated, "and wouldn't cost a cuarto."

The attention now redoubled, for it was whispered in Manila that this man controlled the Captain-General, and all saw the remedy in process of execution. Even Don Custodio himself turned to listen.

"Dig a canal straight from the source to the mouth of the river, passing through Manila; that is, make a new river-channel and fill up the old Pasig. That would save land, shorten communication, and prevent the formation of sandbars."

The project left all his hearers astounded, accustomed as they were to palliative measures.

"It's a Yankee plan!" observed Ben-Zayb, to ingratiate himself with Simoun, who had spent a long time in North America.

All considered the plan wonderful and so indicated by the movements of their heads. Only Don Custodio, the liberal Don Custodio, owing to his independent position and his high offices, thought it his duty to attack a project that did not emanate from himself—that was a usurpation! He coughed, stroked the ends of his mustache, and with a voice as important as though he were at a formal session of the Ayuntamiento, said, "Excuse me, Señor Simoun, my respected friend, if I should say that I am not of your opinion. It would cost a great deal of money and might perhaps destroy some towns."

"Then destroy them!" rejoined Simoun coldly.

"And the money to pay the laborers?"

"Don't pay them! Use the prisoners and convicts!"

"But there aren't enough, Señor Simoun!"

"Then, if there aren't enough, let all the villagers, the old men, the youths, the boys, work. Instead of the fifteen days of obligatory service, let them work three, four, five months for the State, with the additional obligation that each one provide his own food and tools."

The startled Don Custodio turned his head to see if there was any Indian within ear-shot, but fortunately those nearby were rustics, and the two helmsmen seemed to be very much occupied with the windings of the river.

"But, Señor Simoun—"

"Don't fool yourself, Don Custodio," continued Simoun dryly, "only in this way are great enterprises carried out with small means. Thus were constructed the Pyramids, Lake Moeris, and the Colosseum in Rome. Entire provinces came in from the desert, bringing their tubers to feed on. Old men, youths, and boys labored in transporting stones, hewing them, and carrying them on their shoulders under the direction of the official lash, and afterwards, the survivors returned to their homes or perished in the sands of the desert. Then came other provinces, then others, succeeding one another in the work during years. Thus the task was finished, and now we admire them, we travel, we go to Egypt and to Home, we extol the Pharaohs and the Antonines. Don't fool yourself—the dead remain dead, and might only is considered right by posterity."

"But, Señor Simoun, such measures might provoke uprisings," objected Don Custodio, rather uneasy over the turn the affair had taken.

"Uprisings, ha, ha! Did the Egyptian people ever rebel, I wonder? Did the Jewish prisoners rebel against the pious Titus? Man, I thought you were better informed in history!"

Clearly Simoun was either very presumptuous or disregarded conventionalities! To say to Don Custodio's face that he did not know history! It was enough to make any one lose his temper! So it seemed, for Don Custodio forgot himself and retorted, "But the fact is that you're not among Egyptians or Jews!"

"And these people have rebelled more than once," added the Dominican, somewhat timidly. "In the times when they were forced to transport heavy timbers for the construction of ships, if it hadn't been for the clerics—"

"Those times are far away," answered Simoun, with a laugh even drier than usual. "These islands will never again rebel, no matter how much work and taxes they have. Haven't you lauded to me, Padre Salvi," he added, turning to the Franciscan, "the house and hospital at Los Baños, where his Excellency is at present?"

Padre Salvi gave a nod and looked up, evading the question.

"Well, didn't you tell me that both buildings were constructed by forcing the people to work on them under the whip of a lay-brother? Perhaps that wonderful bridge was built in the same way. Now tell me, did these people rebel?"

"The fact is—they have rebelled before," replied the Dominican, "and *ab actu ad posse valet illatio!*"

"No, no, nothing of the kind," continued Simoun, starting down a hatchway to the cabin. "What's said, is said! And you, Padre Sibyla, don't talk either Latin or nonsense. What are you friars good for if the people can rebel?"

Taking no notice of the replies and protests, Simoun descended the small companionway that led below, repeating disdainfully, "Bosh, bosh!"

Padre Sibyla turned pale; this was the first time that he, Vice-Rector of the University, had ever been credited with nonsense. Don Custodio turned green; at no meeting in which he had ever found himself had he encountered such an adversary.

"An American mulatto!" he fumed.

"A British Indian," observed Ben-Zayb in a low tone.

"An American, I tell you, and shouldn't I know?" retorted Don Custodio in ill-humor. "His Excellency has told me so. He's a jeweler whom the latter knew in Havana, and, as I suspect, the one who got him advancement by lending him money. So to repay him he has had him come here to let him have a chance and increase his fortune by selling diamonds—imitations, who knows? And he so ungrateful, that, after getting money from the Indians, he wishes—huh!" The sentence was concluded by a significant wave of the hand.

No one dared to join in this diatribe. Don Custodio could discredit himself with his Excellency, if he wished, but neither Ben-Zayb, nor Padre Irene, nor Padre Salvi, nor the offended Padre Sibyla had any confidence in the discretion of the others.

"The fact is that this man, being an American, thinks no doubt that we are dealing with the redskins. To talk of these matters on a steamer! Compel, force the people! And he's the very person who advised the expedition to the Carolines and the campaign in Mindanao, which is going to bring us to disgraceful ruin. He's the one who has offered to superintend the building of the cruiser, and I say, what does a jeweler, no matter how rich and learned he may be, know about naval construction?"

All this was spoken by Don Custodio in a guttural tone to his neighbor Ben-Zayb, while he gesticulated, shrugged his shoulders, and from time to time with his looks consulted the others, who were nodding their heads ambiguously. The Canon Irene indulged in a rather equivocal smile, which he half hid with his hand as he rubbed his nose.

"I tell you, Ben-Zayb," continued Don Custodio, slapping the journalist on the arm, "all the trouble comes from not consulting the old-timers here. A project in fine words, and especially with a big appropriation, with an appropriation in round numbers, dazzles, meets with acceptance at once, for this!" Here, in further explanation, he rubbed the tip of his thumb against his middle and forefinger.

"There's something in that, there's something in that," Ben-Zayb thought it his duty to remark, since in his capacity of journalist he had to be informed about everything.

"Now look here, before the port works I presented a project, original, simple, useful, economical, and practicable, for clearing away the bar in the lake, and it hasn't been accepted because there wasn't any of that in it." He repeated the movement of his fingers, shrugged his shoulders, and gazed at the others as though to say, "Have you ever heard of such a misfortune?"

"May we know what it was?" asked several, drawing nearer and giving him their attention. The projects of Don Custodio were as renowned as quacks' specifics.

Don Custodio was on the point of refusing to explain it from resentment at not having found any supporters in his diatribe against Simoun. "When there's no danger, you want me to talk, eh? And when there is, you keep quiet!" he was going to say, but that would cause the loss of a good opportunity, and his project, now that it could not be carried out, might at least be known and admired.

After blowing out two or three puffs of smoke, coughing, and spitting through a scupper, he slapped Ben-Zayb on the thigh and asked, "You've seen ducks?"

"I rather think so—we've hunted them on the lake," answered the surprised journalist.

"No, I'm not talking about wild ducks, I'm talking of the domestic ones, of those that are raised in Pateros and Pasig. Do you know what they feed on?"

Ben-Zayb, the only thinking head, did not know—he was not engaged in that business.

"On snails, man, on snails!" exclaimed Padre Camorra. "One doesn't have to be an Indian to know that; it's sufficient to have eyes!"

"Exactly so, on snails!" repeated Don Custodio, flourishing his forefinger. "And do you know where they get them?"

Again the thinking head did not know.

"Well, if you had been in the country as many years as I have, you would know that they fish them out of the bar itself, where they abound, mixed with the sand."

"Then your project?"

"Well, I'm coming to that. My idea was to compel all the towns round about, near the bar, to raise ducks, and you'll see how they, all by themselves, will deepen the channel by fishing for the snails—no more and no less, no more and no less!"

Here Don Custodio extended his arms and gazed triumphantly at the stupefaction of his hearers—to none of them had occurred such an original idea.

"Will you allow me to write an article about that?" asked Ben-Zayb. "In this country there is so little thinking done—"

"But, Don Custodio," exclaimed Doña Victorina with smirks and grimaces, "if everybody takes to raising ducks the *balot* eggs will become abundant. Ugh, how nasty! Rather, let the bar close up entirely!"

1   The Spanish designation for the Christianized Malay of the Philippines was *indio* (Indian), a term used rather contemptuously, the name *filipino* being generally applied in a restricted sense to the children of Spaniards born in the Islands.—Tr.

2   Now generally known as the Mariquina.—Tr.

3   This bridge, constructed in Lukban under the supervision of a Franciscan friar, was jocularly referred to as the *Puente de Capricho,* being apparently an ignorant blunder in the right direction, since it was declared in an official report made by Spanish engineers in 1852 to conform to no known principle of scientific construction, and yet proved to be strong and durable.—Tr.

4   Don Custodio's gesture indicates money.—Tr.

5   Duck eggs, that are allowed to advance well into the duckling stage, then boiled and eaten. The señora is sneering at a custom among some of her own people.—Tr.

ON THE LOWER DECK

There, below, other scenes were being enacted. Seated on benches or small wooden stools among valises, boxes, and baskets, a few feet from the engines, in the heat of the boilers, amid the human smells and the pestilential odor of oil, were to be seen the great majority of the passengers. Some were silently gazing at the changing scenes along the banks, others were playing cards or conversing in the midst of the scraping of shovels, the roar of the engine, the hiss of escaping steam, the swash of disturbed waters, and the shrieks of the whistle. In one corner, heaped up like corpses, slept, or tried to sleep, a number of Chinese pedlers, seasick, pale, frothing through half-opened lips, and bathed in their copious perspiration. Only a few youths, students for the most part, easily recognizable from their white garments and their confident bearing, made bold to move about from stern to bow, leaping over baskets and boxes, happy in the prospect of the approaching vacation. Now they commented on the movements of the engines, endeavoring to recall forgotten notions of physics, now they surrounded the young schoolgirl or the red-lipped *buyera* with her collar of *sampaguitas,* whispering into their ears words that made them smile and cover their faces with their fans.

Nevertheless, two of them, instead of engaging in these fleeting gallantries, stood in the bow talking with a man, advanced in years, but still vigorous and erect. Both these youths seemed to be well known and respected, to judge from the deference shown them by their fellow passengers. The elder, who was dressed in complete black, was the medical student, Basilio, famous for his successful cures and extraordinary treatments, while the other, taller and more robust, although much younger, was Isagani, one of the poets, or at least rimesters, who that year came from the Atenco,[1] a curious character, ordinarily quite taciturn and uncommunicative.

The man talking with them was the rich Capitan Basilio, who was returning from a business trip to Manila.

"Capitan Tiago is getting along about the same as usual, yes, sir," said the student Basilio, shaking his head. "He won't submit to any treatment. At the advice of *a certain person* he is sending me to San Diego under the pretext of looking after his property, but in reality so that he may be left to smoke his opium with complete liberty."

When the student said *a certain person*, he really meant Padre Irene, a great friend and adviser of Capitan Tiago in his last days.

"Opium is one of the plagues of modern times," replied the capitan with the disdain and indignation of a Roman senator. "The ancients knew about it but never abused it. While the addiction to classical studies lasted—mark this well, young men—opium was used solely as a medicine; and besides, tell me who smoke it the most?—Chinamen, Chinamen who don't understand a word of Latin! Ah, if Capitan Tiago had only devoted himself to Cicero—" Here the most classical disgust painted itself on his carefully-shaven Epicurean face. Isagani regarded him with attention: that gentleman was suffering from nostalgia for antiquity.

"But to get back to this academy of Castilian," Capitan Basilio continued, "I assure you, gentlemen, that you won't materialize it."

"Yes, sir, from day to day we're expecting the permit," replied Isagani. "Padre Irene, whom you may have noticed above, and to whom we've presented a team of bays, has promised it to us. He's on his way now to confer with the General." "That doesn't matter. Padre Sibyla is opposed to it."

"Let him oppose it! That's why he's here on the steamer, in order to—at Los Baños before the General."

And the student Basilio filled out his meaning by going through the pantomime of striking his fists together.

"That's understood," observed Capitan Basilio, smiling. "But even though you get the permit, where'll you get the funds?"

"We have them, sir. Each student has contributed a real."

"But what about the professors?"

"We have them: half Filipinos and half Peninsulars."

"And the house?"

"Makaraig, the wealthy Makaraig, has offered one of his."

Capitan Basilio had to give in; these young men had everything arranged.

"For the rest," he said with a shrug of his shoulders, "it's not altogether bad, it's not a bad idea, and now that you can't know Latin at least you may know Castilian. Here you have another instance, namesake, of how we are going backwards. In our times we learned Latin because our books were in Latin; now you study Latin a little but have no Latin books. On the other hand, your books are in Castilian and that language is not taught—*aetas parentum pejor avis tulit nos nequiores!* as Horace said." With this quotation he moved away majestically, like a Roman emperor.

The youths smiled at each other. "These men of the past," remarked Isagani, "find obstacles for everything. Propose a thing to them and instead of seeing its advantages they only fix their attention on the difficulties. They want everything to come smooth and round as a billiard ball."

"He's right at home with your uncle," observed Basilio.

"They talk of past times. But listen—speaking of uncles, what does yours say about Paulita?"

Isagani blushed. "He preached me a sermon about the choosing of a wife. I answered him that there wasn't in Manila another like her—beautiful, well-bred, an orphan—"

"Very wealthy, elegant, charming, with no defect other than a ridiculous aunt," added Basilio, at which both smiled.

"In regard to the aunt, do you know that she has charged me to look for her husband?"

"Doña Victorina? And you've promised, in order to keep your sweetheart."

"Naturally! But the fact is that her husband is actually hidden—in my uncle's house!"

Both burst into a laugh at this, while Isagani continued: "That's why my uncle, being a conscientious man, won't go on the upper deck, fearful that Doña Victorina will ask him about Don Tiburcio. Just imagine, when Doña Victorina learned that I was a steerage passenger she gazed at me with a disdain that—"

At that moment Simoun came down and, catching sight of the two young men, greeted Basilio in a patronizing tone: "Hello, Don

Basilio, you're off for the vacation? Is the gentleman a townsman of yours?"

Basilio introduced Isagani with the remark that he was not a townsman, but that their homes were not very far apart. Isagani lived on the seashore of the opposite coast. Simoun examined him with such marked attention that he was annoyed, turned squarely around, and faced the jeweler with a provoking stare.

"Well, what is the province like?" the latter asked, turning again to Basilio.

"Why, aren't you familiar with it?"

"How the devil am I to know it when I've never set foot in it? I've been told that it's very poor and doesn't buy jewels."

"We don't buy jewels, because we don't need them," rejoined Isagani dryly, piqued in his provincial pride.

A smile played over Simoun's pallid lips. "Don't be offended, young man," he replied. "I had no bad intentions, but as I've been assured that nearly all the money is in the hands of the native priests, I said to myself: the friars are dying for curacies and the Franciscans are satisfied with the poorest, so when they give them up to the native priests the truth must be that the king's profile is unknown there. But enough of that! Come and have a beer with me and we'll drink to the prosperity of your province."

The youths thanked him, but declined the offer.

"You do wrong," Simoun said to them, visibly taken aback. "Beer is a good thing, and I heard Padre Camorra say this morning that the lack of energy noticeable in this country is due to the great amount of water the inhabitants drink."

Isagani was almost as tall as the jeweler, and at this he drew himself up.

"Then tell Padre Camorra," Basilio hastened to say, while he nudged Isagani slyly, "tell him that if he would drink water instead of wine or beer, perhaps we might all be the gainers and he would not give rise to so much talk."

"And tell him, also," added Isagani, paying no attention to his friend's nudges, "that water is very mild and can be drunk, but that it drowns out the wine and beer and puts out the fire, that heated it becomes steam, and that ruffled it is the ocean, that it once destroyed mankind and made the earth tremble to its foundations!"

Simoun raised his head. Although his looks could not be read through the blue goggles, on the rest of his face surprise might be seen. "Rather a good answer," he said. "But I fear that he might get facetious and ask me when the water will be converted into steam and when into an ocean. Padre Camorra is rather incredulous and is a great wag."

"When the fire heats it, when the rivulets that are now scattered through the steep valleys, forced by fatality, rush together in the abyss that men are digging," replied Isagani.

"No, Señor Simoun," interposed Basilio, changing to a jesting tone, "rather keep in mind the verses of my friend Isagani himself:

'Fire you, you say, and water we,
Then as you wish, so let it be;
But let us live in peace and right,
Nor shall the fire e'er see us fight;
So joined by wisdom's glowing flame,
That without anger, hate, or blame,
We form the steam, the fifth element,
Progress and light, life and movement.'"

"Utopia, Utopia!" responded Simoun dryly. "The engine is about to meet—in the meantime, I'll drink my beer." So, without any word of excuse, he left the two friends.

"But what's the matter with you today that you're so quarrelsome?" asked Basilio.

"Nothing. I don't know why, but that man fills me with horror, fear almost."

"I was nudging you with my elbow. Don't you know that he's called the Brown Cardinal?"

"The Brown Cardinal?"

"Or Black Eminence, as you wish."

"I don't understand."

"Richelieu had a Capuchin adviser who was called the Gray Eminence; well, that's what this man is to the General."

"Really?"

"That's what I've heard from *a certain person*,—who always speaks ill of him behind his back and flatters him to his face."

"Does he also visit Capitan Tiago?"

"From the first day after his arrival, and I'm sure that *a certain person* looks upon him as a rival—in the inheritance. I believe that he's going to see the General about the question of instruction in Castilian."

At that moment Isagani was called away by a servant to his uncle.

On one of the benches at the stern, huddled in among the other passengers, sat a native priest gazing at the landscapes that were successively unfolded to his view. His neighbors made room for him, the men on passing taking off their hats, and the gamblers not daring to set their table near where he was. He said little, but neither smoked nor assumed arrogant airs, nor did he disdain to mingle with the other men, returning the salutes with courtesy and affability as if he felt much honored and very grateful. Although advanced in years, with hair almost completely gray, he appeared to be in vigorous health, and even when seated held his body straight and his head erect, but without pride or arrogance. He differed from the ordinary native priests, few enough indeed, who at that period served merely as coadjutors or administered some curacies temporarily, in a certain self-possession and gravity, like one who was conscious of his personal dignity and the sacredness of his office. A superficial examination of his appearance, if not his white hair, revealed at once that he belonged to another epoch, another generation, when the better young men were not afraid to risk their dignity by becoming priests, when the native clergy looked any friar at all in the face, and when their class, not yet degraded and vilified, called for free men and not slaves, superior intelligences and not servile wills. In his sad and serious features was to be read the serenity of a soul fortified by study and meditation, perhaps tried out by deep moral suffering. This priest was Padre Florentino, Isagani's uncle, and his story is easily told.

Scion of a wealthy and influential family of Manila, of agreeable appearance and cheerful disposition, suited to shine in the world, he had never felt any call to the sacerdotal profession, but by reason of some promises or vows, his mother, after not a few struggles and violent disputes, compelled him to enter the seminary. She was a great friend of the Archbishop, had a will of iron, and was as inexorable as is every devout woman who believes that she is interpreting the will of God. Vainly the young Florentine offered resistance, vainly he begged, vainly he pleaded his love affairs, even provoking scandals: priest he had to become at twenty-five years of age, and priest he became. The Archbishop ordained him, his first mass was celebrated with great pomp, three days were given over to feasting, and his mother died happy and content, leaving him all her fortune.

But in that struggle Florentine received a wound from which he never recovered. Weeks before his first mass the woman he loved, in desperation, married a nobody—a blow the rudest he had ever experienced. He lost his moral energy, life became dull and insupportable. If not his virtue and the respect for his office, that unfortunate love affair saved him from the depths into which the regular orders and secular clergymen both fall in the Philippines. He devoted himself to his parishioners as a duty, and by inclination to the natural sciences.

When the events of seventy-two occurred, he feared that the large income his curacy yielded him would attract attention to him, so, desiring peace above everything, he sought and secured his release, living thereafter as a private individual on his patrimonial estate situated on the Pacific coast. He there adopted his nephew, Isagani, who was reported by the malicious to be his own son by his old sweetheart when she became a widow, and by the more serious and better informed, the natural child of a cousin, a lady in Manila.

The captain of the steamer caught sight of the old priest and insisted that he go to the upper deck, saying, "If you don't do so, the friars will think that you don't want to associate with them."

Padre Florentino had no recourse but to accept, so he summoned his nephew in order to let him know where he was going, and to charge him not to come near the upper deck while he was there. "If the captain notices you, he'll invite you also, and we should then be abusing his kindness."

"My uncle's way!" thought Isagani. "All so that I won't have any reason for talking with Doña Victorina."

1   The Jesuit College in Manila, established in 1859.—Tr.

2   Natives of Spain; to distinguish them from the Filipinos, *i.e.,* descendants of Spaniards born in the Philippines. See Glossary: "Indian."—Tr.

3   It was a common saying among the old Filipinos that the Spaniards (white men) were fire (activity), while they themselves were water (passivity).—Tr.

4   he "liberal" demonstrations in Manila, and the mutiny in the Cavite Arsenal, resulting in the garroting of the three native priests to whom this work was dedicated: the first of a series of fatal mistakes, culminating in the execution of the author, that cost Spain the loyalty of the Filipinos.—Tr.

LEGENDS

Ich weiss nicht was soil es bedeuten
Dass ich so traurig bin!

When Padre Florentino joined the group above, the bad humor provoked by the previous discussion had entirely disappeared. Perhaps their spirits had been raised by the attractive houses of the town of Pasig, or the glasses of sherry they had drunk in preparation for the coming meal, or the prospect of a good breakfast. Whatever the cause, the fact was that they were all laughing and joking, even including the lean Franciscan, although he made little noise and his smiles looked like death-grins.

"Evil times, evil times!" said Padre Sibyla with a laugh.

"Get out, don't say that, Vice-Rector!" responded the Canon Irene, giving the other's chair a shove. "In Hongkong you're doing a fine business, putting up every building that—ha, ha!"

"Tut, tut!" was the reply; "you don't see our expenses, and the tenants on our estates are beginning to complain—"

"Here, enough of complaints, *puñales,* else I'll fall to weeping!" cried Padre Camorra gleefully. "We're not complaining, and we haven't either estates or banking-houses. You know that my Indians are beginning to haggle over the fees and to flash schedules on me! Just look how they cite schedules to me now, and none other than those of the Archbishop Basilio Sancho,[1] as if from his time up to now prices had not risen. Ha, ha, ha! Why should a baptism cost less than a chicken? But I play the deaf man, collect what I can, and never complain. We're not avaricious, are we, Padre Salvi?"

At that moment Simoun's head appeared above the hatchway.

"Well, where've you been keeping yourself?" Don Custodio called to him, having forgotten all about their dispute. "You're missing the prettiest part of the trip!"

"Pshaw!" retorted Simoun, as he ascended, "I've seen so many rivers and landscapes that I'm only interested in those that call up legends."

"As for legends, the Pasig has a few," observed the captain, who did not relish any depreciation of the river where he navigated and earned his livelihood. "Here you have that of *Malapad-na-bato,* a rock sacred before the coming of the Spaniards as the abode of spirits. Afterwards, when the superstition had been dissipated and the rock profaned, it was converted into a nest of tulisanes, since from its crest they easily captured the luckless bankas, which had to contend against both the currents and men. Later, in our time, in spite of human interference, there are still told stories about wrecked bankas, and if on rounding it I didn't steer with my six senses, I'd be smashed against its sides. Then you have another legend, that of Doña Jeronima's cave, which Padre Florentino can relate to you."

"Everybody knows that," remarked Padre Sibyla disdainfully.

But neither Simoun, nor Ben-Zayb, nor Padre Irene, nor Padre Camorra knew it, so they begged for the story, some in jest and others from genuine curiosity. The priest, adopting the tone of burlesque with which some had made their request, began like an old tutor relating a story to children.

"Once upon a time there was a student who had made a promise of marriage to a young woman in his country, but it seems that he failed to remember her. She waited for him faithfully year after year, her youth passed, she grew into middle age, and then one day she heard a report that her old sweetheart was the Archbishop of Manila. Disguising herself as a man, she came round the Cape and presented herself before his grace, demanding the fulfilment of his promise. What she asked was of course impossible, so the Archbishop ordered the preparation of the cave that you may have noticed with its entrance covered and decorated with a curtain of vines. There she lived and died and there she is buried. The legend states that Doña Jeronima was so fat that she had to turn sidewise to get into it. Her fame as an enchantress sprung from her custom of throwing into the river the silver dishes which she used in the

33

sumptuous banquets that were attended by crowds of gentlemen. A net was spread under the water to hold the dishes and thus they were cleaned. It hasn't been twenty years since the river washed the very entrance of the cave, but it has gradually been receding, just as the memory of her is dying out among the people."

"A beautiful legend!" exclaimed Ben-Zayb. "I'm going to write an article about it. It's sentimental!"

Doña Victorina thought of dwelling in such a cave and was about to say so, when Simoun took the floor instead.

"But what's your opinion about that, Padre Salvi?" he asked the Franciscan, who seemed to be absorbed in thought. "Doesn't it seem to you as though his Grace, instead of giving her a cave, ought to have placed her in a nunnery—in St. Clara's, for example? What do you say?"

There was a start of surprise on Padre Sibyla's part to notice that Padre Salvi shuddered and looked askance at Simoun.

"Because it's not a very gallant act," continued Simoun quite naturally, "to give a rocky cliff as a home to one with whose hopes we have trifled. It's hardly religious to expose her thus to temptation, in a cave on the banks of a river—it smacks of nymphs and dryads. It would have been more gallant, more pious, more romantic, more in keeping with the customs of this country, to shut her up in St. Clara's, like a new Eloise, in order to visit and console her from time to time."

"I neither can nor should pass judgment upon the conduct of archbishops," replied the Franciscan sourly.

"But you, who are the ecclesiastical governor, acting in the place of our Archbishop, what would you do if such a case should arise?"

Padre Salvi shrugged his shoulders and calmly responded, "It's not worth while thinking about what can't happen. But speaking of legends, don't overlook the most beautiful, since it is the truest: that of the miracle of St. Nicholas, the ruins of whose church you may have noticed. I'm going to relate it to Señor Simoun, as he probably hasn't heard it. It seems that formerly the river, as well as the lake, was infested with caymans, so huge and voracious that they attacked bankas and upset them with a slap of the tail. Our chronicles relate that one day an infidel Chinaman, who up to that time had refused to be converted, was passing in front of the church, when suddenly the devil presented himself to him in the form of a cayman and upset the banka, in order to devour him and carry him off to hell. Inspired by God, the Chinaman at that moment called upon St. Nicholas and instantly the cayman was changed into a stone. The old people say that in their time the monster could easily be recognized in the pieces of stone that were left, and, for my part, I can assure you that I have clearly made out the head, to judge from which the monster must have been enormously large."

"Marvelous, a marvelous legend!" exclaimed Ben-Zayb. "It's good for an article—the description of the monster, the terror of the Chinaman, the waters of the river, the bamboo brakes. Also, it'll do for a study of comparative religions; because, look you, an infidel Chinaman in great distress invoked exactly the saint that he must know only by hearsay and in whom he did not believe. Here there's no room for the proverb that 'a known evil is preferable to an unknown good.' If I should find myself in China and get caught in such a difficulty, I would invoke the obscurest saint in the calendar before Confucius or Buddha. Whether this is due to the manifest superiority of Catholicism or to the inconsequential and illogical inconsistency in the brains of the yellow race, a profound study of anthropology alone will be able to elucidate."

Ben-Zayb had adopted the tone of a lecturer and was describing circles in the air with his forefinger, priding himself on his imagination, which from the most insignificant facts could deduce so many applications and inferences. But noticing that Simoun was preoccupied and thinking that he was pondering over what he, Ben-Zayb, had just said, he inquired what the jeweler was meditating about.

"About two very important questions," answered Simoun; "two questions that you might add to your article. First, what may have become of the devil on seeing himself suddenly confined within a stone? Did he escape? Did he stay there? Was he crushed? Second, if the petrified animals that I have seen in various European museums may not have been the victims of some antediluvian saint?"

The tone in which the jeweler spoke was so serious, while he rested his forehead on the tip of his forefinger in an attitude of deep meditation, that Padre Camorra responded very gravely, "Who knows, who knows?"

"Since we're busy with legends and are now entering the lake," remarked Padre Sibyla, "the captain must know many—"

At that moment the steamer crossed the bar and the panorama spread out before their eyes was so truly magnificent that all were impressed. In front extended the beautiful lake bordered by green shores and blue mountains, like a huge mirror, framed in emeralds and sapphires, reflecting the sky in its glass. On the right were spread out the low shores, forming bays with graceful curves, and dim there in the distance the crags of Sungay, while in the background rose Makiling, imposing and majestic, crowned with fleecy clouds. On the left lay Talim Island with its curious sweep of hills. A fresh breeze rippled over the wide plain of water.

"By the way, captain," said Ben-Zayb, turning around, "do you know in what part of the lake a certain Guevara, Navarra, or Ibarra, was killed?"

The group looked toward the captain, with the exception of Simoun, who had turned away his head as though to look for something on the shore.

"Ah, yes!" exclaimed Doña Victorina. "Where, captain? Did he leave any tracks in the water?"

The good captain winked several times, an indication that he was annoyed, but reading the request in the eyes of all, took a few steps toward the bow and scanned the shore.

"Look over there," he said in a scarcely audible voice, after making sure that no strangers were near. "According to the officer who conducted the pursuit, Ibarra, upon finding himself surrounded, jumped out of his banka there near the Kinabutasan² and, swimming under water, covered all that distance of more than two miles, saluted by bullets every time that he raised his head to breathe. Over yonder is where they lost track of him, and a little farther on near the shore they discovered something like the color of blood. And now I think of it, it's just thirteen years, day for day, since this happened."

"So that his corpse—" began Ben-Zayb.

"Went to join his father's," replied Padre Sibyla. "Wasn't he also another filibuster, Padre Salvi?"

"That's what might be called cheap funerals, Padre Camorra, eh?" remarked Ben-Zayb.

"I've always said that those who won't pay for expensive funerals are filibusters," rejoined the person addressed, with a merry laugh.

"But what's the matter with you, Señor Simoun?" inquired Ben-Zayb, seeing that the jeweler was motionless and thoughtful. "Are you seasick—an old traveler like you? On such a drop of water as this!"

"I want to tell you," broke in the captain, who had come to hold all those places in great affection, "that you can't call this a drop of water. It's larger than any lake in Switzerland and all those in Spain put together. I've seen old sailors who got seasick here."

---

1   Archbishop of Manila from 1767 to 1787.—Tr.

2   "Between this island (Talim) and Halahala point extends a strait a mile wide and a league long, which the Indians call 'Kinabutasan,' a name that in their language means 'place that was cleft open'; from which it is inferred that in other times the island was joined to the mainland and was separated from it by some severe earthquake, thus leaving this strait: of this there is an old tradition among the Indians."—Fray Martinez de Zuñiga's *Estadismo* (1803).

CABESANG TALES

Those who have read the first part of this story will perhaps remember an old wood-cutter who lived in the depths of the forest. Tandang Selo is still alive, and though his hair has turned completely white, he yet preserves his good health. He no longer hunts or cuts firewood, for his fortunes have improved and he works only at making brooms.

His son Tales (abbreviation of Telesforo) had worked at first on shares on the lands of a capitalist, but later, having become the owner of two carabaos and several hundred pesos, determined to work on his own account, aided by his father, his wife, and his three children. So they cut down and cleared away some thick woods which were situated on the borders of the town and which they believed belonged to no one. During the labors of cleaning and cultivating the new land, the whole family fell ill with malaria and the mother died, along with the eldest daughter, Lucia, in the flower of her age. This, which was the natural consequence of breaking up new soil infested with various kinds of bacteria, they attributed to the anger of the woodland spirit, so they were resigned and went on with their labor, believing him pacified.

But when they began to harvest their first crop a religious corporation, which owned land in the neighboring town, laid claim to the fields, alleging that they fell within their boundaries, and to prove it they at once started to set up their marks. However, the administrator of the religious order left to them, for humanity's sake, the usufruct of the land on condition that they pay a small sum annually—a mere bagatelle, twenty or thirty pesos. Tales, as peaceful a man as could be found, was as much opposed to lawsuits as any one and more submissive to the friars than most people; so, in order not to smash a *palyok* against a *kawali* (as he said, for to him the friars were iron pots and he a clay jar), he had the weakness to yield to their claim, remembering that he did not know Spanish and had no money to pay lawyers.

Besides, Tandang Selo said to him, "Patience! You would spend more in one year of litigation than in ten years of paying what the white padres demand. And perhaps they'll pay you back in masses! Pretend that those thirty pesos had been lost in gambling or had fallen into the water and been swallowed by a cayman."

The harvest was abundant and sold well, so Tales planned to build a wooden house in the barrio of Sagpang, of the town of Tiani, which adjoined San Diego.

Another year passed, bringing another good crop, and for this reason the friars raised the rent to fifty pesos, which Tales paid in order not to quarrel and because he expected to sell his sugar at a good price.

"Patience! Pretend that the cayman has grown some," old Selo consoled him.

That year he at last saw his dream realized: to live in the barrio of Sagpang in a wooden house. The father and grandfather then thought of providing some education for the two children, especially the daughter Juliana, or Juli, as they called her, for she gave promise of being accomplished and beautiful. A boy who was a friend of the family, Basilio, was studying in Manila, and he was of as lowly origin as they.

But this dream seemed destined not to be realized. The first care the community took when they saw the family prospering was to appoint as cabeza de barangay its most industrious member, which left only Tano, the son, who was only fourteen years old. The father was therefore called *Cabesang* Tales and had to order a sack coat, buy a felt hat, and prepare to spend his money. In order to avoid any quarrel with the curate or the government, he settled from his own pocket the shortages in the tax-lists, paying for those who had died or moved away, and he lost considerable time in making the collections and on his trips to the capital.

"Patience! Pretend that the cayman's relatives have joined him," advised Tandang Selo, smiling placidly.

"Next year you'll put on a long skirt and go to Manila to study like the young ladies of the town," Cabesang Tales told his daughter every time he heard her talking of Basilio's progress.

But that next year did not come, and in its stead there was another increase in the rent. Cabesang Tales became serious and scratched his head. The clay jar was giving up all its rice to the iron pot.

When the rent had risen to two hundred pesos, Tales was not content with scratching his head and sighing; he murmured and protested. The friar-administrator then told him that if he could not pay, some one else would be assigned to cultivate that land—many who desired it had offered themselves.

He thought at first that the friar was joking, but the friar was talking seriously, and indicated a servant of his to take possession of the land. Poor Tales turned pale, he felt a buzzing in his ears, he saw in the red mist that rose before his eyes his wife and daughter, pallid, emaciated, dying, victims of the intermittent fevers—then he saw the thick forest converted into productive fields, he saw the stream of sweat watering its furrows, he saw himself plowing under the hot sun, bruising his feet against the stones and roots, while this friar had been driving about in his carriage with the wretch who was to get the land following like a slave behind his master. No, a thousand times, no! First let the fields sink into the depths of the earth and bury them all! Who was this intruder that he should have any right to his land? Had he brought from his own country a single handful of that soil? Had he crooked a single one of his fingers to pull up the roots that ran through it?

Exasperated by the threats of the friar, who tried to uphold his authority at any cost in the presence of the other tenants, Cabesang Tales rebelled and refused to pay a single cuarto, having ever before himself that red mist, saying that he would give up his fields to the first man who could irrigate it with blood drawn from his own veins.

Old Selo, on looking at his son's face, did not dare to mention the cayman, but tried to calm him by talking of clay jars, reminding him that the winner in a lawsuit was left without a shirt to his back.

"We shall all be turned to clay, father, and without shirts we were born," was the reply.

So he resolutely refused to pay or to give up a single span of his land unless the friars should first prove the legality of their claim by exhibiting a title-deed of some kind. As they had none, a lawsuit followed, and Cabesang Tales entered into it, confiding that some at least, if not all, were lovers of justice and respecters of the law.

"I serve and have been serving the King with my money and my services," he said to those who remonstrated with him. "I'm asking for justice and he is obliged to give it to me."

Drawn on by fatality, and as if he had put into play in the lawsuit the whole future of himself and his children, he went on spending his savings to pay lawyers, notaries, and solicitors, not to mention the officials and clerks who exploited his ignorance and his needs. He moved to and fro between the village and the capital, passed his days without eating and his nights without sleeping, while his talk was always about briefs, exhibits, and appeals. There was then seen a struggle such as was never before carried on under the skies of the Philippines: that of a poor Indian, ignorant and friendless, confiding in the justness and righteousness of his cause, fighting against a powerful corporation before which Justice bowed her head, while the judges let fall the scales and surrendered the sword. He fought as tenaciously as the ant which bites when it knows that it is going to be crushed, as does the fly which looks into space only through a pane of glass. Yet the clay jar defying the iron pot and smashing itself into a thousand pieces had in it something impressive—it had the sublimeness of desperation!

On the days when his journeys left him free he patrolled his fields armed with a shotgun, saying that the tulisanes were hovering around and he had need of defending himself in order not to fall into their hands and thus lose his lawsuit. As if to improve his marksmanship, he shot at birds and fruits, even the butterflies, with such accurate aim that the friar-administrator did not dare to go to Sagpang without an escort of civil-guards, while the friar's hireling, who gazed from afar at the threatening figure of Tales wandering over the fields like a sentinel upon the walls, was terror stricken and refused to take the property away from him.

But the local judges and those at the capital, warned by the experience of one of their number who had been summarily dismissed, dared not give him the decision, fearing their own dismissal. Yet they were not really bad men, those judges, they were upright and conscientious, good citizens, excellent fathers, dutiful sons—and they were able to appreciate poor Tales' situation better than Tales himself could. Many of them were versed in the scientific and historical basis of property, they knew that the friars by their own statutes could not own property, but they also knew that to come from far across the sea with an appointment secured with great difficulty, to undertake the duties of the position with the best intentions, and now to lose it because an Indian fancied that justice had to be done on earth as in heaven—that surely was an idea! They had their families and greater needs surely than that Indian: one had a mother to provide for, and what duty is more sacred than that of caring for a mother? Another had sisters, all of marriageable age; that other there had many little children who expected their daily bread and who, like fledglings in a nest, would surely die of hunger the day he was out of a job; even the very least of them had there, far away, a wife who would be in distress if the monthly remittance failed. All these moral and conscientious judges tried everything in their power in the way of counsel, advising Cabesang Tales to pay the rent demanded. But Tales, like all simple souls, once he had seen what was just, went straight toward it. He demanded proofs, documents, papers, title-deeds, but the friars had none of these, resting their case on his concessions in the past.

Cabesang Tales' constant reply was: "If every day I give alms to a beggar to escape annoyance, who will oblige me to continue my gifts if he abuses my generosity?"

From this stand no one could draw him, nor were there any threats that could intimidate him. In vain Governor M—made a trip expressly to talk to him and frighten him. His reply to it all was: "You may do what you like, Mr. Governor, I'm ignorant and powerless. But I've cultivated those fields, my wife and daughter died while helping me clear them, and I won't give them up to any one but him who can do more with them than I've done. Let him first irrigate them with his blood and bury in them his wife and daughter!"

The upshot of this obstinacy was that the honorable judges gave the decision to the friars, and everybody laughed at him, saying that lawsuits are not won by justice. But Cabesang Tales appealed, loaded his shotgun, and patrolled his fields with deliberation.

During this period his life seemed to be a wild dream. His son, Tano, a youth as tall as his father and as good as his sister, was conscripted, but he let the boy go rather than purchase a substitute.

"I have to pay the lawyers," he told his weeping daughter. "If I win the case I'll find a way to get him back, and if I lose it I won't have any need for sons."

So the son went away and nothing more was heard of him except that his hair had been cropped and that he slept under a cart. Six months later it was rumored that he had been seen embarking for the Carolines; another report was that he had been seen in the uniform of the Civil Guard.

"Tano in the Civil Guard! *'Susmariosep!*'" exclaimed several, clasping their hands. "Tano, who was so good and so honest! *Requimternam!*"

The grandfather went many days without speaking to the father, Juli fell sick, but Cabesang Tales did not shed a single tear, although for two days he never left the house, as if he feared the looks of reproach from the whole village or that he would be called the executioner of his son. But on the third day he again sallied forth with his shotgun.

Murderous intentions were attributed to him, and there were well-meaning persons who whispered about that he had been heard to threaten that he would bury the friar-administrator in the furrows of his fields, whereat the friar was frightened at him in earnest. As a result of this, there came a decree from the Captain-General forbidding the use of firearms and ordering that they be taken up. Cabesang Tales had to hand over his shotgun but he continued his rounds armed with a long bolo.

"What are you going to do with that bolo when the tulisanes have firearms?" old Selo asked him.

"I must watch my crops," was the answer. "Every stalk of cane growing there is one of my wife's bones."

The bolo was taken up on the pretext that it was too long. He then took his father's old ax and with it on his shoulder continued his sullen rounds.

Every time he left the house Tandang Selo and Juli trembled for his life. The latter would get up from her loom, go to the window, pray, make vows to the saints, and recite novenas. The grandfather was at times unable to finish the handle of a broom and talked of returning to the forest—life in that house was unbearable.

At last their fears were realized. As the fields were some distance from the village, Cabesang Tales, in spite of his ax, fell into the hands of tulisanes who had revolvers and rifles. They told him that since he had money to pay judges and lawyers he must have some also for the outcasts and the hunted. They therefore demanded a ransom of five hundred pesos through the medium of a rustic, with the warning that if anything happened to their messenger, the captive would pay for it with his life. Two days of grace were allowed.

This news threw the poor family into the wildest terror, which was augmented when they learned that the Civil Guard was going out in pursuit of the bandits. In case of an encounter, the first victim would be the captive—this they all knew. The old man was paralyzed, while the pale and frightened daughter tried often to talk but could not. Still, another thought more terrible, an idea more cruel, roused them from their stupor. The rustic sent by the tulisanes said that the band would probably have to move on, and if they were slow in sending the ransom the two days would elapse and Cabesang Tales would have his throat cut.

This drove those two beings to madness, weak and powerless as they were. Tandang Selo got up, sat down, went outside, came back again, knowing not where to go, where to seek aid. Juli appealed to her images, counted and recounted her money, but her two hundred pesos did not increase or multiply. Soon she dressed herself, gathered together all her jewels, and asked the advice of her grandfather, if she should go to see the gobernadorcillo, the judge, the notary, the lieutenant of the Civil Guard. The old man said yes to everything, or when she said no, he too said no. At length came the neighbors, their relatives and friends, some poorer than others, in their simplicity magnifying the fears. The most active of all was Sister Bali, a great *panguinguera,* who had been to Manila to practise religious exercises in the nunnery of the Sodality.

Juli was willing to sell all her jewels, except a locket set with diamonds and emeralds which Basilio had given her, for this locket had a history: a nun, the daughter of Capitan Tiago, had given it to a leper, who, in return for professional treatment, had made a present of it to Basilio. So she could not sell it without first consulting him.

Quickly the shell-combs and earrings were sold, as well as Juli's rosary, to their richest neighbor, and thus fifty pesos were added, but two hundred and fifty were still lacking. The locket might be pawned, but Juli shook her head. A neighbor suggested that the house be sold and Tandang Selo approved the idea, satisfied to return to the forest and cut firewood as of old, but Sister Bali observed that this could not be done because the owner was not present.

"The judge's wife once sold me her *tapis* for a peso, but her husband said that the sale did not hold because it hadn't received his approval. *Abá!* He took back the *tapis* and she hasn't returned the peso yet, but I don't pay her when she wins at *panguingui, abá!* In that way I've collected twelve cuartos, and for that alone I'm going to play with her. I can't bear to have people fail to pay what they owe me, *abá!*"

Another neighbor was going to ask Sister Bali why then did not she settle a little account with her, but the quick *panguinguera* suspected this and added at once: "Do you know, Juli, what you can do? Borrow two hundred and fifty pesos on the house, payable when the lawsuit is won."

This seemed to be the best proposition, so they decided to act upon it that same day. Sister Bali offered to accompany her, and together they visited the houses of all the rich folks in Tiani, but no one would accept the proposal. The case, they said, was already lost, and to show favors to an enemy of the friars was to expose themselves to their vengeance. At last a pious woman took pity on the girl and lent the money on condition that Juli should remain with her as a servant until the debt was paid. Juli would not have so very much to do: sew, pray, accompany her to mass, and fast for her now and then. The girl accepted with tears in her eyes, received the money, and promised to enter her service on the following day, Christmas.

When the grandfather heard of that sale he fell to weeping like a child. What, that granddaughter whom he had not allowed to walk in the sun lest her skin should be burned, Juli, she of the delicate fingers and rosy feet! What, that girl, the prettiest in the village and perhaps in the whole town, before whose window many gallants had vainly passed the night playing and singing! What, his only granddaughter, the sole joy of his fading eyes, she whom he had dreamed of seeing dressed in a long skirt, talking Spanish, and holding herself erect waving a painted fan like the daughters of the wealthy—she to become a servant, to be scolded and reprimanded, to ruin her fingers, to sleep anywhere, to rise in any manner whatsoever!

So the old grandfather wept and talked of hanging or starving himself to death. "If you go," he declared, "I'm going back to the forest and will never set foot in the town."

Juli soothed him by saying that it was necessary for her father to return, that the suit would be won, and they could then ransom her from her servitude.

The night was a sad one. Neither of the two could taste a bite and the old man refused to lie down, passing the whole night seated in a corner, silent and motionless. Juli on her part tried to sleep, but for a long time could not close her eyes. Somewhat relieved about her father's fate, she now thought of herself and fell to weeping, but stifled her sobs so that the old man might not hear them. The next day she would be a servant, and it was the very day Basilio was accustomed to come from Manila with presents for her. Henceforward she would have to give up that love; Basilio, who was going to be a doctor, couldn't marry a pauper. In fancy she saw him going to the church in company with the prettiest and richest girl in the town, both well-dressed, happy and smiling, while she, Juli, followed her mistress, carrying novenas, buyos, and the cuspidor. Here the girl felt a lump rise in her throat, a sinking at her heart, and begged the Virgin to let her die first.

But—said her conscience—he will at least know that I preferred to pawn myself rather than the locket he gave me.

This thought consoled her a little and brought on empty dreams. Who knows but that a miracle might happen? She might find the two hundred and fifty pesos under the image of the Virgin—she had read of many similar miracles. The sun might not rise nor morning come, and meanwhile the suit would be won. Her father might return, or Basilio put in his appearance, she might find a bag of gold in the garden, the tulisanes would send the bag of gold, the curate, Padre Camorra, who was always teasing her, would come with the tulisanes. So her ideas became more and more confused, until at length, worn out by fatigue and sorrow, she went to sleep with dreams of her childhood in the depths of the forest:

she was bathing in the torrent along with her two brothers, there were little fishes of all colors that let themselves be caught like fools, and she became impatient because she found no pleasure in catchnig such foolish little fishes! Basilio was under the water, but Basilio for some reason had the face of her brother Tano. Her new mistress was watching them from the bank.

---

1   The reference is to the novel *Noli Me Tangere* (*The Social Cancer*), the author's first work, of which, the present is in a way a continuation.—Tr.

A COCHERO'S CHRISTMAS EVE

Basilio reached San Diego just as the Christmas Eve procession was passing through the streets. He had been delayed on the road for several hours because the cochero, having forgotten his cedula, was held up by the Civil Guard, had his memory jogged by a few blows from a rifle-butt, and afterwards was taken before the commandant. Now the carromata was again detained to let the procession pass, while the abused cochero took off his hat reverently and recited a paternoster to the first image that came along, which seemed to be that of a great saint. It was the figure of an old man with an exceptionally long beard, seated at the edge of a grave under a tree filled with all kinds of stuffed birds. A *kalan* with a clay jar, a mortar, and a *kalikut* for mashing buyo were his only utensils, as if to indicate that he lived on the border of the tomb and was doing his cooking there. This was the Methuselah of the religious iconography of the Philippines; his colleague and perhaps contemporary is called in Europe Santa Claus, and is still more smiling and agreeable.

"In the time of the saints," thought the cochero, "surely there were no civil-guards, because one can't live long on blows from rifle-butts."

Behind the great old man came the three Magian Kings on ponies that were capering about, especially that of the negro Melchior, which seemed to be about to trample its companions.

"No, there couldn't have been any civil-guards," decided the cochero, secretly envying those fortunate times, "because if there had been, that negro who is cutting up such capers beside those two Spaniards"—Gaspar and Bathazar—"would have gone to jail."

Then, observing that the negro wore a crown and was a king, like the other two, the Spaniards, his thoughts naturally turned to the king of the Indians, and he sighed. "Do you know, sir," he asked Basilio respectfully, "if his right foot is loose yet?"

Basilio had him repeat the question. "Whose right foot?"

"The King's!" whispered the cochero mysteriously.

"What King's?"

"Our King's, the King of the Indians."

Basilio smiled and shrugged his shoulders, while the cochero again sighed. The Indians in the country places preserve the legend that their king, imprisoned and chained in the cave of San Mateo, will come some day to free them. Every hundredth year he breaks one of his chains, so that he now has his hands and his left foot loose—only the right foot remains bound. This king causes the earthquakes when he struggles or stirs himself, and he is so strong that in shaking hands with him it is necessary to extend to him a bone, which he crushes in his grasp. For some unexplainable reason the Indians call him King Bernardo, perhaps by confusing him with Bernardo del Carpio.[1]

"When he gets his right foot loose," muttered the cochero, stifling another sigh, "I'll give him my horses, and offer him my services even to death, for he'll free us from the Civil Guard." With a melancholy gaze he watched the Three Kings move on.

The boys came behind in two files, sad and serious as though they were there under compulsion. They lighted their way, some with torches, others with tapers, and others with paper lanterns on bamboo poles, while they recited the rosary at the top of their voices, as though quarreling with somebody. Afterwards came St. Joseph on a modest float, with a look of sadness and resignation on his face, carrying his stalk of lilies, as he moved along between two civil-guards as though he were a prisoner. This enabled the cochero to understand the expression on the saint's face, but whether the sight of the guards troubled him or he had no great respect for a saint who would travel in such company, he did not recite a single requiem.

Behind St. Joseph came the girls bearing lights, their heads covered with handkerchiefs knotted under their chins, also reciting the rosary, but with less wrath than the boys. In their midst were to be seen several lads dragging along little rabbits made of Japanese paper, lighted by red candles, with their short paper tails erect. The lads brought those toys into the procession to enliven the birth of the Messiah. The little animals, fat and round as eggs, seemed to be so pleased that at times they would take a leap, lose their balance, fall, and catch fire. The owner would then hasten to extinguish such burning enthusiasm, puffing and blowing until he finally beat out the fire, and then, seeing his toy destroyed, would fall to weeping. The cochero observed with sadness that the race of little paper animals disappeared each year, as if they had been attacked by the pest like the living animals. He, the abused Sinong, remembered his two magnificent horses, which, at the advice of the curate, he had caused to be blessed to save them from plague, spending therefor ten pesos —for neither the government nor the curates have found any better remedy for the epizootic—and they had died after all. Yet he consoled himself by remembering also that after the shower of holy water, the Latin phrases of the padre, and the ceremonies, the horses had become so vain and self-important that they would not even allow him, Sinong, a good Christian, to put them in harness, and he had not dared to whip them, because a tertiary sister had said that they were *sanctified*.

The procession was closed by the Virgin dressed as the Divine Shepherd, with a pilgrim's hat of wide brim and long plumes to indicate the journey to Jerusalem. That the birth might be made more explicable, the curate had ordered her figure to be stuffed with rags and cotton under her skirt, so that no one could be in any doubt as to her condition. It was a very beautiful image, with the same sad expression of all the images that the Filipinos make, and a mien somewhat ashamed, doubtless at the way in which the curate had arranged her. In front came several singers and behind, some musicians with the usual civil-guards. The curate, as was to be expected after what he had done, was not in his place, for that year he was greatly displeased at having to use all his diplomacy and shrewdness to convince the townspeople that they should pay thirty pesos for each Christmas mass instead of the usual twenty. "You're turning filibusters!" he had said to them.

The cochero must have been greatly preoccupied with the sights of the procession, for when it had passed and Basilio ordered him to go on, he did not notice that the lamp on his carromata had gone out. Neither did Basilio notice it, his attention being devoted to gazing at the houses, which were illuminated inside and out with little paper lanterns of fantastic shapes and colors, stars surrounded by hoops with long streamers which produced a pleasant murmur when shaken by the wind, and fishes of movable heads and tails, having a glass of oil inside, suspended from the eaves of the windows in the delightful fashion of a happy and homelike fiesta. But he also noticed that the lights were flickering, that the stars were being eclipsed, that this year had fewer ornaments and hangings than the former, which in turn had had even fewer than the year preceding it. There was scarcely any music in the streets, while the agreeable noises of the kitchen were not to be heard in all the houses, which the youth ascribed to the fact that for some time things had been going badly, the sugar did not bring a good price, the rice crops had failed, over half the live stock had died, but the taxes rose and increased for some inexplicable reason, while the abuses of the Civil Guard became more frequent to kill off the happiness of the people in the towns.

He was just pondering over this when an energetic "Halt!" resounded. They were passing in front of the barracks and one of the guards had noticed the extinguished lamp of the carromata, which could not go on without it. A hail of insults fell about the poor cochero, who vainly excused himself with the length of the procession. He would be arrested for violating the ordinances and afterwards advertised in the newspapers, so the peaceful and prudent Basilio left the carromata and went his way on foot, carrying his valise. This was San Diego, his native town, where he had not a single relative.

The only house wherein there seemed to be any mirth was Capitan Basilio's. Hens and chickens cackled their death chant to the accompaniment of dry and repeated strokes, as of meat pounded on a chopping-block, and the sizzling of grease in the frying-pans. A feast was going on in the house, and even into the street there passed a certain draught of air, saturated with the succulent odors of stews and confections. In the entresol Basilio saw Sinang, as small as when our readers knew her before, although a little rounder and plumper since her marriage. Then to his great surprise he made out, further in at the back of the room, chatting with Capitan Basilio, the curate, and the alferez of the Civil Guard, no less than the jeweler Simoun, as ever with his blue goggles and his nonchalant air.

"It's understood, Señor Simoun," Capitan Basilio was saying, "that we'll go to Tiani to see your jewels."

"I would also go," remarked the alferez, "because I need a watch-chain, but I'm so busy—if Capitan Basilio would undertake—"

Capitan Basilio would do so with the greatest pleasure, and as he wished to propitiate the soldier in order that he might not be molested in the persons of his laborers, he refused to accept the money which the alferez was trying to get out of his pocket.

"It's my Christmas gift!"

"I can't allow you, Capitan, I can't permit it!"

"All right! We'll settle up afterwards," replied Capitan Basilio with a lordly gesture.

Also, the curate wanted a pair of lady's earrings and requested the capitan to buy them for him. "I want them first class. Later we'll fix up the account."

"Don't worry about that, Padre," said the good man, who wished to be at peace with the Church also. An unfavorable report on the curate's part could do him great damage and cause him double the expense, for those earrings were a forced present. Simoun in the meantime was praising his jewels.

"That fellow is fierce!" mused the student. "He does business everywhere. And if I can believe *a certain person,* he buys from some gentlemen for a half of their value the same jewels that he himself has sold for presents. Everybody in this country prospers but us!"

He made his way to his house, or rather Capitan Tiago's, now occupied by a trustworthy man who had held him in great esteem since the day when he had seen him perform a surgical operation with the same coolness that he would cut up a chicken. This man was now waiting to give him the news. Two of the laborers were prisoners, one was to be deported, and a number of carabaos had died.

"The same old story," exclaimed Basilio, in a bad humor. "You always receive me with the same complaints." The youth was not overbearing, but as he was at times scolded by Capitan Tiago, he liked in his turn to chide those under his orders.

The old man cast about for something new. "One of our tenants has died, the old fellow who took care of the woods, and the curate refused to bury him as a pauper, saying that his master is a rich man."

"What did he die of?"

"Of old age."

"Get out! To die of old age! It must at least have been some disease." Basilio in his zeal for making autopsies wanted diseases.

"Haven't you anything new to tell me? You take away my appetite relating the same old things. Do you know anything of Sagpang?"

The old man then told him about the kidnapping of Cabesang Tales. Basilio became thoughtful and said nothing more—his appetite had completely left him.

---

1   This legend is still current among the Tagalogs. It circulates in various forms, the commonest being that the king was so confined for defying the lightning; and it takes no great stretch of the imagination to fancy in this idea a reference to the firearms used by the Spanish conquerors. Quite recently (January 1909), when the nearly extinct volcano of Banahao shook itself and scattered a few tons of mud over the surrounding landscape, the people thereabout recalled this old legend, saying that it was their King Bernardo making another effort to get that right foot loose.—Tr.

2   The reference is to *Noli Me Tangere,* in which Sinang appears.

BASILIO

When the bells began their chimes for the midnight mass and those who preferred a good sleep to fiestas and ceremonies arose grumbling at the noise and movement, Basilio cautiously left the house, took two or three turns through the streets to see that he was not watched or followed, and then made his way by unfrequented paths to the road that led to the ancient wood of the Ibarras, which had been acquired by Capitan Tiago when their property was confiscated and sold. As Christmas fell under the waning moon that year, the place was wrapped in darkness. The chimes had ceased, and only the tolling sounded through the darkness of the night amid the murmur of the breeze-stirred branches and the measured roar of the waves on the neighboring lake, like the deep respiration of nature sunk in profound sleep.

Awed by the time and place, the youth moved along with his head down, as if endeavoring to see through the darkness. But from time to time he raised it to gaze at the stars through the open spaces between the treetops and went forward parting the bushes or tearing away the lianas that obstructed his path. At times he retraced his steps, his foot would get caught among the plants, he stumbled over a projecting root or a fallen log. At the end of a half-hour he reached a small brook on the opposite side of which arose a hillock, a black and shapeless mass that in the darkness took on the proportions of a mountain. Basilio crossed the brook on the stones that showed black against the shining surface of the water, ascended the hill, and made his way to a small space enclosed by old and crumbling walls. He approached the balete tree that rose in the center, huge, mysterious, venerable, formed of roots that extended up and down among the confusedly-interlaced trunks.

Pausing before a heap of stones he took off his hat and seemed to be praying. There his mother was buried, and every time he came to the town his first visit was to that neglected and unknown grave. Since he must visit Cabesang Tales' family the next day, he had taken advantage of the night to perform this duty. Seated on a stone, he seemed to fall into deep thought. His past rose before him like a long black film, rosy at first, then shadowy with spots of blood, then black, black, gray, and then light, ever lighter. The end could not be seen, hidden as it was by a cloud through which shone lights and the hues of dawn.

Thirteen years before to the day, almost to the hour, his mother had died there in the deepest distress, on a glorious night when the moon shone brightly and the Christians of the world were engaged in rejoicing. Wounded and limping, he had reached there in pursuit of her—she mad and terrified, fleeing from her son as from a ghost. There she had died, and there had come a stranger who had commanded him to build a funeral pyre. He had obeyed mechanically and when he returned he found a second stranger by the side of the other's corpse. What a night and what a morning those were! The stranger helped him raise the pyre, whereon they burned the corpse of the first, dug the grave in which they buried his mother, and then after giving him some pieces of money told him to leave the place. It was the first time that he had seen that man—tall, with blood-shot eyes, pale lips, and a sharp nose.

Entirely alone in the world, without parents or brothers and sisters, he left the town whose authorities inspired in him such great fear and went to Manila to work in some rich house and study at the same time, as many do. His journey was an Odyssey of sleeplessness and startling surprises, in which hunger counted for little, for he ate the fruits in the woods, whither he retreated whenever he made out from afar the uniform of the Civil Guard, a sight that recalled the origin of all his misfortunes. Once in Manila, ragged and sick, he went from door to door offering his services. A boy from the provinces who knew not a single word of Spanish, and sickly besides! Discouraged, hungry, and miserable, he wandered about the streets, attracting attention by the wretchedness of his clothing. How often was he tempted to throw himself under the feet of the horses that flashed by, drawing carriages shining with silver and varnish, thus to end his misery at once! Fortunately, he saw Capitan Tiago, accompanied by Aunt Isabel. He had known them since the days in San Diego, and in his joy believed that in them he saw almost fellow-townsfolk. He followed the carriage until he lost sight of it, and then made inquiries for the house. As it was the very day that Maria Clara entered the nunnery and Capitan Tiago was accordingly depressed, he was admitted as a servant, without pay, but instead with leave to study, if he so wished, in San Juan de Letran.[1]

Dirty, poorly dressed, with only a pair of clogs for footwear, at the end of several months' stay in Manila, he entered the first year of Latin. On seeing his clothes, his classmates drew away from him, and the professor, a handsome Dominican, never asked him a question, but frowned every time he looked at him. In the eight months that the class continued, the only words that passed between them were his name read from the roll and the daily *adsum* with which the student responded. With what bitterness he left the class each day, and, guessing the reason for the treatment accorded him, what tears sprang into his eyes and what complaints were stifled in his heart! How he had wept and sobbed over the grave of his mother, relating to her his hidden sorrows, humiliations, and affronts, when at the approach of Christmas Capitan Tiago had taken him back to San Diego! Yet he memorized the lessons without omitting a comma, although he understood scarcely any part of them. But at length he became resigned, noticing that among the three or four hundred in his class only about forty merited the honor of being questioned, because they attracted the professor's attention by their appearance, some prank, comicality, or other cause. The greater part of the students congratulated themselves that they thus escaped the work of thinking and understanding the subject. "One goes to college, not to learn and study, but to gain credit for the course, so if the book can be memorized, what more can be asked—the year is thus gained."[2]

Basilio passed the examinations by answering the solitary question asked him, like a machine, without stopping or breathing, and in the amusement of the examiners won the passing certificate. His nine companions—they were examined in batches of ten in order to save time—did not have such good luck, but were condemned to repeat the year of brutalization.

In the second year the game-cock that he tended won a large sum and he received from Capitan Tiago a big tip, which he immediately invested in the purchase of shoes and a felt hat. With these and the clothes given him by his employer, which he made over to fit his person, his appearance became more decent, but did not get beyond that. In such a large class a great deal was needed to attract the professor's attention, and the student who in the first year did not make himself known by some special quality, or did not capture the good-will of the professors, could with difficulty make himself known in the rest of his school-days. But Basilio kept on, for perseverance was his chief trait.

His fortune seemed to change somewhat when he entered the third year. His professor happened to be a very jolly fellow, fond of jokes and of making the students laugh, complacent enough in that he almost always had his favorites recite the lessons—in fact, he was satisfied with anything. At this time Basilio now wore shoes and a clean and well-ironed camisa. As his professor noticed that he laughed very little at the jokes and that his large eyes seemed to be asking something like an eternal question, he took him for a fool, and one day decided to make him conspicuous by calling on him for the lesson. Basilio recited it from beginning to end, without hesitating over a single letter, so the professor called him a parrot and told a story to make the class laugh. Then to increase the hilarity and justify the epithet he asked several questions, at the same time winking to his favorites, as if to say to them, "You'll see how we're going to amuse ourselves."

Basilio now understood Spanish and answered the questions with the plain intention of making no one laugh. This disgusted everybody, the expected absurdity did not materialize, no one could laugh, and the good friar never pardoned him for having defrauded the hopes of the class and disappointed his own prophecies. But who would expect anything worth while to come from a head so badly combed and placed on an Indian poorly shod, classified until recently among the arboreal animals? As in other centers of learning, where the teachers are honestly desirous that the students should learn, such discoveries usually delight the instructors, so in a college managed by men convinced that for the most part knowledge is an evil, at least for the students, the episode of Basilio produced a bad impression and he was not questioned again during the year. Why should he be, when he made no one laugh?

Quite discouraged and thinking of abandoning his studies, he passed to the fourth year of Latin. Why study at all, why not sleep like the others and trust to luck?

One of the two professors was very popular, beloved by all, passing for a sage, a great poet, and a man of advanced ideas. One day when he accompanied the collegians on their walk, he had a dispute with some cadets, which resulted in a skirmish and a challenge. No doubt recalling his brilliant youth, the professor preached a crusade and promised good marks to all who during the promenade on the following Sunday would take part in the fray. The week was a lively one—there were occasional encounters in which canes and sabers were crossed, and in one of these Basilio distinguished himself. Borne in triumph by the students and presented to the professor, he thus became known to him and came to be his favorite. Partly for this reason and partly from his diligence, that year he received the highest marks, medals included, in view of which Capitan Tiago, who, since his daughter had become a nun, exhibited some aversion to the friars, in a fit of good humor induced him to transfer to the Ateneo Municipal, the fame of which was then in its apogee.

Here a new world opened before his eyes—a system of instruction that he had never dreamed of. Except for a few superfluities and some childish things, he was filled with admiration for the methods there used and with gratitude for the zeal of the instructors. His eyes at times filled with tears when he thought of the four previous years during which, from lack of means, he had been unable to study at that center. He had to make extraordinary efforts to get himself to the level of those who had had a good preparatory course, and it might be said that in that one year he learned the whole five of the secondary curricula. He received his bachelor's degree, to the great satisfaction of his instructors, who in the examinations showed themselves to be proud of him before the Dominican examiners sent there to inspect the school. One of these, as if to dampen such great enthusiasm a little, asked him where he had studied the first years of Latin.

"In San Juan de Letran, Padre," answered Basilio.

"Aha! Of course! He's not bad,—in Latin," the Dominican then remarked with a slight smile.

From choice and temperament he selected the course in medicine. Capitan Tiago preferred the law, in order that he might have a lawyer free, but knowledge of the laws is not sufficient to secure clientage in the Philippines—it is necessary to win the cases, and for this friendships are required, influence in certain spheres, a good deal of astuteness. Capitan Tiago finally gave in, remembering that medical students get on intimate terms with corpses, and for some time he had been seeking a poison to put on the gaffs of his game-cocks, the best he had been able to secure thus far being the blood of a Chinaman who had died of syphilis.

With equal diligence, or more if possible, the young man continued this course, and after the third year began to render medical services with such great success that he was not only preparing a brilliant future for himself but also earning enough to dress well and save some money. This was the last year of the course and in two months he would be a physician; he would come back to the town, he would marry Juliana, and they would be happy. The granting of his licentiateship was not only assured, but he expected it to be the crowning act of his school-days, for he had been designated to deliver the valedictory at the graduation, and already he saw himself in the rostrum, before the whole faculty, the object of public attention. All those heads, leaders of Manila science, half-hidden in their colored capes; all the women who came there out of curiosity and who years before had gazed at him, if not with disdain, at least with indifference; all those men whose carriages had once been about to crush him down in the mud like a dog: they would listen attentively, and he was going to say something to them that would not be trivial, something that had never before resounded in that place, he was going to forget himself in order to aid the poor students of the future—and he would make his entrance on his work in the world with that speech.

---

1   The Dominican school of secondary instruction in Manila.—Tr.

2   "The studies of secondary instruction given in Santo Tomas, in the college of San Juan de Letran, and of San José, and in the private schools, had the defects inherent in the plan of instruction which the friars developed in the Philippines. It suited their plans that scientific and literary knowledge should not become general nor very extensive, for which reason they took but little interest in the study of those subjects or in the quality of the instruction. Their educational establishments were places of luxury for the children of wealthy and well-to-do families rather than establishments in which to perfect and develop the minds of the Filipino

youth. It is true they were careful to give them a religious education, tending to make them respect the omnipotent power (*sic*) of the monastic corporations.

"The intellectual powers were made dormant by devoting a greater part of the time to the study of Latin, to which they attached an extraordinary importance, for the purpose of discouraging pupils from studying the exact and experimental sciences and from gaining a knowledge of true literary studies.

"The philosophic system explained was naturally the scholastic one, with an exceedingly refined and subtle logic, and with deficient ideas upon physics. By the study of Latin, and their philosophic systems, they converted their pupils into automatic machines rather than into practical men prepared to battle with life."—*Census of the Philippine Islands (Washington, 1905), Volume III, pp. 601, 602.*

SIMOUN

Over these matters Basilio was pondering as he visited his mother's grave. He was about to start back to the town when he thought he saw a light flickering among the trees and heard the snapping of twigs, the sound of feet, and rustling of leaves. The light disappeared but the noises became more distinct, coming directly toward where he was. Basilio was not naturally superstitious, especially after having carved up so many corpses and watched beside so many death-beds, but the old legends about that ghostly spot, the hour, the darkness, the melancholy sighing of the wind, and certain tales heard in his childhood, asserted their influence over his mind and made his heart beat violently.

The figure stopped on the other side of the balete, but the youth could see it through an open space between two roots that had grown in the course of time to the proportions of tree-trunks. It produced from under its coat a lantern with a powerful reflecting lens, which it placed on the ground, thereby lighting up a pair of riding-boots, the rest of the figure remaining concealed in the darkness. The figure seemed to search its pockets and then bent over to fix a shovel-blade on the end of a stout cane. To his great surprise Basilio thought he could make out some of the features of the jeweler Simoun, who indeed it was.

The jeweler dug in the ground and from time to time the lantern illuminated his face, on which were not now the blue goggles that so completely disguised him. Basilio shuddered: that was the same stranger who thirteen years before had dug his mother's grave there, only now he had aged somewhat, his hair had turned white, he wore a beard and a mustache, but yet his look was the same, the bitter expression, the same cloud on his brow, the same muscular arms, though somewhat thinner now, the same violent energy. Old impressions were stirred in the boy: he seemed to feel the heat of the fire, the hunger, the weariness of that time, the smell of freshly turned earth. Yet his discovery terrified him—that jeweler Simoun, who passed for a British Indian, a Portuguese, an American, a mulatto, the Brown Cardinal, his Black Eminence, the evil genius of the Captain-General as many called him, was no other than the mysterious stranger whose appearance and disappearance coincided with the death of the heir to that land! But of the two strangers who had appeared, which was Ibarra, the living or the dead?

This question, which he had often asked himself whenever Ibarra's death was mentioned, again came into his mind in the presence of the human enigma he now saw before him. The dead man had had two wounds, which must have been made by firearms, as he knew from what he had since studied, and which would be the result of the chase on the lake. Then the dead man must have been Ibarra, who had come to die at the tomb of his forefathers, his desire to be cremated being explained by his residence in Europe, where cremation is practised. Then who was the other, the living, this jeweler Simoun, at that time with such an appearance of poverty and wretchedness, but who had now returned loaded with gold and a friend of the authorities? There was the mystery, and the student, with his characteristic cold-bloodedness, determined to clear it up at the first opportunity.

Simoun dug away for some time, but Basilio noticed that his old vigor had declined—he panted and had to rest every few moments. Fearing that he might be discovered, the boy made a sudden resolution. Rising from his seat and issuing from his hiding-place, he asked in the most matter-of-fact tone, "Can I help you, sir?"

Simoun straightened up with the spring of a tiger attacked at his prey, thrust his hand in his coat pocket, and stared at the student with a pale and lowering gaze.

"Thirteen years ago you rendered me a great service, sir," went on Basilio unmoved, "in this very place, by burying my mother, and I should consider myself happy if I could serve you now."

Without taking his eyes off the youth Simoun drew a revolver from his pocket and the click of a hammer being cocked was heard. "For whom do you take me?" he asked, retreating a few paces.

"For a person who is sacred to me," replied Basilio with some emotion, for he thought his last moment had come. "For a person whom all, except me, believe to be dead, and whose misfortunes I have always lamented."

An impressive silence followed these words, a silence that to the youth seemed to suggest eternity. But Simoun, after some hesitation, approached him and placing a hand on his shoulder said in a moving tone: "Basilio, you possess a secret that can ruin me and now you have just surprised me in another, which puts me completely in your hands, the divulging of which would upset all my plans. For my own security and for the good of the cause in which I labor, I ought to seal your lips forever, for what is the life of one man compared to the end I seek? The occasion is fitting; no one knows that I have come here; I am armed; you are defenceless; your death would be attributed to the outlaws, if not to more supernatural causes—yet I'll let you live and trust that I shall not regret it. You have toiled, you have struggled with energetic perseverance, and like myself, you have your scores to settle with society. Your brother was murdered, your mother driven to insanity, and society has prosecuted neither the assassin nor the executioner. You and I are the dregs of justice and instead of destroying we ought to aid each other."

Simoun paused with a repressed sigh, and then slowly resumed, while his gaze wandered about: "Yes, I am he who came here thirteen years ago, sick and wretched, to pay the last tribute to a great and noble soul that was willing to die for me. The victim of a vicious system, I have wandered over the world, working night and day to amass a fortune and carry out my plan. Now I have returned to destroy that system, to precipitate its downfall, to hurl it into the abyss toward which it is senselessly rushing, even though I may have to shed oceans of tears and blood. It has condemned itself, it stands condemned, and I don't want to die before I have seen it in fragments at the foot of the precipice!"

Simoun extended both his arms toward the earth, as if with that gesture he would like to hold there the broken remains. His voice took on a sinister, even lugubrious tone, which made the student shudder.

"Called by the vices of the rulers, I have returned to these islands, and under the cloak of a merchant have visited the towns. My gold has opened a way for me and wheresoever I have beheld greed in the most execrable forms, sometimes hypocritical, sometimes shameless, sometimes cruel, fatten on the dead organism, like a vulture on a corpse, I have asked myself—why was there not, festering in its vitals, the corruption, the ptomaine, the poison of the tombs, to kill the foul bird? The corpse was letting itself be consumed, the vulture was gorging itself with meat, and because it was not possible for me to give it life so that it might turn against its destroyer, and because the corruption developed slowly, I have stimulated greed, I have abetted it. The cases of injustice and the abuses multiplied themselves; I have instigated crime and acts of cruelty, so that the people might become accustomed to the idea of death. I have stirred up trouble so that to escape from it some remedy might be found; I have placed obstacles in the way of trade so that the country, impoverished and reduced to misery, might no longer be afraid of anything; I have excited desires to plunder the treasury, and as this has not been enough to bring about a popular uprising, I have wounded the people in their most sensitive fiber; I have made the vulture itself insult the very corpse that it feeds upon and hasten the corruption.

"Now, when I was about to get the supreme rottenness, the supreme filth, the mixture of such foul products brewing poison, when the greed was beginning to irritate, in its folly hastening to seize whatever came to hand, like an old woman caught in a conflagration, here you come with your cries of Hispanism, with chants of confidence in the government, in what cannot come to pass, here you have a body palpitating with heat and life, young, pure, vigorous, throbbing with blood, with enthusiasm, suddenly come forth to offer itself again as fresh food!

"Ah, youth is ever inexperienced and dreamy, always running after the butterflies and flowers! You have united, so that by your efforts you may bind your fatherland to Spain with garlands of roses when in reality you are forging upon it chains harder than the diamond! You ask for equal rights, the Hispanization of your customs, and you don't see that what you are begging for is suicide, the destruction of your nationality, the annihilation of your fatherland, the consecration of tyranny! What will you be in the future? A people without character, a nation without liberty— everything you have will be borrowed, even your very defects! You beg for Hispanization, and do not pale with shame when they deny it you! And even if they should grant it to you, what then—what have you gained? At best, a country of pronunciamentos, a land of civil wars, a republic of the greedy and the malcontents, like some of the republics of South America! To what are you tending now, with your instruction in Castilian, a pretension that would be ridiculous were it not for its deplorable consequences! You wish to add one more language to the forty odd that are spoken in the islands, so that you may understand one another less and less."

"On the contrary," replied Basilio, "if the knowledge of Castilian may bind us to the government, in exchange it may also unite the islands among themselves."

"A gross error!" rejoined Simoun. "You are letting yourselves be deceived by big words and never go to the bottom of things to examine the results in their final analysis. Spanish will never be the general language of the country, the people will never talk it, because the conceptions of their brains and the feelings of their hearts cannot be expressed in that language—each people has its own tongue, as it has its own way of thinking! What are you going to do with Castilian, the few of you who will speak it? Kill off your own originality, subordinate your thoughts to other brains, and instead of freeing yourselves, make yourselves slaves indeed! Nine-tenths of those of you who pretend to be enlightened are renegades to your country! He among you who talks that language neglects his own in such a way that he neither writes nor understands it, and how many have I not seen who pretended not to know a single word of it! But fortunately, you have an imbecile government! While Russia enslaves Poland by forcing the Russian language upon it, while Germany prohibits French in the conquered provinces, your government strives to preserve yours, and you in return, a remarkable people under an incredible government, you are trying to despoil yourselves of your own nationality! One and all you forget that while a people preserves its language, it preserves the marks of its liberty, as a man preserves his independence while he holds to his own way of thinking. Language is the thought of the peoples. Luckily, your independence is assured; human passions are looking out for that!"

Simoun paused and rubbed his hand over his forehead. The waning moon was rising and sent its faint light down through the branches of the trees, and with his white locks and severe features, illuminated from below by the lantern, the jeweler appeared to be the fateful spirit of the wood planning some evil.

Basilio was silent before such bitter reproaches and listened with bowed head, while Simoun resumed: "I saw this movement started and have passed whole nights of anguish, because I understood that among those youths there were exceptional minds and hearts, sacrificing themselves for what they thought to be a good cause, when in reality they were working against their own country. How many times have I wished to speak to you young men, to reveal myself and undeceive you! But in view of the reputation I enjoy, my words would have been wrongly interpreted and would perhaps have had a counter effect. How many times have I not longed to approach your Makaraig, your Isagani! Sometimes I thought of their death, I wished to destroy them—"

Simoun checked himself.

"Here's why I let you live, Basilio, and by such imprudence I expose myself to the risk of being some day betrayed by you. But you know who I am, you know how much I must have suffered— then believe in me! You are not of the common crowd, which sees in the jeweler Simoun the trader who incites the authorities to commit abuses in order that the abused may buy jewels. I am the Judge who wishes to castigate this system by making use of its own defects, to make war on it by flattering it. I need your help, your influence among the youth, to combat these senseless desires for Hispanization, for assimilation, for equal rights. By that road you will become only a poor copy, and the people should look higher. It is madness to attempt to influence the thoughts of the rulers—they have their plan outlined, the bandage covers their eyes, and besides losing time uselessly, you are deceiving the people with vain hopes and are helping to bend their necks before the tyrant. What you should do is to take advantage of their prejudices to serve your needs. Are they unwilling that you be assimilated with the Spanish people? Good enough! Distinguish yourselves then by revealing yourselves in your own character, try to lay the foundations of the Philippine fatherland! Do they deny you hope? Good! Don't depend on them, depend upon yourselves and work! Do they deny you representation in their Cortes? So much the better! Even should you succeed in sending representatives of your own choice, what are you going to accomplish there except to be overwhelmed among so many voices, and sanction with your presence the abuses and wrongs that are afterwards perpetrated? The fewer rights they allow you, the more reason you will have later to throw off the yoke, and return evil for evil. If they are unwilling to teach you their language, cultivate your own, extend it, preserve to the people their own way of thinking, and instead of aspiring to be a province, aspire to be a nation! Instead of subordinate thoughts, think independently, to the end that neither by right, nor custom, nor language, the Spaniard can be considered the master here, nor even be looked upon as a part of the country, but ever as an invader, a foreigner, and sooner or later you will have your liberty! Here's why I let you live!"

Basilio breathed freely, as though a great weight had been lifted from him, and after a brief pause, replied: "Sir, the honor you do me in confiding your plans to me is too great for me not to be frank with you, and tell you that what you ask of me is beyond my power. I am no politician, and if I have signed the petition for instruction in Castilian it has been because I saw in it an advantage to our studies and nothing more. My destiny is different; my aspiration reduces itself to alleviating the physical sufferings of my fellow men."

The jeweler smiled. "What are physical sufferings compared to moral tortures? What is the death of a man in the presence of the death of a society? Some day you will perhaps be a great physician, if they let you go your way in peace, but greater yet will be he who can inject a new idea into this anemic people! You, what are you doing for the land that gave you existence, that supports your life, that affords you knowledge? Don't you realize that that is a useless life which is not consecrated to a great idea? It is a stone wasted in the fields without becoming a part of any edifice."

"No, no, sir!" replied Basilio modestly, "I'm not folding my arms, I'm working like all the rest to raise up from the ruins of the past a people whose units will be bound together—that each one may feel in himself the conscience and the life of the whole. But however enthusiastic our generation may be, we understand that in this great social fabric there must be a division of labor. I have chosen my task and will devote myself to science."

"Science is not the end of man," declared Simoun.

"The most civilized nations are tending toward it."

"Yes, but only as a means of seeking their welfare."

"Science is more eternal, it's more human, it's more universal!" exclaimed the youth in a transport of enthusiasm. "Within a few centuries, when humanity has become redeemed and enlightened, when there are no races, when all peoples are free, when there are neither tyrants nor slaves, colonies nor mother countries, when justice rules and man is a citizen of the world, the pursuit of science alone will remain, the word patriotism will be equivalent to fanaticism, and he who prides himself on patriotic ideas will doubtless be isolated as a dangerous disease, as a menace to the social order."

Simoun smiled sadly. "Yes, yes," he said with a shake of his head, "yet to reach that condition it is necessary that there be no tyrannical and no enslaved peoples, it is necessary that man go about freely, that he know how to respect the rights of others in their own individuality, and for this there is yet much blood to be shed, the struggle forces itself forward. To overcome the ancient fanaticism that bound consciences it was necessary that many should perish in the holocausts, so that the social conscience in horror declared the individual conscience free. It is also necessary that all answer the question which with each day the fatherland asks them, with its fettered hands extended! Patriotism can only be a crime in a tyrannical people, because then it is rapine under a beautiful name, but however perfect humanity may become, patriotism will always be a virtue among oppressed peoples, because it will at all times mean love of justice, of liberty, of personal dignity—nothing of chimerical dreams, of effeminate idyls! The greatness of a man is not in living before his time, a thing almost impossible, but in understanding its desires, in responding to its needs, and in guiding it on its forward way. The geniuses that are commonly believed to have existed before their time, only appear so because those who judge them see from a great distance, or take as representative of the age the line of stragglers!"

Simoun fell silent. Seeing that he could awake no enthusiasm in that unresponsive mind, he turned to another subject and asked with a change of tone: "And what are you doing for the memory of your mother and your brother? Is it enough that you come here every year, to weep like a woman over a grave?" And he smiled sarcastically.

The shot hit the mark. Basilio changed color and advanced a step.

"What do you want me to do?" he asked angrily.

"Without means, without social position, how may I bring their murderers to justice? I would merely be another victim, shattered like a piece of glass hurled against a rock. Ah, you do ill to recall this to me, since it is wantonly reopening a wound!"

"But what if I should offer you my aid?"

Basilio shook his head and remained pensive. "All the tardy vindications of justice, all the revenge in the world, will not restore a single hair of my mother's head, or recall a smile to my brother's lips. Let them rest in peace—what should I gain now by avenging them?"

"Prevent others from suffering what you have suffered, that in the future there be no brothers murdered or mothers driven to madness. Resignation is not always a virtue; it is a crime when it encourages tyrants: there are no despots where there are no slaves! Man is in his own nature so wicked that he always abuses complaisance. I thought as you do, and you know what my fate was. Those who caused your misfortunes are watching you day and night, they suspect that you are only biding your time, they take your eagerness to learn, your love of study, your very complaisance, for burning desires for revenge. The day they can get rid of you they will do with you as they did with me, and they will not let you grow to manhood, because they fear and hate you!"

"Hate me? Still hate me after the wrong they have done me?" asked the youth in surprise.

Simoun burst into a laugh. "'It is natural for man to hate those whom he has wronged,' said Tacitus, confirming the *quos laeserunt et oderunt* of Seneca. When you wish to gauge the evil or the good that one people has done to another, you have only to observe whether it hates or loves. Thus is explained the reason why many who have enriched themselves here in the high offices they have filled, on their return to the Peninsula relieve themselves by slanders and insults against those who have been their victims. *Proprium humani ingenii est odisse quern laeseris!*"

"But if the world is large, if one leaves them to the peaceful enjoyment of power, if I ask only to be allowed to work, to live—"

"And to rear meek-natured sons to send them afterwards to submit to the yoke," continued Simoun, cruelly mimicking Basilio's tone. "A fine future you prepare for them, and they have to thank you for a life of humiliation and suffering! Good enough, young man! When a body is inert, it is useless to galvanize it. Twenty years of continuous slavery, of systematic humiliation, of constant prostration, finally create in the mind a twist that cannot be straightened by the labor of a day. Good and evil instincts are inherited and transmitted from father to son. Then let your idylic ideas live, your dreams of a slave who asks only for a bandage to wrap the chain so that it may rattle less and not ulcerate his skin! You hope for a little home and some ease, a wife and a handful of rice—here is your ideal man of the Philippines! Well, if they give it to you, consider yourself fortunate."

Basilio, accustomed to obey and bear with the caprices and humors of Capitan Tiago. was now dominated by Simoun, who appeared to him terrible and sinister on a background bathed in tears and blood. He tried to explain himself by saying that he did not consider himself fit to mix in politics, that he had no political opinions because he had never studied the question, but that he was always ready to lend his services the day they might be needed, that for the moment he saw only one need, the enlightenment of the people.

Simoun stopped him with a gesture, and, as the dawn was coming, said to him: "Young man, I am not warning you to keep my secret, because I know that discretion is one of your good qualities, and even though you might wish to sell me, the jeweler Simoun, the friend of the authorities and of the religious corporations, will always be given more credit than the student Basilio, already suspected of filibusterism, and, being a native, so much the more marked and watched, and because in the profession you are entering upon you will encounter powerful rivals. After all, even though you have not corresponded to my hopes, the day on which you change your mind, look me up at my house in the Escolta, and I'll be glad to help you."

Basilio thanked him briefly and went away.

"Have I really made a mistake?" mused Simoun, when he found himself alone. "Is it that he doubts me and meditates his plan of revenge so secretly that he fears to tell it even in the solitude of the night? Or can it be that the years of servitude have extinguished in his heart every human sentiment and there remain only the animal desires to live and reproduce? In that case the type is deformed and will have to be cast over again. Then the hecatomb is preparing: let the unfit perish and only the strongest survive!"

Then he added sadly, as if apostrophizing some one: "Have patience, you who left me a name and a home, have patience! I have lost all—country, future, prosperity, your very tomb, but have patience! And thou, noble spirit, great soul, generous heart, who didst live with only one thought and didst sacrifice thy life without asking the gratitude or applause of any one, have patience, have patience! The methods that I use may perhaps not be thine, but they are the most direct. The day is coming, and when it brightens I myself will come to announce it to you who are now indifferent. Have patience!"

MERRY CHRISTMAS!

When Juli opened her sorrowing eyes, she saw that the house was still dark, but the cocks were crowing. Her first thought was that perhaps the Virgin had performed the miracle and the sun was not going to rise, in spite of the invocations of the cocks. She rose, crossed herself, recited her morning prayers with great devotion, and with as little noise as possible went out on the *batalan*.

There was no miracle—the sun was rising and promised a magnificent morning, the breeze was delightfully cool, the stars were paling in the east, and the cocks were crowing as if to see who could crow best and loudest. That had been too much to ask—it were much easier to request the Virgin to send the two hundred and fifty pesos. What would it cost the Mother of the Lord to give them? But underneath the image she found only the letter of her father asking for the ransom of five hundred pesos. There was nothing to do but go, so, seeing that her grandfather was not stirring, she thought him asleep and began to prepare breakfast. Strange, she was calm, she even had a desire to laugh! What had she had last night to afflict her so? She was not going very far, she could come every second day to visit the house, her grandfather could see her, and as for Basilio, he had known for some time the bad turn her father's affairs had taken, since he had often said to her, "When I'm a physician and we are married, your father won't need his fields."

"What a fool I was to cry so much," she said to herself as she packed her *tampipi*. Her fingers struck against the locket and she pressed it to her lips, but immediately wiped them from fear of contagion, for that locket set with diamonds and emeralds had come from a leper. Ah, then, if she should catch that disease she could not get married.

As it became lighter, she could see her grandfather seated in a corner, following all her movements with his eyes, so she caught up her *tampipi* of clothes and approached him smilingly to kiss his hand. The old man blessed her silently, while she tried to appear merry. "When father comes back, tell him that I have at last gone to college—my mistress talks Spanish. It's the cheapest college I could find."

Seeing the old man's eyes fill with tears, she placed the *tampipi* on her head and hastily went downstairs, her slippers slapping merrily on the wooden steps. But when she turned her head to look again at the house, the house wherein had faded her childhood dreams and her maiden illusions, when she saw it sad, lonely, deserted, with the windows half closed, vacant and dark like a dead man's eyes, when she heard the low rustling of the bamboos, and saw them nodding in the fresh morning breeze as though bidding her farewell, then her vivacity disappeared; she stopped, her eyes filled with tears, and letting herself fall in a sitting posture on a log by the wayside she broke out into disconsolate tears.

Juli had been gone several hours and the sun was quite high overhead when Tandang Selo gazed from the window at the people in their festival garments going to the town to attend the high mass. Nearly all led by the hand or carried in their arms a little boy or girl decked out as if for a fiesta.

Christmas day in the Philippines is, according to the elders, a fiesta for the children, who are perhaps not of the same opinion and who, it may be supposed, have for it an instinctive dread. They are roused early, washed, dressed, and decked out with everything new, dear, and precious that they possess—high silk shoes, big hats, woolen or velvet suits, without overlooking four or five scapularies, which contain texts from St. John, and thus burdened they are carried to the high mass, where for almost an hour they are subjected to the heat and the human smells from so many crowding, perspiring people, and if they are not made to recite the rosary they must remain quiet, bored, or asleep. At each movement or antic that may soil their clothing they are pinched and scolded, so the fact is that they do not laugh or feel happy, while in their round eyes can be read a protest against so much embroidery and a longing for the old shirt of week-days.

Afterwards, they are dragged from house to house to kiss their relatives' hands. There they have to dance, sing, and recite all the amusing things they know, whether in the humor or not, whether comfortable or not in their fine clothes, with the eternal pinchings and scoldings if they play any of their tricks. Their relatives give them cuartos which their parents seize upon and of which they hear nothing more. The only positive results they are accustomed to get from the fiesta are the marks of the aforesaid pinchings, the vexations, and at best an attack of indigestion from gorging themselves with candy and cake in the houses of kind relatives. But such is the custom, and Filipino children enter the world through these ordeals, which afterwards prove the least sad, the least hard, of their lives.

Adult persons who live independently also share in this fiesta, by visiting their parents and their parents' relatives, crooking their knees, and wishing them a merry Christmas. Their Christmas gift consists of a sweetmeat, some fruit, a glass of water, or some insignificant present.

Tandang Selo saw all his friends pass and thought sadly that this year he had no Christmas gift for anybody, while his granddaughter had gone without hers, without wishing him a merry Christmas. Was it delicacy on Juli's part or pure forgetfulness?

When he tried to greet the relatives who called on him, bringing their children, he found to his great surprise that he could not articulate a word. Vainly he tried, but no sound could he utter. He placed his hands on his throat, shook his head, but without effect. When he tried to laugh, his lips trembled convulsively and the only noise produced was a hoarse wheeze like the blowing of bellows.

The women gazed at him in consternation. "He's dumb, he's dumb!" they cried in astonishment, raising at once a literal pandemonium.

PILATES

When the news of this misfortune became known in the town, some lamented it and others shrugged their shoulders. No one was to blame, and no one need lay it on his conscience.

The lieutenant of the Civil Guard gave no sign: he had received an order to take up all the arms and he had performed his duty. He had chased the tulisanes whenever he could, and when they captured Cabesang Tales he had organized an expedition and brought into the town, with their arms bound behind them, five or six rustics who looked suspicious, so if Cabesang Tales did not show up it was because he was not in the pockets or under the skins of the prisoners, who were thoroughly shaken out.

The friar-administrator shrugged his shoulders: he had nothing to do with it, it was a matter of tulisanes and he had merely done his duty. True it was that if he had not entered the complaint, perhaps the arms would not have been taken up, and poor Tales would not have been captured; but he, Fray Clemente, had to look after his own safety, and that Tales had a way of staring at him as if picking out a good target in some part of his body. Self-defense is natural. If there are tulisanes, the fault is not his, it is not his duty to run them down—that belongs to the Civil Guard. If Cabesang Tales, instead of wandering about his fields, had stayed at home, he would not have been captured. In short, that was a punishment from heaven upon those who resisted the demands of his corporation.

When Sister Penchang, the pious old woman in whose service Juli had entered, learned of it, she ejaculated several *'Susmarioseps*, crossed herself, and remarked, "Often God sends these trials because we are sinners or have sinning relatives, to whom we should have taught piety and we haven't done so."

Those *sinning relatives* referred to Juliana, for to this pious woman Juli was a great sinner. "Think of a girl of marriageable age who doesn't yet know how to pray! *Jesús*, how scandalous! If the wretch doesn't say the *Diós te salve María* without stopping at *es contigo*, and the *Santa María* without a pause after *pecadores*, as every good Christian who fears God ought to do! She doesn't know the *oremus gratiam*, and says *mentibus* for *méntibus*. Anybody hearing her would think she was talking about something else. '*Susmariosep!*'"

Greatly scandalized, she made the sign of the cross and thanked God, who had permitted the capture of the father in order that the daughter might be snatched from sin and learn the virtues which, according to the curates, should adorn every Christian woman. She therefore kept the girl constantly at work, not allowing her to return to the village to look after her grandfather. Juli had to learn how to pray, to read the books distributed by the friars, and to work until the two hundred and fifty pesos should be paid.

When she learned that Basilio had gone to Manila to get his savings and ransom Juli from her servitude, the good woman believed that the girl was forever lost and that the devil had presented himself in the guise of the student. Dreadful as it all was, how true was that little book the curate had given her! Youths who go to Manila to study are ruined and then ruin the others. Thinking to rescue Juli, she made her read and re-read the book called *Tandang Basio Macunat*,[1] charging her always to go and see the curate in the convento,[2] as did the heroine, who is so praised by the author, a friar.

Meanwhile, the friars had gained their point. They had certainly won the suit, so they took advantage of Cabesang Tales' captivity to turn the fields over to the one who had asked for them, without the least thought of honor or the faintest twinge of shame. When the former owner returned and learned what had happened, when he saw his fields in another's possession,—those fields that had cost the lives of his wife and daughter,—when he saw his father dumb and his daughter working as a servant, and when he himself received an order from the town council, transmitted through the headman of the village, to move out of the house within three days, he said nothing; he sat down at his father's side and spoke scarcely once during the whole day.

1   The nature of this booklet, in Tagalog, is made clear in several passages. It was issued by the Franciscans, but proved too outspoken for even Latin refinement, and was suppressed by the Order itself.—Tr.

2   The rectory or parish house.

WEALTH AND WANT

On the following day, to the great surprise of the village, the jeweler Simoun, followed by two servants, each carrying a canvas-covered chest, requested the hospitality of Cabesang Tales, who even in the midst of his wretchedness did not forget the good Filipino customs—rather, he was troubled to think that he had no way of properly entertaining the stranger. But Simoun brought everything with him, servants and provisions, and merely wished to spend the day and night in the house because it was the largest in the village and was situated between San Diego and Tiani, towns where he hoped to find many customers.

Simoun secured information about the condition of the roads and asked Cabesang Tales if his revolver was a sufficient protection against the tulisanes.

"They have rifles that shoot a long way," was the rather absent-minded reply.

"This revolver does no less," remarked Simoun, firing at an areca-palm some two hundred paces away.

Cabesang Tales noticed that some nuts fell, but remained silent and thoughtful.

Gradually the families, drawn by the fame of the jeweler's wares, began to collect. They wished one another merry Christmas, they talked of masses, saints, poor crops, but still were there to spend their savings for jewels and trinkets brought from Europe. It was known that the jeweler was the friend of the Captain-General, so it wasn't lost labor to get on good terms with him, and thus be prepared for contingencies.

Capitan Basilio came with his wife, daughter, and son-in-law, prepared to spend at least three thousand pesos. Sister Penchang was there to buy a diamond ring she had promised to the Virgin of Antipolo. She had left Juli at home memorizing a booklet the curate had sold her for four cuartos, with forty days of indulgence granted by the Archbishop to every one who read it or listened to it read.

"*Jesús!*" said the pious woman to Capitana Tika, "that poor girl has grown up like a mushroom planted by the *tikbalang*. I've made her read the book at the top of her voice at least fifty times and she doesn't remember a single word of it. She has a head like a sieve—full when it's in the water. All of us hearing her, even the dogs and cats, have won at least twenty years of indulgence."

Simoun arranged his two chests on the table, one being somewhat larger than the other. "You don't want plated jewelry or imitation gems. This lady," turning to Sinang, "wants real diamonds."

"That's it, yes, sir, diamonds, old diamonds, antique stones, you know," she responded. "Papa will pay for them, because he likes antique things, antique stones." Sinang was accustomed to joke about the great deal of Latin her father understood and the little her husband knew.

"It just happens that I have some antique jewels," replied Simoun, taking the canvas cover from the smaller chest, a polished steel case with bronze trimmings and stout locks. "I have necklaces of Cleopatra's, real and genuine, discovered in the Pyramids; rings of Roman senators and knights, found in the ruins of Carthage."

"Probably those that Hannibal sent back after the battle of Cannae!" exclaimed Capitan Basilio seriously, while he trembled with pleasure. The good man, thought he had read much about the ancients, had never, by reason of the lack of museums in Filipinas, seen any of the objects of those times.

"I have brought besides costly earrings of Roman ladies, discovered in the villa of Annius Mucius Papilinus in Pompeii."

Capitan Easilio nodded to show that he understood and was eager to see such precious relics. The women remarked that they also wanted things from Rome, such as rosaries blessed by the Pope, holy relics that would take away sins without the need of confessions, and so on.

When the chest was opened and the cotton packing removed, there was exposed a tray filled with rings, reliquaries, lockets, crucifixes, brooches, and such like. The diamonds set in among variously colored stones flashed out brightly and shimmered among golden flowers of varied hues, with petals of enamel, all of peculiar designs and rare Arabesque workmanship.

Simoun lifted the tray and exhibited another filled with quaint jewels that would have satisfied the imaginations of seven débutantes on the eves of the balls in their honor. Designs, one more fantastic than the other, combinations of precious stones and pearls worked into the figures of insects with azure backs and transparent forewings, sapphires, emeralds, rubies, turquoises, diamonds, joined to form dragon-flies, wasps, bees, butterflies, beetles, serpents, lizards, fishes, sprays of flowers. There were diadems, necklaces of pearls and diamonds, so that some of the girls could not withhold a *nakú* of admiration, and Sinang gave a cluck with her tongue, whereupon her mother pinched her to prevent her from encouraging the jeweler to raise his prices, for Capitana Tika still pinched her daughter even after the latter was married.

"Here you have some old diamonds," explained the jeweler. "This ring belonged to the Princess Lamballe and those earrings to one of Marie Antoinette's ladies." They consisted of some beautiful solitaire diamonds, as large as grains of corn, with somewhat bluish lights, and pervaded with a severe elegance, as though they still reflected in their sparkles the shuddering of the Reign of Terror.

"Those two earrings!" exclaimed Sinang, looking at her father and instinctively covering the arm next to her mother.

"Something more ancient yet, something Roman," said Capitan Basilio with a wink.

The pious Sister Penchang thought that with such a gift the Virgin of Antipolo would be softened and grant her her most vehement desire: for some time she had begged for a wonderful miracle to which her name would be attached, so that her name might be immortalized on earth and she then ascend into heaven, like the Capitana Ines of the curates. She inquired the price and Simoun asked three thousand pesos, which made the good woman cross herself—'*Susmariosep!*

Simoun now exposed the third tray, which was filled with watches, cigar-and match-cases decorated with the rarest enamels, reliquaries set with diamonds and containing the most elegant miniatures.

The fourth tray, containing loose gems, stirred a murmur of admiration. Sinang again clucked with her tongue, her mother again pinched her, although at the same time herself emitting a *'Susmaria* of wonder.

No one there had ever before seen so much wealth. In that chest lined with dark-blue velvet, arranged in trays, were the wonders of the *Arabian Nights,* the dreams of Oriental fantasies. Diamonds as large as peas glittered there, throwing out attractive rays as if they were about to melt or burn with all the hues of the spectrum; emeralds from Peru, of varied forms and shapes; rubies from India, red as drops of blood; sapphires from Ceylon, blue and white; turquoises from Persia; Oriental pearls, some rosy, some lead-colored, others black. Those who have at night seen a great rocket burst in the azure darkness of the sky into thousands of colored lights, so bright that they make the eternal stars look dim, can imagine the aspect the tray presented.

As if to increase the admiration of the beholders, Simoun took the stones out with his tapering brown fingers, gloating over their crystalline hardness, their luminous stream, as they poured from his hands like drops of water reflecting the tints of the rainbow. The reflections from so many facets, the thought of their great value, fascinated the gaze of every one.

Cabesang Tales, who had approached out of curiosity, closed his eyes and drew back hurriedly, as if to drive away an evil thought. Such great riches were an insult to his misfortunes; that man had come there to make an exhibition of his immense wealth on the very day that he, Tales, for lack of money, for lack of protectors, had to abandon the house raised by his own hands.

"Here you have two black diamonds, among the largest in existence," explained the jeweler. "They're very difficult to cut because they're the very hardest. This somewhat rosy stone is also a diamond, as is this green one that many take for an emerald. Quiroga the Chinaman offered me six thousand pesos for it in order to present it to a very influential lady, and yet it is not the green ones that are the most valuable, but these blue ones."

He selected three stones of no great size, but thick and well-cut, of a delicate azure tint.

"For all that they are smaller than the green," he continued, "they cost twice as much. Look at this one, the smallest of all, weighing not more than two carats, which cost me twenty thousand pesos and which I won't sell for less than thirty. I had to make a special trip to buy it. This other one, from the mines of Golconda, weighs three and a half carats and is worth over seventy thousand. The Viceroy of India, in a letter I received the day before yesterday, offers me twelve thousand pounds sterling for it."

Before such great wealth, all under the power of that man who talked so unaffectedly, the spectators felt a kind of awe mingled with dread. Sinang clucked several times and her mother did not pinch her, perhaps because she too was overcome, or perhaps because she reflected that a jeweler like Simoun was not going to try to gain five pesos more or less as a result of an exclamation more or less indiscreet. All gazed at the gems, but no one showed any desire to handle them, they were so awe-inspiring. Curiosity was blunted by wonder. Cabesang Tales stared out into the field, thinking that with a single diamond, perhaps the very smallest there, he could recover his daughter, keep his house, and perhaps rent another farm. Could it be that those gems were worth more than a man's home, the safety of a maiden, the peace of an old man in his declining days?

As if he guessed the thought, Simoun remarked to those about him: "Look here—with one of these little blue stones, which appear so innocent and inoffensive, pure as sparks scattered over the arch of heaven, with one of these, seasonably presented, a man was able to have his enemy deported, the father of a family, as a disturber of the peace; and with this other little one like it, red as one's heart-blood, as the feeling of revenge, and bright as an orphan's tears, he was restored to liberty, the man was returned to his home, the father to his children, the husband to the wife, and a whole family saved from a wretched future."

. He slapped the chest and went on in a loud tone in bad Tagalog: "Here I have, as in a medicine-chest, life and death, poison and balm, and with this handful I can drive to tears all the inhabitants of the Philippines!"

The listeners gazed at him awe-struck, knowing him to be right. In his voice there could be detected a strange ring, while sinister flashes seemed to issue from behind the blue goggles.

Then as if to relieve the strain of the impression made by the gems on such simple folk, he lifted up the tray and exposed at the bottom the *sanctum sanctorum*. Cases of Russian leather, separated by layers of cotton, covered a bottom lined with gray velvet. All expected wonders, and Sinang's husband thought he saw carbuncles, gems that flashed fire and shone in the midst of the shadows. Capitan Basilio was on the threshold of immortality: he was going to behold something real, something beyond his dreams.

"This was a necklace of Cleopatra's," said Simoun, taking out carefully a flat case in the shape of a half-moon. "It's a jewel that can't be appraised, an object for a museum, only for a rich government."

It was a necklace fashioned of bits of gold representing little idols among green and blue beetles, with a vulture's head made from a single piece of rare jasper at the center between two extended wings—the symbol and decoration of Egyptian queens.

Sinang turned up her nose and made a grimace of childish depreciation, while Capitan Basilio, with all his love for antiquity, could not restrain an exclamation of disappointment.

"It's a magnificent jewel, well-preserved, almost two thousand years old."

"Pshaw!" Sinang made haste to exclaim, to prevent her father's falling into temptation.

"Fool!" he chided her, after overcoming his first disappointment. "How do you know but that to this necklace is due the present condition of the world? With this Cleopatra may have captivated Caesar, Mark Antony! This has heard the burning declarations of love from the greatest warriors of their time, it has listened to speeches in the purest and most elegant Latin, and yet you would want to wear it!"

"I? I wouldn't give three pesos for it."

"You could give twenty, silly," said Capitana Tika in a judicial tone. "The gold is good and melted down would serve for other jewelry."

"This is a ring that must have belonged to Sulla," continued Simoun, exhibiting a heavy ring of solid gold with a seal on it.

"With that he must have signed the death-wrarrants during his dictatorship!" exclaimed Capitan Basilio, pale with emotion. He examined it and tried to decipher the seal, but though he turned it over and over he did not understand paleography, so he could not read it.

"What a finger Sulla had!" he observed finally. "This would fit two of ours—as I've said, we're degenerating!"

"I still have many other jewels—"

"If they're all that kind, never mind!" interrupted Sinang. "I think I prefer the modern."

Each one selected some piece of jewelry, one a ring, another a watch, another a locket. Capitana Tika bought a reliquary that contained a fragment of the stone on which Our Saviour rested at his third fall; Sinang a pair of earrings; and Capitan Basilio the watch-chain for the alferez, the lady's earrings for the curate, and other gifts. The families from the town of Tiani, not to be outdone by those of San Diego, in like manner emptied their purses.

Simoun bought or exchanged old jewelry, brought there by economical mothers, to whom it was no longer of use.

"You, haven't you something to sell?" he asked Cabesang Tales, noticing the latter watching the sales and exchanges with covetous eyes, but the reply was that all his daughter's jewels had been sold, nothing of value remained.

"What about Maria Clara's locket?" inquired Sinang.

"True!" the man exclaimed, and his eyes blazed for a moment.

"It's a locket set with diamonds and emeralds," Sinang told the jeweler. "My old friend wore it before she became a nun."

Simoun said nothing, but anxiously watched Cabesang Tales, who, after opening several boxes, found the locket. He examined it carefully, opening and shutting it repeatedly. It was the same locket that Maria Clara had worn during the fiesta in San Diego and which she had in a moment of compassion given to a leper.

"I like the design," said Simoun. "How much do you want for it?"

Cabesang Tales scratched his head in perplexity, then his ear, then looked at the women.

"I've taken a fancy to this locket," Simoun went on. "Will you take a hundred, five hundred pesos? Do you want to exchange it for something else? Take your choice here!"

Tales stared foolishly at Simoun, as if in doubt of what he heard. "Five hundred pesos?" he murmured.

"Five hundred," repeated the jeweler in a voice shaking with emotion.

Cabesang Tales took the locket and made several turns about the room, with his heart beating violently and his hands trembling. Dared he ask more? That locket could save him, this was an excellent opportunity, such as might not again present itself.

The women winked at him to encourage him to make the sale, excepting Penchang, who, fearing that Juli would be ransomed, observed piously: "I would keep it as a relic. Those who have seen Maria Clara in the nunnery say she has got so thin and weak that she can scarcely talk and it's thought that she'll die a saint. Padre Salvi speaks very highly of her and he's her confessor. That's why Juli didn't want ito give it up, but rather preferred to pawn herself."

This speech had its effect—the thought of his daughter restrained Tales. "If you will allow me," he said, "I'll go to the town to consult my daughter. I'll be back before night."

This was agreed upon and Tales set out at once. But when he found himself outside of the village, he made out at a distance, on a path, that entered the woods, the friar-administrator and a man whom he recognized as the usurper of his land. A husband seeing his wife enter a private room with another man could not feel more wrath or jealousy than Cabesang Tales experienced when he saw them moving over his fields, the fields cleared by him, which he had thought to leave to his children. It seemed to him that they were mocking him, laughing at his powerlessness. There flashed into his memory what he had said about never giving up his fields except to him who irrigated them with his own blood and buried in them his wife and daughter.

He stopped, rubbed his hand over his forehead, and shut his eyes. When he again opened them, he saw that the man had turned to laugh and that the friar had caught his sides as though to save himself from bursting with merriment, then he saw them point toward his house and laugh again.

A buzz sounded in his ears, he felt the crack of a whip around his chest, the red mist reappeared before his eyes, he again saw the corpses of his wife and daughter, and beside them the usurper with the friar laughing and holding his sides. Forgetting everything else, he turned aside into the path they had taken, the one leading to his fields.

Simoun waited in vain for Cabesang Tales to return that night. But the next morning when he arose he noticed that the leather holster of his revolver was empty. Opening it he found inside a scrap of paper wrapped around the locket set with emeralds and diamonds, with these few lines written on it in Tagalog:

"Pardon, sir, that in my own house I relieve you of what belongs to you, but necessity drives me to it. In exchange for your revolver I leave the locket you desired so much. I need the weapon, for I am going out to join the tulisanes.

"I advise you not to keep on your present road, because if you fall into our power, not then being my guest, we will require of you a large ransom.

Telesforo Juan de Dios."

"At last I've found my man!" muttered Simoun with a deep breath. "He's somewhat scrupulous, but so much the better—he'll keep his promises."

He then ordered a servant to go by boat over the lake to Los Baños with the larger chest and await him there. He would go on overland, taking the smaller chest, the one containing his famous jewels. The arrival of four civil-guards completed his good humor. They came to arrest Cabesang Tales and not finding him took Tandang Selo away instead.

Three murders had been committed during the night. The friar-administrator and the new tenant of Cabesang Tales' land had been found dead, with their heads split open and their mouths full of earth, on the border of the fields. In the town the wife of the usurper was found dead at dawn, her mouth also filled with earth and her throat cut, with a fragment of paper beside her, on which was the name *Tales*, written in blood as though traced by a finger.

Calm yourselves, peaceful inhabitants of Kalamba! None of you are named Tales, none of you have committed any crime! You are called Luis Habaña, Matías Belarmino, Nicasio Eigasani, Cayetano de Jesús, Mateo Elejorde, Leandro Lopez, Antonino Lopez, Silvestre Ubaldo, Manuel Hidalgo, Paciano Mercado, your name is the whole village of Kalamba.' You cleared your fields, on them you have spent the labor of your whole lives, your savings, your vigils and privations, and you have been despoiled of them, driven from your homes, with the rest forbidden to show you hospitality! Not content with outraging justice, they[2] have trampled upon the sacred traditions of your country! You have served Spain and the King, and when in their name you have asked for justice, you were banished without trial, torn from your wives' arms and your children's caresses! Any one of you has suffered more than Cabesang Tales, and yet none, not one of you, has received justice! Neither pity nor humanity has been shown you—you have been persecuted beyond the tomb, as was Mariano Herbosa![3] Weep or laugh, there in those lonely isles where you wander vaguely, uncertain of the future! Spain, the generous Spain, is watching over you, and sooner or later you will have justice!

---

[1] Friends of the author, who suffered in Weyler's expedition, mentioned below.—Tr.

[2] The Dominican corporation, at whose instigation Captain-General Valeriano Weyler sent a battery of artillery to Kalamba to destroy the property of tenants who were contesting in the courts the friars' titles to land there. The author's family were the largest sufferers.—Tr.

[3] A relative of the author, whose body was dragged from the tomb and thrown to the dogs, on the pretext that he had died without receiving final absolution.—Tr.

LOS BAÑOS

His Excellency, the Captain-General and Governor of the Philippine Islands, had been hunting in Bosoboso. But as he had to be accompanied by a band of music,—since such an exalted personage was not to be esteemed less than the wooden images carried in the processions,—and as devotion to the divine art of St. Cecilia has not yet been popularized among the deer and wild boars of Bosoboso, his Excellency, with the band of music and train of friars, soldiers, and clerks, had not been able to catch a single rat or a solitary bird.

The provincial authorities foresaw dismissals and transfers, the poor gobernadorcillos and cabezas de barangay were restless and sleepless, fearing that the mighty hunter in his wrath might have a notion to make up with their persons for the lack of submissiveness on the part of the beasts of the forest, as had been done years before by an alcalde who had traveled on the shoulders of impressed porters because he found no horses gentle enough to guarantee his safety. There was not lacking an evil rumor that his Excellency had decided to take some action, since in this he saw the first symptoms of a rebellion which should be strangled in its infancy, that a fruitless hunt hurt the prestige of the Spanish name, that he already had his eye on a wretch to be dressed up as a deer, when his Excellency, with clemency that Ben-Zayb lacked words to extol sufficiently, dispelled all the fears by declaring that it pained him to sacrifice to his pleasure the beasts of the forest.

But to tell the truth, his Excellency was secretly very well satisfied, for what would have happened had he missed a shot at a deer, one of those not familiar with political etiquette? What would the prestige of the sovereign power have come to then? A Captain-General of the Philippines missing a shot, like a raw hunter? What would have been said by the Indians, among whom there were some fair huntsmen? The integrity of the fatherland would have been endangered.

So it was that his Excellency, with a sheepish smile, and posing as a disappointed hunter, ordered an immediate return to Los Baños. During the journey he related with an indifferent air his hunting exploits in this or that forest of the Peninsula, adopting a tone somewhat depreciative, as suited the case, toward hunting in Filipinas. The bath in Dampalit, the hot springs on the shore of the lake, card-games in the palace, with an occasional excursion to some neighboring waterfall, or the lake infested with caymans, offered more attractions and fewer risks to the integrity of the fatherland.

Thus on one of the last days of December, his Excellency found himself in the sala, taking a hand at cards while he awaited the breakfast hour. He had come from the bath, with the usual glass of coconut-milk and its soft meat, so he was in the best of humors for granting favors and privileges. His good humor was increased by his winning a good many hands, for Padre Irene and Padre Sibyla, with whom he was playing, were exercising all their skill in secretly trying to lose, to the great irritation of Padre Camorra, who on account of his late arrival only that morning was not informed as to the game they were playing on the General. The friar-artilleryman was playing in good faith and with great care, so he turned red and bit his lip every time Padre Sibyla seemed inattentive or blundered, but he dared not say a word by reason of the respect he felt for the Dominican. In exchange he took his revenge out on Padre Irene, whom he looked upon as a base fawner and despised for his coarseness. Padre Sibyla let him scold, while the humbler Padre Irene tried to excuse himself by rubbing his long nose. His Excellency was enjoying it and took advantage, like the good tactician that the Canon hinted he was, of all the mistakes of his opponents. Padre Camorra was ignorant of the fact that across the table they were playing for the intellectual development of the Filipinos, the instruction in Castilian, but had he known it he would doubtless have joyfully entered into that *game*.

The open balcony admitted the fresh, pure breeze and revealed the lake, whose waters murmured sweetly around the base of the edifice, as if rendering homage. On the right, at a distance, appeared Talim Island, a deep blue in the midst of the lake, while almost in front lay the green and deserted islet of Kalamba, in the shape of a half-moon. To the left the picturesque shores were fringed with clumps of bamboo, then a hill overlooking the lake, with wide ricefields beyond, then red roofs amid the deep green of the trees,—the town of Kalamba,—and beyond the shore-line fading into the distance, with the horizon at the back closing down over the water, giving the lake the appearance of a sea and justifying the name the Indians give it of *dagat na tabang*, or fresh-water sea.

At the end of the sala, seated before a table covered with documents, was the secretary. His Excellency was a great worker and did not like to lose time, so he attended to business in the intervals of the game or while dealing the cards. Meanwhile, the bored secretary yawned and despaired. That morning he had worked, as usual, over transfers, suspensions of employees, deportations, pardons, and the like, but had not yet touched the great question that had stirred so much interest—the petition of the students requesting permission to establish an academy of Castilian. Pacing from one end of the room to the other and conversing animatedly but in low tones were to be seen Don Custodio, a high official, and a friar named Padre Fernandez, who hung his head with an air either of meditation or annoyance. From an adjoining room issued the click of balls striking together and bursts of laughter, amid which might be heard the sharp, dry voice of Simoun, who was playing billiards with Ben-Zayb.

Suddenly Padre Camorra arose. "The devil with this game, *puñales!*" he exclaimed, throwing his cards at Padre Irene's head. "*Puñales*, that trick, if not all the others, was assured and we lost by default! *Puñales!* The devil with this game!"

He explained the situation angrily to all the occupants of the sala, addressing himself especially to the three walking about, as if he had selected them for judges. The general played thus, he replied with such a card, Padre Irene had a certain card; he led, and then that fool of a Padre Irene didn't play his card! Padre Irene was giving the game away! It was a devil of a way to play! His mother's son had not come here to rack his brains for nothing and lose his money!

Then he added, turning very red, "If the booby thinks my money grows on every bush! . . . On top of the fact that my Indians are beginning to haggle over payments!" Fuming, and disregarding the excuses of Padre Irene, who tried to explain while he rubbed the tip of his beak in order to conceal his sly smile, he went into the billiardroom.

"Padre Fernandez, would you like to take a hand?" asked Fray Sibyla.

"I'm a very poor player," replied the friar with a grimace.

"Then get Simoun," said the General. "Eh, Simoun! Eh, Mister, won't you try a hand?"

"What is your disposition concerning the arms for sporting purposes?" asked the secretary, taking advantage of the pause.

Simoun thrust his head through the doorway.

"Don't you want to take Padre Camorra's place, Señor Sindbad?" inquired Padre Irene. "You can bet diamonds instead of chips."

"I don't care if I do," replied Simoun, advancing while he brushed the chalk from his hands. "What will you bet?"

"What should we bet?" returned Padre Sibyla. "The General can bet what he likes, but we priests, clerics—"

"Bah!" interrupted Simoun ironically. "You and Padre Irene can pay with deeds of charity, prayers, and virtues, eh?"

"You know that the virtues a person may possess," gravely argued Padre Sibyla, "are not like the diamonds that may pass from hand to hand, to be sold and resold. They are inherent in the being, they are essential attributes of the subject—"

"I'll be satisfied then if you pay me with promises," replied Simoun jestingly. "You, Padre Sibyla, instead of paying me five something or other in money, will say, for example: for five days I renounce poverty, humility, and obedience. You, Padre Irene: I renounce chastity, liberality, and so on. Those are small matters, and I'm putting up my diamonds."

"What a peculiar man this Simoun is, what notions he has!" exclaimed Padre Irene with a smile.

"And *he*," continued Simoun, slapping his Excellency familiarly on the shoulder, "he will pay me with an order for five days in prison, or five months, or an order of deportation made out in blank, or let us say a summary execution by the Civil Guard while my man is being conducted from one town to another."

This was a strange proposition, so the three who had been pacing about gathered around.

"But, Señor Simoun," asked the high official, "what good will you get out of winning promises of virtues, or lives and deportations and summary executions?"

"A great deal! I'm tired of hearing virtues talked about and would like to have the whole of them, all there are in the world, tied up in a sack, in order to throw them into the sea, even though I had to use my diamonds for sinkers."

"What an idea!" exclaimed Padre Irene with another smile. "And the deportations and executions, what of them?"

"Well, to clean the country and destroy every evil seed."

"Get out! You're still sore at the tulisanes. But you were lucky that they didn't demand a larger ransom or keep all your jewels. Man, don't be ungrateful!"

Simoun proceeded to relate how he had been intercepted by a band of tulisanes, who, after entertaining him for a day, had let him go on his way without exacting other ransom than his two fine revolvers and the two boxes of cartridges he carried with him. He added that the tulisanes had charged him with many kind regards for his Excellency, the Captain-General.

As a result of this, and as Simoun reported that the tulisanes were well provided with shotguns, rifles, and revolvers, and against such persons one man alone, no matter how well armed, could not defend himself, his Excellency, to prevent the tulisanes from getting weapons in the future, was about to dictate a new decree forbidding the introduction of sporting arms.

"On the contrary, on the contrary!" protested Simoun, "for me the tulisanes are the most respectable men in the country, they're the only ones who earn their living honestly. Suppose I had fallen into the hands—well, of you yourselves, for example, would you have let me escape without taking half of my jewels, at least?"

Don Custodio was on the point of protesting; that Simoun was really a rude American mulatto taking advantage of his friendship with the Captain-General to insult Padre Irene, although it may be true also that Padre Irene would hardly have set him free for so little.

"The evil is not," went on Simoun, "in that there are tulisanes in the mountains and uninhabited parts—the evil lies in the tulisanes in the towns and cities."

"Like yourself," put in the Canon with a smile.

"Yes, like myself, like all of us! Let's be frank, for no Indian is listening to us here," continued the jeweler. "The evil is that we're not all openly declared tulisanes. When that happens and we all take to the woods, on that day the country will be saved, on that day will rise a new social order which will take care of itself, and his Excellency will be able to play his game in peace, without the necessity of having his attention diverted by his secretary."

The person mentioned at that moment yawned, extending his folded arms above his head and stretching his crossed legs under the table as far as possible, upon noticing which all laughed. His Excellency wished to change the course of the conversation, so, throwing down the cards he had been shuffling, he said half seriously: "Come, come, enough of jokes and cards! Let's get to work, to work in earnest, since we still have a half-hour before breakfast. Are there many matters to be got through with?"

All now gave their attention. That was the day for joining battle over the question of instruction in Castilian, for which purpose Padre Sibyla and Padre Irene had been there several days. It was known that the former, as Vice-Rector, was opposed to the project and that the latter supported it, and his activity was in turn supported by the Countess.

"What is there, what is there?" asked his Excellency impatiently.

"The petition about sporting arms," replied the secretary with a stifled yawn.

"Forbidden!"

"Pardon, General," said the high official gravely, "your Excellency will permit me to invite your attention to the fact that the use of sporting arms is permitted in all the countries of the world."

The General shrugged his shoulders and remarked dryly, "We are not imitating any nation in the world."

Between his Excellency and the high official there was always a difference of opinion, so it was sufficient that the latter offer any suggestion whatsoever to have the former remain stubborn.

The high official tried another tack. "Sporting arms can harm only rats and chickens. They'll say—"

"But are we chickens?" interrupted the General, again shrugging his shoulders. "Am I? I've demonstrated that I'm not."

"But there's another thing," observed the secretary. "Four months ago, when the possession of arms was prohibited, the foreign importers were assured that sporting arms would be admitted."

His Excellency knitted his brows.

"That can be arranged," suggested Simoun.

"How?"

"Very simply. Sporting arms nearly all have a caliber of six millimeters, at least those now in the market. Authorize only the sale of those that haven't these six millimeters."

All approved this idea of Simoun's, except the high official, who muttered into Padre Fernandez's ear that this was not dignified, nor was it the way to govern.

"The schoolmaster of Tiani," proceeded the secretary, shuffling some papers about, "asks for a better location for—"

"What better location can he want than the storehouse that he has all to himself?" interrupted Padre Camorra, who had returned, having forgotten about the card-game.

"He says that it's roofless," replied the secretary, "and that having purchased out of his own pocket some maps and pictures, he doesn't want to expose them to the weather."

"But I haven't anything to do with that," muttered his Excellency. "He should address the head secretary,' the governor of the province, or the nuncio."

"I want to tell you," declared Padre Camorra, "that this little schoolmaster is a discontented filibuster. Just imagine—the heretic teaches that corpses rot just the same, whether buried with great pomp or without any! Some day I'm going to punch him!" Here he doubled up his fists.

"To tell the truth," observed Padre Sibyla, as if speaking only to Padre Irene, "he who wishes to teach, teaches everywhere, in the open air. Socrates taught in the public streets, Plato in the gardens of the Academy, even Christ among the mountains and lakes."

"I've heard several complaints against this schoolmaster," said his Excellency, exchanging a glance with Simoun. "I think the best thing would be to suspend him."

"Suspended!" repeated the secretary.

The luck of that unfortunate, who had asked for help and received his dismissal, pained the high official and he tried to do something for him.

"It's certain," he insinuated rather timidly, "that education is not at all well provided for—"

"I've already decreed large sums for the purchase of supplies," exclaimed his Excellency haughtily, as if to say, "I've done more than I ought to have done."

"But since suitable locations are lacking, the supplies purchased get ruined."

"Everything can't be done at once," said his Excellency dryly. "The schoolmasters here are doing wrong in asking for buildings when those in Spain starve to death. It's great presumption to be better off here than in the mother country itself!"

"Filibusterism—"

"Before everything the fatherland! Before everything else we are Spaniards!" added Ben-Zayb, his eyes glowing with patriotism, but he blushed somewhat when he noticed that he was speaking alone.

"In the future," decided the General, "all who complain will be suspended."

"If my project were accepted—" Don Custodio ventured to remark, as if talking to himself.

"For the construction of schoolhouses?"

"It's simple, practical, economical, and, like all my projects, derived from long experience and knowledge of the country. The towns would have schools without costing the government a cuarto."

"That's easy," observed the secretary sarcastically. "Compel the towns to construct them at their own expense," whereupon all laughed.

"No, sir! No, sir!" cried the exasperated Don Custodio, turning very red. "The buildings are already constructed and only wait to be utilized. Hygienic, unsurpassable, spacious—"

The friars looked at one another uneasily. Would Don Custodio propose that the churches and conventos be converted into schoolhouses?

"Let's hear it," said the General with a frown.

"Well, General, it's very simple," replied Don Custodio, drawing himself up and assuming his hollow voice of ceremony. "The schools are open only on week-days and the cockpits on holidays. Then convert these into schoolhouses, at least during the week."

"Man, man, man!"

"What a lovely idea!"

"What's the matter with you, Don Custodio?"

"That's a grand suggestion!"

"That beats them all!"

"But, gentlemen," cried Don Custodio, in answer to so many exclamations, "let's be practical—what places are more suitable than the cockpits? They're large, well constructed, and under a curse for the use to which they are put during the week-days. From a moral standpoint my project would be acceptable, by serving as a kind of expiation and weekly purification of the temple of chance, as we might say."

"But the fact remains that sometimes there are cockfights during the week," objected Padre Camorra, "and it wouldn't be right when the contractors of the cockpits pay the government—"

"Well, on those days close the school!"

"Man, man!" exclaimed the scandalized Captain-General. "Such an outrage shall never be perpetrated while I govern! To close the schools in order to gamble! Man, man, I'll resign first!" His Excellency was really horrified.

"But, General, it's better to close them for a few days than for months."

"It would be immoral," observed Padre Irene, more indignant even than his Excellency.

"It's more immoral that vice has good buildings and learning none. Let's be practical, gentlemen, and not be carried away by sentiment. In politics there's nothing worse than sentiment. While from humane considerations we forbid the cultivation of opium in our colonies, we tolerate the smoking of it, and the result is that we do not combat the vice but impoverish ourselves."

"But remember that it yields to the government, without any effort, more than four hundred and fifty thousand pesos," objected Padre Irene, who was getting more and more on the governmental side.

"Enough, enough, enough!" exclaimed his Excellency, to end the discussion. "I have my own plans in this regard and will devote special attention to the matter of public instruction. Is there anything else?"

The secretary looked uneasily toward Padre Sibyla and Padre Irene. The cat was about to come out of the bag. Both prepared themselves.

"The petition of the students requesting authorization to open an academy of Castilian," answered the secretary.

A general movement was noted among those in the room. After glancing at one another they fixed their eyes on the General to learn what his disposition would be. For six months the petition had lain there awaiting a decision and had become converted into a kind of *casus belli* in certain circles. His Excellency had lowered his eyes, as if to keep his thoughts from being read.

The silence became embarrassing, as the General understood, so he asked the high official, "What do you think?"

"What should I think, General?" responded the person addressed, with a shrug of his shoulders and a bitter smile. "What should I think but that the petition is just, very just, and that I am surprised that six months should have been taken to consider it."

"The fact is that it involves other considerations," said Padre Sibyla coldly, as he half closed his eyes.

The high official again shrugged his shoulders, like one who did not comprehend what those considerations could be.

"Besides the intemperateness of the demand," went on the Dominican, "besides the fact that it is in the nature of an infringement on our prerogatives—"

Padre Sibyla dared not go on, but looked at Simoun.

"The petition has a somewhat suspicious character," corroborated that individual, exchanging a look with the Dominican, who winked several times.

Padre Irene noticed these things and realized that his cause was almost lost—Simoun was against him.

"It's a peaceful rebellion, a revolution on stamped paper," added Padre Sibyla.

"Revolution? Rebellion?" inquired the high official, staring from one to the other as if he did not understand what they could mean.

"It's headed by some young men charged with being too radical and too much interested in reforms, not to use stronger terms," remarked the secretary, with a look at the Dominican. "Among them is a certain Isagani, a poorly balanced head, nephew of a native priest—"

"He's a pupil of mine," put in Padre Fernandez, "and I'm much pleased with him."

"*Puñales,* I like your taste!" exclaimed Padre Camorra. "On the steamer we nearly had a fight. He's so insolent that when I gave him a shove aside he returned it."

"There's also one Makaragui or Makarai—"

"Makaraig," Padre Irene joined in. "A very pleasant and agreeable young man."

Then he murmured into the General's ear, "He's the one I've talked to you about, he's very rich. The Countess recommends him strongly."

"Ah!"

"A medical student, one Basilio—"

"Of that Basilio, I'll say nothing," observed Padre Irene, raising his hands and opening them, as if to say *Dominus vobiscum.* "He's too deep for me. I've never succeeded in fathoming what he wants or what he is thinking about. It's a pity that Padre Salvi isn't present to tell us something about his antecedents. I believe that I've heard that when a boy he got into trouble with the Civil Guard. His father was killed in—I don't remember what disturbance."

Simoun smiled faintly, silently, showing his sharp white teeth.

"Aha! Aha!" said his Excellency nodding. "That's the kind we have! Make a note of that name."

"But, General," objected the high official, seeing that the matter was taking a bad turn, "up to now nothing positive is known against these young men. Their position is a very just one, and we have no right to deny it on the ground of mere conjectures. My opinion is that the government, by exhibiting confidence in the people and in its own stability, should grant what is asked, then it could freely revoke the permission when it saw that its kindness was being abused—reasons and pretexts would not be wanting, we can watch them. Why cause disaffection among some young men, who later on may feel resentment, when what they ask is commanded by royal decrees?"

Padre Irene, Don Custodio, and Padre Fernandez nodded in agreement.

"But the Indians must not understand Castilian, you know," cried Padre Camorra. "They mustn't learn it, for then they'll enter into arguments with us, and the Indians must not argue, but obey and pay. They mustn't try to interpret the meaning of the laws and the books, they're so tricky and pettifogish! Just as soon as they learn Castilian they become enemies of God and of Spain. Just read the *Tandang Basio Macunat*—that's a book! It tells truths like this!" And he held up his clenched fists.

Padre Sibyla rubbed his hand over his tonsure in sign of impatience. "One word," he began in the most conciliatory tone, though fuming with irritation, "here we're not dealing with the instruction in Castilian alone. Here there is an underhand fight between the students and the University of Santo Tomas. If the students win this, our prestige will be trampled in the dirt, they will say that they've beaten us and will exult accordingly. Then, good-by to moral strength, good-by to everything! The first dike broken down, who will restrain this youth? With our fall we do no more than signal your own. After us, the government!"

"*Puñales*, that's not so!" exclaimed Padre Camorra. "We'll see first who has the biggest fists!"

At this point Padre Fernandez, who thus far in the discussion had merely contented himself with smiling, began to talk. All gave him their attention, for they knew him to be a thoughtful man.

"Don't take it ill of me, Padre Sibyla, if I differ from your view of the affair, but it's my peculiar fate to be almost always in opposition to my brethren. I say, then, that we ought not to be so pessimistic. The instruction in Castilian can be allowed without any risk whatever, and in order that it may not appear to be a defeat of the University, we Dominicans ought to put forth our efforts and be the first to rejoice over it—that should be our policy. To what end are we to be engaged in an everlasting struggle with the people, when after all we are the few and they are the many, when we need them and they do not need us? Wait, Padre Camorra, wait! Admit that now the people may be weak and ignorant—I also believe that—but it will not be true tomorrow or the day after. Tomorrow and the next day they will be the stronger, they will know what is good for them, and we cannot keep it from them, just

99

as it is not possible to keep from children the knowledge of many things when they reach a certain age. I say, then, why should we not take advantage of this condition of ignorance to change our policy completely, to place it upon a basis solid and enduring—on the basis of justice, for example, instead of on the basis of ignorance? There's nothing like being just; that I've always said to my brethren, but they won't believe me. The Indian idolizes justice, like every race in its youth; he asks for punishment when he has done wrong, just as he is exasperated when he has not deserved it. Is theirs a just desire? Then grant it! Let's give them all the schools they want, until they are tired of them. Youth is lazy, and what urges them to activity is our opposition. Our bond of prestige, Padre Sibyla, is about worn out, so let's prepare another, the bond of gratitude, for example. Let's not be fools, let's do as the crafty Jesuits—"

"Padre Fernandez!" Anything could be tolerated by Padre Sibyla except to propose the Jesuits to him as a model. Pale and trembling, he broke out into bitter recrimination. "A Franciscan first! Anything before a Jesuit!" He was beside himself.

"Oh, oh!"

"Eh, Padre—"

A general discussion broke out, regardless of the Captain-General. All talked at once, they yelled, they misunderstood and contradicted one another. Ben-Zayb and Padre Camorra shook their fists in each other's faces, one talking of simpletons and the other of ink-slingers, Padre Sibyla kept harping on the *Capitulum*, and Padre Fernandez on the *Summa* of St. Thomas, until the curate of Los Baños entered to announce that breakfast was served.

His Excellency arose and so ended the discussion. "Well, gentlemen," he said, "we've worked like niggers and yet we're on a vacation. Some one has said that grave matters should he considered at dessert. I'm entirely of that opinion."

"We might get indigestion," remarked the secretary, alluding to the heat of the discussion.

"Then we'll lay it aside until tomorrow."

As they rose the high official whispered to the General, "Your Excellency, the daughter of Cabesang Tales has been here again begging for the release of her sick grandfather, who was arrested in place of her father."

His Excellency looked at him with an expression of impatience and rubbed his hand across his broad forehead. "*Carambas*! Can't one be left to eat his breakfast in peace?"

"This is the third day she has come. She's a poor girl—"

"Oh, the devil!" exclaimed Padre Camorra. "I've just thought of it. I have something to say to the General about that—that's what I came over for—to support that girl's petition."

The General scratched the back of his ear and said, "Oh, go along! Have the secretary make out an order to the lieutenant of the Civil Guard for the old man's release. They sha'n't say that we're not clement and merciful."

He looked at Ben-Zayb. The journalist winked.

---

1   Under the Spanish régime the government paid no attention to education, the schools (!) being under the control of the religious orders and the friar-curates of the towns.—Tr.

2   The cockpits are farmed out annually by the local governments, the terms "contract," and "contractor," having now been softened into "license" and "licensee."—Tr.

PLACIDO PENITENTE

Reluctantly, and almost with tearful eyes, Placido Penitente was going along the Escolta on his way to the University of Santo Tomas. It had hardly been a week since he had come from his town, yet he had already written to his mother twice, reiterating his desire to abandon his studies and go back there to work. His mother answered that he should have patience, that at the least he must be graduated as a bachelor of arts, since it would be unwise to desert his books after four years of expense and sacrifices on both their parts.

Whence came to Penitente this aversion to study, when he had been one of the most diligent in the famous college conducted by Padre Valerio in Tanawan? There Penitente had been considered one of the best Latinists and the subtlest disputants, one who could tangle or untangle the simplest as well as the most abstruse questions. His townspeople considered him very clever, and his curate, influenced by that opinion, already classified him as a filibuster—a sure proof that he was neither foolish nor incapable. His friends could not explain those desires for abandoning his studies and returning: he had no sweethearts, was not a gambler, hardly knew anything about *hunkian* and rarely tried his luck at the more familiar *revesino*. He did not believe in the advice of the curates, laughed at *Tandang Basio Macunat*, had plenty of money and good clothes, yet he went to school reluctantly and looked with repugnance on his books.

On the Bridge of Spain, a bridge whose name alone came from Spain, since even its ironwork came from foreign countries, he fell in with the long procession of young men on their way to the Walled City to their respective schools. Some were dressed in the European fashion and walked rapidly, carrying books and notes, absorbed in thoughts of their lessons and essays—these were the students of the Ateneo. Those from San Juan de Letran were nearly all dressed in the Filipino costume, but were more numerous and carried fewer books. Those from the University are dressed more carefully and elegantly and saunter along carrying canes instead of books. The collegians of the Philippines are not very noisy or turbulent. They move along in a preoccupied manner, such that upon seeing them one would say that before their eyes shone no hope, no smiling future. Even though here and there the line is brightened by the attractive appearance of the schoolgirls of the *Escuela Municipal*,' with their sashes across their shoulders and their books in their hands, followed by their servants, yet scarcely a laugh resounds or a joke can be heard—nothing of song or jest, at best a few heavy jokes or scuffles among the smaller boys. The older ones nearly always proceed seriously and composedly, like the German students.

Placido was proceeding along the Paseo de Magallanes toward the breach—formerly the gate—of Santo Domingo, when he suddenly felt a slap on the shoulder, which made him turn quickly in ill humor.

"Hello, Penitente! Hello, Penitente!"

It was his schoolmate Juanito Pelaez, the *barbero* or pet of the professors, as big a rascal as he could be, with a roguish look and a clownish smile. The son of a Spanish mestizo—a rich merchant in one of the suburbs, who based all his hopes and joys on the boy's talent—he promised well with his roguery, and, thanks to his custom of playing tricks on every one and then hiding behind his companions, he had acquired a peculiar hump, which grew larger whenever he was laughing over his deviltry.

"What kind of time did you have, Penitente?" was his question as he again slapped him on the shoulder.

"So, so," answered Placido, rather bored. "And you?"

"Well, it was great! Just imagine—the curate of Tiani invited me to spend the vacation in his town, and I went. Old man, you know Padre Camorra, I suppose? Well, he's a liberal curate, very jolly, frank, very frank, one of those like Padre Paco. As there were pretty girls, we serenaded them all, he with his guitar and songs and I with my violin. I tell you, old man, we had a great time—there wasn't a house we didn't try!"

He whispered a few words in Placido's ear and then broke out into laughter. As the latter exhibited some surprise, he resumed: "I'll swear to it! They can't help themselves, because with a governmental order you get rid of the father, husband, or brother, and then—merry Christmas! However, we did run up against a little fool, the sweetheart, I believe, of Basilio, you know? Look, what a fool this Basilio is! To have a sweetheart who doesn't know a word of Spanish, who hasn't any money, and who has been a servant! She's as shy as she can be, but pretty. Padre Camorra one night started to club two fellows who were serenading her and I don't know how it was he didn't kill them, yet with all that she was just as shy as ever. But it'll result for her as it does with all the women, all of them!"

Juanito Pelaez laughed with a full mouth, as though he thought this a glorious thing, while Placido stared at him in disgust.

"Listen, what did the professor explain yesterday?" asked Juanito, changing the conversation.

"Yesterday there was no class."

"Oho, and the day before yesterday?"

"Man, it was Thursday!"

"Right! What an ass I am! Don't you know, Placido, that I'm getting to be a regular ass? What about Wednesday?"

"Wednesday? Wait—Wednesday, it was a little wet."

"Fine! What about Tuesday, old man?"

"Tuesday was the professor's nameday and we went to entertain him with an orchestra, present him flowers and some gifts."

"Ah, *carambas!*" exclaimed Juanito, "that I should have forgotten about it! What an ass I am! Listen, did he ask for me?"

Penitente shrugged his shoulders. "I don't know, but they gave him a list of his entertainers."

"*Carambas!* Listen—Monday, what happened?"

"As it was the first school-day, he called the roll and assigned the lesson—about mirrors. Look, from here to here, by memory, word for word. We jump all this section, we take that." He was pointing out with his finger in the "Physics" the portions that were to be learned, when suddenly the book flew through the air, as a result of the slap Juanito gave it from below.

"Thunder, let the lessons go! Let's have a *dia pichido!*"

The students in Manila call *dia pichido* a school-day that falls between two holidays and is consequently suppressed, as though forced out by their wish.

"Do you know that you really are an ass?" exclaimed Placido, picking up his book and papers.

"Let's have a *dia pichido!*" repeated Juanito.

Placido was unwilling, since for only two the authorities were hardly going to suspend a class of more than a hundred and fifty. He recalled the struggles and privations his mother was suffering in order to keep him in Manila, while she went without even the necessities of life.

They were just passing through the breach of Santo Domingo, and Juanito, gazing across the little plaza[2] in front of the old Customs building, exclaimed, "Now I think of it, I'm appointed to take up the collection."

"What collection?"

"For the monument."

"What monument?"

"Get out! For Padre Balthazar, you know."

"And who was Padre Balthazar?"

"Fool! A Dominican, of course—that's why the padres call on the students. Come on now, loosen up with three or four pesos, so that they may see we are sports. Don't let them say afterwards that in order to erect a statue they had to dig down into their own pockets. Do, Placido, it's not money thrown away."

He accompanied these words with a significant wink. Placido recalled the case of a student who had passed through the entire course by presenting canary-birds, so he subscribed three pesos.

"Look now, I'll write your name plainly so that the professor will read it, you see—Placido Penitente, three pesos. Ah, listen! In a couple of weeks comes the nameday of the professor of natural history. You know that he's a good fellow, never marks absences or asks about the lesson. Man, we must show our appreciation!"

"That's right!"

"Then don't you think that we ought to give him a celebration? The orchestra must not be smaller than the one you had for the professor of physics."

"That's right!"

"What do you think about making the contribution two pesos? Come, Placido, you start it, so you'll be at the head of the list."

Then, seeing that Placido gave the two pesos without hesitation, he added, "Listen, put up four, and afterwards I'll return you two. They'll serve as a decoy."

"Well, if you're going to return them to me, why give them to you? It'll be sufficient, for you to write four."

"Ah, that's right! What an ass I am! Do you know, I'm getting to be a regular ass! But let me have them anyhow, so that I can show them."

Placido, in order not to give the lie to the priest who christened him, gave what was asked, just as they reached the University.

In the entrance and along the walks on each side of it were gathered the students, awaiting the appearance of the professors. Students of the preparatory year of law, of the fifth of the secondary course, of the preparatory in medicine, formed lively groups. The latter were easily distinguished by their clothing and by a certain air that was lacking in the others, since the greater part of them came from the Ateneo Municipal. Among them could be seen the poet Isagani, explaining to a companion the theory of the refraction of light. In another group they were talking, disputing, citing the statements of the professor, the text-books, and scholastic principles; in yet another they were gesticulating and waving their books in the air or making demonstrations with their canes by drawing diagrams on the ground; farther on, they were entertaining themselves in watching the pious women go into the neighboring church, all the students making facetious remarks. An old woman leaning on a young girl limped piously, while the girl moved along wrrith downcast eyes, timid and abashed to pass before so many curious eyes. The old lady, catching up her coffee-colored skirt, of the Sisterhood of St. Rita, to reveal her big feet and white stockings, scolded her companion and shot furious glances at the staring bystanders.

"The rascals!" she grunted. "Don't look at them, keep your eyes down."

Everything was noticed; everything called forth jokes and comments. Now it was a magnificent victoria which stopped at the door to set down a family of votaries on their way to visit the Virgin of the Rosary[3] on her favorite day, while the inquisitive sharpened their eyes to get a glimpse of the shape and size of the young ladies' feet as they got out of the carriages; now it was a student who came out of the door with devotion still shining in his eyes, for he had passed through the church to beg the Virgin's help in understanding his lesson and to see if his sweetheart was there, to exchange a few glances with her and go on to his class with the recollection of her loving eyes.

Soon there was noticed some movement in the groups, a certain air of expectancy, while Isagani paused and turned pale. A carriage drawn by a pair of well-known white horses had stopped at the door. It was that of Paulita Gomez, and she had already jumped down, light as a bird, without giving the rascals time to see her foot. With a bewitching whirl of her body and a sweep of her hand she arranged the folds of her skirt, shot a rapid and apparently careless glance toward Isagani, spoke to him and smiled. Doña Victorina descended in her turn, gazed over her spectacles, saw Juanito Pelaez, smiled, and bowed to him affably.

Isagani, flushed with excitement, returned a timid salute, while Juanito bowed profoundly, took off his hat, and made the same gesture as the celebrated clown and caricaturist Panza when he received applause.

"Heavens, what a girl!" exclaimed one of the students, starting forward. "Tell the professor that I'm seriously ill." So Tadeo, as this invalid youth was known, entered the church to follow the girl.

Tadeo went to the University every day to ask if the classes would be held and each time seemed to be more and more astonished that they would. He had a fixed idea of a latent and eternal *holiday*, and expected it to come any day. So each morning, after vainly proposing that they play truant, he would go away alleging important business, an appointment, or illness, just at the very moment when his companions were going to their classes. But by some occult, thaumaturgic art Tadeo passed the examinations, was beloved by the professors, and had before him a promising future.

Meanwhile, the groups began to move inside, for the professor of physics and chemistry had put in his appearance. The students appeared to be cheated in their hopes and went toward the interior of the building with exclamations of discontent. Placido went along with the crowd.

"Penitente, Penitente!" called a student with a certain mysterious air. "Sign this!"

"What is it?"

"Never mind—sign it!"

It seemed to Placido that some one was twitching his ears. He recalled the story of a cabeza de barangay in his town who, for having signed a document that he did not understand, was kept a prisoner for months and months, and came near to deportation. An uncle of Placido's, in order to fix the lesson in his memory, had given him a severe ear-pulling, so that always whenever he heard signatures spoken of, his ears reproduced the sensation.

"Excuse me, but I can't sign anything without first understanding what it's about."

"What a fool you are! If two *celestial carbineers* have signed it, what have you to fear?"

The name of *celestial carbineers* inspired confidence, being, as it was, a sacred company created to aid God in the warfare against the evil spirit and to prevent the smuggling of heretical contraband into the markets of the New Zion.'

Placido was about to sign to make an end of it, because he was in a hurry,—already his classmates were reciting the *O Thoma*,—but again his ears twitched, so he said, "After the class! I want to read it first."

"It's very long, don't you see? It concerns the presentation of a counter-petition, or rather, a protest. Don't you understand? Makaraig and some others have asked that an academy of Castilian be opened, which is a piece of genuine foolishness—"

"All right, all right, after awhile. They're already beginning," answered Placido, trying to get away.

"But your professor may not call the roll—"

"Yes, yes; but he calls it sometimes. Later on, later on! Besides, I don't want to put myself in opposition to Makaraig."

"But it's not putting yourself in opposition, it's only—"

Placido heard no more, for he was already far away, hurrying to his class. He heard the different voices—*adsum, adsum*—the roll was being called! Hastening his steps he got to the door just as the letter Q was reached.

"*Tinamáan ñg—!*" he muttered, biting his lips.

He hesitated about entering, for the mark was already down against him and was not to be erased. One did not go to the class to learn but in order not to get this absence mark, for the class was reduced to reciting the lesson from memory, reading the book, and at the most answering a few abstract, profound, captious, enigmatic questions. True, the usual preachment was never lacking—the same as ever, about humility, submission, and respect to the clerics, and he, Placido, was humble, submissive, and respectful. So he was about to turn away when he remembered that the examinations were approaching and his professor had not yet asked him a question nor appeared to notice him—this would be a good opportunity to attract his attention and become known! To be known was to gain a year, for if it cost nothing to suspend one who was not known, it required a hard heart not to be touched by the sight of a youth who by his daily presence was a reproach over a year of his life wasted.

So Placido went in, not on tiptoe as was his custom, but noisily on his heels, and only too well did he succeed in his intent! The professor stared at him, knitted his brows, and shook his head, as though to say, "Ah, little impudence, you'll pay for that!"

---

1   The "Municipal School for Girls" was founded by the municipality of Manila in 1864 ... The institution was in charge of the Sisters of Charity.—*Census of the Philippine Islands, Vol. III, p. 615.*

2   Now known as Plaza España.—Tr.

3   Patroness of the Dominican Order. She was formally and sumptuously recrowned a queen of the skies in 1907.—Tr.

4   A burlesque on an association of students known as the *Milicia Angelica*, organized by the Dominicans to strengthen their hold on the people. The name used is significant, "carbineers" being the local revenue officers, notorious in their later days for graft and abuse.—Tr.

5   "Tinamáan ñg lintik!"—a Tagalog exclamation of anger, disappointment, or dismay, regarded as a very strong expression, equivalent to profanity. Literally, "May the lightning strike you!"—Tr.

THE CLASS IN PHYSICS

The classroom was a spacious rectangular hall with large grated windows that admitted an abundance of light and air. Along the two sides extended three wide tiers of stone covered with wood, filled with students arranged in alphabetical order. At the end opposite the entrance, under a print of St. Thomas Aquinas, rose the professor's chair on an elevated platform with a little stairway on each side. With the exception of a beautiful blackboard in a narra frame, scarcely ever used, since there was still written on it the *viva* that had appeared on the opening day, no furniture, either useful or useless, was to be seen. The walls, painted white and covered with glazed tiles to prevent scratches, were entirely bare, having neither a drawing nor a picture, nor even an outline of any physical apparatus. The students had no need of any, no one missed the practical instruction in an extremely experimental science; for years and years it has been so taught and the country has not been upset, but continues just as ever. Now and then some little instrument descended from heaven and was exhibited to the class from a distance, like the monstrance to the prostrate worshipers—look, but touch not! From time to time, when some complacent professor appeared, one day in the year was set aside for visiting the mysterious laboratory and gazing from without at the puzzling apparatus arranged in glass cases. No one could complain, for on that day there were to be seen quantities of brass and glassware, tubes, disks, wheels, bells, and the like—the exhibition did not get beyond that, and the country was not upset.

Besides, the students were convinced that those instruments had not been purchased for them—the friars would be fools! The laboratory was intended to be shown to the visitors and the high officials who came from the Peninsula, so that upon seeing it they would nod their heads with satisfaction, while their guide would smile, as if to say, "Eh, you thought you were going to find some backward monks! Well, we're right up with the times—we have a laboratory!"

The visitors and high officials, after being handsomely entertained, would then write in their *Travels* or *Memoirs*: "The Royal and Pontifical University of Santo Tomas of Manila, in charge of the enlightened Dominican Order, possesses a magnificent physical laboratory for the instruction of youth. Some two hundred and fifty students annually study this subject, but whether from apathy, indolence, the limited capacity of the Indian, or some other ethnological or incomprehensible reason, up to now there has not developed a Lavoisier, a Secchi, or a Tyndall, not even in miniature, in the Malay-Filipino race."

Yet, to be exact, we will say that in this laboratory are held the classes of thirty or forty *advanced* students, under the direction of an instructor who performs his duties well enough, but as the greater part of these students come from the Ateneo of the Jesuits, where science is taught practically in the laboratory itself, its utility does not come to be so great as it would be if it could be utilized by the two hundred and fifty who pay their matriculation fees, buy their books, memorize them, and waste a year to know nothing afterwards. As a result, with the exception of some rare usher or janitor who has had charge of the museum for years, no one has ever been known to get any advantage from the lessons memorized with so great effort.

But let us return to the class. The professor was a young Dominican, who had filled several chairs in San Juan de Letran with zeal and good repute. He had the reputation of being a great logician as well as a profound philosopher, and was one of the most promising in his clique. His elders treated him with consideration, while the younger men envied him, for there were also cliques among them. This was the third year of his professorship and, although the first in which he had taught physics and chemistry, he already passed for a sage, not only with the complaisant students but also among the other nomadic professors. Padre Millon did not belong to the common crowd who each year change their subject in order to acquire scientific knowledge, students among other students, with the difference only that they follow a single course, that they quiz instead of being quizzed, that they have a better

111

knowledge of Castilian, and that they are not examined at the completion of the course. Padre Millon went deeply into science, knew the physics of Aristotle and Padre Amat, read carefully his "Ramos," and sometimes glanced at "Ganot." With all that, he would often shake his head with an air of doubt, as he smiled and murmured: "*transeat.*" In regard to chemistry, no common knowledge was attributed to him after he had taken as a premise the statement of St. Thomas that water is a mixture and proved plainly that the Angelic Doctor had long forestalled Berzelius, Gay-Lussac, Bunsen, and other more or less presumptuous materialists. Moreover, in spite of having been an instructor in geography, he still entertained certain doubts as to the rotundity of the earth and smiled maliciously when its rotation and revolution around the sun were mentioned, as he recited the verses

> "El mentir de las estrellas
> Es un cómodo mentir."

He also smiled maliciously in the presence of certain physical theories and considered visionary, if not actually insane, the Jesuit Secchi, to whom he imputed the making of triangulations on the host as a result of his astronomical mania, for which reason it was said that he had been forbidden to celebrate mass. Many persons also noticed in him some aversion to the sciences that he taught, but these vagaries were trifles, scholarly and religious prejudices that were easily explained, not only by the fact that the physical sciences were eminently practical, of pure observation and deduction, while his forte was philosophy, purely speculative, of abstraction and induction, but also because, like any good Dominican, jealous of the fame of his order, he could hardly feel any affection for a science in which none of his brethren had excelled—he was the first who did not accept the chemistry of St. Thomas Aquinas—and in which so much renown had been acquired by hostile, or rather, let us say, rival orders.

This was the professor who that morning called the roll and directed many of the students to recite the lesson from memory, word for word. The phonographs got into operation, some well, some ill, some stammering, and received their grades. He who recited without an error earned a good mark and he who made more than three mistakes a bad mark.

A fat boy with a sleepy face and hair as stiff and hard as the bristles of a brush yawned until he seemed to be about to dislocate his jaws, and stretched himself with his arms extended as though he were in his bed. The professor saw this and wished to startle him.

"Eh, there, sleepy-head! What's this? Lazy, too, so it's sure you don't know the lesson, ha?"

Padre Millon not only used the depreciative *tu* with the students, like a good friar, but he also addressed them in the slang of the markets, a practise that he had acquired from the professor of canonical law: whether that reverend gentleman wished to humble the students or the sacred decrees of the councils is a question not yet settled, in spite of the great attention that has been given to it.

This question, instead of offending the class, amused them, and many laughed—it was a daily occurrence. But the sleeper did not laugh; he arose with a bound, rubbed his eyes, and, as though a steam-engine were turning the phonograph, began to recite.

"The name of mirror is applied to all polished surfaces intended to produce by the reflection of light the images of the objects placed before said surfaces. From the substances that form these surfaces, they are divided into metallic mirrors and glass mirrors—"

"Stop, stop, stop!" interrupted the professor. "Heavens, what a rattle! We are at the point where the mirrors are divided into metallic and glass, eh? Now if I should present to you a block of wood, a piece of kamagon for instance, well polished and varnished, or a slab of black marble well burnished, or a square of jet, which would reflect the images of objects placed before them, how would you classify those mirrors?"

Whether he did not know what to answer or did not understand the question, the student tried to get out of the difficulty by demonstrating that he knew the lesson, so he rushed on like a torrent.

"The first are composed of brass or an alloy of different metals and the second of a sheet of glass, with its two sides well polished, one of which has an amalgam of tin adhering to it."

"Tut, tut, tut! That's not it! I say to you '*Dominus vobiscum*,' and you answer me with '*Requiescat in pace!*'"

The worthy professor then repeated the question in the vernacular of the markets, interspersed with *cosas* and *abás* at every moment.

The poor youth did not know how to get out of the quandary: he doubted whether to include the kamagon with the metals, or the marble with glasses, and leave the jet as a neutral substance, until Juanito Pelaez maliciously prompted him:

"The mirror of kamagon among the wooden mirrors."

The incautious youth repeated this aloud and half the class was convulsed with laughter.

"A good sample of wood you are yourself!" exclaimed the professor, laughing in spite of himself. "Let's see from what you would define a mirror—from a surface *per se, in quantum est superficies*, or from a substance that forms the surface, or from the substance upon which the surface rests, the raw material, modified by the attribute 'surface,' since it is clear that, surface being an accidental property of bodies, it cannot exist without substance. Let's see now—what do you say?"

"I? Nothing!" the wretched boy was about to reply, for he did not understand what it was all about, confused as he was by so many surfaces and so many accidents that smote cruelly on his ears, but a sense of shame restrained him. Filled with anguish and breaking into a cold perspiration, he began to repeat between his teeth: "The name of mirror is applied to all polished surfaces—"

"*Ergo, per te*, the mirror is the surface," angled the professor. "Well, then, clear up this difficulty. If the surface is the mirror, it must be of no consequence to the 'essence' of the mirror what may be found behind this surface, since what is behind it does not affect the 'essence' that is before it, *id est*, the surface, *quae super faciem est, quia vocatur superficies, facies ea quae supra videtur*. Do you admit that or do you not admit it?"

The poor youth's hair stood up straighter than ever, as though acted upon by some magnetic force.

"Do you admit it or do you not admit it?"

"Anything! Whatever you wish, Padre," was his thought, but he did not dare to express it from fear of ridicule. That was a dilemma indeed, and he had never been in a worse one. He had a vague idea that the most innocent thing could not be admitted to the friars but that they, or rather their estates and curacies, would get out of it all the results and advantages imaginable. So his good angel prompted him to deny everything with all the energy of his soul and refractoriness of his hair, and he was about to shout a proud *nego*, for the reason that he who denies everything does not compromise himself in anything, as a certain lawyer had once told him; but the evil habit of disregarding the dictates of one's own conscience, of having little faith in legal folk, and of seeking aid from others where one is sufficient unto himself, was his undoing. His companions, especially Juanito Pelaez, were making signs to him to admit it, so he let himself be carried away by his evil destiny and exclaimed, "*Concedo*, Padre," in a voice as faltering as though he were saying, "*In manus tuas commendo spiritum meum.*"

"*Concedo antecedentum*," echoed the professor, smiling maliciously. "*Ergo*, I can scratch the mercury off a looking-glass, put in its place a piece of *bibinka*, and we shall still have a mirror, eh? Now what shall we have?"

The youth gazed at his prompters, but seeing them surprised and speechless, contracted his features into an expression of bitterest reproach. "*Deus meus, Deus meus, quare dereliquiste me*," said his troubled eyes, while his lips muttered "*Linintikan!*" Vainly he coughed, fumbled at his shirt-bosom, stood first on one foot and then on the other, but found no answer.

"Come now, what have we?" urged the professor, enjoying the effect of his reasoning.

"*Bibinka!*" whispered Juanito Pelaez. "*Bibinka!*"

"Shut up, you fool!" cried the desperate youth, hoping to get out of the difficulty by turning it into a complaint.

"Let's see, Juanito, if you can answer the question for me," the professor then said to Pelaez, who was one of his pets.

The latter rose slowly, not without first giving Penitente, who followed him on the roll, a nudge that meant, "Don't forget to prompt me."

"*Nego consequentiam*, Padre," he replied resolutely.

"Aha, then *probo consequentiam! Per te*, the polished surface constitutes the 'essence' of the mirror—"

"*Nego suppositum!*" interrupted Juanito, as he felt Placido pulling at his coat.

"How? *Per te—*"

"*Nego!*"

"*Ergo,* you believe that what is behind affects what is in front?"

"Nego!" the student cried with still more ardor, feeling another jerk at his coat.

Juanito, or rather Placido, who was prompting him, was unconsciously adopting Chinese tactics: not to admit the most inoffensive foreigner in order not to be invaded.

"Then where are we?" asked the professor, somewhat disconcerted, and looking uneasily at the refractory student. "Does the substance behind affect, or does it not affect, the surface?"

To this precise and categorical question, a kind of ultimatum, Juanito did not know what to reply and his coat offered no suggestions. In vain he made signs to Placido, but Placido himself was in doubt. Juanito then took advantage of a moment in which the professor was staring at a student who was cautiously and secretly taking off the shoes that hurt his feet, to step heavily on Placido's toes and whisper, "Tell me, hurry up, tell me!"

"I distinguish—Get out! What an ass you are!" yelled Placido unreservedly, as he stared with angry eyes and rubbed his hand over his patent-leather shoe.

The professor heard the cry, stared at the pair, and guessed what had happened.

"Listen, you meddler," he addressed Placido, "I wasn't questioning you, but since you think you can save others, let's see if you can save yourself, *salva te ipsum,* and decide this question."

Juanito sat down in content, and as a mark of gratitude stuck out his tongue at his prompter, who had arisen blushing with shame and muttering incoherent excuses.

For a moment Padre Millon regarded him as one gloating over a favorite dish. What a good thing it would be to humiliate and hold up to ridicule that dudish boy, always smartly dressed, with head erect and serene look! It would be a deed of charity, so the charitable professor applied himself to it with all his heart, slowly repeating the question.

"The book says that the metallic mirrors are made of brass and an alloy of different metals—is that true or is it not true?"

"So the book says, Padre."

"*Liber dixit, ergo ita est.* Don't pretend that you know more than the book does. It then adds that the glass mirrors are made of a sheet of glass whose two surfaces are well polished, one of them having applied to it an amalgam of tin, *nota bene*, an amalgam of tin! Is that true?"

"If the book says so, Padre."

"Is tin a metal?"

"It seems so, Padre. The book says so."

"It is, it is, and the word amalgam means that it is compounded with mercury, which is also a metal. *Ergo*, a glass mirror is a metallic mirror; *ergo*, the terms of the distinction are confused; *ergo*, the classification is imperfect—how do you explain that, meddler?"

He emphasized the *ergos* and the familiar "you's" with indescribable relish, at the same time winking, as though to say, "You're done for."

"It means that, it means that—" stammered Placido.

"It means that you haven't learned the lesson, you petty meddler, you don't understand it yourself, and yet you prompt your neighbor!"

The class took no offense, but on the contrary many thought the epithet funny and laughed. Placido bit his lips.

"What's your name?" the professor asked him.

"Placido," was the curt reply.

"Aha! Placido Penitente, although you look more like Placido the Prompter—or the Prompted. But, *Penitent*, I'm going to impose some *penance* on you for your promptings."

Pleased with his play on words, he ordered the youth to recite the lesson, and the latter, in the state of mind to which he was reduced, made more than three mistakes. Shaking his head up and down, the professor slowly opened the register and slowly scanned it while he called off the names in a low voice.

"Palencia—Palomo—Panganiban—Pedraza—Pelado—Pelaez—Penitents, aha! Placido Penitente, fifteen unexcused absences—"

Placido started up. "Fifteen absences, Padre?"

"Fifteen unexcused absences," continued the professor, "so that you only lack one to be dropped from the roll."

"Fifteen absences, fifteen absences," repeated Placido in amazement. "I've never been absent more than four times, and with today, perhaps five."

"Jesso, jesso, monseer," replied the professor, examining the youth over his gold eye-glasses. "You confess that you have missed five times, and God knows if you may have missed oftener. *Atqui*, as I rarely call the roll, every time I catch any one I put five marks against him; *ergo*, how many are five times five? Have you forgotten the multiplication table? Five times five?"

"Twenty-five."

"Correct, correct! Thus you've still got away with ten, because I have caught you only three times. Huh, if I had caught you every time—Now, how many are three times five?"

"Fifteen."

"Fifteen, right you are!" concluded the professor, closing the register. "If you miss once more—out of doors with you, get out! Ah, now a mark for the failure in the daily lesson."

He again opened the register, sought out the name, and entered the mark. "Come, only one mark," he said, "since you hadn't any before."

"But, Padre," exclaimed Placido, restraining himself, "if your Reverence puts a mark against me for failing in the lesson, your Reverence owes it to me to erase the one for absence that you have put against me for today."

His Reverence made no answer. First he slowly entered the mark, then contemplated it with his head on one side,—the mark must be artistic,—closed the register, and asked with great sarcasm, "*Abá*, and why so, sir?"

"Because I can't conceive, Padre, how one can be absent from the class and at the same time recite the lesson in it. Your Reverence is saying that to be is not to be."

"*Nakú*, a metaphysician, but a rather premature one! So you can't conceive of it, eh? *Sed patet experientia* and *contra experientiam negantem, fusilibus est arguendum*, do you understand? And can't you conceive, with your philosophical head, that one can be absent from the class and not know the lesson at the same time? Is it a fact that absence necessarily implies knowledge? What do you say to that, philosophaster?"

This last epithet was the drop of water that made the full cup overflow. Placido enjoyed among his friends the reputation of being a philosopher, so he lost his patience, threw down his book, arose, and faced the professor.

"Enough, Padre, enough! Your Reverence can put all the marks against me that you wish, but you haven't the right to insult me. Your Reverence may stay with the class, I can't stand any more." Without further farewell, he stalked away.

The class was astounded; such an assumption of dignity had scarcely ever been seen, and who would have thought it of Placido Penitente? The surprised professor bit his lips and shook his head threateningly as he watched him depart. Then in a trembling voice he began his preachment on the same old theme, delivered however with more energy and more eloquence. It dealt with the growing arrogance, the innate ingratitude, the presumption, the lack of respect for superiors, the pride that the spirit of darkness infused in the young, the lack of manners, the absence of courtesy, and so on. From this he passed to coarse jests and sarcasm over the presumption which some good-for-nothing "prompters" had of teaching their teachers by establishing an academy for instruction in Castilian.

"Aha, aha!" he moralized, "those who the day before yesterday scarcely knew how to say, 'Yes, Padre,' 'No, Padre,' now want to know more than those who have grown gray teaching them. He who wishes to learn, will learn, academies or no academies! Undoubtedly that fellow who has just gone out is one of those in the project. Castilian is in good hands with such guardians! When are you going to get the time to attend the academy if you have scarcely enough to fulfill your duties in the regular classes? We wish that you may all know Spanish and that you pronounce it well, so that you won't split our ear-drums with your twist of expression and your 'p's';' but first business and then pleasure: finish your studies first, and afterwards learn Castilian, and all become clerks, if you so wish."

So he went on with his harangue until the bell rang and the class was over. The two hundred and thirty-four students, after reciting their prayers, went out as ignorant as when they went in, but breathing more freely, as if a great weight had been lifted from them. Each youth had lost another hour of his life and with it a portion of his dignity and self-respect, and in exchange there was an increase of discontent, of aversion to study, of resentment in their hearts. After all this ask for knowledge, dignity, gratitude!

De nobis, post haec, tristis sententia fertur!

Just as the two hundred and thirty-four spent their class hours, so the thousands of students who preceded them have spent theirs, and, if matters do not mend, so will those yet to come spend theirs, and be brutalized, while wounded dignity and youthful enthusiasm will be converted into hatred and sloth, like the waves that become polluted along one part of the shore and roll on one after another, each in succession depositing a larger sediment of filth. But yet He who from eternity watches the consequences of a deed develop like a thread through the loom of the centuries, He who weighs the value of a second and has ordained for His creatures as an elemental law progress and development, He, if He is just, will demand a strict accounting from those who must render it, of the millions of intelligences darkened and blinded, of human dignity trampled upon in millions of His creatures, and of the incalculable time lost and effort wasted! And if the teachings of the Gospel are based on truth, so also will these have to answer—the millions and millions who do not know how to preserve the light of their intelligences and their dignity of mind, as the master demanded an accounting from the cowardly servant for the talent that he let be taken from him.

---

1   "To lie about the stars is a safe kind of lying."—Tr.
2   Throughout this chapter the professor uses the familiar *tu* in addressing the students, thus giving his remarks a contemptuous tone.—Tr.
3   The professor speaks these words in vulgar dialect.
4   To confuse the letters *p* and *f* in speaking Spanish was a common error among uneducated Filipinos.—Tr.

IN THE HOUSE OF THE STUDENTS

The house where Makaraig lived was worth visiting. Large and spacious, with two entresols provided with elegant gratings, it seemed to be a school during the first hours of the morning and pandemonium from ten o'clock on. During the boarders' recreation hours, from the lower hallway of the spacious entrance up to the main floor, there was a bubbling of laughter, shouts, and movement. Boys in scanty clothing played *sipa* or practised gymnastic exercises on improvised trapezes, while on the staircase a fight was in progress between eight or nine armed with canes, sticks, and ropes, but neither attackers nor attacked did any great damage, their blows generally falling sidewise upon the shoulders of the Chinese pedler who was there selling his outlandish mixtures and indigestible pastries. Crowds of boys surrounded him, pulled at his already disordered queue, snatched pies from him, haggled over the prices, and committed a thousand deviltries. The Chinese yelled, swore, forswore, in all the languages he could jabber, not omitting his own; he whimpered, laughed, pleaded, put on a smiling face when an ugly one would not serve, or the reverse.

He cursed them as devils, savages, *no kilistanos* but that mattered nothing. A whack would bring his face around smiling, and if the blow fell only upon his shoulders he would calmly continue his business transactions, contenting himself with crying out to them that he was not in the game, but if it struck the flat basket on which were placed his wares, then he would swear never to come again, as he poured out upon them all the imprecations and anathemas imaginable. Then the boys would redouble their efforts to make him rage the more, and when at last his vocabulary was exhausted and they were satiated with his fearful mixtures, they paid him religiously, and sent him away happy, winking, chuckling to himself, and receiving as caresses the light blows from their canes that the students gave him as tokens of farewell.

Concerts on the piano and violin, the guitar, and the accordion, alternated with the continual clashing of blades from the fencing lessons. Around a long, wide table the students of the Ateneo prepared their compositions or solved their problems by the side of others writing to their sweethearts on pink perforated note-paper covered with drawings. Here one was composing a melodrama at the side of another practising on the flute, from which he drew wheezy notes. Over there, the older boys, students in professional courses, who affected silk socks and embroidered slippers, amused themselves in teasing the smaller boys by pulling their ears, already red from repeated fillips, while two or three held down a little fellow who yelled and cried, defending himself with his feet against being reduced to the condition in which he was born, kicking and howling. In one room, around a small table, four were playing *revesino* with laughter and jokes, to the great annoyance of another who pretended to be studying his lesson but who was in reality waiting his turn to play.

Still another came in with exaggerated wonder, scandalized as he approached the table. "How wicked you are! So early in the morning and already gambling! Let's see, let's see! You fool, take it with the three of spades!" Closing his book, he too joined in the game.

Cries and blows were heard. Two boys were fighting in the adjoining room—a lame student who was very sensitive about his infirmity and an unhappy newcomer from the provinces who was just commencing his studies. He was working over a treatise on philosophy and reading innocently in a loud voice, with a wrong accent, the Cartesian principle: "*Cogito, ergo sum!*"

The little lame boy (*el cojito*) took this as an insult and the others intervened to restore peace, but in reality only to sow discord and come to blows themselves.

In the dining-room a young man with a can of sardines, a bottle of wine, and the provisions that he had just brought from his town, was making heroic efforts to the end that his friends might participate in his lunch, while they were offering in their turn heroic resistance to his invitation. Others were bathing on the azotea, playing firemen with the water from the well, and joining in combats with pails of water, to the great delight of the spectators.

But the noise and shouts gradually died away with the coming of leading students, summoned by Makaraig to report to them the progress of the academy of Castilian. Isagani was cordially greeted, as was also the Peninsular, Sandoval, who had come to Manila as a government employee and was finishing his studies, and who had completely identified himself with the cause of the Filipino students. The barriers that politics had established between the races had disappeared in the schoolroom as though dissolved by the zeal of science and youth.

From lack of lyceums and scientific, literary, or political centers, Sandoval took advantage of all the meetings to cultivate his great oratorical gifts, delivering speeches and arguing on any subject, to draw forth applause from his friends and listeners. At that moment the subject of conversation was the instruction in Castilian, but as Makaraig had not yet arrived conjecture was still the order of the day.

"What can have happened?"

"What has the General decided?"

"Has he refused the permit?"

"Has Padre Irene or Padre Sibyla won?"

Such were the questions they asked one another, questions that could be answered only by Makaraig.

Among the young men gathered together there were optimists like Isagani and Sandoval, who saw the thing already accomplished and talked of congratulations and praise from the government for the patriotism of the students—outbursts of optimism that led Juanito Pelaez to claim for himself a large part of the glory of founding the society.

All this was answered by the pessimist Pecson, a chubby youth with a wide, clownish grin, who spoke of outside influences, whether the Bishop A., the Padre B., or the Provincial C., had been consulted or not, whether or not they had advised that the whole association should be put in jail—a suggestion that made Juanito Pelaez so uneasy that he stammered out, "*Carambas*, don't you drag me into—"

Sandoval, as a Peninsular and a liberal, became furious at this. "But pshaw!" he exclaimed, "that is holding a bad opinion of his

Excellency! I know that he's quite a friar-lover, but in such a matter as this he won't let the friars interfere. Will you tell me, Pecson, on what you base your belief that the General has no judgment of his own?"

"I didn't say that, Sandoval," replied Pecson, grinning until he exposed his wisdom-tooth. "For me the General has *his own* judgment, that is, the judgment of all those within his reach. That's plain!"

"You're dodging—cite me a fact, cite me a fact!" cried Sandoval. "Let's get away from hollow arguments, from empty phrases, and get on the solid ground of facts,"—this with an elegant gesture. "Facts, gentlemen, facts! The rest is prejudice—I won't call it filibusterism."

Pecson smiled like one of the blessed as he retorted, "There comes the filibusterism. But can't we enter into a discussion without resorting to accusations?"

Sandoval protested in a little extemporaneous speech, again demanding facts.

"Well, not long ago there was a dispute between some private persons and certain friars, and the acting Governor rendered a decision that it should be settled by the Provincial of the Order concerned," replied Pecson, again breaking out into a laugh, as though he were dealing with an insignificant matter, he cited names and dates, and promised documents that would prove how justice was dispensed.

"But, on what ground, tell me this, on what ground can they refuse permission for what plainly appears to be extremely useful and necessary?" asked Sandoval.

Pecson shrugged his shoulders. "It's that it endangers the integrity of the fatherland," he replied in the tone of a notary reading an allegation.

"That's pretty good! What has the integrity of the fatherland to do with the rules of syntax?"

"The Holy Mother Church has learned doctors—what do I know? Perhaps it is feared that we may come to understand the laws so that we can obey them. What will become of the Philippines on the day when we understand one another?"

Sandoval did not relish the dialectic and jesting turn of the conversation; along that path could rise no speech worth the while.

"Don't make a joke of things!" he exclaimed. "This is a serious matter."

"The Lord deliver me from joking when there are friars concerned!"

"But, on what do you base—"

"On the fact that, the hours for the classes having to come at night," continued Pecson in the same tone, as if he were quoting known and recognized formulas, "there may be invoked as an obstacle the immorality of the thing, as was done in the case of the school at Malolos."

"Another! But don't the classes of the Academy of Drawing, and the novenaries and the processions, cover themselves with the mantle of night?"

"The scheme affects the dignity of the University," went on the chubby youth, taking no notice of the question.

"Affects nothing! The University has to accommodate itself to the needs of the students. And granting that, what is a university then? Is it an institution to discourage study? Have a few men banded themselves together in the name of learning and instruction in order to prevent others from becoming enlightened?"

"The fact is that movements initiated from below are regarded as discontent—"

"What about projects that come from above?" interpolated one of the students. "There's the School of Arts and Trades!"

"Slowly, slowly, gentlemen," protested Sandoval. "I'm not a friar-lover, my liberal views being well known, but render unto Caesar that which is Caesar's. Of that School of Arts and Trades, of which I have been the most enthusiastic supporter and the realization of which I shall greet as the first streak of dawn for these fortunate islands, of that School of Arts and Trades the friars have taken charge—"

"Or the cat of the canary, which amounts to the same thing," added Pecson, in his turn interrupting the speech.

"Get out!" cried Sandoval, enraged at the interruption, which had caused him to lose the thread of his long, well-rounded sentence. "As long as we hear nothing bad, let's not be pessimists, let's not be unjust, doubting the liberty and independence of the government."

Here he entered upon a defense in beautiful phraseology of the government and its good intentions, a subject that Pecson dared not break in upon.

"The Spanish government," he said among other things, "has given you everything, it has denied you nothing! We had absolutism in Spain and you had absolutism here; the friars covered our soil with conventos, and conventos occupy a third part of Manila; in Spain the garrote prevails and here the garrote is the extreme punishment; we are Catholics and we have made you Catholics; we were scholastics and scholasticism sheds its light in your college halls; in short, gentlemen, we weep when you weep, we suffer when you suffer, we have the same altars, the same courts, the same punishments, and it is only just that we should give you our rights and our joys."

As no one interrupted him, he became more and more enthusiastic, until he came to speak of the future of the Philippines.

"As I have said, gentlemen, the dawn is not far distant. Spain is now breaking the eastern sky for her beloved Philippines, and the times are changing, as I positively know, faster than we imagine. This government, which, according to you, is vacillating and weak, should be strengthened by our confidence, that we may make it see that it is the custodian of our hopes. Let us remind it by our conduct (should it ever forget itself, which I do not believe can happen) that we have faith in its good intentions and that it should be guided by no other standard than justice and the welfare of all the governed. No, gentlemen," he went on in a tone more and more declamatory, "we must not admit at all in this matter the possibility of a consultation with other more or less hostile entities, as such a supposition would imply our resignation to the fact. Your conduct up to the present has been frank, loyal, without vacillation, above suspicion; you have addressed it simply and directly; the reasons you have presented could not be more sound; your aim is to lighten the labor of the teachers in the first years and to facilitate study among the hundreds of students who fill the college halls and for whom one solitary professor cannot suffice. If up to the present the petition has not been granted, it has been for the reason, as I feel sure, that there has been a great deal of material accumulated, but I predict that the campaign is won, that the summons of Makaraig is to announce to us the victory, and tomorrow we shall see our efforts crowned with the applause and appreciation of the country, and who knows, gentlemen, but that the government may confer upon you some handsome decoration of merit, benefactors as you are of the fatherland!"

Enthusiastic applause resounded. All immediately believed in the triumph, and many in the decoration.

"Let it be remembered, gentlemen," observed Juanito, "that I was one of the first to propose it."

The pessimist Pecson was not so enthusiastic. "Just so we don't get that decoration on our ankles," he remarked, but fortunately for Pelaez this comment was not heard in the midst of the applause.

When they had quieted down a little, Pecson replied, "Good, good, very good, but one supposition: if in spite of all that, the General consults and consults and consults, and afterwards refuses the permit?"

This question fell like a dash of cold water. All turned to Sandoval, who was taken aback. "Then—" he stammered.

"Then?"

"Then," he exclaimed in a burst of enthusiasm, still excited by the applause, "seeing that in writing and in printing it boasts of desiring your enlightenment, and yet hinders and denies it when called upon to make it a reality—then, gentlemen, your efforts will not have been in vain, you will have accomplished what no one else has been able to do. Make them drop the mask and fling down the gauntlet to you!"

"Bravo, bravo!" cried several enthusiastically.

"Good for Sandoval! Hurrah for the gauntlet!" added others.

"Let them fling down the gauntlet to us!" repeated Pecson disdainfully. "But afterwards?"

Sandoval seemed to be cut short in his triumph, but with the vivacity peculiar to his race and his oratorical temperament he had an immediate reply.

"Afterwards?" he asked. "Afterwards, if none of the Filipinos dare to accept the challenge, then I, Sandoval, in the name of Spain, will take up the gauntlet, because such a policy would give the lie to the good intentions that she has always cherished toward her provinces, and because he who is thus faithless to the trust reposed in him and abuses his unlimited authority deserves neither the protection of the fatherland nor the support of any Spanish citizen!"

The enthusiasm of his hearers broke all bounds. Isagani embraced him, the others following his example. They talked of the fatherland, of union, of fraternity, of fidelity. The Filipinos declared that if there were only Sandovals in Spain all would be Sandovals in the Philippines. His eyes glistened, and it might well be believed that if at that moment any kind of gauntlet had been flung at him he would have leaped upon any kind of horse to ride to death for the Philippines.

The "cold water" alone replied: "Good, that's very good, Sandoval. I could also say the same if I were a Peninsular, but not being one, if I should say one half of what you have, you yourself would take me for a filibuster."

Sandoval began a speech in protest, but was interrupted.

"Rejoice, friends, rejoice! Victory!" cried a youth who entered at that moment and began to embrace everybody.

"Rejoice, friends! Long live the Castilian tongue!"

An outburst of applause greeted this announcement. They fell to embracing one another and their eyes filled with tears. Pecson alone preserved his skeptical smile.

The bearer of such good news was Makaraig, the young man at the head of the movement. This student occupied in that house, by himself, two rooms, luxuriously furnished, and had his servant and a cochero to look after his carriage and horses. He was of robust carriage, of refined manners, fastidiously dressed, and very rich. Although studying law only that he might have an academic degree, he enjoyed a reputation for diligence, and as a logician in the scholastic way had no cause to envy the most frenzied quibblers of the University faculty. Nevertheless he was not very far behind in regard to modern ideas and progress, for his fortune enabled him to have all the books and magazines that a watchful censor was unable to keep out. With these qualifications and his reputation for courage, his fortunate associations in his earlier years, and his refined and delicate courtesy, it was not strange that he should exercise such great influence over his associates and that he should have been chosen to carry out such a difficult undertaking as that of the instruction in Castilian.

After the first outburst of enthusiasm, which in youth always takes hold in such exaggerated forms, since youth finds everything beautiful, they wanted to be informed how the affair had been managed.

"I saw Padre Irene this morning," said Makaraig with a certain air of mystery.

"Hurrah for Padre Irene!" cried an enthusiastic student.

"Padre Irene," continued Makaraig, "has told me about everything that took place at Los Baños. It seems that they disputed for at least a week, he supporting and defending our case against all of them, against Padre Sibyla, Padre Fernandez, Padre Salvi, the General, the jeweler Simoun—"

"The jeweler Simoun!" interrupted one of his listeners. "What has that Jew to do with the affairs of our country? We enrich him by buying—"

"Keep quiet!" admonished another impatiently, anxious to learn how Padre Irene had been able to overcome such formidable opponents.

"There were even high officials who were opposed to our project, the Head Secretary, the Civil Governor, Quiroga the Chinaman—"

"Quiroga the Chinaman! The pimp of the—"

"Shut up!"

"At last," resumed Makaraig, "they were going to pigeonhole the petition and let it sleep for months and months, when Padre Irene remembered the Superior Commission of Primary Instruction and proposed, since the matter concerned the teaching of the Castilian tongue, that the petition be referred to that body for a report upon it."

"But that Commission hasn't been in operation for a long time," observed Pecson.

"That's exactly what they replied to Padre Irene, and he answered that this was a good opportunity to revive it, and availing himself of the presence of Don Custodio, one of its members, he proposed on the spot that a committee should be appointed. Don Custodio's activity being known and recognized, he was named as arbiter and the petition is now in his hands. He promised that he would settle it this month."

"Hurrah for Don Custodio!"

"But suppose Don Custodio should report unfavorably upon it?" inquired the pessimist Pecson.

Upon this they had not reckoned, being intoxicated with the thought that the matter would not be pigeonholed, so they all turned to Makaraig to learn how it could be arranged.

"The same objection I presented to Padre Irene, but with his sly smile he said to me: 'We've won a great deal, we have succeeded in getting the matter on the road to a decision, the opposition sees itself forced to join battle.' If we can bring some influence to bear upon Don Custodio so that he, in accordance with his liberal tendencies, may report favorably, all is won, for the General showed himself to be absolutely neutral."

Makaraig paused, and an impatient listener asked, "How can we influence him?"

"Padre Irene pointed out to me two ways—"

"Quiroga," some one suggested.

"Pshaw, great use Quiroga—"

"A fine present."

"No, that won't do, for he prides himself upon being incorruptible."

"Ah, yes, I know!" exclaimed Pecson with a laugh. "Pepay the dancing girl." "Ah, yes, Pepay the dancing girl," echoed several.

This Pepay was a showy girl, supposed to be a great friend of Don Custodio. To her resorted the contractors, the employees, the intriguers, when they wanted to get something from the celebrated councilor. Juanito Pelaez, who was also a great friend of the dancing girl, offered to look after the matter, but Isagani shook his head, saying that it was sufficient that they had made use of Padre Irene and that it would be going too far to avail themselves of Pepay in such an affair.

"Show us the other way."

"The other way is to apply to his attorney and adviser, Señor Pasta, the oracle before whom Don Custodio bows."

"I prefer that," said Isagani. "Señor Pasta is a Filipino, and was a schoolmate of my uncle's. But how can we interest him?"

"There's the *quid*," replied Makaraig, looking earnestly at Isagani. "Señor Pasta has a dancing girl—I mean, a seamstress."

Isagani again shook his head.

"Don't be such a puritan," Juanito Pelaez said to him. "The end justifies the means! I know the seamstress, Matea, for she has a shop where a lot of girls work."

"No, gentlemen," declared Isagani, "let's first employ decent methods. I'll go to Señor Pasta and, if I don't accomplish anything, then you can do what you wish with the dancing girls and seamstresses."

They had to accept this proposition, agreeing that Isagani should talk to Señor Pasta that very day, and in the afternoon report to his associates at the University the result of the interview.

---

1   *No cristianos*, not Christians, *i.e.*, savages.—Tr.

SEÑOR PASTA

Isagani presented himself in the house of the lawyer, one of the most talented minds in Manila, whom the friars consulted in their great difficulties. The youth had to wait some time on account of the numerous clients, but at last his turn came and he entered the office, or *bufete*, as it is generally called in the Philippines. The lawyer received him with a slight cough, looking down furtively at his feet, but he did not rise or offer a seat, as he went on writing. This gave Isagani an opportunity for observation and careful study of the lawyer, who had aged greatly. His hair was gray and his baldness extended over nearly the whole crown of his head. His countenance was sour and austere.

There was complete silence in the study, except for the whispers of the clerks and understudies who were at work in an adjoining room. Their pens scratched as though quarreling with the paper.

At length the lawyer finished what he was writing, laid down his pen, raised his head, and, recognizing the youth, let his face light up with a smile as he extended his hand affectionately.

"Welcome, young man! But sit down, and excuse me, for I didn't know that it was you. How is your uncle?"

Isagani took courage, believing that his case would get on well. He related briefly what had been done, the while studying the effect of his words. Señor Pasta listened impassively at first and, although he was informed of the efforts of the students, pretended ignorance, as if to show that he had nothing to do with such childish matters, but when he began to suspect what was wanted of him and heard mention of the Vice-Rector, friars, the Captain-General, a project, and so on, his face slowly darkened and he finally exclaimed, "This is the land of projects! But go on, go on!"

Isagani was not yet discouraged. He spoke of the manner in which a decision was to be reached and concluded with an expression of the confidence which the young men entertained that he, Señor Pasta, would *intercede* in their behalf in case Don Custodio should consult him, as was to be expected. He did not dare to say would *advise*, deterred by the wry face the lawyer put on.

But Señor Pasta had already formed his resolution, and it was not to mix at all in the affair, either as consulter or consulted. He was familiar with what had occurred at Los Baños, he knew that there existed two factions, and that Padre Irene was not the only champion on the side of the students, nor had he been the one who proposed submitting the petition to the Commission of Primary Instruction, but quite the contrary. Padre Irene, Padre Fernandez, the Countess, a merchant who expected to sell the materials for the new academy, and the high official who had been citing royal decree after royal decree, were about to triumph, when Padre Sibyla, wishing to gain time, had thought of the Commission. All these facts the great lawyer had present in his mind, so that when Isagani had finished speaking, he determined to confuse him with evasions, tangle the matter up, and lead the conversation to other subjects.

"Yes," he said, pursing his lips and scratching his head, "there is no one who surpasses me in love for the country and in aspirations toward progress, but—I can't compromise myself, I don't know whether you clearly understand my position, a position that is very delicate, I have so many interests, I have to labor within the limits of strict prudence, it's a risk—"

The lawyer sought to bewilder the youth with an exuberance of words, so he went on speaking of laws and decrees, and talked so much that instead of confusing the youth, he came very near to entangling himself in a labyrinth of citations.

"In no way do we wish to compromise you," replied Isagani with great calmness. "God deliver us from injuring in the least the persons whose lives are so useful to the rest of the Filipinos! But, as little versed as I may be in the laws, royal decrees, writs, and resolutions that obtain in this country, I can't believe that there can be any harm in furthering the high purposes of the government, in trying to secure a proper interpretation of these purposes. We are seeking the same end and differ only about the means."

The lawyer smiled, for the youth had allowed himself to wander away from the subject, and there where the former was going to entangle him he had already entangled himself.

"That's exactly the *quid*, as is vulgarly said. It's clear that it is laudable to aid the government, when one aids it submissively, following out its desires and the true spirit of the laws in agreement with the just beliefs of the governing powers, and when not in contradiction to the fundamental and general way of thinking of the persons to whom is intrusted the common welfare of the individuals that form a social organism. Therefore, it is criminal, it is punishable, because it is offensive to the high principle of authority, to attempt any action contrary to its initiative, even supposing it to be better than the governmental proposition, because such action would injure its prestige, which is the elementary basis upon which all colonial edifices rest."

Confident that this broadside had at least stunned Isagani, the old lawyer fell back in his armchair, outwardly very serious, but laughing to himself.

Isagani, however, ventured to reply. "I should think that governments, the more they are threatened, would be all the more careful to seek bases that are impregnable. The basis of prestige for colonial governments is the weakest of all, since it does not depend upon themselves but upon the consent of the governed, while the latter are willing to recognize it. The basis of justice or reason would seem to be the most durable."

The lawyer raised his head. How was this—did that youth dare to reply and argue with him, *him*, Señor Pasta? Was he not yet bewildered with his big words?

"Young man, you must put those considerations aside, for they are dangerous," he declared with a wave of his hand. "What I advise is that you let the government attend to its own business."

"Governments are established for the welfare of the peoples, and in order to accomplish this purpose properly they have to follow the suggestions of the citizens, who are the ones best qualified to understand their own needs."

"Those who constitute the government are also citizens, and among the most enlightened."

"But, being men, they are fallible, and ought not to disregard the opinions of others."

"They must be trusted, they have to attend to everything."

"There is a Spanish proverb which says, 'No tears, no milk,' in other words, 'To him who does not ask, nothing is given.'"

"Quite the reverse," replied the lawyer with a sarcastic smile; "with the government exactly the reverse occurs—"

But he suddenly checked himself, as if he had said too much and wished to correct his imprudence. "The government has given us things that we have not asked for, and that we could not ask for, because to ask—to ask, presupposes that it is in some way incompetent and consequently is not performing its functions. To suggest to it a course of action, to try to guide it, when not really antagonizing it, is to presuppose that it is capable of erring, and as I have already said to you such suppositions are menaces to the existence of colonial governments. The common crowd overlooks this and the young men who set to work thoughtlessly do not know, do not comprehend, do not try to comprehend the counter-effect of asking, the menace to order there is in that idea—"

"Pardon me," interrupted Isagani, offended by the arguments the jurist was using with him, "but when by legal methods people ask a government for something, it is because they think it good and disposed to grant a blessing, and such action, instead of irritating it, should flatter it—to the mother one appeals, never to the stepmother. The government, in my humble opinion, is not an omniscient being that can see and anticipate everything, and even if it could, it ought not to feel offended, for here you have the church itself doing nothing but asking and begging of God, who sees and knows everything, and you yourself ask and demand many things in the courts of this same government, yet neither God nor the courts have yet taken offense. Every one realizes that the government, being the human institution that it is, needs the support of all the people, it needs to be made to see and feel the reality of things. You yourself are not convinced of the truth of your objection, you yourself know that it is a tyrannical and despotic government which, in order to make a display of force and independence, denies everything through fear or distrust, and that the tyrannized and enslaved peoples are the only ones whose duty it is never to ask for anything. A people that hates its government ought to ask for nothing but that it abdicate its power."

The old lawyer grimaced and shook his head from side to side, in sign of discontent, while he rubbed his hand over his bald pate and said in a tone of condescending pity: "Ahem! those are bad doctrines, bad theories, ahem! How plain it is that you are young and inexperienced in life. Look what is happening with the inexperienced young men who in Madrid are asking for so many reforms. They are accused of filibusterism, many of them don't dare return here, and yet, what are they asking for? Things holy, ancient, and recognized as quite harmless. But there are matters that can't be explained, they're so delicate. Let's see—I confess to you that there are other reasons besides those expressed that might lead a sensible government to deny systematically the wishes of the people—no—but it may happen that we find ourselves under rulers so fatuous and ridiculous—but there are always other reasons, even though what is asked be quite just—different governments encounter different conditions—"

The old man hesitated, stared fixedly at Isagani, and then with a sudden resolution made a sign with his hand as though he would dispel some idea.

"I can guess what you mean," said Isagani, smiling sadly. "You mean that a colonial government, for the very reason that it is imperfectly constituted and that it is based on premises—"

"No, no, not that, no!" quickly interrupted the old lawyer, as he sought for something among his papers. "No, I meant—but where are my spectacles?"

"There they are," replied Isagani.

The old man put them on and pretended to look over some papers, but seeing that the youth was waiting, he mumbled, "I wanted to tell you something, I wanted to say—but it has slipped from my mind. You interrupted me in your eagerness—but it was an insignificant matter. If you only knew what a whirl my head is in, I have so much to do!"

Isagani understood that he was being dismissed. "So," he said, rising, "we—"

"Ah, you will do well to leave the matter in the hands of the government, which will settle it as it sees fit. You say that the Vice-Rector is opposed to the teaching of Castilian. Perhaps he may be, not as to the fact but as to the form. It is said that the Rector who is on his way will bring a project for reform in education.

Wait a while, give time a chance, apply yourself to your studies as the examinations are near, and—*carambas!*—you who already speak Castilian and express yourself easily, what are you bothering yourself about? What interest have you in seeing it specially taught? Surely Padre Florentino thinks as I do! Give him my regards."

"My uncle," replied Isagani, "has always admonished me to think of others as much as of myself. I didn't come for myself, I came in the name of those who are in worse condition."

"What the devil! Let them do as you have done, let them singe their eyebrows studying and come to be bald like myself, stuffing whole paragraphs into their memories! I believe that if you talk Spanish it is because you have studied it—you're not of Manila or of Spanish parents! Then let them learn it as you have, and do as I have done: I've been a servant to all the friars, I've prepared their chocolate, and while with my right hand I stirred it, with the left I held a grammar, I learned, and, thank God! have never needed other teachers or academies or permits from the government. Believe me, he who wishes to learn, learns and becomes wise!"

"But how many among those who wish to learn come to be what you are? One in ten thousand, and more!"

"Pish! Why any more?" retorted the old man, shrugging his shoulders. "There are too many lawyers now, many of them become mere clerks. Doctors? They insult and abuse one another, and even kill each other in competition for a patient. Laborers, sir, laborers, are what we need, for agriculture!"

Isagani realized that he was losing time, but still could not forbear replying: "Undoubtedly, there are many doctors and lawyers, but I won't say there are too many, since we have towns that lack them entirely, and if they do abound in quantity, perhaps they are deficient in quality. Since the young men can't be prevented from studying, and no other professions are open to us, why let them waste their time and effort? And if the instruction, deficient as it is, does not keep many from becoming lawyers and doctors, if we must finally have them, why not have good ones? After all, even if the sole wish is to make the country a country of farmers and laborers, and condemn in it all intellectual activity, I don't see any evil in enlightening those same farmers and laborers, in giving them at least an education that will aid them in perfecting themselves and in perfecting their work, in placing them in a condition to understand many things of which they are at present ignorant."

"Bah, bah, bah!" exclaimed the lawyer, drawing circles in the air with his hand to dispel the ideas suggested. "To be a good farmer no great amount of rhetoric is needed. Dreams, illusions, fancies! Eh, will you take a piece of advice?"

He arose and placed his hand affectionately on the youth's shoulder, as he continued: "I'm going to give you one, and a very good one, because I see that you are intelligent and the advice will not be wasted. You're going to study medicine? Well, confine yourself to learning how to put on plasters and apply leeches, and don't ever try to improve or impair the condition of your kind. When you become a licentiate, marry a rich and devout girl, try to make cures and charge well, shun everything that has any relation to the general state of the country, attend mass, confession, and communion when the rest do, and you will see afterwards how you will thank me, and I shall see it, if I am still alive. Always remember that charity begins at home, for man ought not to seek on earth more than the greatest amount of happiness for himself, as Bentham says. If you involve yourself in quixotisms you will have no career, nor will you get married, nor will you ever amount to anything. All will abandon you, your own countrymen will be the first to laugh at your simplicity. Believe me, you will remember me and see that I am right, when you have gray hairs like myself, gray hairs such as these!"

Here the old lawyer stroked his scanty white hair, as he smiled sadly and shook his head.

"When I have gray hairs like those, sir," replied Isagani with equal sadness, "and turn my gaze back over my past and see that I have worked only for myself, without having done what I plainly could and should have done for the country that has given me everything, for the citizens that have helped me to live—then, sir, every gray hair will be a thorn, and instead of rejoicing, they will shame me!"

So saying, he took his leave with a profound bow. The lawyer remained motionless in his place, with an amazed look on his face. He listened to the footfalls that gradually died away, then resumed his seat.

"Poor boy!" he murmured, "similar thoughts also crossed my mind once! What more could any one desire than to be able to say: 'I have done this for the good of the fatherland, I have consecrated my life to the welfare of others!' A crown of laurel, steeped in aloes, dry leaves that cover thorns and worms! That is not life, that does not get us our daily bread, nor does it bring us honors—the laurel would hardly serve for a salad, nor produce ease, nor aid us in winning lawsuits, but quite the reverse! Every country has its code of ethics, as it has its climate and its diseases, different from the climate and the diseases of other countries."

After a pause, he added: "Poor boy! If all should think and act as he does, I don't say but that—Poor boy! Poor Florentino!"

THE TRIBULATIONS OF A CHINESE

In the evening of that same Saturday, Quiroga, the Chinese, who aspired to the creation of a consulate for his nation, gave a dinner in the rooms over his bazaar, located in the Escolta. His feast was well attended: friars, government employees, soldiers, merchants, all of them his customers, partners or patrons, were to be seen there, for his store supplied the curates and the conventos with all their necessities, he accepted the chits of all the employees, and he had servants who were discreet, prompt, and complaisant. The friars themselves did not disdain to pass whole hours in his store, sometimes in view of the public, sometimes in the chambers with agreeable company.

That night, then, the sala presented a curious aspect, being filled with friars and clerks seated on Vienna chairs, stools of black wood, and marble benches of Cantonese origin, before little square tables, playing cards or conversing among themselves, under the brilliant glare of the gilt chandeliers or the subdued light of the Chinese lanterns, which were brilliantly decorated with long silken tassels. On the walls there was a lamentable medley of landscapes in dim and gaudy colors, painted in Canton or Hongkong, mingled with tawdry chromos of odalisks, half-nude women, effeminate lithographs of Christ, the deaths of the just and of the sinners— made by Jewish houses in Germany to be sold in the Catholic countries. Nor were there lacking the Chinese prints on red paper representing a man seated, of venerable aspect, with a calm, smiling face, behind whom stood a servant, ugly, horrible, diabolical, threatening, armed with a lance having a wide, keen blade. Among the Indians some call this figure Mohammed, others Santiago,' we do not know why, nor do the Chinese themselves give a very clear explanation of this popular pair. The pop of champagne corks, the rattle of glasses, laughter, cigar smoke, and that odor peculiar to a

Chinese habitation—a mixture of punk, opium, and dried fruits—completed the collection.

Dressed as a Chinese mandarin in a blue-tasseled cap, Quiroga moved from room to room, stiff and straight, but casting watchful glances here and there as though to assure himself that nothing was being stolen. Yet in spite of this natural distrust, he exchanged handshakes with each guest, greeted some with a smile sagacious and humble, others with a patronizing air, and still others with a certain shrewd look that seemed to say, "I know! You didn't come on my account, you came for the dinner!"

And Quiroga was right! That fat gentleman who is now praising him and speaking of the advisability of a Chinese consulate in Manila, intimating that to manage it there could be no one but Quiroga, is the Señor Gonzalez who hides behind the pseudonym *Pitili* when he attacks Chinese immigration through the columns of the newspapers. That other, an elderly man who closely examines the lamps, pictures, and other furnishings with grimaces and ejaculations of disdain, is Don Timoteo Pelaez, Juanito's father, a merchant who inveighs against the Chinese competition that is ruining his business. The one over there, that thin, brown individual with a sharp look and a pale smile, is the celebrated originator of the dispute over Mexican pesos, which so troubled one of Quiroga's protéges: that government clerk is regarded in Manila as very clever. That one farther on, he of the frowning look and unkempt mustache, is a government official who passes for a most meritorious fellow because he has the courage to speak ill of the business in lottery tickets carried on between Quiroga and an exalted dame in Manila society. The fact is that two thirds of the tickets go to China and the few that are left in Manila are sold at a premium of a half-real. The honorable gentleman entertains the conviction that some day he will draw the first prize, and is in a rage at finding himself confronted with such tricks.

The dinner, meanwhile, was drawing to an end. From the dining-room floated into the sala snatches of toasts, interruptions, bursts and ripples of laughter. The name of Quiroga was often heard mingled with the words "consul," "equality," "justice." The amphitryon himself did not eat European dishes, so he contented himself with drinking a glass of wine with his guests from time to time, promising to dine with those who were not seated at the first table.

Simoun, who was present, having already dined, was in the sala talking with some merchants, who were complaining of business conditions: everything was going wrong, trade was paralyzed, the European exchanges were exorbitantly high. They sought information from the jeweler or insinuated to him a few ideas, with the hope that these would be communicated to the Captain-General. To all the remedies suggested Simoun responded with a sarcastic and unfeeling exclamation about nonsense, until one of them in exasperation asked him for his opinion.

"My opinion?" he retorted. "Study how other nations prosper, and then do as they do."

"And why do they prosper, Señor Simoun?"

Simoun replied with a shrug of his shoulders.

"The port works, which weigh so heavily upon commerce, and the port not yet completed!" sighed Don Timoteo Pelaez. "A Penelope's web, as my son says, that is spun and unspun. The taxes—"

"You complaining!" exclaimed another. "Just as the General has decreed the destruction of houses of light materials! And you with a shipment of galvanized iron!"

"Yes," rejoined Don Timoteo, "but look what that decree cost me! Then, the destruction will not be carried out for a month, not until Lent begins, and other shipments may arrive. I would have wished them destroyed right away, but—Besides, what are the owners of those houses going to buy from me if they are all poor, all equally beggars?"

"You can always buy up their shacks for a trifle."

"And afterwards have the decree revoked and sell them back at double the price—that's business!"

Simoun smiled his frigid smile. Seeing Quiroga approach, he left the querulous merchants to greet the future consul, who on catching sight of him lost his satisfied expression and assigned a countenance like those of the merchants, while he bent almost double.

Quiroga respected the jeweler greatly, not only because he knew him to be very wealthy, but also on account of his rumored influence with the Captain-General. It was reported that Simoun favored Quiroga's ambitions, that he was an advocate for the consulate, and a certain newspaper hostile to the Chinese had alluded to him in many paraphrases, veiled allusions, and suspension points, in the celebrated controversy with another sheet that was favorable to the queued folk. Some prudent persons added with winks and half-uttered words that his Black Eminence was advising the General to avail himself of the Chinese in order to humble the tenacious pride of the natives.

"To hold the people in subjection," he was reported to have said, "there's nothing like humiliating them and humbling them in their own eyes."

To this end an opportunity had soon presented itself. The guilds of mestizos and natives were continually watching one another, venting their bellicose spirits and their activities in jealousy and distrust. At mass one day the gobernadorcillo of the natives was seated on a bench to the right, and, being extremely thin, happened to cross one of his legs over the other, thus adopting a nonchalant attitude, in order to expose his thighs more and display his pretty shoes. The gobernadorcillo of the guild of mestizos, who was seated on the opposite bench, as he had bunions, and could not cross his legs on account of his obesity, spread his legs wide apart to expose a plain waistcoat adorned with a beautiful gold chain set with diamonds. The two cliques comprehended these maneuvers and joined battle. On the following Sunday all the mestizos, even the thinnest, had large paunches and spread their legs wide apart as though on horseback, while the natives placed one leg over the other, even the fattest, there being one cabeza de barangay who turned a somersault. Seeing these movements, the Chinese all adopted their own peculiar attitude, that of sitting as they do in their shops, with one leg drawn back and upward, the other swinging loose. There resulted protests and petitions, the police rushed to arms ready to start a civil war, the curates rejoiced, the Spaniards were amused and made money out of everybody, until the General settled the quarrel by ordering that every one should sit as the Chinese did, since they were the heaviest contributors, even though they were not the best Catholics. The difficulty for the mestizos and natives then was that their trousers were too tight to permit of their imitating the Chinese. But to make the intention of humiliating them the more evident, the measure was carried out with great pomp and ceremony, the church being surrounded by a troop of cavalry, while all those within were sweating. The matter was carried to the Cortes, but it was repeated that the Chinese, as the ones who paid, should have their way in the religious ceremonies, even though they apostatized and laughed at Christianity immediately after. The natives and the mestizos had to be content, learning thus not to waste time over such fatuity.[1]

Quiroga, with his smooth tongue and humble smile, was lavishly and flatteringly attentive to Simoun. His voice was caressing and his bows numerous, but the jeweler cut his blandishments short by asking brusquely:

"Did the bracelets suit her?"

At this question all Quiroga's liveliness vanished like a dream. His caressing voice became plaintive; he bowed lower, gave the Chinese salutation of raising his clasped hands to the height of his face, and groaned: "Ah, Señor Simoun! I'm lost, I'm ruined!"[1]

"How, Quiroga, lost and ruined when you have so many bottles of champagne and so many guests?"

Quiroga closed his eyes and made a grimace. Yes, the affair of that afternoon, that affair of the bracelets, had ruined him. Simoun smiled, for when a Chinese merchant complains it is because all is going well, and when he makes a show that things are booming it is quite certain that he is planning an assignment or flight to his own country.

"You didn't know that I'm lost, I'm ruined? Ah, Señor Simoun, I'm *busted!*" To make his condition plainer, he illustrated the word by making a movement as though he were falling in collapse.

Simoun wanted to laugh, but restrained himself and said that he knew nothing, nothing at all, as Quiroga led him to a room and closed the door. He then explained the cause of his misfortune.

Three diamond bracelets that he had secured from Simoun on pretense of showing them to his wife were not for her, a poor native shut up in her room like a Chinese woman, but for a beautiful and charming lady, the friend of a powerful man, whose influence was needed by him in a certain deal in which he could clear some six thousand pesos. As he did not understand feminine tastes and wished to be gallant, the Chinese had asked for the three finest bracelets the jeweler had, each priced at three to four thousand pesos. With affected simplicity and his most caressing smile, Quiroga had begged the lady to select the one she liked best, and the lady, more simple and caressing still, had declared that she liked all three, and had kept them.

Simoun burst out into laughter.

"Ah, sir, I'm lost, I'm ruined!" cried the Chinese, slapping himself lightly with his delicate hands; but the jeweler continued his laughter.

"Ugh, bad people, surely not a real lady," went on the Chinaman, shaking his head in disgust. "What! She has no decency, while me, a Chinaman, me always polite! Ah, surely she not a real lady—a *cigarrera* has more decency!"

"They've caught you, they've caught you!" exclaimed Simoun, poking him in the chest.

"And everybody's asking for loans and never pays—what about that? Clerks, officials, lieutenants, soldiers—" he checked them off on his long-nailed fingers—"ah, Señor Simoun, I'm lost, I'm *busted*!"

"Get out with your complaints," said Simoun. "I've saved you from many officials that wanted money from you. I've lent it to them so that they wouldn't bother you, even when I knew that they couldn't pay."

"But, Señor Simoun, you lend to officials; I lend to women, sailors, everybody."

"I bet you get your money back."

"Me, money back? Ah, surely you don't understand! When it's lost in gambling they never pay. Besides, you have a consul, you can force them, but I haven't."

Simoun became thoughtful. "Listen, Quiroga," he said, somewhat abstractedly, "I'll undertake to collect what the officers and sailors owe you. Give me their notes."

Quiroga again fell to whining: they had never given him any notes.

"When they come to you asking for money, send them to me. I want to help you."

The grateful Quiroga thanked him, but soon fell to lamenting again about the bracelets. "A *cigarrera* wouldn't be so shameless!" he repeated.

"The devil!" exclaimed Simoun, looking askance at the Chinese, as though studying him. "Exactly when I need the money and thought that you could pay me! But it can all be arranged, as

I don't want you to fail for such a small amount. Come, a favor, and I'll reduce to seven the nine thousand pesos you owe me. You can get anything you wish through the Customs—boxes of lamps, iron, copper, glassware, Mexican pesos—you furnish arms to the conventos, don't you?"

The Chinese nodded affirmation, but remarked that he had to do a good deal of bribing. "I furnish the padres everything!"

"Well, then," added Simoun in a low voice, "I need you to get in for me some boxes of rifles that arrived this evening. I want you to keep them in your warehouse; there isn't room for all of them in my house."

Quiroga began to show symptoms of fright.

"Don't get scared, you don't run any risk. These rifles are to be concealed, a few at a time, in various dwellings, then a search will be instituted, and many people will be sent to prison. You and I can make a haul getting them set free. Understand me?"

Quiroga wavered, for he was afraid of firearms. In his desk he had an empty revolver that he never touched without turning his head away and closing his eyes.

"If you can't do it, I'll have to apply to some one else, but then I'll need the nine thousand pesos to cross their palms and shut their eyes."

"All right, all right!" Quiroga finally agreed. "But many people will be arrested? There'll be a search, eh?"

When Quiroga and Simoun returned to the sala they found there, in animated conversation, those who had finished their dinner, for the champagne had loosened their tongues and stirred their brains. They were talking rather freely.

In a group where there were a number of government clerks, some ladies, and Don Custodio, the topic was a commission sent to India to make certain investigations about footwear for the soldiers.

"Who compose it?" asked an elderly lady.

"A colonel, two other officers, and his Excellency's nephew."

"Four?" rejoined a clerk. "What a commission! Suppose they disagree—are they competent?"

"That's what I asked," replied a clerk. "It's said that one civilian ought to go, one who has no military prejudices—a shoemaker, for instance."

"That's right," added an importer of shoes, "but it wouldn't do to send an Indian or a Chinaman, and the only Peninsular shoemaker demanded such large fees—"

"But why do they have to make any investigations about footwear?" inquired the elderly lady. "It isn't for the Peninsular artillerymen. The Indian soldiers can go barefoot, as they do in their towns.'"

"Exactly so, and the treasury would save more," corroborated another lady, a widow who was not satisfied with her pension.

"But you must remember," remarked another in the group, a friend of the officers on the commission, "that while it's true they go barefoot in the towns, it's not the same as moving about under orders in the service. They can't choose the hour, nor the road, nor rest when they wish. Remember, madam, that, with the noonday sun overhead and the earth below baking like an oven, they have to march over sandy stretches, where there are stones, the sun above and fire below, bullets in front—"

"It's only a question of getting used to it!"

"Like the donkey that got used to not eating! In our present campaign the greater part of our losses have been due to wounds on the soles of the feet. Remember the donkey, madam, remember the donkey!"

"But, my dear sir," retorted the lady, "look how much money is wasted on shoe-leather. There's enough to pension many widows and orphans in order to maintain our prestige. Don't smile, for I'm not talking about myself, and I have my pension, even though a very small one, insignificant considering the services my husband rendered, but I'm talking of others who are dragging out miserable lives! It's not right that after so much persuasion to come and so many hardships in crossing the sea they should end here by dying of hunger. What you say about the soldiers may be true, but the fact is that I've been in the country more than three years, and I haven't seen any soldier limping."

"In that I agree with the lady," said her neighbor. "Why issue them shoes when they were born without them?"

"And why shirts?"

"And why trousers?"

"Just calculate what we should economize on soldiers clothed only in their skins!" concluded he who was defending the army.

In another group the conversation was more heated. Ben-Zayb was talking and declaiming, while Padre Camorra, as usual, was constantly interrupting him. The friar-journalist, in spite of his respect for the cowled gentry, was always at loggerheads with Padre Camorra, whom he regarded as a silly half-friar, thus giving himself the appearance of being independent and refuting the accusations of those who called him Fray Ibañez. Padre Camorra liked his adversary, as the latter was the only person who would take seriously what he styled his arguments. They were discussing magnetism, spiritualism, magic, and the like. Their words flew through the air like the knives and balls of jugglers, tossed back and forth from one to the other.

That year great attention had been attracted in the Quiapo fair by a head, wrongly called a sphinx, exhibited by Mr. Leeds, an American. Glaring advertisements covered the walls of the houses, mysterious and funereal, to excite the curiosity of the public. Neither Ben-Zayb nor any of the padres had yet seen it; Juanito Pelaez was the only one who had, and he was describing his wonderment to the party.

Ben-Zayb, as a journalist, looked for a natural explanation. Padre Camorra talked of the devil, Padre Irene smiled, Padre Salvi remained grave.

"But, Padre, the devil doesn't need to come—we are sufficient to damn ourselves—"

"It can't be explained any other way."

"If science—"

"Get out with science, *puñales!*"

"But, listen to me and I'll convince you. It's all a question of optics. I haven't yet seen the head nor do I know how it looks, but this gentleman"—indicating Juanito Pelaez—"tells us that it does not look like the talking heads that are usually exhibited. So be it! But the principle is the same—it's all a question of optics. Wait! A mirror is placed thus, another mirror behind it, the image is reflected—I say, it is purely a problem in physics."

Taking down from the walls several mirrors, he arranged them, turned them round and round, but, not getting the desired result, concluded: "As I say, it's nothing more or less than a question of optics."

"But what do you want mirrors for, if Juanito tells us that the head is inside a box placed on the table? I see in it spiritualism, because the spiritualists always make use of tables, and I think that Padre Salvi, as the ecclesiastical governor, ought to prohibit the exhibition."

Padre Salvi remained silent, saying neither yes nor no.

"In order to learn if there are devils or mirrors inside it," suggested Simoun, "the best thing would be for you to go and see the famous sphinx."

The proposal was a good one, so it was accepted, although Padre Salvi and Don Custodio showed some repugnance. They at a fair, to rub shoulders with the public, to see sphinxes and talking heads! What would the natives say? These might take them for mere men, endowed with the same passions and weaknesses as others. But Ben-Zayb, with his journalistic ingenuity, promised to request Mr. Leeds not to admit the public while they were inside. They would be honoring him sufficiently by the visit not to admit of his refusal, and besides he would not charge any admission fee. To give a show of probability to this, he concluded: "Because, remember, if I should expose the trick of the mirrors to the public, it would ruin the poor American's business." Ben-Zayb was a conscientious individual.

About a dozen set out, among them our acquaintances, Padres Salvi, Camorra, and Irene, Don Custodio, Ben-Zayb, and Juanito Pelaez. Their carriages set them down at the entrance to the Quiapo Plaza.

---

1   The patron saint of Spain, St. James.—Tr.
2   Houses of bamboo and nipa, such as form the homes of the masses of the natives.—Tr.
3   "In this paragraph Rizal alludes to an incident that had very serious results. There was annually celebrated in Binondo a certain religious festival, principally at the expense of the Chinese mestizos. The latter finally petitioned that their gobernadorcillo be given the presidency of it, and this was granted, thanks to the fact that the parish priest (the Dominican, Fray José Hevia Campomanes) held to the opinion that the presidency belonged to those who paid the most. The Tagalogs protested, alleging their better right to it, as the genuine sons of the country, not to mention the historical precedent, but the friar, who was looking after his own interests, did not yield. General Terrero (Governor, 1885–1888), at the advice of his liberal councilors, finally had the parish priest removed and for the time being decided the affair in favor of the Tagalogs. The matter reached

the Colonial Office (*Ministerio de Ultramar*) and the Minister was not even content merely to settle it in the way the friars desired, but made amends to Padre Hevia by appointing him a bishop."—*W. E. Retana, who was a journalist in Manila at the time, in a note to this chapter.*

Childish and ridiculous as this may appear now, it was far from being so at the time, especially in view of the supreme contempt with which the pugnacious Tagalog looks down upon the meek and complaisant Chinese and the mortal antipathy that exists between the two races.—Tr.

4   It is regrettable that Quiroga's picturesque butchery of Spanish and Tagalog—the dialect of the Manila Chinese—cannot be reproduced here. Only the thought can be given. There is the same difficulty with *r's*, *d's*, and *l's* that the Chinese show in English.—Tr.

5   Up to the outbreak of the insurrection in 1896, the only genuinely Spanish troops in the islands were a few hundred artillerymen, the rest being natives, with Spanish officers.—Tr.

THE QUIAPO FAIR

It was a beautiful night and the plaza presented a most animated aspect. Taking advantage of the freshness of the breeze and the splendor of the January moon, the people filled the fair to see, be seen, and amuse themselves. The music of the cosmoramas and the lights of the lanterns gave life and merriment to every one. Long rows of booths, brilliant with tinsel and gauds, exposed to view clusters of balls, masks strung by the eyes, tin toys, trains, carts, mechanical horses, carriages, steam-engines with diminutive boilers, Lilliputian tableware of porcelain, pine Nativities, dolls both foreign and domestic, the former red and smiling, the latter sad and pensive like little ladies beside gigantic children. The beating of drums, the roar of tin horns, the wheezy music of the accordions and the hand-organs, all mingled in a carnival concert, amid the coming and going of the crowd, pushing, stumbling over one another, with their faces turned toward the booths, so that the collisions were frequent and often amusing. The carriages were forced to move slowly, with the *tabí* of the cocheros repeated every moment. Met and mingled government clerks, soldiers, friars, students, Chinese, girls with their mammas or aunts, all greeting, signaling, calling to one another merrily.

Padre Camorra was in the seventh heaven at the sight of so many pretty girls. He stopped, looked back, nudged Ben-Zayb, chuckled and swore, saying, "And that one, and that one, my ink-slinger? And that one over there, what say you?" In his contentment he even fell to using the familiar *tu* toward his friend and adversary. Padre Salvi stared at him from time to time, but he took little note of Padre Salvi. On the contrary, he pretended to stumble so that he might brush against the girls, he winked and made eyes at them.

"*Puñales!*" he kept saying to himself. "When shall I be the curate of Quiapo?"

Suddenly Ben-Zayb let go an oath, jumped aside, and slapped his hand on his arm; Padre Camorra in his excess of enthusiasm had pinched him. They were approaching a dazzling señorita who was attracting the attention of the whole plaza, and Padre Camorra, unable to restrain his delight, had taken Ben-Zayb's arm as a substitute for the girl's.

It was Paulita Gomez, the prettiest of the pretty, in company with Isagani, followed by Doña Victorina. The young woman was resplendent in her beauty: all stopped and craned their necks, while they ceased their conversation and followed her with their eyes— even Doña Victorina was respectfully saluted.

Paulita was arrayed in a rich camisa and pañuelo of embroidered piña, different from those she had worn that morning to the church. The gauzy texture of the piña set off her shapely head, and the Indians who saw her compared her to the moon surrounded by fleecy clouds. A silk rose-colored skirt, caught up in rich and graceful folds by her little hand, gave majesty to her erect figure, the movement of which, harmonizing with her curving neck, displayed all the triumphs of vanity and satisfied coquetry. Isagani appeared to be rather disgusted, for so many curious eyes fixed upon the beauty of his sweetheart annoyed him. The stares seemed to him robbery and the girl's smiles faithlessness.

Juanito saw her and his hump increased when he spoke to her. Paulita replied negligently, while Doña Victorina called to him, for Juanito was her favorite, she preferring him to Isagani.

"What a girl, what a girl!" muttered the entranced Padre Camorra.

"Come, Padre, pinch yourself and let me alone," said Ben-Zayb fretfully.

"What a girl, what a girl!" repeated the friar. "And she has for a sweetheart a pupil of mine, the boy I had the quarrel with."

"Just my luck that she's not of my town," he added, after turning his head several times to follow her with his looks. He was even tempted to leave his companions to follow the girl, and Ben-Zayb had difficulty in dissuading him. Paulita's beautiful figure moved on, her graceful little head nodding with inborn coquetry.

Our promenaders kept on their way, not without sighs on the part of the friar-artilleryman, until they reached a booth surrounded by sightseers, who quickly made way for them. It was a shop of little wooden figures, of local manufacture, representing in all shapes and sizes the costumes, races, and occupations of the country: Indians, Spaniards, Chinese, mestizos, friars, clergymen, government clerks, gobernadorcillos, students, soldiers, and so on.

Whether the artists had more affection for the priests, the folds of whose habits were better suited to their esthetic purposes, or whether the friars, holding such an important place in Philippine life, engaged the attention of the sculptor more, the fact was that, for one cause or another, images of them abounded, well-turned and finished, representing them in the sublimest moments of their lives—the opposite of what is done in Europe, where they are pictured as sleeping on casks of wine, playing cards, emptying tankards, rousing themselves to gaiety, or patting the cheeks of a buxom girl. No, the friars of the Philippines were different: elegant, handsome, well-dressed, their tonsures neatly shaven, their features symmetrical and serene, their gaze meditative, their expression saintly, somewhat rosy-cheeked, cane in hand and patent-leather shoes on their feet, inviting adoration and a place in a glass case. Instead of the symbols of gluttony and incontinence of their brethren in Europe, those of Manila carried the book, the crucifix, and the palm of martyrdom; instead of kissing the simple country lasses, those of Manila gravely extended the hand to be kissed by children and grown men doubled over almost to kneeling; instead of the full refectory and dining-hall, their stage in Europe, in Manila they had the oratory, the study-table; instead of the mendicant friar who goes from door to door with his donkey and sack, begging alms, the friars of the Philippines scattered gold from full hands among the miserable Indians.

"Look, here's Padre Camorra!" exclaimed Ben-Zayb, upon whom the effect of the champagne still lingered. He pointed to a picture of a lean friar of thoughtful mien who was seated at a table with his head resting on the palm of his hand, apparently writing a sermon by the light of a lamp. The contrast suggested drew laughter from the crowd.

Padre Camorra, who had already forgotten about Paulita, saw what was meant and laughing his clownish laugh, asked in turn, "Whom does this other figure resemble, Ben-Zayb?"

It was an old woman with one eye, with disheveled hair, seated on the ground like an Indian idol, ironing clothes. The sad-iron was carefully imitated, being of copper with coals of red tinsel and smoke-wreaths of dirty twisted cotton.

"Eh, Ben-Zayb, it wasn't a fool who designed that" asked Padre Camorra with a laugh.

"Well, I don't see the point," replied the journalist.

"But, *puñales*, don't you see the title, *The Philippine Press*? That utensil with which the old woman is ironing is here called the press!"

All laughed at this, Ben-Zayb himself joining in good-naturedly.

Two soldiers of the Civil Guard, appropriately labeled, were placed behind a man who was tightly bound and had his face covered by his hat. It was entitled *The Country of Abaka,* and from appearances they were going to shoot him.

Many of our visitors were displeased with the exhibition. They talked of rules of art, they sought proportion—one said that this figure did not have seven heads, that the face lacked a nose, having only three, all of which made Padre Camorra somewhat thoughtful, for he did not comprehend how a figure, to be correct, need have four noses and seven heads. Others said, if they were muscular, that they could not be Indians; still others remarked that it was not sculpture, but mere carpentry. Each added his spoonful of criticism, until Padre Camorra, not to be outdone, ventured to ask for at least thirty legs for each doll, because, if the others wanted noses, couldn't he require feet? So they fell to discussing whether the Indian had or had not any aptitude for sculpture, and whether it would be advisable to encourage that art, until there arose a general dispute, which was cut short by Don Custodio's declaration that the Indians had the aptitude, but that they should devote themselves exclusively to the manufacture of saints.

"One would say," observed Ben-Zayb, who was full of bright ideas that night, "that this Chinaman is Quiroga, but on close examination it looks like Padre Irene. And what do you say about that British Indian? He looks like Simoun!"

Fresh peals of laughter resounded, while Padre Irene rubbed his nose.

"That's right!"

"It's the very image of him!"

"But where is Simoun? Simoun should buy it."

But the jeweler had disappeared, unnoticed by any one.

"*Puñales!*" exclaimed Padre Camorra, "how stingy the American is! He's afraid we would make him pay the admission for all of us into Mr. Leeds' show."

"No!" rejoined Ben-Zayb, "what he's afraid of is that he'll compromise himself. He may have foreseen the joke in store for his friend Mr. Leeds and has got out of the way."

Thus, without purchasing the least trifle, they continued on their way to see the famous sphinx. Ben-Zayb offered to manage the affair, for the American would not rebuff a journalist who could take revenge in an unfavorable article. "You'll see that it's all a question of mirrors," he said, "because, you see—" Again he plunged into a long demonstration, and as he had no mirrors at hand to discredit his theory he tangled himself up in all kinds of blunders and wound up by not knowing himself what he was saying. "In short, you'll see how it's all a question of optics."

---

1   Abaka is the fiber obtained from the leaves of the *Musa textilis* and is known commercially as Manila hemp. As it is exclusively a product of the Philippines, it may be taken here to symbolize the country.—Tr.

LEGERDEMAIN

Mr. Leeds, a genuine Yankee, dressed completely in black, received his visitors with great deference. He spoke Spanish well, from having been for many years in South America, and offered no objection to their request, saying that they might examine everything, both before and after the exhibition, but begged that they remain quiet while it was in progress. Ben-Zayb smiled in pleasant anticipation of the vexation he had prepared for the American.

The room, hung entirely in black, was lighted by ancient lamps burning alcohol. A rail wrapped in black velvet divided it into two almost equal parts, one of which was filled with seats for the spectators and the other occupied by a platform covered with a checkered carpet. In the center of this platform was placed a table, over which was spread a piece of black cloth adorned with skulls and cabalistic signs. The *mise en scène* was therefore lugubrious and had its effect upon the merry visitors. The jokes died away, they spoke in whispers, and however much some tried to appear indifferent, their lips framed no smiles. All felt as if they had entered a house where there was a corpse, an illusion accentuated by an odor of wax and incense. Don Custodio and Padre Salvi consulted in whispers over the expediency of prohibiting such shows.

Ben-Zayb, in order to cheer the dispirited group and embarrass Mr. Leeds, said to him in a familiar tone: "Eh, Mister, since there are none but ourselves here and we aren't Indians who can be fooled, won't you let us see the trick? We know of course that it's purely a question of optics, but as Padre Camorra won't be convinced—"

Here he started to jump over the rail, instead of going through the proper opening, while Padre Camorra broke out into protests, fearing that Ben-Zayb might be right.

"And why not, sir?" rejoined the American. "But don't break anything, will you?"

The journalist was already on the platform. "You will allow me, then?" he asked, and without waiting for the permission, fearing that it might not be granted, raised the cloth to look for the mirrors that he expected should be between the legs of the table. Ben-Zayb uttered an exclamation and stepped back, again placed both hands under the table and waved them about; he encountered only empty space. The table had three thin iron legs, sunk into the floor.

The journalist looked all about as though seeking something.

"Where are the mirrors?" asked Padre Camorra.

Ben-Zayb looked and looked, felt the table with his fingers, raised the cloth again, and rubbed his hand over his forehead from time to time, as if trying to remember something.

"Have you lost anything?" inquired Mr. Leeds.

"The mirrors, Mister, where are the mirrors?"

"I don't know where yours are—mine are at the hotel. Do you want to look at yourself? You're somewhat pale and excited."

Many laughed, in spite of their weird impressions, on seeing the jesting coolness of the American, while Ben-Zayb retired, quite abashed, to his seat, muttering, "It can't be. You'll see that he doesn't do it without mirrors. The table will have to be changed later."

Mr. Leeds placed the cloth on the table again and turning toward his illustrious audience, asked them, "Are you satisfied? May we begin?"

"Hurry up! How cold-blooded he is!" said the widow.

"Then, ladies and gentlemen, take your seats and get your questions ready."

Mr. Leeds disappeared through a doorway and in a few moments returned with a black box of worm-eaten wood, covered with inscriptions in the form of birds, beasts, and human heads.

"Ladies and gentlemen," he began solemnly, "once having had occasion to visit the great pyramid of Khufu, a Pharaoh of the fourth dynasty, I chanced upon a sarcophagus of red granite in a forgotten chamber. My joy was great, for I thought that I had found a royal mummy, but what was my disappointment on opening the coffin, at the cost of infinite labor, to find nothing more than this box, which you may examine."

He handed the box to those in the front row. Padre Camorra drew back in loathing, Padre Salvi looked at it closely as if he enjoyed sepulchral things, Padre Irene smiled a knowing smile, Don Custodio affected gravity and disdain, while Ben-Zayb hunted for his mirrors—there they must be, for it was a question of mirrors.

"It smells like a corpse," observed one lady, fanning herself furiously. "Ugh!"

"It smells of forty centuries," remarked some one with emphasis.

Ben-Zayb forgot about his mirrors to discover who had made this remark. It was a military official who had read the history of Napoleon.

Ben-Zayb felt jealous and to utter another epigram that might annoy Padre Camorra a little said, "It smells of the Church."

"This box, ladies and gentlemen," continued the American, "contained a handful of ashes and a piece of papyrus on which were written some words. Examine them yourselves, but I beg of you not to breathe heavily, because if any of the dust is lost my sphinx will appear in a mutilated condition."

The humbug, described with such seriousness and conviction, was gradually having its effect, so much so that when the box was passed around, no one dared to breathe. Padre Camorra, who had so often depicted from the pulpit of Tiani the torments and sufferings of hell, while he laughed in his sleeves at the terrified looks of the sinners, held his nose, and Padre Salvi—the same Padre Salvi who had on All Souls' Day prepared a phantasmagoria of the souls in purgatory with flames and transparencies illuminated with alcohol lamps and covered with tinsel, on the high altar of the church in a suburb, in order to get alms and orders for masses—the lean and taciturn Padre Salvi held his breath and gazed suspiciously at that handful of ashes.

"*Memento, homo, quia pulvis es!*" muttered Padre Irene with a smile.

"Pish!" sneered Ben-Zayb—the same thought had occurred to him, and the Canon had taken the words out of his mouth.

"Not knowing what to do," resumed Mr. Leeds, closing the box carefully, "I examined the papyrus and discovered two words whose meaning was unknown to me. I deciphered them, and tried to pronounce them aloud. Scarcely had I uttered the first word when I felt the box slipping from my hands, as if pressed down by an enormous weight, and it glided along the floor, whence I vainly endeavored to remove it. But my surprise was converted into terror when it opened and I found within a human head that stared at me fixedly. Paralyzed with fright and uncertain what to do in the presence of such a phenomenon, I remained for a time stupefied, trembling like a person poisoned with mercury, but after a while recovered myself and, thinking that it was a vain illusion, tried to divert my attention by reading the second word. Hardly had I pronounced it when the box closed, the head disappeared, and in its place I again found the handful of ashes. Without suspecting it I had discovered the two most potent words in nature, the words of creation and destruction, of life and of death!"

He paused for a few moments to note the effect of his story, then with grave and measured steps approached the table and placed the mysterious box upon it.

"The cloth, Mister!" exclaimed the incorrigible Ben-Zayb.

"Why not?" rejoined Mr. Leeds, very complaisantly.

Lifting the box with his right hand, he caught up the cloth with his left, completely exposing the table sustained by its three legs. Again he placed the box upon the center and with great gravity turned to his audience.

"Here's what I want to see," said Ben-Zayb to his neighbor. "You notice how he makes some excuse."

Great attention was depicted on all countenances and silence reigned. The noise and roar of the street could be distinctly heard, but all were so affected that a snatch of dialogue which reached them produced no effect.

"Why can't we go in?" asked a woman's voice.

"*Abá*, there's a lot of friars and clerks in there," answered a man. "The sphinx is for them only."

"The friars are inquisitive too," said the woman's voice, drawing away. "They don't want us to know how they're being fooled. Why, is the head a friar's *querida?*"

In the midst of a profound silence the American announced in a tone of emotion: "Ladies and gentlemen, with a word I am now going to reanimate the handful of ashes, and you will talk with a being that knows the past, the present, and much of the future!"

Here the prestidigitator uttered a soft cry, first mournful, then lively, a medley of sharp sounds like imprecations and hoarse notes like threats, which made Ben-Zayb's hair stand on end.

"*Deremof!*" cried the American.

The curtains on the wall rustled, the lamps burned low, the table creaked. A feeble groan responded from the interior of the box. Pale and uneasy, all stared at one another, while one terrified señora caught hold of Padre Salvi.

The box then opened of its own accord and presented to the eyes of the audience a head of cadaverous aspect, surrounded by long and abundant black hair. It slowly opened its eyes and looked around the whole audience. Those eyes had a vivid radiance, accentuated by their cavernous sockets, and, as if deep were calling unto deep, fixed themselves upon the profound, sunken eyes of the trembling Padre Salvi, who was staring unnaturally, as though he saw a ghost.

"Sphinx," commanded Mr. Leeds, "tell the audience who you are."

A deep silence prevailed, while a chill wind blew through the room and made the blue flames of the sepulchral lamps flicker. The most skeptical shivered.

"I am Imuthis," declared the head in a funereal, but strangely menacing, voice. "I was born in the time of Amasis and died under the Persian domination, when Cambyses was returning from his disastrous expedition into the interior of Libya. I had come to complete my education after extensive travels through Greece, Assyria, and Persia, and had returned to my native laud to dwell in it until Thoth should call me before his terrible tribunal. But to my undoing, on passing through Babylonia, I discovered an awful secret—the secret of the false Smerdis who usurped the throne, the bold Magian Gaumata who governed as an impostor. Fearing that I would betray him to Cambyses, he determined upon my ruin through the instrumentality of the Egyptian priests, who at that time ruled my native country. They were the owners of two-thirds of the land, the monopolizers of learning, they held the people down in ignorance and tyranny, they brutalized them, thus making them fit to pass without resistance from one domination to another. The invaders availed themselves of them, and knowing their usefulness, protected and enriched them. The rulers not only depended on their will, but some were reduced to mere instruments of theirs. The Egyptian priests hastened to execute Gaumata's orders, with greater zeal from their fear of me, because they were afraid that I would reveal their impostures to the people. To accomplish their purpose, they made use of a young priest of Abydos, who passed for a saint."

A painful silence followed these words. That head was talking of priestly intrigues and impostures, and although referring to another age and other creeds, all the friars present were annoyed, possibly because they could see in the general trend of the speech some analogy to the existing situation. Padre Salvi was in the grip of convulsive shivering; he worked his lips and with bulging eyes followed the gaze of the head as though fascinated. Beads of sweat began to break out on his emaciated face, but no one noticed this, so deeply absorbed and affected were they.

"What was the plot concocted by the priests of your country against you?" asked Mr. Leeds.

The head uttered a sorrowful groan, which seemed to come from the bottom of the heart, and the spectators saw its eyes, those fiery eyes, clouded and filled with tears. Many shuddered and felt their hair rise. No, that was not an illusion, it was not a trick: the head was the victim and what it told was its own story.

"Ay!" it moaned, shaking with affliction, "I loved a maiden, the daughter of a priest, pure as light, like the freshly opened lotus! The young priest of Abydos also desired her and planned a rebellion, using my name and some papyri that he had secured from my beloved. The rebellion broke out at the time when Cambyses was returning in rage over the disasters of his unfortunate campaign. I was accused of being a rebel, was made a prisoner, and having effected my escape was killed in the chase on Lake Moeris. From out of eternity I saw the imposture triumph. I saw the priest of Abydos night and day persecuting the maiden, who had taken refuge in a temple of Isis on the island of Philae. I saw him persecute and harass her, even in the subterranean chambers, I saw him drive her mad with terror and suffering, like a huge bat pursuing a white dove. Ah, priest, priest of Abydos, I have returned to life to expose your infamy, and after so many years of silence, I name thee murderer, hypocrite, liar!"

A dry, hollow laugh accompanied these words, while a choked voice responded, "No! Mercy!"

It was Padre Salvi, who had been overcome with terror and with arms extended was slipping in collapse to the floor.

"What's the matter with your Reverence? Are you ill?" asked Padre Irene.

"The heat of the room—"

"This odor of corpses we're breathing here—"

"Murderer, slanderer, hypocrite!" repeated the head. "I accuse you—murderer, murderer, murderer!"

Again the dry laugh, sepulchral and menacing, resounded, as though that head were so absorbed in contemplation of its wrongs that it did not see the tumult that prevailed in the room.

"Mercy! She still lives!" groaned Padre Salvi, and then lost consciousness. He was as pallid as a corpse. Some of the ladies thought it their duty to faint also, and proceeded to do so.

"He is out of his head! Padre Salvi!"

"I told him not to eat that bird's-nest soup," said Padre Irene. "It has made him sick."

"But he didn't eat anything," rejoined Don Custodio shivering. "As the head has been staring at him fixedly, it has mesmerized him."

So disorder prevailed, the room seemed to be a hospital or a battlefield. Padre Salvi looked like a corpse, and the ladies, seeing that no one was paying them any attention, made the best of it by recovering.

Meanwhile, the head had been reduced to ashes, and Mr. Leeds, having replaced the cloth on the table, bowed his audience out.

"This show must be prohibited," said Don Custodio on leaving. "It's wicked and highly immoral."

"And above all, because it doesn't use mirrors," added Ben-Zayb, who before going out of the room tried to assure himself finally, so he leaped over the rail, went up to the table, and raised the cloth: nothing, absolutely nothing! On the following day he wrote an article in which he spoke of occult sciences, spiritualism, and the like.

An order came immediately from the ecclesiastical governor prohibiting the show, but Mr. Leeds had already disappeared, carrying his secret with him to Hongkong.

---

1   Yet Ben-Zayb was not very much mistaken. The three legs of the table have grooves in them in which slide the mirrors hidden below the platform and covered by the squares of the carpet. By placing the box upon the table a spring is pressed and the mirrors rise gently. The cloth is then removed, with care to raise it instead of letting it slide off, and then there is the ordinary table of the talking heads. The table is connected with the bottom of the box. The exhibition ended, the prestidigitator again covers the table, presses another spring, and the mirrors descend.—*Author's note.*

THE FUSE

Placido Penitente left the class with his heart overflowing with bitterness and sullen gloom in his looks. He was worthy of his name when not driven from his usual course, but once irritated he was a veritable torrent, a wild beast that could only be stopped by the death of himself or his foe. So many affronts, so many pinpricks, day after day, had made his heart quiver, lodging in it to sleep the sleep of lethargic vipers, and they now were awaking to shake and hiss with fury. The hisses resounded in his ears with the jesting epithets of the professor, the phrases in the slang of the markets, and he seemed to hear blows and laughter. A thousand schemes for revenge rushed into his brain, crowding one another, only to fade immediately like phantoms in a dream. His vanity cried out to him with desperate tenacity that he must do something.

"Placido Penitente," said the voice, "show these youths that you have dignity, that you are the son of a valiant and noble province, where wrongs are washed out with blood. You're a Batangan, Placido Penitente! Avenge yourself, Placido Penitente!"

The youth groaned and gnashed his teeth, stumbling against every one in the street and on the Bridge of Spain, as if he were seeking a quarrel. In the latter place he saw a carriage in which was the Vice-Rector, Padre Sibyla, accompanied by Don Custodio, and he had a great mind to seize the friar and throw him into the river.

He proceeded along the Escolta and was tempted to assault two Augustinians who were seated in the doorway of Quiroga's bazaar, laughing and joking with other friars who must have been inside in joyous conversation, for their merry voices and sonorous laughter could be heard. Somewhat farther on, two cadets blocked up the sidewalk, talking with the clerk of a warehouse, who was in his shirtsleeves. Penitents moved toward them to force a passage and they, perceiving his dark intention, good-humoredly made way for him. Placido was by this time under the influence of the *amok*, as the Malayists say.

As he approached his home—the house of a silversmith where he lived as a boarder—he tried to collect his thoughts and make a plan—to return to his town and avenge himself by showing the friars that they could not with impunity insult a youth or make a joke of him. He decided to write a letter immediately to his mother, Cabesang Andang, to inform her of what had happened and to tell her that the schoolroom had closed forever for him. Although there was the Ateneo of the Jesuits, where he might study that year, yet it was not very likely that the Dominicans would grant him the transfer, and, even though he should secure it, in the following year he would have to return to the University.

"They say that we don't know how to avenge ourselves!" he muttered. "Let the lightning strike and we'll see!"

But Placido was not reckoning upon what awaited him in the house of the silversmith. Cabesang Andang had just arrived from Batangas, having come to do some shopping, to visit her son, and to bring him money, jerked venison, and silk handkerchiefs.

The first greetings over, the poor woman, who had at once noticed her son's gloomy look, could no longer restrain her curiosity and began to ask questions. His first explanations Cabesang Andang regarded as some subterfuge, so she smiled and soothed her son, reminding him of their sacrifices and privations. She spoke of Capitana Simona's son, who, having entered the seminary, now carried himself in the town like a bishop, and Capitana Simona already considered herself a Mother of God, clearly so, for her son was going to be another Christ.

"If the son becomes a priest," said she, "the mother won't have to pay us what she owes us. Who will collect from her then?"

But on seeing that Placido was speaking seriously and reading in his eyes the storm that raged within him, she realized that what he was telling her was unfortunately the strict truth. She remained silent for a while and then broke out into lamentations.

"Ay!" she exclaimed. "I promised your father that I would care for you, educate you, and make a lawyer of you! I've deprived myself of everything so that you might go to school! Instead of joining the *panguingui* where the stake is a half peso, I Ve gone only where it's a half real, enduring the bad smells and the dirty cards.

Look at my patched camisa; for instead of buying new ones I've spent the money in masses and presents to St. Sebastian, even though I don't have great confidence in his power, because the curate recites the masses fast and hurriedly, he's an entirely new saint and doesn't yet know how to perform miracles, and isn't made of *batikulin* but of *lanete*. Ay, what will your father say to me when I die and see him again!"

So the poor woman lamented and wept, while Placido became gloomier and let stifled sighs escape from his breast.

"What would I get out of being a lawyer?" was his response.

"What will become of you?" asked his mother, clasping her hands. "They'll call you a filibuster and garrote you. I've told you that you must have patience, that you must be humble. I don't tell you that you must kiss the hands of the curates, for I know that you have a delicate sense of smell, like your father, who couldn't endure European cheese.' But we have to suffer, to be silent, to say yes to everything. What are we going to do? The friars own everything, and if they are unwilling, no one will become a lawyer or a doctor. Have patience, my son, have patience!"

"But I've had a great deal, mother, I've suffered for months and months."

Cabesang Andang then resumed her lamentations. She did not ask that he declare himself a partizan of the friars, she was not one herself—it was enough to know that for one good friar there were ten bad, who took the money from the poor and deported the rich. But one must be silent, suffer, and endure—there was no other course. She cited this man and that one, who by being *patient* and humble, even though in the bottom of his heart he hated his masters, had risen from servant of the friars to high office; and such another who was rich and could commit abuses, secure of having patrons who would protect him from the law, yet who had been nothing more than a poor sacristan, humble and obedient, and who had married a pretty girl whose son had the curate for a godfather. So Cabesang Andang continued her litany of humble and *patient* Filipinos, as she called them, and was about to cite others who by not being so had found themselves persecuted and exiled, when Placido on some trifling pretext left the house to wander about the streets.

He passed through Sibakong, Tondo, San Nicolas, and Santo Cristo, absorbed in his ill-humor, without taking note of the sun or the hour, and only when he began to feel hungry and discovered that he had no money, having given it all for celebrations and contributions, did he return to the house. He had expected that he would not meet his mother there, as she was in the habit, when in Manila, of going out at that hour to a neighboring house where *panguingui* was played, but Cabesang Andang was waiting to propose her plan. She would avail herself of the procurator of the Augustinians to restore her son to the good graces of the Dominicans.

Placido stopped her with a gesture. "I'll throw myself into the sea first," he declared. "I'll become a tulisan before I'll go back to the University."

Again his mother began her preachment about patience and humility, so he went away again without having eaten anything, directing his steps toward the quay where the steamers tied up. The sight of a steamer weighing anchor for Hongkong inspired him with an idea—to go to Hongkong, to run away, get rich there, and make war on the friars.

The thought of Hongkong awoke in his mind the recollection of a story about frontals, cirials, and candelabra of pure silver, which the piety of the faithful had led them to present to a certain church. The friars, so the silversmith told, had sent to Hongkong to have duplicate frontals, cirials, and candelabra made of German silver, which they substituted for the genuine ones, these being melted down and coined into Mexican pesos. Such was the story he had heard, and though it was no more than a rumor or a story, his resentment gave it the color of truth and reminded him of other tricks of theirs in that same style. The desire to live free, and certain half-formed plans, led him to decide upon Hongkong. If the corporations sent all their money there, commerce must be flourishing and he could enrich himself.

"I want to be free, to live free!"

Night surprised him wandering along San Fernando, but not meeting any sailor he knew, he decided to return home. As the night was beautiful, with a brilliant moon transforming the squalid city into a fantastic fairy kingdom, he went to the fair. There he wandered back and forth, passing booths without taking any notice of the articles in them, ever with the thought of Hongkong, of living free, of enriching himself.

He was about to leave the fair when he thought he recognized the jeweler Simoun bidding good-by to a foreigner, both of them speaking in English. To Placido every language spoken in the Philippines by Europeans, when not Spanish, had to be English, and besides, he caught the name Hongkong. If only the jeweler would recommend him to that foreigner, who must be setting out for Hongkong!

Placido paused. He was acquainted with the jeweler, as the latter had been in his town peddling his wares, and he had accompanied him on one of his trips, when Simoun had made himself very amiable indeed, telling him of the life in the universities of the free countries—what a difference!

So he followed the jeweler. "Señor Simoun, Señor Simoun!" he called.

The jeweler was at that moment entering his carriage. Recognizing Placido, he checked himself.

"I want to ask a favor of you, to say a few words to you."

Simoun made a sign of impatience which Placido in his perturbation did not observe. In a few words the youth related what had happened and made known his desire to go to Hongkong.

"Why?" asked Simoun, staring fixedly at Placido through his blue goggles.

Placido did not answer, so Simoun threw back his head, smiled his cold, silent smile and said, "All right! Come with me. To Calle Iris!" he directed the cochero.

Simoun remained silent throughout the whole drive, apparently absorbed in meditation of a very important nature. Placido kept quiet, waiting for him to speak first, and entertained himself in watching the promenaders who were enjoying the clear moonlight: pairs of infatuated lovers, followed by watchful mammas or aunts; groups of students in white clothes that the moonlight made whiter still; half-drunken soldiers in a carriage, six together, on their way to visit some nipa temple dedicated to Cytherea; children playing their games and Chinese selling sugar-cane. All these filled the streets, taking on in the brilliant moonlight fantastic forms and ideal outlines. In one house an orchestra was playing waltzes, and couples might be seen dancing under the bright lamps and chandeliers—what a sordid spectacle they presented in comparison with the sight the streets afforded! Thinking of Hongkong, he asked himself if the moonlit nights in that island were so poetical and sweetly melancholy as those of the Philippines, and a deep sadness settled down over his heart.

Simoun ordered the carriage to stop and both alighted, just at the moment when Isagani and Paulita Gomez passed them murmuring sweet inanities. Behind them came Doña Victorina with Juanito Pelaez, who was talking in a loud voice, busily gesticulating, and appearing to have a larger hump than ever. In his preoccupation Pelaez did not notice his former schoolmate.

"There's a fellow who's happy!" muttered Placido with a sigh, as he gazed toward the group, which became converted into vaporous silhouettes, with Juanito's arms plainly visible, rising and falling like the arms of a windmill.

"That's all he's good for," observed Simoun. "It's fine to be young!"

To whom did Placido and Simoun each allude?

The jeweler made a sign to the young man, and they left the street to pick their way through a labyrinth of paths and passageways among various houses, at times leaping upon stones to avoid the mudholes or stepping aside from the sidewalks that were badly constructed and still more badly tended. Placido was surprised to see the rich jeweler move through such places as if he were familiar with them. They at length reached an open lot where a wretched hut stood off by itself surrounded by banana-plants and areca-palms. Some bamboo frames and sections of the same material led Placido to suspect that they were approaching the house of a pyrotechnist.

Simoun rapped on the window and a man's face appeared.

"Ah, sir!" he exclaimed, and immediately came outside.

"Is the powder here?" asked Simoun.

"In sacks. I'm waiting for the shells."

"And the bombs?"

"Are all ready."

"All right, then. This very night you must go and inform the lieutenant and the corporal. Then keep on your way, and in Lamayan you will find a man in a banka. You will say *Cabesa* and he will answer *Tales*. It's necessary that he be here tomorrow. There's no time to be lost."

Saying this, he gave him some gold coins.

"How's this, sir?" the man inquired in very good Spanish. "Is there any news?"

"Yes, it'll be done within the coming week."

"The coming week!" exclaimed the unknown, stepping backward. "The suburbs are not yet ready, they hope that the General will withdraw the decree. I thought it was postponed until the beginning of Lent."

Simoun shook his head. "We won't need the suburbs," he said. "With Cabesang Tales' people, the ex-carbineers, and a regiment, we'll have enough. Later, Maria Clara may be dead. Start at once!"

The man disappeared. Placido, who had stood by and heard all of this brief interview, felt his hair rise and stared with startled eyes at Simoun, who smiled.

"You're surprised," he said with his icy smile, "that this Indian, so poorly dressed, speaks Spanish well? He was a schoolmaster who persisted in teaching Spanish to the children and did not stop until he had lost his position and had been deported as a disturber of the public peace, and for having been a friend of the unfortunate Ibarra. I got him back from his deportation, where he had been working as a pruner of coconut-palms, and have made him a pyrotechnist."

They returned to the street and set out for Trozo. Before a wooden house of pleasant and well-kept appearance was a Spaniard on crutches, enjoying the moonlight. When Simoun accosted him, his attempt to rise was accompanied by a stifled groan.

"You're ready?" Simoun inquired of him.

"I always am!"

"The coming week?"

"So soon?"

"At the first cannon-shot!"

He moved away, followed by Placido, who was beginning to ask himself if he were not dreaming.

"Does it surprise you," Simoun asked him, "to see a Spaniard so young and so afflicted with disease? Two years ago he was as robust as you are, but his enemies succeeded in sending him to Balabak to work in a penal settlement, and there he caught the rheumatism and fever that are dragging him into the grave. The poor devil had married a very beautiful woman."

As an empty carriage was passing, Simoun hailed it and with Placido directed it to his house in the Escolta, just at the moment when the clocks were striking half-past ten.

Two hours later Placido left the jeweler's house and walked gravely and thoughtfully along the Escolta, then almost deserted, in spite of the fact that the cafés were still quite animated. Now and then a carriage passed rapidly, clattering noisily over the worn pavement.

From a room in his house that overlooked the Pasig, Simoun turned his gaze toward the Walled City, which could be seen through the open windows, with its roofs of galvanized iron gleaming in the moonlight and its somber towers showing dull and gloomy in the midst of the serene night. He laid aside his blue goggles, and his white hair, like a frame of silver, surrounded his energetic bronzed features, dimly lighted by a lamp whose flame was dying out from lack of oil. Apparently wrapped in thought, he took no notice of the fading light and impending darkness.

"Within a few days," he murmured, "when on all sides that accursed city is burning, den of presumptuous nothingness and impious exploitation of the ignorant and the distressed, when the tumults break out in the suburbs and there rush into the terrorized streets my avenging hordes, engendered by rapacity and wrongs, then will I burst the walls of your prison, I will tear you from the clutches of fanaticism, and my white dove, you will be the Phoenix that will rise from the glowing embers! A revolution plotted by men in darkness tore me from your side—another revolution will sweep me into your arms and revive me! That moon, before reaching the apogee of its brilliance, will light the Philippines cleansed of loathsome filth!"

Simoun, stopped suddenly, as though interrupted. A voice in his inner consciousness was asking if he, Simoun, were not also a part of the filth of that accursed city, perhaps its most poisonous ferment. Like the dead who are to rise at the sound of the last trumpet, a thousand bloody specters—desperate shades of murdered men, women violated, fathers torn from their families, vices stimulated and encouraged, virtues mocked, now rose in answer to the mysterious question. For the first time in his criminal career, since in Havana he had by means of corruption and bribery set out to fashion an instrument for the execution of his plans—a man without faith, patriotism, or conscience—for the first time in that life, something within rose up and protested against his actions. He closed his eyes and remained for some time motionless, then rubbed his hand over his forehead, tried to be deaf to his conscience, and felt fear creeping over him. No, he must not analyze himself, he lacked the courage to turn his gaze toward his past. The idea of his courage, his conviction, his self-confidence failing him at the very moment when his work was set before him! As the ghosts of the wretches in whose misfortunes he had taken a hand continued to hover before his eyes, as if issuing from the shining surface of the river to invade the room with appeals and hands extended toward him, as reproaches and laments seemed to fill the air with threats and cries for vengeance, he turned his gaze from the window and for the first time began to tremble.

"No, I must be ill, I can't be feeling well," he muttered. "There are many who hate me, who ascribe their misfortunes to me, but—"

He felt his forehead begin to burn, so he arose to approach the window and inhale the fresh night breeze. Below him the Pasig dragged along its silvered stream, on whose bright surface the foam glittered, winding slowly about, receding and advancing, following the course of the little eddies. The city loomed up on the opposite bank, and its black walls looked fateful, mysterious, losing their sordidness in the moonlight that idealizes and embellishes everything. But again Simoun shivered; he seemed to see before him the severe countenance of his father, dying in prison, but dying for having done good; then the face of another man, severer still, who had given his life for him because he believed that he was going to bring about the regeneration of his country.

"No, I can't turn back," he exclaimed, wiping the perspiration from his forehead. "The work is at hand and its success will justify me! If I had conducted myself as you did, I should have succumbed. Nothing of idealism, nothing of fallacious theories! Fire and steel to the cancer, chastisement to vice, and afterwards destroy the instrument, if it be bad! No, I have planned well, but now I feel feverish, my reason wavers, it is natural—If I have done ill, it has been that I may do good, and the end justifies the means. What I will do is not to expose myself—"

With his thoughts thus confused he lay down, and tried to fall asleep.

On the following morning Placido listened submissively, with a smile on his lips, to his mother's preachment. When she spoke of her plan of interesting the Augustinian procurator he did not protest or object, but on the contrary offered himself to carry it out, in order to save trouble for his mother, whom he begged to return at once to the province, that very day, if possible. Cabesang Andang asked him the reason for such haste.

"Because—because if the procurator learns that you are here he won't do anything until you send him a present and order some masses."

---

1   The Malay method of kissing is quite different from the Occidental. The mouth is placed close to the object and a deep breath taken, often without actually touching the object, being more of a sniff than a kiss.—Tr.

2   Now Calle Tetuan, Santa Cruz. The other names are still in use.—Tr.

THE ARBITER

True it was that Padre Irene had said: the question of the academy of Castilian, so long before broached, was on the road to a solution. Don Custodio, the active Don Custodio, the most active of all the arbiters in the world, according to Ben-Zayb, was occupied with it, spending his days reading the petition and falling asleep without reaching any decision, waking on the following day to repeat the same performance, dropping off to sleep again, and so on continuously.

How the good man labored, the most active of all the arbiters in the world! He wished to get out of the predicament by pleasing everybody—the friars, the high official, the Countess, Padre Irene, and his own liberal principles. He had consulted with Señor Pasta, and Señor Pasta had left him stupefied and confused, after advising him to do a million contradictory and impossible things. He had consulted with Pepay the dancing girl, and Pepay, who had no idea what he was talking about, executed a pirouette and asked him for twenty-five pesos to bury an aunt of hers who had suddenly died for the fifth time, or the fifth aunt who had suddenly died, according to fuller explanations, at the same time requesting that he get a cousin of hers who could read, write, and play the violin, a job as assistant on the public works—all things that were far from inspiring Don Custodio with any saving idea.

Two days after the events in the Quiapo fair, Don Custodio was as usual busily studying the petition, without hitting upon the happy solution. While he yawns, coughs, smokes, and thinks about Pepay's legs and her pirouettes, let us give some account of this exalted personage, in order to understand Padre Sibyla's reason for proposing him as the arbiter of such a vexatious matter and why the other clique accepted him.

Don Custodio de Salazar y Sanchez de Monteredondo, often referred to as *Good Authority*, belonged to that class of Manila society which cannot take a step without having the newspapers heap titles upon them, calling each *indedefatigable, distinguished, zealous, active, profound, intelligent, well-informed, influential,* and so on, as if they feared that he might be confused with some idle and ignorant possessor of the same name. Besides, no harm resulted from it, and the watchful censor was not disturbed. The *Good Authority* resulted from his friendship with Ben-Zayb, when the latter, in his two noisiest controversies, which he carried on for weeks and months in the columns of the newspapers about whether it was proper to wear a high hat, a derby, or a *salakot,* and whether the plural of *carácter* should be *carácteres* or *caractéres,* in order to strengthen his argument always came out with, "We have this on good authority," "We learn this from good authority," later letting it be known, for in Manila everything becomes known, that this *Good Authority* was no other than Don Custodio de Salazar y Sanchez de Monteredondo.

He had come to Manila very young, with a good position that had enabled him to marry a pretty mestiza belonging to one of the wealthiest families of the city. As he had natural talent, boldness, and great self-possession, and knew how to make use of the society in which he found himself, he launched into business with his wife's money, filling contracts for the government, by reason of which he was made alderman, afterwards alcalde, member of the Economic Society, councilor of the administration, president of the directory of the *Obras Pias,* member of the Society of Mercy, director of the Spanish-Filipino Bank, etc., etc. Nor are these *etceteras* to be taken like those ordinarily placed after a long enumeration of titles: Don Custodio, although never having seen a treatise on hygiene, came to be vice-chairman of the Board of Health, for the truth was that of the eight who composed this board only one had to be a physician and he could not be that one. So also he was a member of the Vaccination Board, which was composed of three physicians and seven laymen, among these being the Archbishop and three Provincials. He was a brother in all the confraternities of the common and of the most exalted dignity, and, as we have seen, director of the Superior Commission of Primary Instruction, which usually did not do anything—all these being quite sufficient reason for the newspapers to heap adjectives upon him no less when he traveled than when he sneezed.

In spite of so many offices, Don Custodio was not among those who slept through the sessions, contenting themselves, like lazy and timid delegates, in voting with the majority. The opposite of the numerous kings of Europe who bear the title of King of Jerusalem, Don Custodio made his dignity felt and got from it all the benefit possible, often frowning, making his voice impressive, coughing out his words, often taking up the whole session telling a story, presenting a project, or disputing with a colleague who had placed himself in open opposition to him. Although not past forty, he already talked of acting with circumspection, of letting the figs ripen (adding under his breath "pumpkins"), of pondering deeply and of stepping with careful tread, of the necessity for understanding the country, because the nature of the Indians, because the prestige of the Spanish name, because they were first of all Spaniards, because religion—and so on. Remembered yet in Manila is a speech of his when for the first time it was proposed to light the city with kerosene in place of the old coconut oil: in such an innovation, far from seeing the extinction of the coconut-oil industry, he merely discerned the interests of a certain alderman— because Don Custodio saw a long way—and opposed it with all the resonance of his bucal cavity, considering the project too premature and predicting great social cataclysms. No less celebrated was his opposition to a sentimental serenade that some wished to tender a certain governor on the eve of his departure. Don Custodio, who felt a little resentment over some slight or other, succeeded in insinuating the idea that the rising star was the mortal enemy of the setting one, whereat the frightened promoters of the serenade gave it up.

One day he was advised to return to Spain to be cured of a liver complaint, and the newspapers spoke of him as an Antaeus who had to set foot in the mother country to gain new strength. But the Manila Antaeus found himself a small and insignificant person at the capital. There he was nobody, and he missed his beloved adjectives. He did not mingle with the upper set, and his lack of education prevented him from amounting to much in the academies and scientific centers, while his backwardness and his parish-house politics drove him from the clubs disgusted, vexed, seeing nothing clearly but that there they were forever borrowing money and gambling heavily. He missed the submissive servants of Manila, who endured all his peevishness, and who now seemed to be far preferable; when a winter kept him between a fireplace and an attack of pneumonia, he sighed for the Manila winter during which a single quilt is sufficient, while in summer he missed the easy-chair and the boy to fan him. In short, in Madrid he was only one among many, and in spite of his diamonds he was once taken for a rustic who did not know how to comport himself and at another time for an *Indiano*. His scruples were scoffed at, and he was shamelessly flouted by some borrowers whom he offended. Disgusted with the conservatives, who took no great notice of his advice, as well as with the sponges who rifled his pockets, he declared himself to be of the liberal party and returned within a year to the Philippines, if not sound in his liver, yet completely changed in his beliefs.

The eleven months spent at the capital among café politicians, nearly all retired half-pay office-holders, the various speeches caught here and there, this or that article of the opposition, all the political life that permeates the air, from the barber-shop where amid the scissors-clips the Figaro announces his program to the banquets where in harmonious periods and telling phrases the different shades of political opinion, the divergences and disagreements, are adjusted—all these things awoke in him the farther he got from Europe, like the life-giving sap within the sown seed prevented from bursting out by the thick husk, in such a way that when he reached Manila he believed that he was going to regenerate it and actually had the holiest plans and the purest ideals.

During the first months after his return he was continually talking about the capital, about his good friends, about Minister So-and-So, ex-Minister Such-a-One, the delegate C., the author B., and there was not a political event, a court scandal, of which he was not informed to the last detail, nor was there a public man the secrets of whose private life were unknown to him, nor could anything occur that he had not foreseen, nor any reform be ordered but he had first been consulted. All this was seasoned with attacks on the conservatives in righteous indignation, with apologies of the liberal party, with a little anecdote here, a phrase there from some great man, dropped in as one who did not wish offices and employments, which same he had refused in order not to be beholden to the conservatives. Such was his enthusiasm in these first days that various cronies in the grocery-store which he visited from time to time affiliated themselves with the liberal party and began to style themselves liberals: Don Eulogio Badana, a retired sergeant of carbineers; the honest Armendia, by profession a pilot, and a rampant Carlist; Don Eusebio Picote, customs inspector; and Don Bonifacio Tacon, shoe-and harness-maker.

But nevertheless, from lack of encouragement and of opposition, his enthusiasm gradually waned. He did not read the newspapers that came from Spain, because they arrived in packages, the sight of which made him yawn. The ideas that he had caught having been all expended, he needed reinforcement, and his orators were not there, and although in the casinos of Manila there was enough gambling, and money was borrowed as in Madrid, no speech that would nourish his political ideas was permitted in them. But Don Custodio was not lazy, he did more than wish—he worked. Foreseeing that he was going to leave his bones in the Philippines, he began to consider that country his proper sphere and to devote his efforts to its welfare. Thinking to liberalize it, he commenced to draw up a series of reforms or projects, which were ingenious, to say the least. It was he who, having heard in Madrid mention of the wooden street pavements of Paris, not yet adopted in Spain, proposed the introduction of them in Manila by covering the streets with boards nailed down as they are on the sides of houses; it was he who, deploring the accidents to two-wheeled vehicles, planned to avoid them by putting on at least three wheels; it was also he who, while acting as vice-president of the Board of Health, ordered everything fumigated, even the telegrams that came from infected places; it was also he who, in compassion for the convicts that worked in the sun and with a desire of saving to the government the cost of their equipment, suggested that they be clothed in a simple breech-clout and set to work not by day but at night. He marveled, he stormed, that his projects should encounter objectors, but consoled himself with the reflection that the man who is worth enemies has them, and revenged himself by attacking and tearing to pieces any project, good or bad, presented by others.

As he prided himself on being a liberal, upon being asked what he thought of the Indians he would answer, like one conferring a great favor, that they were fitted for manual labor and the *imitative arts* (meaning thereby music, painting, and sculpture), adding his old postscript that to know them one must have resided many, many years in the country. Yet when he heard of any one of them excelling in something that was not manual labor or an *imitative art*—in chemistry, medicine, or philosophy, for example—he would exclaim: "Ah, he promises fairly, fairly well, he's not a fool!" and feel sure that a great deal of Spanish blood must flow in the veins of such an *Indian*. If unable to discover any in spite of his good intentions, he then sought a Japanese origin, for it was at that time the fashion began of attributing to the Japanese or the Arabs whatever good the Filipinos might have in them. For him the native songs were Arabic music, as was also the alphabet of the ancient Filipinos—he was certain of this, although he did not know Arabic nor had he ever seen that alphabet.

"Arabic, the purest Arabic," he said to Ben-Zayb in a tone that admitted no reply. "At best, Chinese!"

Then he would add, with a significant wink: "Nothing can be, nothing ought to be, original with the Indians, you understand! I like them greatly, but they mustn't be allowed to pride themselves upon anything, for then they would take heart and turn into a lot of wretches."

At other times he would say: "I love the Indians fondly, I've constituted myself their father and defender, but it's necessary to keep everything in its proper place. Some were born to command and others to serve—plainly, that is a truism which can't be uttered very loudly, but it can be put into practise without many words. For look, the trick depends upon trifles. When you wish to reduce a people to subjection, assure it that it is in subjection. The first day it will laugh, the second protest, the third doubt, and the fourth be convinced. To keep the Filipino docile, he must have repeated to him day after day what he is, to convince him that he is incompetent. What good would it do, besides, to have him believe in something else that would make him wretched? Believe me, it's an act of charity to hold every creature in his place—that is order, harmony. That constitutes the *science* of government."

In referring to his policies, Don Custodio was not satisfied with the word *art*, and upon pronouncing the word *government*, he would extend his hand downwards to the height of a man bent over on his knees.

In regard to his religious ideas, he prided himself on being a Catholic, very much a Catholic—ah, Catholic Spain, the land of *María Santísima!* A liberal could be and ought to be a Catholic, when the reactionaries were setting themselves up as gods or saints, just as a mulatto passes for a white man in Kaffirland. But with all that, he ate meat during Lent, except on Good Friday, never went to confession, believed neither in miracles nor the infallibility of the Pope, and when he attended mass, went to the one at ten o'clock, or to the shortest, the military mass. Although in Madrid he had spoken ill of the religious orders, so as not to be out of harmony with his surroundings, considering them anachronisms, and had hurled curses against the Inquisition, while relating this or that lurid or droll story wherein the habits danced, or rather friars without habits, yet in speaking of the Philippines, which should be ruled by special laws, he would cough, look wise, and again extend his hand downwards to that mysterious altitude.

"The friars are necessary, they're a necessary evil," he would declare.

But how he would rage when any Indian dared to doubt the miracles or did not acknowledge the Pope! All the tortures of the Inquisition were insufficient to punish such temerity.

When it was objected that to rule or to live at the expense of ignorance has another and somewhat ugly name and is punished by law when the culprit is a single person, he would justify his position by referring to other colonies. "We," he would announce in his official tone, "can speak out plainly! We're not like the British and the Dutch who, in order to hold people in subjection, make use of the lash. We avail ourselves of other means, milder and surer. The salutary influence of the friars is superior to the British lash."

This last remark made his fortune. For a long time Ben-Zayb continued to use adaptations of it, and with him all Manila. The thinking part of Manila applauded it, and it even got to Madrid, where it was quoted in the Parliament as from *a liberal of long residence there.* The friars, flattered by the comparison and seeing their prestige enhanced, sent him sacks of chocolate, presents which the incorruptible Don Custodio returned, so that Ben-Zayb immediately compared him to Epaminondas. Nevertheless, this modern Epaminondas made use of the rattan in his choleric moments, and advised its use!

At that time the conventos, fearful that he would render a decision favorable to the petition of the students, increased their gifts, so that on the afternoon when we see him he was more perplexed than ever, his reputation for energy was being compromised. It had been more than a fortnight since he had had the petition in his hands, and only that morning the high official, after praising his zeal, had asked for a decision. Don Custodio had replied with mysterious gravity, giving him to understand that it was not yet completed. The high official had smiled a smile that still worried and haunted him.

As we were saying, he yawned and yawned. In one of these movements, at the moment when he opened his eyes and closed his mouth, his attention was caught by a file of red envelopes, arranged in regular order on a magnificent kamagon desk. On the back of each could be read in large letters: PROJECTS.

For a moment he forgot his troubles and Pepay's pirouettes, to reflect upon all that those files contained, which had issued from his prolific brain in his hours of inspiration. How many original ideas, how many sublime thoughts, how many means of ameliorating the woes of the Philippines! Immortality and the gratitude of the country were surely his!

Like an old lover who discovers a moldy package of amorous epistles, Don Custodio arose and approached the desk. The first envelope, thick, swollen, and plethoric, bore the title: PROJECTS IN PROJECT.

"No," he murmured, "they're excellent things, but it would take a year to read them over."

The second, also quite voluminous, was entitled: PROJECTS UNDER CONSIDERATION. "No, not those either."

Then came the PROJECTS NEARING COMPLETION, PROJECTS PRESENTED, PROJECTS REJECTED, PROJECTS APPROVED, PROJECTS POSTPONED. These last envelopes held little, but the least of all was that of the PROJECTS EXECUTED.

Don Custodio wrinkled up his nose—what did it contain? He had completely forgotten what was in it. A sheet of yellowish paper showed from under the flap, as though the envelope were sticking out its tongue. This he drew out and unfolded: it was the famous project for the School of Arts and Trades!

"What the devil!" he exclaimed. "If the Augustinian padres took charge of it—"

Suddenly he slapped his forehead and arched his eyebrows, while a look of triumph overspread his face. "I have reached a decision!" he cried with an oath that was not exactly *eureka*. "My decision is made!"

Repeating his peculiar *eureka* five or six times, which struck the air like so many gleeful lashes, he sat down at his desk, radiant with joy, and began to write furiously.

---

1   The *Sociedad Económica de Amigos del País* for the encouragement of agricultural and industrial development, was established by Basco de Vargas in 1780.—Tr.

2   Funds managed by the government for making loans and supporting charitable enterprises.—Tr.

3   The names are fictitious burlesques.—Tr.

MANILA TYPES

That night there was a grand function at the Teatro de Variedades. Mr. Jouay's French operetta company was giving its initial performance, *Les Cloches de Corneville*. To the eyes of the public was to be exhibited his select troupe, whose fame the newspapers had for days been proclaiming. It was reported that among the actresses was a very beautiful voice, with a figure even more beautiful, and if credit could be given to rumor, her amiability surpassed even her voice and figure.

At half-past seven in the evening there were no more tickets to be had, not even though they had been for Padre Salvi himself in his direct need, and the persons waiting to enter the general admission already formed a long queue. In the ticket-office there were scuffles and fights, talk of filibusterism and races, but this did not produce any tickets, so that by a quarter before eight fabulous prices were being offered for them. The appearance of the building, profusely illuminated, with flowers and plants in all the doors and windows, enchanted the new arrivals to such an extent that they burst out into exclamations and applause. A large crowd surged about the entrance, gazing enviously at those going in, those who came early from fear of missing their seats. Laughter, whispering, expectation greeted the later arrivals, who disconsolately joined the curious crowd, and now that they could not get in contented themselves with watching those who did.

Yet there was one person who seemed out of place amid such great eagerness and curiosity. He was a tall, meager man, who dragged one leg stiffly when he walked, dressed in a wretched brown coat and dirty checkered trousers that fitted his lean, bony limbs tightly. A straw sombrero, artistic in spite of being broken, covered an enormous head and allowed his dirty gray, almost red, hair to straggle out long and kinky at the end like a poet's curls.

But the most notable thing about this man was not his clothing or his European features, guiltless of beard or mustache, but his fiery red face, from which he got the nickname by which he was known, *Camaroncocido.*[1] He was a curious character belonging to a prominent Spanish family, but he lived like a vagabond and a beggar, scoffing at the prestige which he flouted indifferently with his rags. He was reputed to be a kind of reporter, and in fact his gray goggle-eyes, so cold and thoughtful, always showed up where anything publishable was happening. His manner of living was a mystery to all, as no one seemed to know where he ate and slept. Perhaps he had an empty hogshead somewhere.

But at that moment Camaroncocido lacked his usual hard and indifferent expression, something like mirthful pity being reflected in his looks. A funny little man accosted him merrily.

"Friend!" exclaimed the latter, in a raucous voice, as hoarse as a frog's, while he displayed several Mexican pesos, which Camaroncocido merely glanced at and then shrugged his shoulders. What did they matter to him?

The little old man was a fitting contrast to him. Small, very small, he wore on his head a high hat, which presented the appearance of a huge hairy worm, and lost himself in an enormous frock coat, too wide and too long for him, to reappear in trousers too short, not reaching below his calves. His body seemed to be the grandfather and his legs the grandchildren, while as for his shoes he appeared to be floating on the land, for they were of an enormous sailor type, apparently protesting against the hairy worm worn on his head with all the energy of a convento beside a World's Exposition. If Camaroncocido was red, he was brown; while the former, although of Spanish extraction, had not a single hair on his face, yet he, an Indian, had a goatee and mustache, both long, white, and sparse. His expression was lively. He was known as *Tio Quico,*[2] and like his friend lived on publicity, advertising the shows and posting the theatrical announcements, being perhaps the only Filipino who could appear with impunity in a silk hat and frock coat, just as his friend was the first Spaniard who laughed at the prestige of his race.

"The Frenchman has paid me well," he said smiling and showing his picturesque gums, which looked like a street after a conflagration. "I did a good job in posting the bills."

Camaroncocido shrugged his shoulders again. "Quico," he rejoined in a cavernous voice, "if they've given you six pesos for your work, how much will they give the friars?"

Tio Quico threw back his head in his usual lively manner. "To the friars?"

"Because you surely know," continued Camaroncocido, "that all this crowd was secured for them by the conventos."

The fact was that the friars, headed by Padre Salvi, and some lay brethren captained by Don Custodio, had opposed such shows. Padre Camorra, who could not attend, watered at the eyes and mouth, but argued with Ben-Zayb, who defended them feebly, thinking of the free tickets they would send his newspaper. Don Custodio spoke of morality, religion, good manners, and the like.

"But," stammered the writer, "if our own farces with their plays on words and phrases of double meaning—"

"But at least they're in Castilian!" the virtuous councilor interrupted with a roar, inflamed to righteous wrath. "Obscenities in French, man, Ben-Zayb, for God's sake, in French! Never!"

He uttered this *never* with the energy of three Guzmans threatened with being killed like fleas if they did not surrender twenty Tarifas. Padre Irene naturally agreed with Don Custodio and execrated French operetta. Whew, he had been in Paris, but had never set foot in a theater, the Lord deliver him!

Yet the French operetta also counted numerous partizans. The officers of the army and navy, among them the General's aides, the clerks, and many society people were anxious to enjoy the delicacies of the French language from the mouths of genuine *Parisiennes*, and with them were affiliated those who had traveled by the M.M.' and had jabbered a little French during the voyage, those who had visited Paris, and all those who wished to appear learned.

Hence, Manila society was divided into two factions, operettists and anti-operettists. The latter were supported by the elderly ladies, wives jealous and careful of their husbands' love, and by those who were engaged, while those who were free and those who were beautiful declared themselves enthusiastic operettists. Notes and then more notes were exchanged, there were goings and comings, mutual recriminations, meetings, lobbyings, arguments, even talk of an insurrection of the natives, of their indolence, of inferior and superior races, of prestige and other humbugs, so that after much gossip and more recrimination, the permit was granted, Padre Salvi at the same time publishing a pastoral that was read by no one but the proof-reader. There were questionings whether the General had quarreled with the Countess, whether she spent her time in the halls of pleasure, whether His Excellency was greatly annoyed, whether there had been presents exchanged, whether the French consul—, and so on and on. Many names were bandied about: Quiroga the Chinaman's, Simoun's, and even those of many actresses.

Thanks to these scandalous preliminaries, the people's impatience had been aroused, and since the evening before, when the troupe arrived, there was talk of nothing but attending the first performance. From the hour when the red posters announced *Les Cloches de Corneville* the victors prepared to celebrate their triumph. In some offices, instead of the time being spent in reading newspapers and gossiping, it was devoted to devouring the synopsis and spelling out French novels, while many feigned business outside to consult their pocket-dictionaries on the sly. So no business was transacted, callers were told to come back the next day, but the public could not take offense, for they encountered some very polite and affable clerks, who received and dismissed them with grand salutations in the French style. The clerks were practising, brushing the dust off their French, and calling to one another *oui, monsieur, s'il vous plait,* and *pardon!* at every turn, so that it was a pleasure to see and hear them.

But the place where the excitement reached its climax was the newspaper office. Ben-Zayb, having been appointed critic and translator of the synopsis, trembled like a poor woman accused of witchcraft, as he saw his enemies picking out his blunders and throwing up to his face his deficient knowledge of French. When the Italian opera was on, he had very nearly received a challenge for having mistranslated a tenor's name, while an envious rival had immediately published an article referring to him as an ignoramus—him, the foremost thinking head in the Philippines! All the trouble he had had to defend himself! He had had to write at least seventeen articles and consult fifteen dictionaries, so with these salutary recollections, the wretched Ben-Zayb moved about with leaden hands, to say nothing of his feet, for that would be plagiarizing Padre Camorra, who had once intimated that the journalist wrote with them.

"You see, Quico?" said Camaroncocido. "One half of the people have come because the friars told them not to, making it a kind of public protest, and the other half because they say to themselves, 'Do the friars object to it? Then it must be instructive!' Believe me, Quico, your advertisements are a good thing but the pastoral was better, even taking into consideration the fact that it was read by no one."

"Friend, do you believe," asked Tio Quico uneasily, "that on account of the competition with Padre Salvi my business will in the future be prohibited?"

"Maybe so, Quico, maybe so," replied the other, gazing at the sky. "Money's getting scarce."

Tio Quico muttered some incoherent words: if the friars were going to turn theatrical advertisers, he would become a friar. After bidding his friend good-by, he moved away coughing and rattling his silver coins.

With his eternal indifference Camaroncocido continued to wander about here and there with his crippled leg and sleepy looks. The arrival of unfamiliar faces caught his attention, coming as they did from different parts and signaling to one another with a wink or a cough. It was the first time that he had ever seen these individuals on such an occasion, he who knew all the faces and features in the city. Men with dark faces, humped shoulders, uneasy and uncertain movements, poorly disguised, as though they had for the first time put on sack coats, slipped about among the shadows, shunning attention, instead of getting in the front rows where they could see well.

"Detectives or thieves?" Camaroncocido asked himself and immediately shrugged his shoulders. "But what is it to me?"

The lamp of a carriage that drove up lighted in passing a group of four or five of these individuals talking with a man who appeared to be an army officer.

"Detectives! It must be a new corps," he muttered with his shrug of indifference. Soon, however, he noticed that the officer, after speaking to two or three more groups, approached a carriage and seemed to be talking vigorously with some person inside. Camaroncocido took a few steps forward and without surprise thought that he recognized the jeweler Simoun, while his sharp ears caught this short dialogue.

"The signal will be a gunshot!"

"Yes, sir."

"Don't worry—it's the General who is ordering it, but be careful about saying so. If you follow my instructions, you'll get a promotion."

"Yes, sir."

"So, be ready!"

The voice ceased and a second later the carriage drove away. In spite of his indifference Camaroncocido could not but mutter, "Something's afoot—hands on pockets!"

But feeling his own to be empty, he again shrugged his shoulders. What did it matter to him, even though the heavens should fall?

So he continued his pacing about. On passing near two persons engaged in conversation, he caught what one of them, who had rosaries and scapularies around his neck, was saying in Tagalog: "The friars are more powerful than the General, don't be a fool! He'll go away and they'll stay here. So, if we do well, we'll get rich. The signal is a gunshot."

"Hold hard, hold hard," murmured Camaroncocido, tightening his fingers. "On that side the General, on this Padre Salvi. Poor country! But what is it to me?"

Again shrugging his shoulders and expectorating at the same time, two actions that with him were indications of supreme indifference, he continued his observations.

Meanwhile, the carriages were arriving in dizzy streams, stopping directly before the door to set down the members of the select society. Although the weather was scarcely even cool, the ladies sported magnificent shawls, silk neckerchiefs, and even light cloaks. Among the escorts, some who were in frock coats with white ties wore overcoats, while others carried them on their arms to display the rich silk linings.

In a group of spectators, Tadeo, he who was always taken ill the moment the professor appeared, was accompanied by a fellow townsman of his, the novice whom we saw suffer evil consequences from reading wrongly the Cartesian principle. This novice was very inquisitive and addicted to tiresome questions, and Tadeo was taking advantage of his ingenuousness and inexperience to relate to him the most stupendous lies. Every Spaniard that spoke to him, whether clerkling or underling, was presented as a leading merchant, a marquis, or a count, while on the other hand any one who passed him by was a greenhorn, a petty official, a nobody! When pedestrians failed him in keeping up the novice's astonishment, he resorted to the resplendent carriages that came up. Tadeo would bow politely, wave his hand in a friendly manner, and call out a familiar greeting.

"Who's he?"

"Bah!" was the negligent reply. "The Civil Governor, the Vice-Governor, Judge—, Señora—, all friends of mine!"

The novice marveled and listened in fascination, taking care to keep on the left. Tadeo the friend of judges and governors!

Tadeo named all the persons who arrived, when he did not know them inventing titles, biographies, and interesting sketches.

"You see that tall gentleman with dark whiskers, somewhat squint-eyed, dressed in black—he's Judge A—, an intimate friend of the wife of Colonel B—. One day if it hadn't been for me they would have come to blows. Hello, here comes that Colonel! What if they should fight?"

The novice held his breath, but the colonel and the judge shook hands cordially, the soldier, an old bachelor, inquiring about the health of the judge's family.

"Ah, thank heaven!" breathed Tadeo. "I'm the one who made them friends."

"What if they should invite us to go in?" asked the novice timidly.

"Get out, boy! I never accept favors!" retorted Tadeo majestically. "I confer them, but disinterestedly."

The novice bit his lip and felt smaller than ever, while he placed a respectful distance between himself and his fellow townsman.

Tadeo resumed: "That is the musician H—; that one, the lawyer J—, who delivered as his own a speech printed in all the books and was congratulated and admired for it; Doctor K—, that man just getting out of a hansom, is a specialist in diseases of children, so he's called Herod; that's the banker L—, who can talk only of his money and his hoards; the poet M—, who is always dealing with the stars and *the beyond*. There goes the beautiful wife of N—, whom Padre Q—is accustomed to meet when he calls upon the absent husband; the Jewish merchant P—, who came to the islands with a thousand pesos and is now a millionaire. That fellow with the long beard is the physician R—, who has become rich by making invalids more than by curing them."

"Making invalids?"

"Yes, boy, in the examination of the conscripts. Attention! That finely dressed gentleman is not a physician but a homeopathist *sui generis*—he professes completely the *similis similibus*. The young cavalry captain with him is his chosen disciple. That man in a light suit with his hat tilted back is the government clerk whose maxim is never to be polite and who rages like a demon when he sees a hat on any one else's head—they say that he does it to ruin the German hatters. The man just arriving with his family is the wealthy merchant C—, who has an income of over a hundred thousand pesos. But what would you say if I should tell you that he still owes me four pesos, five reales, and twelve cuartos? But who would collect from a rich man like him?"

"That gentleman in debt to you?"

"Sure! One day I got him out of a bad fix. It was on a Friday at half-past six in the morning, I still remember, because I hadn't breakfasted. That lady who is followed by a duenna is the celebrated Pepay, the dancing girl, but she doesn't dance any more now that a very Catholic gentleman and a great friend of mine has—forbidden it. There's the death's-head Z—, who's surely following her to get her to dance again. He's a good fellow, and a great friend of mine, but has one defect—he's a Chinese mestizo and yet calls himself a Peninsular Spaniard. Sssh! Look at Ben-Zayb, him with the face of a friar, who's carrying a pencil and a roll of paper in his hand. He's the great writer, Ben-Zayb, a good friend of mine—he has talent!"

"You don't say! And that little man with white whiskers?"

"He's the official who has appointed his daughters, those three little girls, assistants in his department, so as to get their names on the pay-roll. He's a clever man, very clever! When he makes a mistake he blames it on somebody else, he buys things and pays for them out of the treasury. He's clever, very, very clever!"

Tadeo was about to say more, but suddenly checked himself.

"And that gentleman who has a fierce air and gazes at everybody over his shoulders?" inquired the novice, pointing to a man who nodded haughtily.

But Tadeo did not answer. He was craning his neck to see Paulita Gomez, who was approaching with a friend, Doña Victorina, and Juanito Pelaez. The latter had presented her with a box and was more humped than ever.

Carriage after carriage drove up; the actors and actresses arrived and entered by a separate door, followed by their friends and admirers.

After Paulita had gone in, Tadeo resumed: "Those are the nieces of the rich Captain D——, those coming up in a landau; you see how pretty and healthy they are? Well, in a few years they'll be dead or crazy. Captain D——is opposed to their marrying, and the insanity of the uncle is appearing in the nieces. That's the Señorita E——, the rich heiress whom the world and the conventos are disputing over. Hello, I know that fellow! It's Padre Irene, in disguise, with a false mustache. I recognize him by his nose. And he was so greatly opposed to this!"

The scandalized novice watched a neatly cut coat disappear behind a group of ladies.

"The Three Fates!" went on Tadeo, watching the arrival of three withered, bony, hollow-eyed, wide-mouthed, and shabbily dressed women. "They're called——"

"Atropos?" ventured the novice, who wished to show that he also knew somebody, at least in mythology.

"No, boy, they're called the Weary Waiters—old, censorious, and dull. They pretend to hate everybody—men, women, and children. But look how the Lord always places beside the evil a remedy, only that sometimes it comes late. There behind the Fates, the frights of the city, come those three girls, the pride of their friends, among whom I count myself. That thin young man with goggle-eyes, somewhat stooped, who is wildly gesticulating because he can't get tickets, is the chemist S——, author of many essays and scientific treatises, some of which are notable and have captured prizes. The Spaniards say of him, 'There's some hope for him, some hope for him.' The fellow who is soothing him with his Voltairian smile is the poet T——, a young man of talent, a great friend of mine, and, for the very reason that he has talent, he has thrown away his pen. That fellow who is trying to get in with the actors by the other door is the young physician U——, who has effected some remarkable cures—it's also said of him that he promises well. He's not such a scoundrel as Pelaez but he's cleverer and slyer still. I believe that he'd shake dice with death and win."

"And that brown gentleman with a mustache like hog-bristles?"

"Ah, that's the merchant F——, who forges everything, even his baptismal certificate. He wants to be a Spanish mestizo at any cost, and is making heroic efforts to forget his native language."

"But his daughters are very white."

"Yes, that's the reason rice has gone up in price, and yet they eat nothing but bread."

The novice did not understand the connection between the price of rice and the whiteness of those girls, but he held his peace.

"There goes the fellow that's engaged to one of them, that thin brown youth who is following them with a lingering movement and speaking with a protecting air to the three friends who are laughing at him. He's a martyr to his beliefs, to his consistency."

The novice was filled with admiration and respect for the young man.

"He has the look of a fool, and he is one," continued Tadeo. "He was born in San Pedro Makati and has inflicted many privations upon himself. He scarcely ever bathes or eats pork, because, according to him, the Spaniards don't do those things, and for the same reason he doesn't eat rice and dried fish, although he may be watering at the mouth and dying of hunger. Anything that comes from Europe, rotten or preserved, he considers divine—a month ago Basilio cured him of a severe attack of gastritis, for he had eaten a jar of mustard to prove that he's a European."

At that moment the orchestra struck up a waltz.

"You see that gentleman—that hypochondriac who goes along turning his head from side to side, seeking salutes? That's the celebrated governor of Pangasinan, a good man who loses his appetite whenever any Indian fails to salute him. He would have died if he hadn't issued the proclamation about salutes to which he owes his celebrity. Poor fellow, it's only been three days since he came from the province and look how thin he has become! Oh, here's the great man, the illustrious—open your eyes!"

"Who? That man with knitted brows?"

"Yes, that's Don Custodio, the liberal, Don Custodio. His brows are knit because he's meditating over some important project. If the ideas he has in his head were carried out, this would be a different world! Ah, here comes Makaraig, your housemate."

It was in fact Makaraig, with Pecson, Sandoval, and Isagani. Upon seeing them, Tadeo advanced and spoke to them.

"Aren't you coming in?" Makaraig asked him.

"We haven't been able to get tickets."

"Fortunately, we have a box," replied Makaraig. "Basilio couldn't come. Both of you, come in with us."

Tadeo did not wait for the invitation to be repeated, but the novice, fearing that he would intrude, with the timidity natural to the provincial Indian, excused himself, nor could he be persuaded to enter.

1　"Boiled Shrimp"—Tr.
2　"Uncle Frank."—Tr.
3　Messageries Maritimes, a French line of steamers in the Oriental trade.—Tr.

THE PERFORMANCE

The interior of the theater presented a lively aspect. It was filled from top to bottom, with people standing in the corridors and in the aisles, fighting to withdraw a head from some hole where they had inserted it, or to shove an eye between a collar and an ear. The open boxes, occupied for the most part by ladies, looked like baskets of flowers, whose petals—the fans—shook in a light breeze, wherein hummed a thousand bees. However, just as there are flowers of strong or delicate fragrance, flowers that kill and flowers that console, so from our baskets were exhaled like emanations: there were to be heard dialogues, conversations, remarks that bit and stung. Three or four boxes, however, were still vacant, in spite of the lateness of the hour. The performance had been advertised for half-past eight and it was already a quarter to nine, but the curtain did not go up, as his Excellency had not yet arrived. The gallery-gods, impatient and uncomfortable in their seats, started a racket, clapping their hands and pounding the floor with their canes.

"Boom—boom—boom! Ring up the curtain! Boom—boom—boom!"

The artillerymen were not the least noisy. Emulators of Mars, as Ben-Zayb called them, they were not satisfied with this music; thinking themselves perhaps at a bullfight, they made remarks at the ladies who passed before them in words that are euphemistically called flowers in Madrid, although at times they seem more like foul weeds. Without heeding the furious looks of the husbands, they bandied from one to another the sentiments and longings inspired by so many beauties.

In the reserved seats, where the ladies seemed to be afraid to venture, as few were to be seen there, a murmur of voices prevailed amid suppressed laughter and clouds of tobacco smoke. They discussed the merits of the players and talked scandal, wondering if his Excellency had quarreled with the friars, if his presence at such a show was a defiance or mere curiosity. Others gave no heed to these matters, but were engaged in attracting the attention of the ladies, throwing themselves into attitudes more or less interesting and statuesque, flashing diamond rings, especially when they thought themselves the foci of insistent opera-glasses, while yet another would address a respectful salute to this or that señora or señorita, at the same time lowering his head gravely to whisper to a neighbor, "How ridiculous she is! And such a bore!"

The lady would respond with one of her most gracious smiles and an enchanting nod of her head, while murmuring to a friend sitting near, amid lazy flourishes of her fan, "How impudent he is! He's madly in love, my dear."

Meanwhile, the noise increased. There remained only two vacant boxes, besides that of his Excellency, which was distinguished by its curtains of red velvet. The orchestra played another waltz, the audience protested, when fortunately there arose a charitable hero to distract their attention and relieve the manager, in the person of a man who had occupied a reserved seat and refused to give it up to its owner, the philosopher Don Primitivo. Finding his own arguments useless, Don Primitivo had appealed to an usher. "I don't care to," the hero responded to the latter's protests, placidly puffing at his cigarette. The usher appealed to the manager. "I don't care to," was the response, as he settled back in the seat. The manager went away, while the artillerymen in the gallery began to sing out encouragement to the usurper.

Our hero, now that he had attracted general attention, thought that to yield would be to lower himself, so he held on to the seat, while he repeated his answer to a pair of guards the manager had called in. These, in consideration of the rebel's rank, went in search of their corporal, while the whole house broke out into applause at the firmness of the hero, who remained seated like a Roman senator.

Hisses were heard, and the inflexible gentleman turned angrily to see if they were meant for him, but the galloping of horses resounded and the stir increased. One might have said that a revolution had broken out, or at least a riot, but no, the orchestra had suspended the waltz and was playing the royal march: it was his Excellency, the Captain-General and Governor of the islands, who was entering. All eyes sought and followed him, then lost sight of him, until he finally appeared in his box. After looking all about him and making some persons happy with a lordly salute, he sat down, as though he were indeed the man for whom the chair was waiting. The artillerymen then became silent and the orchestra tore into the prelude.

Our students occupied a box directly facing that of Pepay, the dancing girl. Her box was a present from Makaraig, who had already got on good terms with her in order to propitiate Don Custodio. Pepay had that very afternoon written a note to the illustrious arbiter, asking for an answer and appointing an interview in the theater. For this reason, Don Custodio, in spite of the active opposition he had manifested toward the French operetta, had gone to the theater, which action won him some caustic remarks on the part of Don Manuel, his ancient adversary in the sessions of the Ayuntamiento.

"I've come to judge the operetta," he had replied in the tone of a Cato whose conscience was clear.

So Makaraig was exchanging looks of intelligence with Pepay, who was giving him to understand that she had something to tell him. As the dancing girl's face wore a happy expression, the students augured that a favorable outcome was assured. Sandoval, who had just returned from making calls in other boxes, also assured them that the decision had been favorable, that that very afternoon the Superior Commission had considered and approved it. Every one was jubilant, even Pecson having laid aside his pessimism when he saw the smiling Pepay display a note. Sandoval and Makaraig congratulated one another, Isagani alone remaining cold and unsmiling. What had happened to this young man?

Upon entering the theater, Isagani had caught sight of Paulita in a box, with Juanito Pelaez talking to her. He had turned pale, thinking that he must be mistaken. But no, it was she herself, she who greeted him with a gracious smile, while her beautiful eyes seemed to be asking pardon and promising explanations. The fact was that they had agreed upon Isagani's going first to the theater to see if the show contained anything improper for a young woman, but now he found her there, and in no other company than that of his rival. What passed in his mind is indescribable: wrath, jealousy, humiliation, resentment raged within him, and there were moments even when he wished that the theater would fall in; he had a violent desire to laugh aloud, to insult his sweetheart, to challenge his rival, to make a scene, but finally contented himself with sitting quiet and not looking at her at all. He was conscious of the beautiful plans Makaraig and Sandoval were making, but they sounded like distant echoes, while the notes of the waltz seemed sad and lugubrious, the whole audience stupid and foolish, and several times he had to make an effort to keep back the tears. Of the trouble stirred up by the hero who refused to give up the seat, of the arrival of the Captain-General, he was scarcely conscious. He stared toward the drop-curtain, on which was depicted a kind of gallery with sumptuous red hangings, affording a view of a garden in which a fountain played, yet how sad the gallery looked to him and how melancholy the painted landscape! A thousand vague recollections surged into his memory like distant echoes of music heard in the night, like songs of infancy, the murmur of lonely forests and gloomy rivulets, moonlit nights on the shore of the sea spread wide before his eyes. So the enamored youth considered himself very wretched and stared fixedly at the ceiling so that the tears should not fall from his eyes.

A burst of applause drew him from these meditations. The curtain had just risen, and the merry chorus of peasants of Corneville was presented, all dressed in cotton caps, with heavy wooden sabots on their feet. Some six or seven girls, well-rouged on the lips and cheeks, with large black circles around their eyes to increase their brilliance, displayed white arms, fingers covered with diamonds, round and shapely limbs. While they were chanting the Norman phrase "*Allez, marchez! Allez, marchez!*" they smiled at their different admirers in the reserved seats with such openness that Don Custodio, after looking toward Pepay's box to assure himself that she was not doing the same thing with some other admirer, set down in his note-book this indecency, and to make sure of it lowered his head a little to see if the actresses were not showing their knees.

"Oh, these Frenchwomen!" he muttered, while his imagination lost itself in considerations somewhat more elevated, as he made comparisons and projects.

"*Quoi v'la tous les cancans d'la s'maine!*" sang Gertrude, a proud damsel, who was looking roguishly askance at the Captain-General.

"We're going to have the cancan!" exclaimed Tadeo, the winner of the first prize in the French class, who had managed to make out this word. "Makaraig, they're going to dance the cancan!"

He rubbed his hands gleefully. From the moment the curtain rose, Tadeo had been heedless of the music. He was looking only for the prurient, the indecent, the immoral in actions and dress, and with his scanty French was sharpening his ears to catch the obscenities that the austere guardians of the fatherland had foretold.

Sandoval, pretending to know French, had converted himself into a kind of interpreter for his friends. He knew as much about it as Tadeo, but the published synopsis helped him and his fancy supplied the rest. "Yes," he said, "they're going to dance the cancan—she's going to lead it."

Makaraig and Pecson redoubled their attention, smiling in anticipation, while Isagani looked away, mortified to think that Paulita should be present at such a show and reflecting that it was his duty to challenge Juanito Pelaez the next day.

But the young men waited in vain. Serpolette came on, a charming girl, in her cotton cap, provoking and challenging. "*Hein, qui parle de Serpolette?*" she demanded of the gossips, with her arms akimbo in a combative attitude. Some one applauded, and after him all those in the reserved seats. Without changing her girlish attitude, Serpolette gazed at the person who had started the applause and paid him with a smile, displaying rows of little teeth that looked like a string of pearls in a case of red velvet.

Tadeo followed her gaze and saw a man in a false mustache with an extraordinarily large nose. "By the monk's cowl!" he exclaimed. "It's Irene!"

"Yes," corroborated Sandoval, "I saw him behind the scenes talking with the actresses."

The truth was that Padre Irene, who was a melomaniac of the first degree and knew French well, had been sent to the theater by Padre Salvi as a sort of religious detective, or so at least he told the persons who recognized him. As a faithful critic, who should not be satisfied with viewing the piece from a distance, he wished to examine the actresses at first hand, so he had mingled in the groups of admirers and gallants, had penetrated into the greenroom, where was whispered and talked a French required by the situation, a *market French*, a language that is readily comprehensible for the vender when the buyer seems disposed to pay well.

Serpolette was surrounded by two gallant officers, a sailor, and a lawyer, when she caught sight of him moving about, sticking the tip of his long nose into all the nooks and corners, as though with it he were ferreting out all the mysteries of the stage. She ceased her chatter, knitted her eyebrows, then raised them, opened her lips and with the vivacity of a *Parisienne* left her admirers to hurl herself like a torpedo upon our critic.

"*Tiens, tiens, Toutou! Mon lapin!*" she cried, catching Padre Irene's arm and shaking it merrily, while the air rang with her silvery laugh.

"Tut, tut!" objected Padre Irene, endeavoring to conceal himself.

"*Mais, comment! Toi ici, grosse bête! Et moi qui t'croyais—*"

"*'Tais pas d'tapage, Lily! Il faut m'respecter! 'Suis ici l'Pape!*"

With great difficulty Padre Irene made her listen to reason, for Lily was *enchanteé* to meet in Manila an old friend who reminded her of the *coulisses* of the Grand Opera House. So it was that Padre Irene, fulfilling at the same time his duties as a friend and a critic, had initiated the applause to encourage her, for Serpolette deserved it.

Meanwhile, the young men were waiting for the cancan. Pecson became all eyes, but there was everything except cancan. There was presented the scene in which, but for the timely arrival of the representatives of the law, the women would have come to blows and torn one another's hair out, incited thereto by the mischievous peasants, who, like our students, hoped to see something more than the cancan.

> Scit, scit, scit, scit, scit, scit,
> Disputez-vous, battez-vous,
> Scit, scit, scit, scit, scit, scit,
> Nous allons compter les coups.

The music ceased, the men went away, the women returned, a few at a time, and started a conversation among themselves, of which our friends understood nothing. They were slandering some absent person.

"They look like the Chinamen of the *pansiteria!*" whispered Pecson.

"But, the cancan?" asked Makaraig.

"They're talking about the most suitable place to dance it," gravely responded Sandoval.

"They look like the Chinamen of the *pansiteria,*" repeated Pecson in disgust.

A lady accompanied by her husband entered at that moment and took her place in one of the two vacant boxes. She had the air of a queen and gazed disdainfully at the whole house, as if to say, "I've come later than all of you, you crowd of upstarts and provincials, I've come later than you!" There are persons who go to the theater like the contestants in a mule-race: the last one in, wins, and we know very sensible men who would ascend the scaffold rather than enter a theater before the first act. But the lady's triumph was of short duration—she caught sight of the other box that was still empty, and began to scold her better half, thus starting such a disturbance that many were annoyed.

"Ssh! Ssh!"

"The blockheads! As if they understood French!" remarked the lady, gazing with supreme disdain in all directions, finally fixing her attention on Juanito's box, whence she thought she had heard an impudent hiss.

Juanito was in fact guilty, for he had been pretending to understand everything, holding himself up proudly and applauding at times as though nothing that was said escaped him, and this too without guiding himself by the actors' pantomime, because he scarcely looked toward the stage. The rogue had intentionally remarked to Paulita that, as there was so much more beautiful a woman close at hand, he did not care to strain his eyes looking beyond her. Paulita had blushed, covered her face with her fan, and glanced stealthily toward where Isagani, silent and morose, was abstractedly watching the show.

Paulita felt nettled and jealous. Would Isagani fall in love with any of those alluring actresses? The thought put her in a bad humor, so she scarcely heard the praises that Doña Victorina was heaping upon her own favorite.

Juanito was playing his part well: he shook his head at times in sign of disapproval, and then there could be heard coughs and murmurs in some parts, at other times he smiled in approbation, and a second later applause resounded. Doña Victorina was charmed, even conceiving some vague ideas of marrying the young man the day Don Tiburcio should die—Juanito knew French and De Espadaña didn't! Then she began to flatter him, nor did he perceive the change in the drift of her talk, so occupied was he in watching a Catalan merchant who was sitting next to the Swiss consul. Having observed that they were conversing in French, Juanito was getting his inspiration from their countenances, and thus grandly giving the cue to those about him.

Scene followed scene, character succeeded character, comic and ridiculous like the bailiff and Grenicheux, imposing and winsome like the marquis and Germaine. The audience laughed heartily at the slap delivered by Gaspard and intended for the coward Grenicheux, which was received by the grave bailiff, whose wig went flying through the air, producing disorder and confusion as the curtain dropped.

"Where's the cancan?" inquired Tadeo.

But the curtain rose again immediately, revealing a scene in a servant market, with three posts on which were affixed signs bearing the announcements: *servantes*, *cochers*, and *domestiques*. Juanito, to improve the opportunity, turned to Doña Victorina and said in a loud voice, so that Paulita might hear and he convinced of his learning:

"*Servantes* means servants, *domestiques* domestics."

"And in what way do the *servantes* differ from the *domestiques*?" asked Paulita.

Juanito was not found wanting. "*Domestiques* are those that are domesticated—haven't you noticed that some of them have the air of savages? Those are the *servantes*."

"That's right," added Doña Victorina, "some have very bad manners—and yet I thought that in Europe everybody was cultivated. But as it happens in France,—well, I see!"

"Ssh! Ssh!"

But what was Juanito's predicament when the time came for the opening of the market and the beginning of the sale, and the servants who were to be hired placed themselves beside the signs that indicated their class! The men, some ten or twelve rough characters in livery, carrying branches in their hands, took their place under the sign *domestiques!*

"Those are the domestics," explained Juanito.

"Really, they have the appearance of being only recently domesticated," observed Doña Victorina. "Now let's have a look at the savages."

Then the dozen girls headed by the lively and merry Serpolette, decked out in their best clothes, each wearing a big bouquet of flowers at the waist, laughing, smiling, fresh and attractive, placed themselves, to Juanito's great desperation, beside the post of the *servantes.*

"How's this?" asked Paulita guilelessly. "Are those the savages that you spoke of?"

"No," replied the imperturbable Juanito, "there's a mistake—they've got their places mixed—those coming behind—"

"Those with the whips?"

Juanito nodded assent, but he was rather perplexed and uneasy.

"So those girls are the *cochers?*"

Here Juanito was attacked by such a violent fit of coughing that some of the spectators became annoyed.

"Put him out! Put the consumptive out!" called a voice.

Consumptive! To be called a consumptive before Paulita! Juanito wanted to find the blackguard and make him swallow that "consumptive." Observing that the women were trying to hold him back, his bravado increased, and he became more conspicuously ferocious. But fortunately it was Don Custodio who had made the diagnosis, and he, fearful of attracting attention to himself, pretended to hear nothing, apparently busy with his criticism of the play.

"If it weren't that I am with you," remarked Juanito, rolling his eyes like some dolls that are moved by clockwork, and to make the resemblance more real he stuck out his tongue occasionally.

Thus that night he acquired in Doña Victorina's eyes the reputation of being brave and punctilious, so she decided in her heart that she would marry him just as soon as Don Tiburcio was out of the way. Paulita became sadder and sadder in thinking about how the girls called *cochers* could occupy Isagani's attention, for the name had certain disagreeable associations that came from the slang of her convent school-days.

At length the first act was concluded, the marquis taking away as servants Serpolette and Germaine, the representative of timid beauty in the troupe, and for coachman the stupid Grenicheux. A burst of applause brought them out again holding hands, those who five seconds before had been tormenting one another and were about to come to blows, bowing and smiling here and there to the gallant Manila public and exchanging knowing looks with various spectators.

While there prevailed the passing tumult occasioned by those who crowded one another to get into the greenroom and felicitate the actresses and by those who were going to make calls on the ladies in the boxes, some expressed their opinions of the play and the players.

"Undoubtedly, Serpolette is the best," said one with a knowing air.

"I prefer Germaine, she's an ideal blonde."

"But she hasn't any voice."

"What do I care about the voice?"

"Well, for shape, the tall one."

"Pshaw," said Ben-Zayb, "not a one is worth a straw, not a one is an artist!"

Ben-Zayb was the critic for *El Grito de la Integridad*, and his disdainful air gave him great importance in the eyes of those who were satisfied with so little.

"Serpolette hasn't any voice, nor Germaine grace, nor is that music, nor is it art, nor is it anything!" he concluded with marked contempt. To set oneself up as a great critic there is nothing like appearing to be discontented with everything. Besides, the management had sent only two seats for the newspaper staff.

In the boxes curiosity was aroused as to who could be the possessor of the empty one, for that person, would surpass every one in chic, since he would be the last to arrive. The rumor started somewhere that it belonged to Simoun, and was confirmed: no one had seen the jeweler in the reserved seats, the greenroom, or anywhere else.

"Yet I saw him this afternoon with Mr. Jouay," some one said. "He presented a necklace to one of the actresses."

"To which one?" asked some of the inquisitive ladies.

"To the finest of all, the one who made eyes at his Excellency."

This information was received with looks of intelligence, winks, exclamations of doubt, of confirmation, and half-uttered commentaries.

"He's trying to play the Monte Cristo," remarked a lady who prided herself on being literary.

"Or purveyor to the Palace!" added her escort, jealous of Simoun.

In the students' box, Pecson, Sandoval, and Isagani had remained, while Tadeo had gone to engage Don Custodio in conversation about his projects, and Makaraig to hold an interview with Pepay.

"In no way, as I have observed to you before, friend Isagani," declared Sandoval with violent gestures and a sonorous voice, so that the ladies near the box, the daughters of the rich man who was in debt to Tadeo, might hear him, "in no way does the French language possess the rich sonorousness or the varied and elegant cadence of the Castilian tongue. I cannot conceive, I cannot imagine, I cannot form any idea of French orators, and I doubt that they have ever had any or can have any now in the strict construction of the term orator, because we must not confuse the name orator with the words babbler and charlatan, for these can exist in any country, in all the regions of the inhabited world, among the cold and curt Englishmen as among the lively and impressionable Frenchmen."

Thus he delivered a magnificent review of the nations, with his poetical characterizations and most resounding epithets. Isagani nodded assent, with his thoughts fixed on Paulita, whom he had surprised gazing at him with an expressive look which contained a wealth of meaning. He tried to divine what those eyes were expressing—those eyes that were so eloquent and not at all deceptive.

"Now you who are a poet, a slave to rhyme and meter, a son of the Muses," continued Sandoval, with an elegant wave of his hand, as though he were saluting, on the horizon, the Nine Sisters, "do you comprehend, can you conceive, how a language so harsh and unmusical as French can give birth to poets of such gigantic stature as our Garcilasos, our Herreras, our Esproncedas, our Calderons?"

"Nevertheless," objected Pecson, "Victor Hugo—"

"Victor Hugo, my friend Pecson, if Victor Hugo is a poet, it is because he owes it to Spain, because it is an established fact, it is a matter beyond all doubt, a thing admitted even by the Frenchmen themselves, so envious of Spain, that if Victor Hugo has genius, if he really is a poet, it is because his childhood was spent in Madrid; there he drank in his first impressions, there his brain was molded, there his imagination was colored, his heart modeled, and the most beautiful concepts of his mind born. And after all, who is Victor Hugo? Is he to be compared at all with our modern—"

This peroration was cut short by the return of Makaraig with a despondent air and a bitter smile on his lips, carrying in his hand a note, which he offered silently to Sandoval, who read:

"MY DOVE: Your letter has reached me late, for I have already handed in my decision, and it has been approved. However, as if I had guessed your wish, I have decided the matter according to the desires of your protégés. I'll be at the theater and wait for you after the performance.

"Your duckling,
"CUSTODINING."

"How tender the man is!" exclaimed Tadeo with emotion.

"Well?" said Sandoval. "I don't see anything wrong about this—quite the reverse!"

"Yes," rejoined Makaraig with his bitter smile, "decided favorably! I've just seen Padre Irene."

"What does Padre Irene say?" inquired Pecson.

"The same as Don Custodio, and the rascal still had the audacity to congratulate me. The Commission, which has taken as its own the decision of the arbiter, approves the idea and felicitates the students on their patriotism and their thirst for knowledge—"

"Well?"

"Only that, considering our duties—in short, it says that in order that the idea may not be lost, it concludes that the direction and execution of the plan should be placed in charge of one of the religious corporations, in case the Dominicans do not wish to incorporate the academy with the University."

Exclamations of disappointment greeted the announcement. Isagani rose, but said nothing.

"And in order that we may participate in the management of the academy," Makaraig went on, "we are intrusted with the collection of contributions and dues, with the obligation of turning them over to the treasurer whom the corporation may designate, which treasurer will issue us receipts."

"Then we're tax-collectors!" remarked Tadeo.

"Sandoval," said Pecson, "there's the gauntlet—take it up!"

"Huh! That's not a gauntlet—from its odor it seems more like a sock."

"The funniest, part of it," Makaraig added, "is that Padre Irene has advised us to celebrate the event with a banquet or a torchlight procession—a public demonstration of the students *en masse* to render thanks to all the persons who have intervened in the affair."

"Yes, after the blow, let's sing and give thanks. *Super flumina Babylonis sedimus!*"

"Yes, a banquet like that of the convicts," said Tadeo.

"A banquet at which we all wear mourning and deliver funeral orations," added Sandoval.

"A serenade with the Marseillaise and funeral marches," proposed Isagani.

"No, gentlemen," observed Pecson with his clownish grin, "to celebrate the event there's nothing like a banquet in a *pansitería*, served by the Chinamen without camisas. I insist, without camisas!"

The sarcasm and grotesqueness of this idea won it ready acceptance, Sandoval being the first to applaud it, for he had long wished to see the interior of one of those establishments which at night appeared to be so merry and cheerful.

Just as the orchestra struck up for the second act, the young men arose and left the theater, to the scandal of the whole house.

A CORPSE

Simoun had not, in fact, gone to the theater. Already, at seven o'clock in the evening, he had left his house looking worried and gloomy. His servants saw him return twice, accompanied by different individuals, and at eight o'clock Makaraig encountered him pacing along Calle Hospital near the nunnery of St. Clara, just when the bells of its church were ringing a funeral knell. At nine Camaroncocido saw him again, in the neighborhood of the theater, speak with a person who seemed to be a student, pay the latter's admission to the show, and again disappear among the shadows of the trees.

"What is it to me?" again muttered Camaroncocido. "What do I get out of watching over the populace?"

Basilio, as Makaraig said, had not gone to the show. The poor student, after returning from San Diego, whither he had gone to ransom Juli, his future bride, from her servitude, had turned again to his studies, spending his time in the hospital, in studying, or in nursing Capitan Tiago, whose affliction he was trying to cure.

The invalid had become an intolerable character. During his bad spells, when he felt depressed from lack of opium, the doses of which Basilio was trying to reduce, he would scold, mistreat, and abuse the boy, who bore it resignedly, conscious that he was doing good to one to whom he owed so much, and yielded only in the last extremity. His vicious appetite satisfied, Capitan Tiago would fall into a good humor, become tender, and call him his son, tearfully recalling the youth's services, how well he administered the estates, and would even talk of making him his heir. Basilio would smile bitterly and reflect that in this world complaisance with vice is rewarded better than fulfilment of duty. Not a few times did he feel tempted to give free rein to the craving and conduct his benefactor to the grave by a path of flowers and smiling illusions rather than lengthen his life along a road of sacrifice.

"What a fool I am!" he often said to himself. "People are stupid and then pay for it."

But he would shake his head as he thought of Juli, of the wide future before him. He counted upon living without a stain on his conscience, so he continued the treatment prescribed, and bore everything patiently.

Yet with all his care the sick man, except for short periods of improvement, grew worse. Basilio had planned gradually to reduce the amount of the dose, or at least not to let him injure himself by increasing it, but on returning from the hospital or some visit he would find his patient in the heavy slumber produced by the opium, driveling, pale as a corpse. The young man could not explain whence the drug came: the only two persons who visited the house were Simoun and Padre Irene, the former rarely, while the latter never ceased exhorting him to be severe and inexorable with the treatment, to take no notice of the invalid's ravings, for the main object was to save him.

"Do your duty, young man," was Padre Irene's constant admonition. "Do your duty." Then he would deliver a sermon on this topic with such great conviction and enthusiasm that Basilio would begin to feel kindly toward the preacher. Besides, Padre Irene promised to get him a fine assignment, a good province, and even hinted at the possibility of having him appointed a professor. Without being carried away by illusions, Basilio pretended to believe in them and went on obeying the dictates of his own conscience.

That night, while *Les Cloches de Corneville* was being presented, Basilio was studying at an old table by the light of an oil-lamp, whose thick glass globe partly illuminated his melancholy features. An old skull, some human bones, and a few books carefully arranged covered the table, whereon there was also a pan of water with a sponge. The smell of opium that proceeded from the adjoining bedroom made the air heavy and inclined him to sleep, but he overcame the desire by bathing his temples and eyes from time to time, determined not to go to sleep until he had finished the book, which he had borrowed and must return as soon as possible. It was a volume of the *Medicina Legal y Toxicología* of Dr. Friata, the only book that the professor would use, and Basilio lacked money to buy a copy, since, under the pretext of its being forbidden by the censor in Manila and the necessity for bribing many government employees to get it in, the booksellers charged a high price for it.

So absorbed was the youth in his studies that he had not given any attention at all to some pamphlets that had been sent to him from some unknown source, pamphlets that treated of the Philippines, among which figured those that were attracting the greatest notice at the time because of their harsh and insulting manner of referring to the natives of the country. Basilio had no time to open them, and he was perhaps restrained also by the thought that there is nothing pleasant about receiving an insult or a provocation without having any means of replying or defending oneself. The censorship, in fact, permitted insults to the Filipinos but prohibited replies on their part.

In the midst of the silence that reigned in the house, broken only by a feeble snore that issued now and then from the adjoining bedroom, Basilio heard light footfalls on the stairs, footfalls that soon crossed the hallway and approached the room where he was. Raising his head, he saw the door open and to his great surprise appeared the sinister figure of the jeweler Simoun, who since the scene in San Diego had not come to visit either himself or Capitan Tiago.

"How is the sick man?" he inquired, throwing a rapid glance about the room and fixing his attention on the pamphlets, the leaves of which were still uncut.

"The beating of his heart is scarcely perceptible, his pulse is very weak, his appetite entirely gone," replied Basilio in a low voice with a sad smile. "He sweats profusely in the early morning."

Noticing that Simoun kept his face turned toward the pamphlets and fearing that he might reopen the subject of their conversation in the wood, he went on: "His system is saturated with poison. He may die any day, as though struck by lightning. The least irritation, any excitement may kill him."

"Like the Philippines!" observed Simoun lugubriously.

Basilio was unable to refrain from a gesture of impatience, but he was determined not to recur to the old subject, so he proceeded as if he had heard nothing: "What weakens him the most is the nightmares, his terrors—"

"Like the government!" again interrupted Simoun.

"Several nights ago he awoke in the dark and thought that he had gone blind. He raised a disturbance, lamenting and scolding me, saying that I had put his eyes out. When I entered his room with a light he mistook me for Padre Irene and called me his saviour."

"Like the government, exactly!"

"Last night," continued Basilio, paying no attention, "he got up begging for his favorite game-cock, the one that died three years ago, and I had to give him a chicken. Then he heaped blessings upon me and promised me many thousands—"

At that instant a clock struck half-past ten. Simoun shuddered and stopped the youth with a gesture.

"Basilio," he said in a low, tense voice, "listen to me carefully, for the moments are precious. I see that you haven't opened the pamphlets that I sent you. You're not interested in your country."

The youth started to protest.

"It's useless," went on Simoun dryly. "Within an hour the revolution is going to break out at a signal from me, and tomorrow there'll be no studies, there'll be no University, there'll be nothing but fighting and butchery. I have everything ready and my success is assured. When we triumph, all those who could have helped us and did not do so will be treated as enemies. Basilio, I've come to offer you death or a future!"

"Death or a future!" the boy echoed, as though he did not understand.

"With us or with the government," rejoined Simoun. "With your country or with your oppressors. Decide, for time presses! I've come to save you because of the memories that unite us!"

"With my country or with the oppressors!" repeated Basilio in a low tone. The youth was stupefied. He gazed at the jeweler with eyes in which terror was reflected, he felt his limbs turn cold, while a thousand confused ideas whirled about in his mind. He saw the streets running blood, he heard the firing, he found himself among the dead and wounded, and by the peculiar force of his inclinations fancied himself in an operator's blouse, cutting off legs and extracting bullets.

"The will of the government is in my hands," said Simoun. "I've diverted and wasted its feeble strength and resources on foolish expeditions, dazzling it with the plunder it might seize. Its heads are now in the theater, calm and unsuspecting, thinking of a night of pleasure, but not one shall again repose upon a pillow. I have men and regiments at my disposition: some I have led to believe that the uprising is ordered by the General; others that the friars are bringing it about; some I have bought with promises, with employments, with money; many, very many, are acting from revenge, because they are oppressed and see it as a matter of killing or being killed. Cabesang Tales is below, he has come with me here! Again I ask you—will you come with us or do you prefer to expose yourself to the resentment of my followers? In critical moments, to declare oneself neutral is to be exposed to the wrath of both the contending parties."

Basilio rubbed his hand over his face several times, as if he were trying to wake from a nightmare. He felt that his brow was cold.

"Decide!" repeated Simoun.

"And what—what would I have to do?" asked the youth in a weak and broken voice.

"A very simple thing," replied Simoun, his face lighting up with a ray of hope. "As I have to direct the movement, I cannot get away from the scene of action. I want you, while the attention of the whole city is directed elsewhere, at the head of a company to force the doors of the nunnery of St. Clara and take from there a person whom only you, besides myself and Capitan Tiago, can recognize. You'll run no risk at all."

"Maria Clara!" exclaimed Basilio.

"Yes, Maria Clara," repeated Simoun, and for the first time his voice became human and compassionate. "I want to save her; to save her I have wished to live, I have returned. I am starting the revolution, because only a revolution can open the doors of the nunneries."

"Ay!" sighed Basilio, clasping his hands. "You've come late, too late!"

"Why?" inquired Simoun with a frown.

"Maria Clara is dead!"

Simoun arose with a bound and stood over the youth. "She's dead?" he demanded in a terrible voice.

"This afternoon, at six. By now she must be—"

"It's a lie!" roared Simoun, pale and beside himself. "It's false! Maria Clara lives, Maria Clara must live! It's a cowardly excuse! She's not dead, and this night I'll free her or tomorrow you die!"

Basilio shrugged his shoulders. "Several days ago she was taken ill and I went to the nunnery for news of her. Look, here is Padre Salvi's letter, brought by Padre Irene. Capitan Tiago wept all the evening, kissing his daughter's picture and begging her forgiveness, until at last he smoked an enormous quantity of opium. This evening her knell was tolled."

"Ah!" exclaimed Simoun, pressing his hands to his head and standing motionless. He remembered to have actually heard the knell while he was pacing about in the vicinity of the nunnery.

"Dead!" he murmured in a voice so low that it seemed to be a ghost whispering. "Dead! Dead without my having seen her, dead without knowing that I lived for her—dead!"

Feeling a terrible storm, a tempest of whirlwind and thunder without a drop of water, sobs without tears, cries without words, rage in his breast and threaten to burst out like burning lava long repressed, he rushed precipitately from the room. Basilio heard him descend the stairs with unsteady tread, stepping heavily, he heard a stifled cry, a cry that seemed to presage death, so solemn, deep, and sad that he arose from his chair pale and trembling, but he could hear the footsteps die away and the noisy closing of the door to the street.

"Poor fellow!" he murmured, while his eyes filled with tears. Heedless now of his studies, he let his gaze wander into space as he pondered over the fate of those two beings: he—young, rich, educated, master of his fortunes, with a brilliant future before him; she—fair as a dream, pure, full of faith and innocence, nurtured amid love and laughter, destined to a happy existence, to be adored in the family and respected in the world; and yet of those two beings, filled with love, with illusions and hopes, by a fatal destiny he wandered over the world, dragged ceaselessly through a whirl of blood and tears, sowing evil instead of doing good, undoing virtue and encouraging vice, while she was dying in the mysterious shadows of the cloister where she had sought peace and perhaps found suffering, where she entered pure and stainless and expired like a crushed flower!

Sleep in peace, ill-starred daughter of my hapless fatherland! Bury in the grave the enchantments of youth, faded in their prime! When a people cannot offer its daughters a tranquil home under the protection of sacred liberty, when a man can only leave to his widow blushes, tears to his mother, and slavery to his children, you do well to condemn yourself to perpetual chastity, stifling within you the germ of a future generation accursed! Well for you that you have not to shudder in your grave, hearing the cries of those who groan in darkness, of those who feel that they have wings and yet are fettered, of those who are stifled from lack of liberty! Go, go with your poet's dreams into the regions of the infinite, spirit of woman dim-shadowed in the moonlight's beam, whispered in the bending arches of the bamboo-brakes! Happy she who dies lamented, she who leaves in the heart that loves her a pure picture, a sacred remembrance, unspotted by the base passions engendered by the years! Go, we shall remember you! In the clear air of our native land, under its azure sky, above the billows of the lake set amid sapphire hills and emerald shores, in the crystal streams shaded by the bamboos, bordered by flowers, enlivened by the beetles and butterflies with their uncertain and wavering flight as though playing with the air, in the silence of our forests, in the singing of our rivers, in the diamond showers of our waterfalls, in the resplendent light of our moon, in the sighs of the night breeze, in all that may call up the vision of the beloved, we must eternally see you as we dreamed of you, fair, beautiful, radiant with hope, pure as the light, yet still sad and melancholy in the contemplation of our woes!

DREAMS

Amor, qué astro eres?

On the following day, Thursday, at the hour of sunset, Isagani was walking along the beautiful promenade of Maria Cristina in the direction of the Malecon to keep an appointment which Paulita had that morning given him. The young man had no doubt that they were to talk about what had happened on the previous night, and as he was determined to ask for an explanation, and knew how proud and haughty she was, he foresaw an estrangement. In view of this eventuality he had brought with him the only two letters he had ever received from Paulita, two scraps of paper, whereon were merely a few hurriedly written lines with various blots, but in an even handwriting, things that did not prevent the enamored youth from preserving them with more solicitude than if they had been the autographs of Sappho and the Muse Polyhymnia.

This decision to sacrifice his love on the altar of dignity, the consciousness of suffering in the discharge of duty, did not prevent a profound melancholy from taking possession of Isagani and brought back into his mind the beautiful days, and nights more beautiful still, when they had whispered sweet nothings through the flowered gratings of the entresol, nothings that to the youth took on such a character of seriousness and importance that they seemed to him the only matters worthy of meriting the attention of the most exalted human understanding. He recalled the walks on moonlit nights, the fair, the dark December mornings after the mass of Nativity, the holy water that he used to offer her, when she would thank him with a look charged with a whole epic of love, both of them trembling as their fingers touched. Heavy sighs, like small rockets, issued from his breast and brought back to him all the verses, all the sayings of poets and writers about the inconstancy of woman. Inwardly he cursed the creation of theaters, the French operetta, and vowed to get revenge on Pelaez at the first opportunity. Everything about him appeared under the saddest and somberest colors: the bay, deserted and solitary, seemed more solitary still on account of the few steamers that were anchored in it; the sun was dying behind Mariveles without poetry or enchantment, without the capricious and richly tinted clouds of happier evenings; the Anda monument, in bad taste, mean and squat, without style, without grandeur, looked like a lump of ice-cream or at best a chunk of cake; the people who were promenading along the Malecon, in spite of their complacent and contented air, appeared distant, haughty, and vain; mischievous and bad-mannered, the boys that played on the beach, skipping flat stones over the surface of the water or searching in the sand for mollusks and crustaceans which they caught for the mere fun of catching and killed without benefit to themselves; in short, even the eternal port works to which he had dedicated more than three odes, looked to him absurd, ridiculous child's play.

The port, ah, the port of Manila, a bastard that since its conception had brought tears of humiliation and shame to all! If only after so many tears there were not being brought forth a useless abortion!

Abstractedly he saluted two Jesuits, former teachers of his, and scarcely noticed a tandem in which an American rode and excited the envy of the gallants who were in calesas only. Near the Anda monument he heard Ben-Zayb talking with another person about Simoun, learning that the latter had on the previous night been taken suddenly ill, that he refused to see any one, even the very aides of the General. "Yes!" exclaimed Isagani with a bitter smile, "for him attentions because he is rich. The soldiers return from their expeditions sick and wounded, but no one visits them."

Musing over these expeditions, over the fate of the poor soldiers, over the resistance offered by the islanders to the foreign yoke, he thought that, death for death, if that of the soldiers was glorious because they were obeying orders, that of the islanders was sublime because they were defending their homes.

"A strange destiny, that of some peoples!" he mused. "Because a traveler arrives at their shores, they lose their liberty and become subjects and slaves, not only of the traveler, not only of his heirs, but even of all his countrymen, and not for a generation, but for all time! A strange conception of justice! Such a state of affairs gives ample right to exterminate every foreigner as the most ferocious monster that the sea can cast up!"

He reflected that those islanders, against whom his country was waging war, after all were guilty of no crime other than that of weakness. The travelers also arrived at the shores of other peoples, but finding them strong made no display of their strange pretension. With all their weakness the spectacle they presented seemed beautiful to him, and the names of the enemies, whom the newspapers did not fail to call cowards and traitors, appeared glorious to him, as they succumbed with glory amid the ruins of their crude fortifications, with greater glory even than the ancient Trojan heroes, for those islanders had carried away no Philippine Helen! In his poetic enthusiasm he thought of the young men of those islands who could cover themselves with glory in the eyes of their women, and in his amorous desperation he envied them because they could find a brilliant suicide.

"Ah, I should like to die," he exclaimed, "be reduced to nothingness, leave to my native land a glorious name, perish in its cause, defending it from foreign invasion, and then let the sun afterwards illumine my corpse, like a motionless sentinel on the rocks of the sea!"

The conflict with the Germans[2] came into his mind and he almost felt sorry that it had been adjusted: he would gladly have died for the Spanish-Filipino banner before submitting to the foreigner.

"Because, after all," he mused, "with Spain we are united by firm bonds—the past, history, religion, language—"

Language, yes, language! A sarcastic smile curled his lips. That very night they would hold a banquet in the *pansitería* to *celebrate* the demise of the academy of Castilian.

"Ay!" he sighed, "provided the liberals in Spain are like those we have here, in a little while the mother country will be able to count the number of the faithful!"

Slowly the night descended, and with it melancholy settled more heavily upon the heart of the young man, who had almost lost hope of seeing Paulita. The promenaders one by one left the Malecon for the Luneta, the music from which was borne to him in snatches of melodies on the fresh evening breeze; the sailors on a warship anchored in the river performed their evening drill, skipping about among the slender ropes like spiders; the boats one by one lighted their lamps, thus giving signs of life; while the beach,

> Do el viento riza las calladas olas
> Que con blando murmullo en la ribera
> Se deslizan veloces por sí solas.'

as Alaejos says, exhaled in the distance thin, vapors that the moon, now at its full, gradually converted into mysterious transparent gauze.

A distant sound became audible, a noise that rapidly approached. Isagani turned his head and his heart began to beat violently. A carriage was coming, drawn by white horses, the white horses that he would know among a hundred thousand. In the carriage rode Paulita and her friend of the night before, with Doña Victorina.

Before the young man could take a step, Paulita had leaped to the ground with sylph-like agility and smiled at him with a smile full of conciliation. He smiled in return, and it seemed to him that all the clouds, all the black thoughts that before had beset him, vanished like smoke, the sky lighted up, the breeze sang, flowers covered the grass by the roadside. But unfortunately Doña Victorina was there and she pounced upon the young man to ask him for news of Don Tiburcio, since Isagani had undertaken to discover his hiding-place by inquiry among the students he knew.

"No one has been able to tell me up to now," he answered, and he was telling the truth, for Don Tiburcio was really hidden in the house of the youth's own uncle, Padre Florentino.

"Let him know," declared Doña Victorina furiously, "that I'll call in the Civil Guard. Alive or dead, I want to know where he is—because one has to wait ten years before marrying again."

Isagani gazed at her in fright—Doña Victorina was thinking of remarrying! Who could the unfortunate be?

"What do you think of Juanito Pelaez?" she asked him suddenly.

Juanito! Isagani knew not what to reply. He was tempted to tell all the evil he knew of Pelaez, but a feeling of delicacy triumphed in his heart and he spoke well of his rival, for the very reason that he was such. Doña Victorina, entirely satisfied and becoming enthusiastic, then broke out into exaggerations of Pelaez's merits and was already going to make Isagani a confidant of her new passion when Paulita's friend came running to say that the former's fan had fallen among the stones of the beach, near the Malecon. Stratagem or accident, the fact is that this mischance gave an excuse for the friend to remain with the old woman, while Isagani might talk with Paulita. Moreover, it was a matter of rejoicing to Doña Victorina, since to get Juanito for herself she was favoring Isagani's love.

Paulita had her plan ready. On thanking him she assumed the role of the offended party, showed resentment, and gave him to understand that she was surprised to meet him there when everybody was on the Luneta, even the French actresses.

"You made the appointment for me, how could I be elsewhere?"

"Yet last night you did not even notice that I was in the theater. I was watching you all the time and you never took your eyes off those *cochers*."

So they exchanged parts: Isagani, who had come to demand explanations, found himself compelled to give them and considered himself very happy when Paulita said that she forgave him. In regard to her presence at the theater, he even had to thank her for that: forced by her aunt, she had decided to go in the hope of seeing him during the performance. Little she cared for Juanito Pelaez!

"My aunt's the one who is in love with him," she said with a merry laugh.

Then they both laughed, for the marriage of Pelaez with Doña Victorina made them really happy, and they saw it already an accomplished fact, until Isagani remembered that Don Tiburcio was still living and confided the secret to his sweetheart, after exacting her promise that she would tell no one. Paulita promised, with the mental reservation of relating it to her friend.

This led the conversation to Isagani's town, surrounded by forests, situated on the shore of the sea which roared at the base of the high cliffs. Isagani's gaze lighted up when he spoke of that obscure spot, a flush of pride overspread his cheeks, his voice trembled, his poetic imagination glowed, his words poured forth burning, charged with enthusiasm, as if he were talking of love to his love, and he could not but exclaim:

"Oh, in the solitude of my mountains I feel free, free as the air, as the light that shoots unbridled through space! A thousand cities, a thousand palaces, would I give for that spot in the Philippines, where, far from men, I could feel myself to have genuine liberty. There, face to face with nature, in the presence of the mysterious and the infinite, the forest and the sea, I think, speak, and work like a man who knows not tyrants."

In the presence of such enthusiasm for his native place, an enthusiasm that she did not comprehend, for she was accustomed to hear her country spoken ill of, and sometimes joined in the chorus herself, Paulita manifested some jealousy, as usual making herself the offended party.

But Isagani very quickly pacified her. "Yes," he said, "I loved it above all things before I knew you! It was my delight to wander through the thickets, to sleep in the shade of the trees, to seat myself upon a cliff to take in with my gaze the Pacific which rolled its blue waves before me, bringing to me echoes of songs learned on the shores of free America. Before knowing you, that sea was for me my world, my delight, my love, my dream! When it slept in calm with the sun shining overhead, it was my delight to gaze into the abyss hundreds of feet below me, seeking monsters in the forests of madrepores and coral that were revealed through the limpid blue, enormous serpents that the country folk say leave the forests to dwell in the sea, and there take on frightful forms. Evening, they say, is the time when the sirens appear, and I saw them between the waves—so great was my eagerness that once I thought I could discern them amid the foam, busy in their divine sports, I distinctly heard their songs, songs of liberty, and I made out the sounds of their silvery harps. Formerly I spent hours and hours watching the transformations in the clouds, or gazing at a solitary tree in the plain or a high rock, without knowing why, without being able to explain the vague feelings they awoke in me. My uncle used to preach long sermons to me, and fearing that I would become a hypochondriac, talked of placing me under a doctor's care. But I met you, I loved you, and during the last vacation it seemed that something was lacking there, the forest was gloomy, sad the river that glides through the shadows, dreary the sea, deserted the sky. Ah, if you should go there once, if your feet should press those paths, if you should stir the waters of the rivulet with your fingers, if you should gaze upon the sea, sit upon the cliff, or make the air ring with your melodious songs, my forest would be transformed into an Eden, the ripples of the brook would sing, light would burst from the dark leaves, into diamonds would be converted the dewdrops and into pearls the foam of the sea."

But Paulita had heard that to reach Isagani's home it was necessary to cross mountains where little leeches abounded, and at the mere thought of them the little coward shivered convulsively. Humored and petted, she declared that she would travel only in a carriage or a railway train.

Having now forgotten all his pessimism and seeing only thornless roses about him, Isagani answered, "Within a short time all the islands are going to be crossed with networks of iron rails.

> "'Por donde rápidas
> Y voladoras
> Locomotoras
> Corriendo irán,'

as some one said. Then the most beautiful spots of the islands will be accessible to all."

"Then, but when? When I'm an old woman?"

"Ah, you don't know what we can do in a few years," replied the youth. "You don't realize the energy and enthusiasm that are awakening in the country after the sleep of centuries. Spain heeds us; our young men in Madrid are working day and night, dedicating to the fatherland all their intelligence, all their time, all their strength. Generous voices there are mingled with ours, statesmen who realize that there is no better bond than community of thought and interest. Justice will be meted out to us, and everything points to a brilliant future for all. It's true that we've just met with a slight rebuff, we students, but victory is rolling along the whole line, it is in the consciousness of all! The traitorous repulse that we have suffered indicates the last gasp, the final convulsions of the dying. Tomorrow we shall be citizens of the Philippines, whose destiny will be a glorious one, because it will be in loving hands. Ah, yes, the future is ours! I see it rose-tinted, I see the movement that stirs the life of these regions so long dead, lethargic. I see towns arise along the railroads, and factories everywhere, edifices like that of Mandaloyan! I hear the steam hiss, the trains roar, the engines rattle! I see the smoke rise—their heavy breathing; I smell the oil—the sweat of monsters busy at incessant toil. This port, so slow and laborious of creation, this river where commerce is in its death agony, we shall see covered with masts, giving us an idea of the forests of Europe in winter. This pure air, and these stones, now so clean, will be crowded with coal, with boxes and barrels, the products of human industry, but let it not matter, for we shall move about rapidly in comfortable coaches to seek in the interior other air, other scenes on other shores, cooler temperatures on the slopes of the mountains. The warships of our navy will guard our coasts, the Spaniard and the Filipino will rival each other in zeal to repel all foreign invasion, to defend our homes, and let you bask in peace and smiles, loved and respected. Free from the system of exploitation, without hatred or distrust, the people will labor because then labor will cease to be a despicable thing, it will no longer be servile, imposed upon a slave. Then the Spaniard will not embitter his character with ridiculous pretensions of despotism, but with a frank look and a stout heart we shall extend our hands to one another, and commerce, industry, agriculture, the sciences, will develop under the mantle of liberty, with wise and just laws, as in prosperous England."

Paulita smiled dubiously and shook her head. "Dreams, dreams!" she sighed. "I've heard it said that you have many enemies. Aunt says that this country must always be enslaved."

"Because your aunt is a fool, because she can't live without slaves! When she hasn't them she dreams of them in the future, and if they are not obtainable she forces them into her imagination. True it is that we have enemies, that there will be a struggle, but we shall conquer. The old system may convert the ruins of its castle into formless barricades, but we will take them singing hymns of liberty, in the light of the eyes of you women, to the applause of your lovely hands. But do not be uneasy—the struggle will be a pacific one. Enough that you spur us to zeal, that you awake in us noble and elevated thoughts and encourage us to constancy, to heroism, with your affection for our reward."

Paulita preserved her enigmatic smile and seemed thoughtful, as she gazed toward the river, patting her cheek lightly with her fan. "But if you accomplish nothing?" she asked abstractedly.

The question hurt Isagani. He fixed his eyes on his sweetheart, caught her lightly by the hand, and began: "Listen, if we accomplish nothing—"

He paused in doubt, then resumed: "You know how I love you, how I adore you, you know that I feel myself a different creature when your gaze enfolds me, when I surprise in it the flash of love, but yet if we accomplish nothing, I would dream of another look of yours and would die happy, because the light of pride could burn in your eyes when you pointed to my corpse and said to the world: 'My love died fighting for the rights of my fatherland!'"

"Come home, child, you're going to catch cold," screeched Doña Victorina at that instant, and the voice brought them back to reality. It was time to return, and they kindly invited him to enter the carriage, an invitation which the young man did not give them cause to repeat. As it was Paulita's carriage, naturally Doña Victorina and the friend occupied the back seat, while the two lovers sat on the smaller one in front.

To ride in the same carriage, to have her at his side, to breathe her perfume, to rub against the silk of her dress, to see her pensive with folded arms, lighted by the moon of the Philippines that lends to the meanest things idealism and enchantment, were all dreams beyond Isagani's hopes! What wretches they who were returning alone on foot and had to give way to the swift carriage! In the whole course of the drive, along the beach and down the length of La Sabana, across the Bridge of Spain, Isagani saw nothing but a sweet profile, gracefully set off by beautiful hair, ending in an arching neck that lost itself amid the gauzy piña. A diamond winked at him from the lobe of the little ear, like a star among silvery clouds. He heard faint echoes inquiring for Don Tiburcio de Espadaña, the name of Juanito Pelaez, but they sounded to him like distant bells, the confused noises heard in a dream. It was necessary to tell him that they had reached Plaza Santa Cruz.

1   Referring to the expeditions—*Misión Española Católica*—to the Caroline and Pelew Islands from 1886 to 1895, headed by the Capuchin Fathers, which brought misery and disaster upon the natives of those islands, unprofitable losses and sufferings to the Filipino soldiers engaged in them, discredit to Spain, and decorations of merit to a number of Spanish officers.—Tr.

2   Over the possession of the Caroline and Pelew Islands. The expeditions referred to in the previous note were largely inspired by German activity with regard to those islands, which had always been claimed by Spain, who sold her claim to them to Germany after the loss of the Philippines.—Tr.

3   "Where the wind wrinkles the silent waves, that rapidly break, of their own movement, with a gentle murmur on the shore."—Tr.

4   "Where rapid and winged engines will rush in flight."—Tr.

5   There is something almost uncanny about the general accuracy of the prophecy in these lines, the economic part of which is now so well on the way to realization, although the writer of them would doubtless have been a very much surprised individual had he also foreseen how it would come about. But one of his own expressions was "fire and steel to the cancer," and it surely got them.

On the very day that this passage was translated and this note written, the first commercial liner was tied up at the new docks, which have destroyed the Malecon but raised Manila to the front rank of Oriental seaports, and the final revision is made at Baguio, Mountain Province, amid the "cooler temperatures on the slopes of the mountains." As for the political portion, it is difficult even now to contemplate calmly the blundering fatuity of that bigoted medieval brand of "patriotism" which led the decrepit Philippine government to play the Ancient Mariner and shoot the Albatross that brought this message.—Tr.

SMILES AND TEARS

The sala of the *Pansiteria Macanista de Buen Gusto*[1] that night presented an extraordinary aspect. Fourteen young men of the principal islands of the archipelago, from the pure Indian (if there be pure ones) to the Peninsular Spaniard, were met to hold the banquet advised by Padre Irene in view of the happy solution of the affair about instruction in Castilian. They had engaged all the tables for themselves, ordered the lights to be increased, and had posted on the wall beside the landscapes and Chinese kakemonos this strange versicle:

"GLORY TO CUSTODIO FOR HIS CLEVERNESS AND PANSIT ON EABTH TO THE YOUTHS OF GOOD WILL."

In a country where everything grotesque is covered with a mantle of seriousness, where many rise by the force of wind and hot air, in a country where the deeply serious and sincere may do damage on issuing from the heart and may cause trouble, probably this was the best way to celebrate the ingenious inspiration of the illustrious Don Custodio. The mocked replied to the mockery with a laugh, to the governmental joke with a plate of *pansit*, and yet—!

They laughed and jested, but it could be seen that the merriment was forced. The laughter had a certain nervous ring, eyes flashed, and in more than one of these a tear glistened. Nevertheless, these young men were cruel, they were unreasonable! It was not the first time that their most beautiful ideas had been so treated, that their hopes had been defrauded with big words and small actions: before this Don Custodio there had been many, very many others.

In the center of the room under the red lanterns were placed four round tables, systematically arranged to form a square. Little wooden stools, equally round, served as seats. In the middle of each table, according to the practise of the establishment, were arranged four small colored plates with four pies on each one and four cups of tea, with the accompanying dishes, all of red porcelain. Before each seat was a bottle and two glittering wine-glasses.

Sandoval was curious and gazed about scrutinizing everything, tasting the food, examining the pictures, reading the bill of fare. The others conversed on the topics of the day: about the French actresses, about the mysterious illness of Simoun, who, according to some, had been found wounded in the street, while others averred that he had attempted to commit suicide. As was natural, all lost themselves in conjectures. Tadeo gave his particular version, which according to him came from a reliable source: Simoun had been assaulted by some unknown person in the old Plaza Vivac,[2] the motive being revenge, in proof of which was the fact that Simoun himself refused to make the least explanation. From this they proceeded to talk of mysterious revenges, and naturally of monkish pranks, each one relating the exploits of the curate of his town.

A notice in large black letters crowned the frieze of the room with this warning:

> De esta fonda el cabecilla
> Al publico advierte
> Que nada dejen absolutamente
> Sobre alguna mesa ó silla.[3]

"What a notice!" exclaimed Sandoval. "As if he might have confidence in the police, eh? And what verses! Don Tiburcio converted into a quatrain—two feet, one longer than the other, between two crutches! If Isagani sees them, he'll present them to his future aunt."

"Here's Isagani!" called a voice from the stairway. The happy youth appeared radiant with joy, followed by two Chinese, without camisas, who carried on enormous waiters tureens that gave out an appetizing odor. Merry exclamations greeted them.

Juanito Pelaez was missing, but the hour fixed had already passed, so they sat down happily to the tables. Juanito was always unconventional.

"If in his place we had invited Basilio," said Tadeo, "we should have been better entertained. We might have got him drunk and drawn some secrets from him."

"What, does the prudent Basilio possess secrets?"

"I should say so!" replied Tadeo. "Of the most important kind. There are some enigmas to which he alone has the key: the boy who disappeared, the nun—"

"Gentlemen, the *pansit lang-lang* is the soup *par excellence*!" cried Makaraig. "As you will observe, Sandoval, it is composed of vermicelli, crabs or shrimps, egg paste, scraps of chicken, and I don't know what else. As first-fruits, let us offer the bones to Don Custodio, to see if he will project something with them."

A burst of merry laughter greeted this sally.

"If he should learn—"

"He'd come a-running!" concluded Sandoval. "This is excellent soup—what is it called?"

"*Pansit lang-lang*, that is, Chinese *pansit*, to distinguish it from that which is peculiar to this country."

"Bah! That's a hard name to remember. In honor of Don Custodio, I christen it the *soup project*!"

"Gentlemen," said Makaraig, who had prepared the menu, "there are three courses yet. Chinese stew made of pork—"

"Which should be dedicated to Padre Irene."

"Get out! Padre Irene doesn't eat pork, unless he turns his nose away," whispered a young man from Iloilo to his neighbor.

"Let him turn his nose away!"

"Down with Padre Irene's nose," cried several at once.

"Respect, gentlemen, more respect!" demanded Pecson with comic gravity.

"The third course is a lobster pie—"

"Which should be dedicated to the friars," suggested he of the Visayas.

"For the lobsters' sake," added Sandoval.

"Right, and call it friar pie!"

The whole crowd took this up, repeating in concert, "Friar pie!"

"I protest in the name of one of them," said Isagani.

"And I, in the name of the lobsters," added Tadeo.

"Respect, gentlemen, more respect!" again demanded Pecson with a full mouth.

"The fourth is stewed *pansit*, which is dedicated—to the government and the country!"

All turned toward Makaraig, who went on: "Until recently, gentlemen, the *pansit* was believed to be Chinese or Japanese, but the fact is that, being unknown in China or Japan, it would seem to be Filipino, yet those who prepare it and get the benefit from it are the Chinese—the same, the very, very same that happens to the government and to the Philippines: they seem to be Chinese, but whether they are or not, the Holy Mother has her doctors—all eat and enjoy it, yet characterize it as disagreeable and loathsome, the same as with the country, the same as with the government. All live at its cost, all share in its feast, and afterwards there is no worse country than the Philippines, there is no government more imperfect. Let us then dedicate the *pansit* to the country and to the government."

"Agreed!" many exclaimed.

"I protest!" cried Isagani.

"Respect for the weaker, respect for the victims," called Pecson in a hollow voice, waving a chicken-bone in the air.

"Let's dedicate the *pansit* to Quiroga the Chinaman, one of the four powers of the Filipino world," proposed Isagani.

"No, to his Black Eminence."

"Silence!" cautioned one mysteriously. "There are people in the plaza watching us, and walls have ears."

True it was that curious groups were standing by the windows, while the talk and laughter in the adjoining houses had ceased altogether, as if the people there were giving their attention to what was occurring at the banquet. There was something extraordinary about the silence.

"Tadeo, deliver your speech," Makaraig whispered to him.

It had been agreed that Sandoval, who possessed the most oratorical ability, should deliver the last toast as a summing up.

Tadeo, lazy as ever, had prepared nothing, so he found himself in a quandary. While disposing of a long string of vermicelli, he meditated how to get out of the difficulty, until he recalled a speech learned in school and decided to plagiarize it, with adulterations.

"Beloved brethren in project!" he began, gesticulating with two Chinese chop-sticks.

"Brute! Keep that chop-stick out of my hair!" cried his neighbor.

"Called by you to fill the void that has been left in—"

"Plagiarism!" Sandoval interrupted him. "That speech was delivered by the president of our lyceum."

"Called by your election," continued the imperturbable Tadeo, "to fill the void that has been left in my mind"—pointing to his stomach—"by a man famous for his Christian principles and for his inspirations and projects, worthy of some little remembrance, what can one like myself say of him, I who am very hungry, not having breakfasted?"

"Have a neck, my friend!" called a neighbor, offering that portion of a chicken.

"There is one course, gentlemen, the treasure of a people who are today a tale and a mockery in the world, wherein have thrust their hands the greatest gluttons of the western regions of the earth—" Here he pointed with his chopsticks to Sandoval, who was struggling with a refractory chicken-wing.

"And eastern!" retorted the latter, describing a circle in the air with his spoon, in order to include all the banqueters.

"No interruptions!"

"I demand the floor!"

"I demand pickles!" added Isagani.

"Bring on the stew!"

All echoed this request, so Tadeo sat down, contented with having got out of his quandary.

The dish consecrated to Padre Irene did not appear to be extra good, as Sandoval cruelly demonstrated thus: "Shining with grease outside and with pork inside! Bring on the third course, the friar pie!"

The pie was not yet ready, although the sizzling of the grease in the frying-pan could be heard. They took advantage of the delay to drink, begging Pecson to talk.

Pecson crossed himself gravely and arose, restraining his clownish laugh with an effort, at the same time mimicking a certain Augustinian preacher, then famous, and beginning in a murmur, as though he were reading a text.

"*Si tripa plena laudal Deum, tripa famelica laudabit fratres*—if the full stomach praises God, the hungry stomach will praise the friars. Words spoken by the Lord Custodio through the mouth of Ben-Zayb, in the journal *El Grito de la Integridad*, the second article, absurdity the one hundred and fifty-seventh.

"Beloved brethren in Christ: Evil blows its foul breath over the verdant shores of Frailandia, commonly called the Philippine Archipelago. No day passes but the attack is renewed, but there is heard some sarcasm against the reverend, venerable, infallible corporations, defenseless and unsupported. Allow me, brethren, on this occasion to constitute myself a knight-errant to sally forth in defense of the unprotected, of the holy corporations that have reared us, thus again confirming the saving idea of the adage—a full stomach praises God, which is to say, a hungry stomach will praise the friars."

"Bravo, bravo!"

"Listen," said Isagani seriously, "I want you to understand that, speaking of friars, I respect one."

Sandoval was getting merry, so he began to sing a shady couplet about the friars.

"Hear me, brethren!" continued Pecson. "Turn your gaze toward the happy days of your infancy, endeavor to analyze the present and ask yourselves about the future. What do you find? Friars, friars, and friars! A friar baptized you, confirmed you, visited you in school with loving zeal; a friar heard your first secret; he was the first to bring you into communion with God, to set your feet upon the pathway of life; friars were your first and friars will be your last teachers; a friar it is who opens the hearts of your sweethearts, disposing them to heed your sighs; a friar marries you, makes you travel over different islands to afford you changes of climate and diversion; he will attend your death-bed, and even though you mount the scaffold, there will the friar be to accompany you with his prayers and tears, and you may rest assured that he will not desert you until he sees you thoroughly dead. Nor does his charity end there—dead, he will then endeavor to bury you with all pomp, he will fight that your corpse pass through the church to receive his supplications, and he will only rest satisfied when he can deliver you into the hands of the Creator, purified here on earth, thanks to temporal punishments, tortures, and humiliations.

Learned in the doctrines of Christ, who closes heaven against the rich, they, our redeemers and genuine ministers of the Saviour, seek every means to lift away our sins and bear them far, far off, there where the accursed Chinese and Protestants dwell, to leave us this air, limpid, pure, healthful, in such a way that even should we so wish afterwards, we could not find a real to bring about our condemnation.

"If, then, their existence is necessary to our happiness, if wheresoever we turn we must encounter their delicate hands, hungering for kisses, that every day smooth the marks of abuse from our countenances, why not adore them and fatten them—why demand their impolitic expulsion? Consider for a moment the immense void that their absence would leave in our social system. Tireless workers, they improve and propagate the races! Divided as we are, thanks to our jealousies and our susceptibilities, the friars unite us in a common lot, in a firm bond, so firm that many are unable to move their elbows. Take away the friar, gentlemen, and you will see how the Philippine edifice will totter; lacking robust shoulders and hairy limbs to sustain it, Philippine life will again become monotonous, without the merry note of the playful and gracious friar, without the booklets and sermons that split our sides with laughter, without the amusing contrast between grand pretensions and small brains, without the actual, daily representations of the tales of Boccaccio and La Fontaine! Without the girdles and scapularies, what would you have our women do in the future—save that money and perhaps become miserly and covetous? Without the masses, novenaries, and processions, where will you find games of *panguingui* to entertain them in their hours of leisure? They would then have to devote themselves to their household duties and instead of reading diverting stories of miracles, we should then have to get them works that are not extant.

"Take away the friar and heroism will disappear, the political virtues will fall under the control of the vulgar. Take him away and the Indian will cease to exist, for the friar is the Father, the Indian is the Word! The former is the sculptor, the latter the statue, because all that we are, think, or do, we owe to the friar—to his patience, his toil, his perseverance of three centuries to modify the form Nature gave us. The Philippines without the friar and without the

Indian—what then would become of the unfortunate government in the hands of the Chinamen?"

"It will eat lobster pie," suggested Isagani, whom Pecson's speech bored.

"And that's what we ought to be doing. Enough of speeches!"

As the Chinese who should have served the courses did not put in his appearance, one of the students arose and went to the rear, toward the balcony that overlooked the river. But he returned at once, making mysterious signs.

"We're watched! I've seen Padre Sibyla's pet!"

"Yes?" ejaculated Isagani, rising.

"It's no use now. When he saw me he disappeared."

Approaching the window he looked toward the plaza, then made signs to his companions to come nearer. They saw a young man leave the door of the *pansitería*, gaze all about him, then with some unknown person enter a carriage that waited at the curb. It was Simoun's carriage.

"Ah!" exclaimed Makaraig. "The slave of the Vice-Rector attended by the Master of the General!"

---

1   These establishments are still a notable feature of native life in Manila. Whether the author adopted a title already common or popularized one of his own invention, the fact is that they are now invariably known by the name used here. The use of *macanista* was due to the presence in Manila of a large number of Chinese from Macao.—Tr.

2   Originally, Plaza San Gabriel, from the Dominican mission for the Chinese established there; later, as it became a commercial center, Plaza Vivac; and now known as Plaza Cervantes, being the financial center of Manila.—Tr.

3   "The manager of this restaurant warns the public to leave absolutely nothing on any table or chair."—Tr.

PASQUINADES

Very early the next morning Basilio arose to go to the hospital. He had his plans made: to visit his patients, to go afterwards to the University to see about his licentiateship, and then have an interview with Makaraig about the expense this would entail, for he had used up the greater part of his savings in ransoming Juli and in securing a house where she and her grandfather might live, and he had not dared to apply to Capitan Tiago, fearing that such a move would be construed as an advance on the legacy so often promised him.

Preoccupied with these thoughts, he paid no attention to the groups of students who were at such an early hour returning from the Walled City, as though the classrooms had been closed, nor did he even note the abstracted air of some of them, their whispered conversations, or the mysterious signals exchanged among them. So it was that when he reached San Juan de Dios and his friends asked him about the conspiracy, he gave a start, remembering what Simoun had planned, but which had miscarried, owing to the unexplained accident to the jeweler. Terrified, he asked in a trembling voice, at the same time endeavoring to feign ignorance, "Ah, yes, what conspiracy?"

"It's been discovered," replied one, "and it seems that many are implicated in it."

With an effort Basilio controlled himself. "Many implicated?" he echoed, trying to learn something from the looks of the others. "Who?"

"Students, a lot of students."

Basilio did not think it prudent to ask more, fearing that he would give himself away, so on the pretext of visiting his patients he left the group. One of the clinical professors met him and placing his hand mysteriously on the youth's shoulder—the professor was a friend of his—asked him in a low voice, "Were you at that supper last night?"

In his excited frame of mind Basilio thought the professor had said *night before last*, which was the time of his interview with Simoun. He tried to explain. "I assure you," he stammered, "that as Capitan Tiago was worse—and besides I had to finish that book—"

"You did well not to attend it," said the professor. "But you're a member of the students' association?"

"I pay my dues."

"Well then, a piece of advice: go home at once and destroy any papers you have that may compromise you."

Basilio shrugged his shoulders—he had no papers, nothing more than his clinical notes.

"Has Señor Simoun—"

"Simoun has nothing to do with the affair, thank God!" interrupted the physician. "He was opportunely wounded by some unknown hand and is now confined to his bed. No, other hands are concerned in this, but hands no less terrible."

Basilio drew a breath of relief. Simoun was the only one who could compromise him, although he thought of Cabesang Tales.

"Are there tulisanes—"

"No, man, nothing more than students."

Basilio recovered his serenity. "What has happened then?" he made bold to ask.

"Seditious pasquinades have been found; didn't you know about them?"

"Where?"

"In the University."

"Nothing more than that?"

"Whew! What more do you want?" asked the professor, almost in a rage. "The pasquinades are attributed to the students of the association—but, keep quiet!"

The professor of pathology came along, a man who had more the look of a sacristan than of a physician. Appointed by the powerful mandate of the Vice-Rector, without other merit than unconditional servility to the corporation, he passed for a spy and an informer in the eyes of the rest of the faculty.

The first professor returned his greeting coldly, and winked to Basilio, as he said to him, "Now I know that Capitan Tiago smells like a corpse—the crows and vultures have been gathering around him." So saying, he went inside.

Somewhat calmed, Basilio now ventured to inquire for more details, but all that he could learn was that pasquinades had been found on the doors of the University, and that the Vice-Rector had ordered them to be taken down and sent to the Civil Government. It was said that they were filled with threats of assassination, invasion, and other braggadocio.

The students made their comments on the affair. Their information came from the janitor, who had it from a servant in Santo Tomas, who had it from an usher. They prognosticated future suspensions and imprisonments, even indicating who were to be the victims—naturally the members of the association.

Basilio then recalled Simoun's words: "The day in which they can get rid of you, you will not complete your course."

"Could he have known anything?" he asked himself. "We'll see who is the most powerful."

Recovering his serenity, he went on toward the University, to learn what attitude it behooved him to take and at the same time to see about his licentiateship. He passed along Calle Legazpi, then down through Beaterio, and upon arriving at the corner of this street and Calle Solana saw that something important must indeed have happened. Instead of the former lively, chattering groups on the sidewalks were to be seen civil-guards making the students move on, and these latter issuing from the University silent, some gloomy, some agitated, to stand off at a distance or make their way home.

The first acquaintance he met was Sandoval, but Basilio called to him in vain. He seemed to have been smitten deaf. "Effect of fear on the gastro-intestinal juices," thought Basilio.

Later he met Tadeo, who wore a Christmas face—at last that eternal holiday seemed to be realized.

"What has happened, Tadeo?"

"We'll have no school, at least for a week, old man! Sublime! Magnificent!" He rubbed his hands in glee.

"But what has happened?"

"They're going to arrest all of us in the association."

"And are you glad of that?"

"There'll be no school, there'll be no school!" He moved away almost bursting with joy.

Basilio saw Juanito Pelaez approaching, pale and suspicious. This time his hump had reached its maximum, so great was his haste to get away. He had been one of the most active promoters of the association while things were running smoothly.

"Eh, Pelaez, what's happened?"

"Nothing, I know nothing. I didn't have anything to do with it," he responded nervously. "I was always telling you that these things were quixotisms. It's the truth, you know I've said so to you?"

Basilio did not remember whether he had said so or not, but to humor him replied, "Yes, man, but what's happened?"

"It's the truth, isn't it? Look, you're a witness: I've always been opposed—you're a witness, don't forget it!"

"Yes, man, but what's going on?"

"Listen, you're a witness! I've never had anything to do with the members of the association, except to give them advice. You're not going to deny it now. Be careful, won't you?"

"No, no, I won't deny it, but for goodness' sake, what has happened?"

But Juanito was already far away. He had caught a glimpse of a guard approaching and feared arrest.

Basilio then went on toward the University to see if perhaps the secretary's office might be open and if he could glean any further news. The office was closed, but there was an extraordinary commotion in the building. Hurrying up and down the stairways were friars, army officers, private persons, old lawyers and doctors, there doubtless to offer their services to the endangered cause.

At a distance he saw his friend Isagani, pale and agitated, but radiant with youthful ardor, haranguing some fellow students with his voice raised as though he cared little that he be heard by everybody.

"It seems preposterous, gentlemen, it seems unreal, that an incident so insignificant should scatter us and send us into flight like sparrows at whom a scarecrow has been shaken! But is this the first time that students have gone to prison for the sake of liberty? Where are those who have died, those who have been shot? Would you apostatize now?"

"But who can the fool be that wrote such pasquinades?" demanded an indignant listener.

"What does that matter to us?" rejoined Isagani. "We don't have to find out, let them find out! Before we know how they are drawn up, we have no need to make any show of agreement at a time like this. There where the danger is, there must we hasten, because honor is there! If what the pasquinades say is compatible with our dignity and our feelings, be he who he may that wrote them, he has done well, and we ought to be grateful to him and hasten to add our signatures to his! If they are unworthy of us, our conduct and our consciences will in themselves protest and defend us from every accusation!"

Upon hearing such talk, Basilio, although he liked Isagani very much, turned and left. He had to go to Makaraig's house to see about the loan.

Near the house of the wealthy student he observed whisperings and mysterious signals among the neighbors, but not comprehending what they meant, continued serenely on his way and entered the doorway. Two guards advanced and asked him what he wanted. Basilio realized that he had made a bad move, but he could not now retreat.

"I've come to see my friend Makaraig," he replied calmly.

The guards looked at each other. "Wait here," one of them said to him. "Wait till the corporal comes down."

Basilio bit his lips and Simoun's words again recurred to him. Had they come to arrest Makaraig?—was his thought, but he dared not give it utterance. He did not have to wait long, for in a few moments Makaraig came down, talking pleasantly with the corporal. The two were preceded by a warrant officer.

"What, you too, Basilio?" he asked.

"I came to see you—"

"Noble conduct!" exclaimed Makaraig laughing. "In time of calm, you avoid us."

The corporal asked Basilio his name, then scanned a list. "Medical student, Calle Anloague?" he asked.

Basilio bit his lip.

"You've saved us a trip," added the corporal, placing his hand on the youth's shoulder. "You're under arrest!"

"What, I also?"

Makaraig burst out into laughter.

"Don't worry, friend. Let's get into the carriage, while I tell you about the supper last night."

With a graceful gesture, as though he were in his own house, he invited the warrant officer and the corporal to enter the carriage that waited at the door.

"To the Civil Government!" he ordered the cochero.

Now that Basilio had again regained his composure, he told Makaraig the object of his visit. The rich student did not wait for him to finish, but seized his hand. "Count on me, count on me, and to the festivities celebrating our graduation we'll invite these gentlemen," he said, indicating the corporal and the warrant officer.

THE FRIAR AND THE FILIPINO

Vox populi, vox Dei

We left Isagani haranguing his friends. In the midst of his enthusiasm an usher approached him to say that Padre Fernandez, one of the higher professors, wished to talk with him.

Isagani's face fell. Padre Fernandez was a person greatly respected by him, being the *one* always excepted by him whenever the friars were attacked.

"What does Padre Fernandez want?" he inquired.

The usher shrugged his shoulders and Isagani reluctantly followed him.

Padre Fernandez, the friar whom we met in Los Baños, was waiting in his cell, grave and sad, with his brows knitted as if he were in deep thought. He arose as Isagani entered, shook hands with him, and closed the door. Then he began to pace from one end of the room to the other. Isagani stood waiting for him to speak.

"Señor Isagani," he began at length with some emotion, "from the window I've heard you speaking, for though I am a consumptive I have good ears, and I want to talk with you. I have always liked the young men who express themselves clearly and have their own way of thinking and acting, no matter that their ideas may differ from mine. You young men, from what I have heard, had a supper last night. Don't excuse yourself—"

"I don't intend to excuse myself!" interrupted Isagani.

"So much the better—it shows that you accept the consequences of your actions. Besides, you would do ill in retracting, and I don't blame you, I take no notice of what may have been said there last night, I don't accuse you, because after all you're free to say of the Dominicans what seems best to you, you are not a pupil of ours—only this year have we had the pleasure of having you, and we shall probably not have you longer. Don't think that I'm going to invoke considerations of gratitude; no, I'm not going to waste my time in stupid vulgarisms. I've had you summoned here because I believe that you are one of the few students who act from conviction, and, as I like men of conviction, I'm going to explain myself to Señor Isagani."

Padre Fernandez paused, then continued his walk with bowed head, his gaze riveted on the floor.

"You may sit down, if you wish," he remarked. "It's a habit of mine to walk about while talking, because my ideas come better then."

Isagani remained standing, with his head erect, waiting for the professor to get to the point of the matter.

"For more than eight years I have been a professor here," resumed Padre Fernandez, still continuing to pace back and forth, "and in that time I've known and dealt with more than twenty-five hundred students. I've taught them, I've tried to educate them, I've tried to inculcate in them principles of justice and of dignity, and yet in these days when there is so much murmuring against us I've not seen one who has the temerity to maintain his accusations when he finds himself in the presence of a friar, not even aloud in the presence of any numbers. Young men there are who behind our backs calumniate us and before us kiss our hands, with a base smile begging kind looks from us! Bah! What do you wish that we should do with such creatures?"

"The fault is not all theirs, Padre," replied Isagani. "The fault lies partly with those who have taught them to be hypocrites, with those who have tyrannized over freedom of thought and freedom of speech. Here every independent thought, every word that is not an echo of the will of those in power, is characterized as filibusterism, and you know well enough what that means. A fool would he be who to please himself would say aloud what he thinks, who would lay himself liable to suffer persecution!"

"What persecution have you had to suffer?" asked Padre Fernandez, raising his head. "Haven't I let you express yourself freely in my class? Nevertheless, you are an exception that, if what you say is true, I must correct, so as to make the rule as general as possible and thus avoid setting a bad example."

Isagani smiled. "I thank you, but I will not discuss with you whether I am an exception. I will accept your qualification so that you may accept mine: you also are an exception, and as here we are not going to talk about exceptions, nor plead for ourselves, at least, I mean, *I'm not*, I beg of my *professor* to change the course of the conversation."

In spite of his liberal principles, Padre Fernandez raised his head and stared in surprise at Isagani. That young man was more independent than he had thought—although he called him *professor*, in reality he was dealing with him as an equal, since he allowed himself to offer suggestions. Like a wise diplomat, Padre Fernandez not only recognized the fact but even took his stand upon it.

"Good enough!" he said. "But don't look upon me as your professor. I'm a friar and you are a Filipino student, nothing more nor less! Now I ask you—what do the Filipino students want of us?"

The question came as a surprise; Isagani was not prepared for it. It was a thrust made suddenly while they were preparing their defense, as they say in fencing. Thus startled, Isagani responded with a violent stand, like a beginner defending himself.

"That you do your duty!" he exclaimed.

Fray Fernandez straightened up—that reply sounded to him like a cannon-shot. "That we do our duty!" he repeated, holding himself erect. "Don't we, then, do our duty? What duties do you ascribe to us?"

"Those which you voluntarily placed upon yourselves on joining the order, and those which afterwards, once in it, you have been willing to assume. But, as a Filipino student, I don't think myself called upon to examine your conduct with reference to your statutes, to Catholicism, to the government, to the Filipino people, and to humanity in general—those are questions that you have to settle with your founders, with the Pope, with the government, with the whole people, and with God. As a Filipino student, I will confine myself to your duties toward us. The friars in general, being the local supervisors of education in the provinces, and the Dominicans in particular, by monopolizing in their hands all the studies of the Filipino youth, have assumed the obligation to its eight millions of inhabitants, to Spain, and to humanity, of which we form a part, of steadily bettering the young plant, morally and physically, of training it toward its happiness, of creating a people honest, prosperous, intelligent, virtuous, noble, and loyal. Now I ask you in my turn—have the friars fulfilled that obligation of theirs?"

"We're fulfilling—"

"Ah, Padre Fernandez," interrupted Isagani, "you with your hand on *your* heart can say that you are fulfilling it, but with your hand on the heart of your order, on the heart of all the orders, you cannot say that without deceiving yourself. Ah, Padre Fernandez, when I find myself in the presence of a person whom I esteem and respect, I prefer to be the accused rather than the accuser, I prefer to defend myself rather than take the offensive. But now that we have entered upon the discussion, let us carry it to the end! How do they fulfill their obligation, those who look after education in the towns? By hindering it! And those who here monopolize education, those who try to mold the mind of youth, to the exclusion of all others whomsoever, how do they carry out their mission? By curtailing knowledge as much as possible, by extinguishing all ardor and enthusiasm, by trampling on all dignity, the soul's only refuge, by inculcating in us worn-out ideas, rancid beliefs, false principles incompatible with a life of progress! Ah, yes, when it is a question of feeding convicts, of providing for the maintenance of criminals, the government calls for bids in order to find the purveyor who offers the best means of subsistence, he who at least will not let them perish from hunger, but when it is a question of morally feeding a whole people, of nourishing the intellect of youth, the healthiest part, that which is later to be the country and the all, the government not only does not ask for any bid, but restricts the power to that very body which makes a boast of not desiring education, of wishing no advancement. What should we say if the purveyor for the prisons, after securing the contract by intrigue, should then leave the prisoners to languish in want, giving them only what is stale and rancid, excusing himself afterwards by saying that it is not convenient for the prisoners to enjoy good health, because good health brings merry thoughts, because merriment improves the man, and the man ought not to be improved, because it is to the purveyor's interest that there be many criminals? What should we say if afterwards the government and the purveyor should agree between themselves that of the ten or twelve cuartos which one received for each criminal, the other should receive five?"

Padre Fernandek bit his lip. "Those are grave charges," he said, "and you are overstepping the limits of our agreement."

"No, Padre, not if I continue to deal with the student question. The friars—and I do not say, you friars, since I do not confuse you with the common herd—the friars of all the orders have constituted themselves our mental purveyors, yet they say and shamelessly proclaim that it is not expedient for us to become enlightened, because some day we shall declare ourselves free! That is just the same as not wishing the prisoner to be well-fed so that he may improve and get out of prison. Liberty is to man what education is to the intelligence, and the friars' unwillingness that we have it is the origin of our discontent."

"Instruction is given only to those who deserve it," rejoined Padre Fernandez dryly. "To give it to men without character and without morality is to prostitute it."

"Why are there men without character and without morality?"

The Dominican shrugged his shoulders. "Defects that they imbibe with their mothers' milk, that they breathe in the bosom of the family—how do I know?"

"Ah, no, Padre Fernandez!" exclaimed the young man impetuously. "You have not dared to go into the subject deeply, you have not wished to gaze into the depths from fear of finding yourself there in the darkness of your brethren. What we are, you have made us. A people tyrannized over is forced to be hypocritical; a people denied the truth must resort to lies; and he who makes himself a tyrant breeds slaves. There is no morality, you say, so let it be—even though statistics can refute you in that here are not committed crimes like those among other peoples, blinded by the fumes of their moralizers. But, without attempting now to analyze what it is that forms the character and how far the education received determines morality, I will agree with you that we are defective. Who is to blame for that? You who for three centuries and a half have had in your hands our education, or we who submit to everything? If after three centuries and a half the artist has been able to produce only a caricature, stupid indeed he must be!"

"Or bad enough the material he works upon."

"Stupider still then, when, knowing it to be bad, he does not give it up, but goes on wasting time. Not only is he stupid, but he is a cheat and a robber, because he knows that his work is useless, yet continues to draw his salary. Not only is he stupid and a thief, he is a villain in that he prevents any other workman from trying his skill to see if he might not produce something worth while! The deadly jealousy of the incompetent!"

The reply was sharp and Padre Fernandez felt himself caught. To his gaze Isagani appeared gigantic, invincible, convincing, and for the first time in his life he felt beaten by a Filipino student. He repented of having provoked the argument, but it was too late to turn back. In this quandary, finding himself confronted with such a formidable adversary, he sought a strong shield and laid hold of the government.

"You impute all the faults to us, because you see only us, who are near," he said in a less haughty tone. "It's natural and doesn't surprise me. A person hates the soldier or policeman who arrests him and not the judge who sends him to prison. You and we are both dancing to the same measure of music—if at the same note you lift your foot in unison with us, don't blame us for it, it's the music that is directing our movements. Do you think that we friars have no consciences and that we do not desire what is right? Do you believe that we do not think about you, that we do not heed our duty, that we only eat to live, and live to rule? Would that it were so! But we, like you, follow the cadence, finding ourselves between Scylla and Charybdis: either you reject us or the government rejects us. The government commands, and he who commands, commands,—and must be obeyed!"

"From which it may be inferred," remarked Isagani with a bitter smile, "that the government wishes our demoralization."

"Oh, no, I didn't mean that! What I meant to say is that there are beliefs, there are theories, there are laws, which, dictated with the best intention, produce the most deplorable consequences. I'll explain myself better by citing an example. To stamp out a small evil, there are dictated many laws that cause greater evils still: '*corruptissima in republica plurimae leges,*' said Tacitus. To prevent one case of fraud, there are provided a million and a half preventive or humiliating regulations, which produce the immediate effect of awakening in the public the desire to elude and mock such regulations. To make a people criminal, there's nothing more needed than to doubt its virtue. Enact a law, not only here, but even in Spain, and you will see how the means of evading it will be sought, and this is for the very reason that the legislators have overlooked the fact that the more an object is hidden, the more a sight of it is desired. Why are rascality and astuteness regarded as great qualities in the Spanish people, when there is no other so noble, so proud, so chivalrous as it? Because our legislators, with the best intentions, have doubted its nobility, wounded its pride, challenged its chivalry! Do you wish to open in Spain a road among the rocks? Then place there an imperative notice forbidding the passage, and the people, in order to protest against the order, will leave the highway to clamber over the rocks. The day on which some legislator in Spain forbids virtue and commands vice, then all will become virtuous!"

The Dominican paused for a brief space, then resumed: "But you may say that we are getting away from the subject, so I'll return to it. What I can say to you, to convince you, is that the vices from which you suffer ought to be ascribed by you neither to us nor to the government. They are due to the imperfect organization of our social system: *qui multum probat, nihil probat*, one loses himself through excessive caution, lacking what is necessary and having too much of what is superfluous."

"If you admit those defects in your social system," replied Isagani, "why then do you undertake to regulate alien societies, instead of first devoting your attention to yourselves?"

"We're getting away from the subject, young man. The theory in accomplished facts must be accepted."

"So let it be! I accept it because it is an accomplished fact, but I will further ask: why, if your social organization is defective, do you not change it or at least give heed to the cry of those who are injured by it?"

"We're still far away. Let's talk about what the students want from the friars."

"From the moment when the friars hide themselves behind the government, the students have to turn to it."

This statement was true and there appeared no means of ignoring it.

"I'm not the government and I can't answer for its acts. What do the students wish us to do for them within the limits by which we are confined?"

"Not to oppose the emancipation of education but to favor it."

The Dominican shook his head. "Without stating my own opinion, that is asking us to commit suicide," he said.

"On the contrary, it is asking you for room to pass in order not to trample upon and crush you."

"Ahem!" coughed Padre Fernandez, stopping and remaining thoughtful. "Begin by asking something that does not cost so much, something that any one of us can grant without abatement of dignity or privilege, for if we can reach an understanding and dwell in peace, why this hatred, why this distrust?"

"Then let's get down to details."

"Yes, because if we disturb the foundation, we'll bring down the whole edifice."

"Then let's get down to details, let's leave the region of abstract principles," rejoined Isagani with a smile, "and *also without stating my own opinion*,"—the youth accented these words—"the students would desist from their attitude and soften certain asperities if the professors would try to treat them better than they have up to the present. That is in their hands."

"What?" demanded the Dominican. "Have the students any complaint to make about my conduct?"

"Padre, we agreed from the start not to talk of yourself or of myself, we're speaking generally. The students, besides getting no great benefit out of the years spent in the classes, often leave there remnants of their dignity, if not the whole of it."

Padre Fernandez again bit his lip. "No one forces them to study—the fields are uncultivated," he observed dryly.

"Yes, there is something that impels them to study," replied Isagani in the same tone, looking the Dominican full in the face. "Besides the duty of every one to seek his own perfection, there is the desire innate in man to cultivate his intellect, a desire the more powerful here in that it is repressed. He who gives his gold and his life to the State has the right to require of it opportunity better to get that gold and better to care for his life. Yes, Padre, there is something that impels them, and that something is the government itself. It is you yourselves who pitilessly ridicule the uncultured Indian and deny him his rights, on the ground that he is ignorant. You strip him and then scoff at his nakedness."

Padre Fernandez did not reply, but continued to pace about feverishly, as though very much agitated.

"You say that the fields are not cultivated," resumed Isagani in a changed tone, after a brief pause. "Let's not enter upon an analysis of the reason for this, because we should get far away. But you, Padre Fernandez, you, a teacher, you, a learned man, do you wish a people of peons and laborers? In your opinion, is the laborer the perfect state at which man may arrive in his development? Or is it that you wish knowledge for yourself and labor for the rest?"

"No, I want knowledge for him who deserves it, for him who knows how to use it," was the reply. "When the students demonstrate that they love it, when young men of conviction appear, young men who know how to maintain their dignity and make it respected, then there will be knowledge, then there will be considerate professors! If there are now professors who resort to abuse, it is because there are pupils who submit to it."

"When there are professors, there will be students!"

"Begin by reforming yourselves, you who have need of change, and we will follow."

"Yes," said Isagani with a bitter laugh, "let us begin it, because the difficulty is on our side. Well you know what is expected of a pupil who stands before a professor—you yourself, with all your love of justice, with all your kind sentiments, have been restraining yourself by a great effort while I have been telling you bitter truths, you yourself, Padre Fernandez! What good has been secured by him among us who has tried to inculcate other ideas? What evils have not fallen upon you because you have tried to be just and perform your duty?"

"Señor Isagani," said the Dominican, extending his hand, "although it may seem that nothing practical has resulted from this conversation, yet something has been gained. I'll talk to my brethren about what you have told me and I hope that something can be done. Only I fear that they won't believe in your existence."

"I fear the same," returned Isagani, shaking the Dominican's hand. "I fear that my friends will not believe in your existence, as you have revealed yourself to me today."

Considering the interview at an end, the young man took his leave.

Padre Fernandez opened the door and followed him with his gaze until he disappeared around a corner in the corridor. For some time he listened to the retreating footsteps, then went back into his cell and waited for the youth to appear in the street.

He saw him and actually heard him say to a friend who asked where he was going: "To the Civil Government! I'm going to see the pasquinades and join the others!"

His startled friend stared at him as one would look at a person who is about to commit suicide, then moved away from him hurriedly.

"Poor boy!" murmured Padre Fernandez, feeling his eyes moisten. "I grudge you to the Jesuits who educated you."

But Padre Fernandez was completely mistaken; the Jesuits repudiated Isagani[2] when that afternoon they learned that he had been arrested, saying that he would compromise them. "That young man has thrown himself away, he's going to do us harm! Let it be understood that he didn't get those ideas here."

Nor were the Jesuits wrong. No! Those ideas come only from God through the medium of Nature.

---

1   "We do not believe in the verisimilitude of this dialogue, fabricated by the author in order to refute the arguments of the friars, whose pride was so great that it would not permit any Isagani to tell them these truths face to face. The *invention* of Padre Fernandez as a Dominican professor is a stroke of generosity on Rizal's part, in conceding that there could have existed *any* friar capable of talking frankly with an *Indian*."—*W. E. Retana, in note to this chapter in the edition published by him at Barcelona in 1908.* Retana ought to know of what he is writing, for he was in the employ of the friars for several years and later in Spain wrote extensively for the journal supported by them to defend their position in the Philippines. He has also been charged with having strongly urged Rizal's execution in 1896. Since 1898, however, he has doubled about, or, perhaps more aptly, performed a journalistic somersault—having written a diffuse biography and other works dealing with Rizal. He is strong in unassorted facts, but his comments, when not inane and wearisome, approach a maudlin wail over "spilt milk," so the above is given at its face value only.—Tr.

2   Quite suggestive of, and perhaps inspired by, the author's own experience.—Tr.

TATAKUT

With prophetic inspiration Ben-Zayb had been for some days past maintaining in his newspaper that education was disastrous, very disastrous for the Philippine Islands, and now in view of the events of that Friday of pasquinades, the writer crowed and chanted his triumph, leaving belittled and overwhelmed his adversary *Horatius*, who in the *Pirotecnia* had dared to ridicule him in the following manner:

> From our contemporary, *El Grito*:
> "Education is disastrous, very disastrous, for the Philippine Islands."
> Admitted.
> For some time *El Grito* has pretended to represent the Filipino people—*ergo*, as Fray Ibañez would say, if he knew Latin.
> But Fray Ibañez turns Mussulman when he writes, and we know how the Mussulmans dealt with education. *In witness whereof*, as a royal preacher said, the Alexandrian library!

Now he was right, he, Ben-Zayb! He was the only one in the islands who thought, the only one who foresaw events!

Truly, the news that seditious pasquinades had been found on the doors of the University not only took away the appetite from many and disturbed the digestion of others, but it even rendered the phlegmatic Chinese uneasy, so that they no longer dared to sit in their shops with one leg drawn up as usual, from fear of losing time in extending it in order to put themselves into flight. At eight o'clock in the morning, although the sun continued on its course and his Excellency, the Captain-General, did not appear at the head of his victorious cohorts, still the excitement had increased. The friars who were accustomed to frequent Quiroga's bazaar did not put in their appearance, and this symptom presaged terrific cataclysms. If the sun had risen a square and the saints appeared only in pantaloons, Quiroga would not have been so greatly alarmed, for he would have taken the sun for a gaming-table and the sacred images for gamblers who had lost their camisas, but for the friars not to come, precisely when some novelties had just arrived for them!

By means of a provincial friend of his, Quiroga forbade entrance into his gaming-houses to every Indian who was not an old acquaintance, as the future Chinese consul feared that they might get possession of the sums that the wretches lost there. After arranging his bazaar in such a way that he could close it quickly in case of need, he had a policeman accompany him for the short distance that separated his house from Simoun's. Quiroga thought this occasion the most propitious for making use of the rifles and cartridges that he had in his warehouse, in the way the jeweler had pointed out; so that on the following days there would be searches made, and then—how many prisoners, how many terrified people would give up their savings! It was the game of the old carbineers, in slipping contraband cigars and tobacco-leaves under a house, in order to pretend a search and force the unfortunate owner to bribery or fines, only now the art had been perfected and, the tobacco monopoly abolished, resort was had to the prohibited arms.

But Simoun refused to see any one and sent word to the Chinese that he should leave things as they were, whereupon he went to see Don Custodio to inquire whether he should fortify his bazaar, but neither would Don Custodio receive him, being at the time engaged in the study of a project for defense in case of a siege. He thought of Ben-Zayb as a source of information, but finding the writer armed to the teeth and using two loaded revolvers for paper-weights, took his leave in the shortest possible time, to shut himself up in his house and take to his bed under pretense of illness.

At four in the afternoon the talk was no longer of simple pasquinades. There were whispered rumors of an understanding between the students and the outlaws of San Mateo, it was certain that in the *pansitería* they had conspired to surprise the city, there was talk of German ships outside the bay to support the movement, of a band of young men who under the pretext of protesting and demonstrating their Hispanism had gone to the Palace to place themselves at the General's orders but had been arrested because it was discovered that they were armed. Providence had saved his Excellency, preventing him from receiving those precocious criminals, as he was at the time in conference with the Provincials, the Vice-Rector, and with Padre Irene, Padre Salvi's representative. There was considerable truth in these rumors, if we have to believe Padre Irene, who in the afternoon went to visit Capitan Tiago. According to him, certain persons had advised his Excellency to improve the opportunity in order to inspire terror and administer a lasting lesson to the filibusters.

"A number shot," one had advised, "some two dozen reformers deported at once, in the silence of the night, would extinguish forever the flames of discontent."

"No," rejoined another, who had a kind heart, "sufficient that the soldiers parade through the streets, a troop of cavalry, for example, with drawn sabers—sufficient to drag along some cannon, that's enough! The people are timid and will all retire into their houses."

"No, no," insinuated another. "This is the opportunity to get rid of the enemy. It's not sufficient that they retire into their houses, they should be made to come out, like evil humors by means of plasters. If they are inclined to start riots, they should be stirred up by secret agitators. I am of the opinion that the troops should be resting on their arms and appearing careless and indifferent, so the people may be emboldened, and then in case of any disturbance— out on them, action!"

"The end justifies the means," remarked another. "Our end is our holy religion and the integrity of the fatherland. Proclaim a state of siege, and in case of the least disturbance, arrest all the rich and educated, and—clean up the country!"

"If I hadn't got there in time to counsel moderation," added Padre Irene, speaking to Capitan Tiago, "it's certain that blood would now be flowing through the streets. I thought of you, Capitan— The partizans of force couldn't do much with the General, and they missed Simoun. Ah, if Simoun had not been taken ill—"

With the arrest of Basilio and the search made later among his books and papers, Capitan Tiago had become much worse. Now Padre Irene had come to augment his terror with hair-raising tales. Ineffable fear seized upon the wretch, manifesting itself first by a light shiver, which was rapidly accentuated, until he was unable to speak. With his eyes bulging and his brow covered with sweat, he caught Padre Irene's arm and tried to rise, but could not, and then, uttering two groans, fell heavily back upon the pillow. His eyes were wide open and he was slavering—but he was dead. The terrified Padre Irene fled, and, as the dying man had caught hold of him, in his flight he dragged the corpse from the bed, leaving it sprawling in the middle of the room.

By night the terror had reached a climax. Several incidents had occurred to make the timorous believe in the presence of secret agitators.

During a baptism some cuartos were thrown to the boys and naturally there was a scramble at the door of the church. It happened that at the time there was passing a bold soldier, who, somewhat preoccupied, mistook the uproar for a gathering of filibusters and hurled himself, sword in hand, upon the boys. He went into the church, and had he not become entangled in the curtains suspended from the choir he would not have left a single head on shoulders. It was but the matter of a moment for the timorous to witness this and take to flight, spreading the news that the revolution had begun. The few shops that had been kept open were now hastily closed, there being Chinese who even left bolts of cloth outside, and not a few women lost their slippers in their flight through the streets. Fortunately, there was only one person wounded and a few bruised, among them the soldier himself, who suffered a fall fighting with the curtain, which smelt to him of filibusterism. Such prowess gained him great renown, and a renown so pure that it is to be wished all fame could be acquired in like manner—mothers would then weep less and earth would be more populous!

In a suburb the inhabitants caught two unknown individuals burying arms under a house, whereupon a tumult arose and the people pursued the strangers in order to kill them and turn their bodies over to the authorities, but some one pacified the excited crowd by telling them that it would be sufficient to hand over the *corpora delictorum*, which proved to be some old shotguns that would surely have killed the first person who tried to fire them.

"All right," exclaimed one braggart, "if they want us to rebel, let's go ahead!" But he was cuffed and kicked into silence, the women pinching him as though he had been the owner of the shotguns.

In Ermita the affair was more serious, even though there was less excitement, and that when there were shots fired. A certain cautious government employee, armed to the teeth, saw at nightfall an object near his house, and taking it for nothing less than a student, fired at it twice with a revolver. The object proved to be a policeman, and they buried him—*pax Christi! Mutis!*

In Dulumbayan various shots also resounded, from which there resulted the death of a poor old deaf man, who had not heard the sentinel's *quién vive*, and of a hog that had heard it and had not answered *España!* The old man was buried with difficulty, since there was no money to pay for the obsequies, but the hog was eaten.

In Manila,[1] in a confectionery near the University much frequented by the students, the arrests were thus commented upon.

"And have they arrested Tadeo?"[2] asked the proprietess.

"*Abá!*" answered a student who lived in Parian, "he's already shot!"

"Shot! *Nakú!* He hasn't paid what he owes me."

"Ay, don't mention that or you'll be taken for an accomplice. I've already burnt the book[3] you lent me. There might be a search and it would be found. Be careful!"

"Did you say that Isagani is a prisoner?"

"Crazy fool, too, that Isagani," replied the indignant student. "They didn't try to catch him, but he went and surrendered. Let him bust himself—he'll surely be shot."

The señora shrugged her shoulders. "He doesn't owe me anything. And what about Paulita?"

"She won't lack a husband. Sure, she'll cry a little, and then marry a Spaniard."

The night was one of the gloomiest. In the houses the rosary was recited and pious women dedicated paternosters and requiems to each of the souls of their relatives and friends. By eight o'clock hardly a pedestrian could be seen—only from time to time was heard the galloping of a horse against whose sides a saber clanked noisily, then the whistles of the watchmen, and carriages that whirled along at full speed, as though pursued by mobs of filibusters.

Yet terror did not reign everywhere. In the house of the silversmith, where Placido Penitente boarded, the events were commented upon and discussed with some freedom.

"I don't believe in the pasquinades," declared a workman, lank and withered from operating the blowpipe. "To me it looks like Padre Salvi's doings."

"Ahem, ahem!" coughed the silversmith, a very prudent man, who did not dare to stop the conversation from fear that he would be considered a coward. The good man had to content himself with coughing, winking to his helper, and gazing toward the street, as if to say, "They may be watching us!"

"On account of the operetta," added another workman.

"Aha!" exclaimed one who had a foolish face, "I told you so!"

"Ahem!" rejoined a clerk, in a tone of compassion, "the affair of the pasquinades is true, Chichoy, and I can give you the explanation."

Then he added mysteriously, "It's a trick of the Chinaman Quiroga's!"

"Ahem, ahem!" again coughed the silversmith, shifting his quid of buyo from one cheek to the other.

"Believe me, Chichoy, of Quiroga the Chinaman! I heard it in the office."

"*Nakú*, it's certain then," exclaimed the simpleton, believing it at once.

"Quiroga," explained the clerk, "has a hundred thousand pesos in Mexican silver out in the bay. How is he to get it in? Very easily. Fix up the pasquinades, availing himself of the question of the students, and, while every-body is excited, grease the officials' palms, and in the cases come!"

"Just it! Just it!" cried the credulous fool, striking the table with his fist. "Just it! That's why Quiroga did it! That's why—" But he had to relapse into silence as he really did not know what to say about Quiroga.

"And we must pay the damages?" asked the indignant Chichoy.

"Ahem, ahem, a-h-hem!" coughed the silversmith, hearing steps in the street.

The footsteps approached and all in the shop fell silent.

"St. Pascual Bailon is a great saint," declared the silversmith hypocritically, in a loud voice, at the same time winking to the others. "St. Pascual Bailon—"

At that moment there appeared the face of Placido Penitente, who was accompanied by the pyrotechnician that we saw receiving orders from Simoun. The newcomers were surrounded and importuned for news.

"I haven't been able to talk with the prisoners," explained Placido. "There are some thirty of them."

"Be on your guard," cautioned the pyrotechnician, exchanging a knowing look with Placido. "They say that to-night there's going to be a massacre."

"Aha! Thunder!" exclaimed Chichoy, looking about for a weapon. Seeing none, he caught up his blowpipe.

The silversmith sat down, trembling in every limb. The credulous simpleton already saw himself beheaded and wept in anticipation over the fate of his family.

"No," contradicted the clerk, "there's not going to be any massacre. The adviser of"—he made a mysterious gesture—"is fortunately sick."

"Simoun!"

"Ahem, ahem, a-h-hem!"

Placido and the pyrotechnician exchanged another look.

"If he hadn't got sick—"

"It would look like a revolution," added the pyrotechnician negligently, as he lighted a cigarette in the lamp chimney. "And what should we do then?"

"Then we'd start a real one, now that they're going to massacre us anyhow—"

The violent fit of coughing that seized the silversmith prevented the rest of this speech from being heard, but Chichoy must have been saying terrible things, to judge from his murderous gestures with the blowpipe and the face of a Japanese tragedian that he put on.

"Rather say that he's playing off sick because he's afraid to go out. As may be seen—"

The silversmith was attacked by another fit of coughing so severe that he finally asked all to retire.

"Nevertheless, get ready," warned the pyrotechnician. "If they want to force us to kill or be killed—"

Another fit of coughing on the part of the poor silversmith prevented further conversation, so the workmen and apprentices retired to their homes, carrying with them hammers and saws, and other implements, more or less cutting, more or less bruising, disposed to sell their lives dearly. Placido and the pyrotechnician went out again.

"Prudence, prudence!" cautioned the silversmith in a tearful voice.

"You'll take care of my widow and orphans!" begged the credulous simpleton in a still more tearful voice, for he already saw himself riddled with bullets and buried.

That night the guards at the city gates were replaced with Peninsular artillerymen, and on the following morning as the sun rose, Ben-Zayb, who had ventured to take a morning stroll to examine the condition of the fortifications, found on the glacis near the Luneta the corpse of a native girl, half-naked and abandoned. Ben-Zayb was horrified, but after touching it with his cane and gazing toward the gates proceeded on his way, musing over a sentimental tale he might base upon the incident.

However, no allusion to it appeared in the newspapers on the following days, engrossed as they were with the falls and slippings caused by banana-peels. In the dearth of news Ben-Zayb had to comment at length on a cyclone that had destroyed in America whole towns, causing the death of more than two thousand persons. Among other beautiful things he said:

"*The sentiment of charity*, MORE PREVALENT IN CATHOLIC COUNTRIES THAN IN OTHERS, and the thought of Him who, influenced by that same feeling, sacrificed himself for *humanity, moves (sic)* us to compassion over the misfortunes of our kind and to render thanks that *in this country*, so scourged by cyclones, there are not enacted scenes so desolating as that which the inhabitants of the United States mus have witnessed!"

Horatius did not miss the opportunity, and, also without mentioning the dead, or the murdered native girl, or the assaults, answered him in his *Pirotecnia*:

"After such great charity and such great humanity, Fray Ibañez—I mean, Ben-Zayb—brings himself to pray for the Philippines.

But he is understood.

Because he is not Catholic, and the sentiment of charity is most prevalent," etc.'

---

1   The Walled City, the original Manila, is still known to the Spaniards and older natives exclusively as such, the other districts being referred to by their distinctive names.—Tr.

2   Nearly all the dialogue in this chapter is in the mongrel Spanish-Tagalog "market language," which cannot be reproduced in English.—Tr.

3   Doubtless a reference to the author's first work, *Noli Me Tangere*, which was tabooed by the authorities.—Tr.

4   Such inanities as these are still a feature of Manila journalism.—Tr.

EXIT CAPITAN TIAGO

Talis vita, finis ita

Capitan Tiago had a good end—that is, a quite exceptional funeral. True it is that the curate of the parish had ventured the observation to Padre Irene that Capitan Tiago had died without confession, but the good priest, smiling sardonically, had rubbed the tip of his nose and answered:

"Why say that to me? If we had to deny the obsequies to all who die without confession, we should forget the *De profundis!* These restrictions, as you well know, are enforced when the impenitent is also insolvent. But Capitan Tiago—out on you! You've buried infidel Chinamen, and with a requiem mass!"

Capitan Tiago had named Padre Irene as his executor and willed his property in part to St. Clara, part to the Pope, to the Archbishop, the religious corporations, leaving twenty pesos for the matriculation of poor students. This last clause had been dictated at the suggestion of Padre Irene, in his capacity as protector of studious youths. Capitan Tiago had annulled a legacy of twenty-five pesos that he had left to Basilio, in view of the ungrateful conduct of the boy during the last few days, but Padre Irene had restored it and announced that he would take it upon his own purse and conscience.

In the dead man's house, where were assembled on the following day many old friends and acquaintances, considerable comment was indulged in over a miracle. It was reported that, at the very moment when he was dying, the soul of Capitan Tiago had appeared to the nuns surrounded by a brilliant light. God had saved him, thanks to the pious legacies, and to the numerous masses he had paid for. The story was commented upon, it was recounted vividly, it took on particulars, and was doubted by no one. The appearance of Capitan Tiago was minutely described—of course the frock coat, the cheek bulged out by the quid of buyo, without omitting the game-cock and the opium-pipe. The senior sacristan, who was present, gravely affirmed these facts with his head and reflected that, after death, he would appear with his cup of white *tajú*, for without that refreshing breakfast he could not comprehend happiness either on earth or in heaven.

On this subject, because of their inability to discuss the events of the preceding day and because there were gamblers present, many strange speculations were developed. They made conjectures as to whether Capitan Tiago would invite St. Peter to a *soltada*, whether they would place bets, whether the game-cocks were immortal, whether invulnerable, and in this case who would be the referee, who would win, and so on: discussions quite to the taste of those who found sciences, theories, and systems, based on a text which they esteem infallible, revealed or dogmatic. Moreover, there were cited passages from novenas, books of miracles, sayings of the curates, descriptions of heaven, and other embroidery. Don Primitivo, the philosopher, was in his glory quoting opinions of the theologians.

"Because no one can lose," he stated with great authority. "To lose would cause hard feelings and in heaven there can't be any hard feelings."

"But some one has to win," rejoined the gambler Aristorenas. "The fun lies in winning!"

"Well, both win, that's easy!"

This idea of both winning could not be admitted by Aristorenas, for he had passed his life in the cockpit and had always seen one cock lose and the other win—at best, there was a tie. Vainly Don Primitivo argued in Latin. Aristorenas shook his head, and that too when Don Primitivo's Latin was easy to understand, for he talked of *an gallus talisainus, acuto tari armatus, an gallus beati Petri bulikus sasabungÞus sit,* and so on, until at length he decided to resort to the argument which many use to convince and silence their opponents.

"You're going to be damned, friend Martin, you're falling into heresy! *Cave ne cadas!* I'm not going to play monte with you any more, and we'll not set up a bank together. You deny the omnipotence of God, *peccatum mortale!* You deny the existence of the Holy Trinity—

three are one and one is three! Take care! You indirectly deny that two natures, two understandings, and two wills can have only one memory! Be careful! *Quicumque non crederit anathema sit!*"

Martin Aristorenas shrank away pale and trembling, while Quiroga, who had listened with great attention to the argument, with marked deference offered the philosopher a magnificent cigar, at the same time asking in his caressing voice: "Surely, one can make a contract for a cockpit with Kilisto,² ha? When I die, I'll be the contractor, ha?"

Among the others, they talked more of the deceased; at least they discussed what kind of clothing to put on him. Capitan Tinong proposed a Franciscan habit—and fortunately, he had one, old, threadbare, and patched, a precious object which, according to the friar who gave it to him as alms in exchange for thirty-six pesos, would preserve the corpse from the flames of hell and which reckoned in its support various pious anecdotes taken from the books distributed by the curates. Although he held this relic in great esteem, Capitan Tinong was disposed to part with it for the sake of his intimate friend, whom he had not been able to visit during his illness. But a tailor objected, with good reason, that since the nuns had seen Capitan Tiago ascending to heaven in a frock coat, in a frock coat he should be dressed here on earth, nor was there any necessity for preservatives and fire-proof garments. The deceased had attended balls and fiestas in a frock coat, and nothing else would be expected of him in the skies—and, wonderful to relate, the tailor accidentally happened to have one ready, which he would part with for thirty-two pesos, four cheaper than the Franciscan habit, because he didn't want to make any profit on Capitan Tiago, who had been his customer in life and would now be his patron in heaven. But Padre Irene, trustee and executor, rejected both proposals and ordered that the Capitan be dressed in one of his old suits of clothes, remarking with holy unction that God paid no attention to clothing.

The obsequies were, therefore, of the very first class. There were responsories in the house, and in the street three friars officiated, as though one were not sufficient for such a great soul. All the rites and ceremonies possible were performed, and it is reported that there were even *extras*, as in the benefits for actors. It was indeed a delight: loads of incense were burned, there were plenty of Latin chants, large quantities of holy water were expended, and Padre Irene, out of regard for his old friend, sang the *Dies Irae* in a falsetto voice from the choir, while the neighbors suffered real headaches from so much knell-ringing.

Doña Patrocinio, the ancient rival of Capitan Tiago in religiosity, actually wanted to die on the next day, so that she might order even more sumptuous obsequies. The pious old lady could not bear the thought that he, whom she had long considered vanquished forever, should in dying come forward again with so much pomp. Yes, she desired to die, and it seemed that she could hear the exclamations of the people at the funeral: "This indeed is what you call a funeral! This indeed is to know how to die, Doña Patrocinio!"

---

1   "Whether there would be a *talisain* cock, armed with a sharp gaff, whether the blessed Peter's fighting-cock would be a *bulik*—"

    Talisain and *bulik* are distinguishing terms in the vernacular for fighting-cocks, *tari* and *sasabungþin* the Tagalog terms for "gaff" and "game-cock," respectively.

    The Tagalog terminology of the cockpit and monkish Latin certainly make a fearful and wonderful mixture—nor did the author have to resort to his imagination to get samples of it.—Tr.

2   This is Quiroga's pronunciation of *Christo.*—Tr.

JULI

The death of Capitan Tiago and Basilio's imprisonment were soon reported in the province, and to the honor of the simple inhabitants of San Diego, let it be recorded that the latter was the incident more regretted and almost the only one discussed. As was to be expected, the report took on different forms, sad and startling details were given, what could not be understood was explained, the gaps being filled by conjectures, which soon passed for accomplished facts, and the phantoms thus created terrified their own creators.

In the town of Tiani it was reported that at least, at the very least, the young man was going to be deported and would very probably be murdered on the journey. The timorous and pessimistic were not satisfied with this but even talked about executions and courts-martial—January was a fatal month; in January the Cavite affair had occurred, and *they* even though curates, had been garroted, so a poor Basilio without protectors or friends—

"I told him so!" sighed the Justice of the Peace, as if he had at some time given advice to Basilio. "I told him so."

"It was to be expected," commented Sister Penchang. "He would go into the church and when he saw that the holy water was somewhat dirty he wouldn't cross himself with it. He talked about germs and disease, *abá*, it's the chastisement of God! He deserved it, and he got it! As though the holy water could transmit diseases! Quite the contrary, *abá!*"

She then related how she had cured herself of indigestion by moistening her stomach with holy water, at the same time reciting the *Sanctus Deus*, and she recommended the remedy to those present when they should suffer from dysentery, or an epidemic occurred, only that then they must pray in Spanish:

Santo Diós,
Santo fuerte,
Santo inmortal,
¡Libranos, Señor, de la peste
Y de todo mal!²

"It's an infallible remedy, but you must apply the holy water to the part affected," she concluded.

But there were many persons who did not believe in these things, nor did they attribute Basilio's imprisonment to the chastisement of God. Nor did they take any stock in insurrections and pasquinades, knowing the prudent and ultra-pacific character of the boy, but preferred to ascribe it to revenge on the part of the friars, because of his having rescued from servitude Juli, the daughter of a tulisan who was the mortal enemy of a certain powerful corporation. As they had quite a poor idea of the morality of that same corporation and could recall cases of petty revenge, their conjecture was believed to have more probability and justification.

"What a good thing I did when I drove her from my house!" said Sister Penchang. "I don't want to have any trouble with the friars, so I urged her to find the money."

The truth was, however, that she regretted Juli's liberty, for Juli prayed and fasted for her, and if she had stayed a longer time, would also have done penance. Why, if the curates pray for us and Christ died for our sins, couldn't Juli do the same for Sister Penchang?

When the news reached the hut where the poor Juli and her grandfather lived, the girl had to have it repeated to her. She stared at Sister Bali, who was telling it, as though without comprehension, without ability to collect her thoughts. Her ears buzzed, she felt a sinking at the heart and had a vague presentiment that this event would have a disastrous influence on her own future. Yet she tried to seize upon a ray of hope, she smiled, thinking that Sister Bali was joking with her, a rather strong joke, to be sure, but she forgave her beforehand if she would acknowledge that it was such. But Sister Bali made a cross with one of her thumbs and a forefinger, and kissed it, to prove that she was telling the truth. Then the smile faded forever from the girl's lips, she turned pale, frightfully pale, she felt her strength leave her and for the first time in her life she lost consciousness, falling into a swoon.

When by dint of blows, pinches, dashes of water, crosses, and the application of sacred palms, the girl recovered and remembered the situation, silent tears sprang from her eyes, drop by drop, without sobs, without laments, without complaints! She thought about Basilio, who had had no other protector than Capitan Tiago, and who now, with the Capitan dead, was left completely unprotected and in prison. In the Philippines it is a well-known fact that patrons are needed for everything, from the time one is christened until one dies, in order to get justice, to secure a passport, or to develop an industry. As it was said that his imprisonment was due to revenge on account of herself and her father, the girl's sorrow turned to desperation. Now it was her duty to liberate him, as he had done in rescuing her from servitude, and the inner voice which suggested the idea offered to her imagination a horrible means.

"Padre Camorra, the curate," whispered the voice. Juli gnawed at her lips and became lost in gloomy meditation.

As a result of her father's crime, her grandfather had been arrested in the hope that by such means the son could be made to appear. The only one who could get him his liberty was Padre Camorra, and Padre Camorra had shown himself to be poorly satisfied with her words of gratitude, having with his usual frankness asked for some sacrifices—since which time Juli had tried to avoid meeting him. But the curate made her kiss his hand, he twitched her nose and patted her cheeks, he joked with her, winking and laughing, and laughing he pinched her. Juli was also the cause of the beating the good curate had administered to some young men who were going about the village serenading the girls. Malicious ones, seeing her pass sad and dejected, would remark so that she might hear: "If she only wished it, Cabesang Tales would be pardoned."

Juli reached her home, gloomy and with wandering looks. She had changed greatly, having lost her merriment, and no one ever saw her smile again. She scarcely spoke and seemed to be afraid to look at her own face. One day she was seen in the town with a big spot of soot on her forehead, she who used to go so trim and neat. Once she asked Sister Bali if the people who committed suicide went to hell.

"Surely!" replied that woman, and proceeded to describe the place as though she had been there.

Upon Basilio's imprisonment, the simple and grateful relatives had planned to make all kinds of sacrifices to save the young man, but as they could collect among themselves no more than thirty pesos, Sister Bali, as usual, thought of a better plan.

"What we must do is to get some advice from the town clerk," she said. To these poor people, the town clerk was what the Delphic oracle was to the ancient Greeks.

"By giving him a real and a cigar," she continued, "he'll tell you all the laws so that your head bursts listening to him. If you have a peso, he'll save you, even though you may be at the foot of the scaffold. When my friend Simon was put in jail and flogged for not being able to give evidence about a robbery perpetrated near his house, *abá*, for two reales and a half and a string of garlics, the town clerk got him out. And I saw Simon myself when he could scarcely walk and he had to stay in bed at least a month. Ay, his flesh rotted as a result and he died!"

Sister Bali's advice was accepted and she herself volunteered to interview the town clerk. Juli gave her four reales and added some strips of jerked venison her grand-father had got, for Tandang Selo had again devoted himself to hunting.

But the town clerk could do nothing—the prisoner was in Manila, and his power did not extend that far. "If at least he were at the capital, then—" he ventured, to make a show of his authority, which he knew very well did not extend beyond the boundaries of Tiani, but he had to maintain his prestige and keep the jerked venison. "But I can give you a good piece of advice, and it is that you go with Juli to see the Justice of the Peace. But it's very necessary that Juli go."

The Justice of the Peace was a very rough fellow, but if he should see Juli he might conduct himself less rudely—this is wherein lay the wisdom of the advice.

With great gravity the honorable Justice listened to Sister Bali, who did the talking, but not without staring from time to time at the girl, who hung her head with shame. People would say that she was greatly interested in Basilio, people who did not remember her debt of gratitude, nor that his imprisonment, according to report, was on her account.

After belching three or four times, for his Honor had that ugly habit, he said that the only person who could save Basilio was Padre Camorra, *in case he should care to do so.* Here he stared meaningly at the girl and advised her to deal with the curate in person.

"You know what influence he has,—he got your grand-father out of jail. A report from him is enough to deport a new-born babe or save from death a man with the noose about his neck."

Juli said nothing, but Sister Bali took this advice as though she had read it in a novena, and was ready to accompany the girl to the convento. It so happened that she was just going there to get as alms a scapulary in exchange for four full reales.

But Juli shook her head and was unwilling to go to the convento. Sister Bali thought she could guess the reason—Padre Camorra was reputed to be very fond of the women and was very frolicsome—so she tried to reassure her. "You've nothing to fear if I go with you. Haven't you read in the booklet *Tandang Basio,* given you by the curate, that the girls should go to the convento, even without the knowledge of their elders, to relate what is going on at home? *Abá,* that book is printed with the permission of the Archbishop!"

Juli became impatient and wished to cut short such talk, so she begged the pious woman to go if she wished, but his Honor observed with a belch that the supplications of a youthful face were more moving than those of an old one, the sky poured its dew over the fresh flowers in greater abundance than over the withered ones. The metaphor was fiendishly beautiful.

Juli did not reply and the two left the house. In the street the girl firmly refused to go to the convento and they returned to their village. Sister Bali, who felt offended at this lack of confidence in herself, on the way home relieved her feelings by administering a long preachment to the girl.

The truth was that the girl could not take that step without damning herself in her own eyes, besides being cursed of men and cursed of God! It had been intimated to her several times, whether with reason or not, that if she would make that sacrifice her father would be pardoned, and yet she had refused, in spite of the cries of her conscience reminding her of her filial duty. Now must she make it for Basilio, her sweetheart? That would be to fall to the sound of mockery and laughter from all creation. Basilio himself would despise her! No, never! She would first hang herself or leap from some precipice. At any rate, she was already damned for being a wicked daughter.

The poor girl had besides to endure all the reproaches of her relatives, who, knowing nothing of what had passed between her and Padre Camovra, laughed at her fears. Would Padre Camorra fix his attention upon a country girl when there were so many others in the town? Hero the good women cited names of unmarried girls, rich and beautiful, who had been more or less unfortunate. Meanwhile, if they should shoot Basilio?

Juli covered her ears and stared wildly about, as if seeking a voice that might plead for her, but she saw only her grandfather, who was dumb and had his gaze fixed on his hunting-spear.

That night she scarcely slept at all. Dreams and nightmares, some funereal, some bloody, danced before her sight and woke her often, bathed in cold perspiration. She fancied that she heard shots, she imagined that she saw her father, that father who had done so much for her, fighting in the forests, hunted like a wild beast because she had refused to save him. The figure of her father was transformed and she recognized Basilio, dying, with looks of reproach at her. The wretched girl arose, prayed, wept, called upon her mother, upon death, and there was even a moment when, overcome with terror, if it had not been night-time, she would have run straight to the convento, let happen what would.

With the coming of day the sad presentiments and the terrors of darkness were partly dissipated. The light inspired hopes in her. But the news of the afternoon was terrible, for there was talk of persons shot, so the next night was for the girl frightful. In her desperation she decided to give herself up as soon as day dawned and then kill herself afterwards—anything, rather than enditre such tortures! But the dawn brought new hope and she would not go to church or even leave the house. She was afraid she would yield.

So passed several days in praying and cursing, in calling upon God and wishing for death. The day gave her a slight respite and she trusted in some miracle. The reports that came from Manila, although they reached there magnified, said that of the prisoners some had secured their liberty, thanks to patrons and influence. Some one had to be sacrificed—who would it be? Juli shuddered and returned home biting her finger-nails. Then came the night with its terrors, which took on double proportions and seemed to be converted into realities. Juli feared to fall asleep, for her slumbers were a continuous nightmare. Looks of reproach would flash across her eyelids just as soon as they were closed, complaints and laments pierced her ears. She saw her father wandering about hungry, without rest or repose; she saw Basilio dying in the road, pierced by two bullets, just as she had seen the corpse of that neighbor who had been killed while in the charge of the Civil Guard. She saw the bonds that cut into the flesh, she saw the blood pouring from the mouth, she heard Basilio calling to her, "Save me! Save me! You alone can save me!" Then a burst of laughter would resound and she would turn her eyes to see her father gazing at her with eyes full of reproach. Juli would wake up, sit up on her *petate*, and draw her hands across her forehead to arrange her hair—cold sweat, like the sweat of death, moistened it!

"Mother, mother!" she sobbed.

Meanwhile, they who were so carelessly disposing of people's fates, he who commanded the legal murders, he who violated justice and made use of the law to maintain himself by force, slept in peace.

At last a traveler arrived from Manila and reported that all the prisoners had been set free, all except Basilio, who had no protector. It was reported in Manila, added the traveler, that the young man would be deported to the Carolines, having been forced to sign a petition beforehand, in which he declared that he asked it voluntarily.' The traveler had seen the very steamer that was going to take him away.

This report put an end to all the girl's hesitation. Besides, her mind was already quite weak from so many nights of watching and horrible dreams. Pale and with unsteady eyes, she sought out Sister Bali and, in a voice that was cause for alarm, told her that she was ready, asking her to accompany her. Sister Bali thereupon rejoiced and tried to soothe her, but Juli paid no attention to her, apparently intent only upon hurrying to the convento. She had decked herself out in her finest clothes, and even pretended to be quite gay, talking a great deal, although in a rather incoherent way.

So they set out. Juli went ahead, becoming impatient that her companion lagged behind. But as they neared the town, her nervous energy began gradually to abate, she fell silent and wavered in her resolution, lessened her pace and soon dropped behind, so that Sister Bali had to encourage her.

"We'll get there late," she remonstrated.

Juli now followed, pale, with downcast eyes, which she was afraid to raise. She felt that the whole world was staring at her and pointing its finger at her. A vile name whistled in her ears, but still she disregarded it and continued on her way. Nevertheless, when they came in sight of the convento, she stopped and began to tremble.

"Let's go home, let's go home," she begged, holding her companion back.

Sister Bali had to take her by the arm and half drag her along, reassuring her and telling her about the books of the friars. She would not desert her, so there was nothing to fear. Padre Camorra had other things in mind—Juli was only a poor country girl.

But upon arriving at the door of the convento, Juli firmly refused to go in, catching hold of the wall.

"No, no," she pleaded in terror. "No, no, no! Have pity!"

"But what a fool—"

Sister Bali pushed her gently along, Juli, pallid and with wild features, offering resistance. The expression of her face said that she saw death before her.

"All right, let's go back, if you don't want to!" at length the good woman exclaimed in irritation, as she did not believe there was any real danger. Padre Camorra, in spite of all his reputation, would dare do nothing before her.

"Let them carry poor Basilio into exile, let them shoot him on the way, saying that he tried to escape," she added. "When he's dead, then remorse will come. But as for myself, I owe him no favors, so he can't reproach me!"

That was the decisive stroke. In the face of that reproach, with wrath and desperation mingled, like one who rushes to suicide, Juli closed her eyes in order not to see the abyss into which she was hurling herself and resolutely entered the convento. A sigh that sounded like the rattle of death escaped from her lips. Sister Bali followed, telling her how to act.

That night comments were mysteriously whispered about certain events which had occurred that afternoon. A girl had leaped from a window of the convento, falling upon some stones and killing herself. Almost at the same time another woman had rushed out of the convento to run through the streets shouting and screaming like a lunatic. The prudent townsfolk dared not utter any names and many mothers pinched their daughters for letting slip expressions that might compromise them.

Later, very much later, at twilight, an old man came from a village and stood calling at the door of the convento, which was closed and guarded by sacristans. The old man beat the door with his fists and with his head, while he littered cries stifled and inarticulate, like those of a dumb person, until he was at length driven away by blows and shoves. Then he made his way to the gobernadorcillo's house, but was told that the gobernadorcillo was not there, he was at the convento; he went to the Justice of the Peace, but neither was the Justice of the Peace at home—he had been summoned to the convento; he went to the teniente-mayor, but he too was at the convento; he directed his steps to the barracks, but the lieutenant of the Civil Guard was at the convento. The old man then returned to his village, weeping like a child. His wails were heard in the middle of the night, causing men to bite their lips and women to clasp their hands, while the dogs slunk fearfully back into the houses with their tails between their legs.

"Ah, God, God!" said a poor woman, lean from fasting, "in Thy presence there is no rich, no poor, no white, no black—Thou wilt grant us justice!"

"Yes," rejoined her husband, "just so that God they preach is not a pure invention, a fraud! They themselves are the first not to believe in Him."

At eight o'clock in the evening it was rumored that more than seven friars, proceeding from neighboring towns, were assembled in the convento to hold a conference. On the following day, Tandang Selo disappeared forever from the village, carrying with him his hunting-spear.

---

1   The native priests Burgos, Gomez, and Zamora, charged with complicity in the uprising of 1872, and executed.—Tr.
2   This versicle, found in the booklets of prayer, is common on the scapularies, which, during the late insurrection, were easily converted into the *anting-anting*, or amulets, worn by the fanatics.—Tr.
3   This practise—secretly compelling suspects to sign a request to be transferred to some other island—was by no means a figment of the author's imagination, but was extensively practised to anticipate any legal difficulties that might arise.—Tr.

THE HIGH OFFICIAL

L'Espagne et sa, vertu, l'Espagne et sa grandeur
Tout s'en va!—Victor Hugo

The newspapers of Manila were so engrossed in accounts of a notorious murder committed in Europe, in panegyrics and puffs for various preachers in the city, in the constantly increasing success of the French operetta, that they could scarcely devote space to the crimes perpetrated in the provinces by a band of tulisanes headed by a fierce and terrible leader who was called *Matanglawin.*[1] Only when the object of the attack was a convento or a Spaniard there then appeared long articles giving frightful details and asking for martial law, energetic measures, and so on. So it was that they could take no notice of what had occurred in the town of Tiani, nor was there the slightest hint or allusion to it. In private circles something was whispered, but so confused, so vague, and so little consistent, that not even the name of the victim was known, while those who showed the greatest interest forgot it quickly, trusting that the affair had been settled in some way with the wronged family. The only one who knew anything certain was Padre Camorra, who had to leave the town, to be transferred to another or to remain for some time in the convento in Manila.

"Poor Padre Camorra!" exclaimed Ben-Zayb in a fit of generosity. "He was so jolly and had such a good heart!"

It was true that the students had recovered their liberty, thanks to the exertions of their relatives, who did not hesitate at expense, gifts, or any sacrifice whatsoever. The first to see himself free, as was to be expected, was Makaraig, and the last Isagani, because Padre Florentine did not reach Manila until a week after the events. So many acts of clemency secured for the General the title of clement and merciful, which Ben-Zayb hastened to add to his long list of adjectives.

The only one who did not obtain his liberty was Basilio, since he was also accused of having in his possession prohibited books. We don't know whether this referred to his text-book on legal medicine or to the pamphlets that were found, dealing with the Philippines, or both together—the fact is that it was said that prohibited literature was being secretly sold, and upon the unfortunate boy fell all the weight of the rod of justice.

It was reported that his Excellency had been thus advised: "It's necessary that there be some one, so that the prestige of authority may be sustained and that it may not be said that we made a great fuss over nothing. Authority before everything. It's necessary that some one be made an example of. Let there be just one, one who, according to Padre Irene, was the servant of Capitan Tiago—there'll be no one to enter a complaint—"

"Servant and student?" asked his Excellency. "That fellow, then! Let it be he!"

"Your Excellency will pardon me," observed the high official, who happened to be present, "but I've been told that this boy is a medical student and his teachers speak well of him. If he remains a prisoner he'll lose a year, and as this year he finishes—"

The high official's interference in behalf of Basilio, instead of helping, harmed him. For some time there had been between this official and his Excellency strained relations and bad feelings, augmented by frequent clashes.

"Yes? So much the greater reason that he should be kept prisoner; a year longer in his studies, instead of injuring him, will do good, not only to himself but to all who afterwards fall into his hands. One doesn't become a bad physician by extensive practise. So much the more reason that he should remain! Soon the filibustering reformers will say that we are not looking out for the country!" concluded his Excellency with a sarcastic laugh.

The high official realized that he had made a false move and took Basilio's case to heart. "But it seems to me that this young man is the most innocent of all," he rejoined rather timidly.

"Books have been seized in his possession," observed the secretary.

"Yes, works on medicine and pamphlets written by Peninsulars, with the leaves uncut, and besides, what does that signify? Moreover, this young man was not present at the banquet in the *pansitería*, he hasn't mixed up in anything. As I've said, he's the most innocent—"

"So much the better!" exclaimed his Excellency jocosely. "In that way the punishment will prove more salutary and exemplary, since it inspires greater terror. To govern is to act in this way, my dear sir, as it is often expedient to sacrifice the welfare of one to the welfare of many. But I'm doing more—from the welfare of one will result the welfare of all, the principle of endangered authority is preserved, prestige is respected and maintained. By this act of mine I'm correcting my own and other people's faults."

The high official restrained himself with an effort and, disregarding the allusion, decided to take another tack. "But doesn't your Excellency fear the—responsibility?"

"What have I to fear?" rejoined the General impatiently. "Haven't I discretionary powers? Can't I do what I please for the better government of these islands? What have I to fear? Can some menial perhaps arraign me before the tribunals and exact from me responsibility? Even though he had the means, he would have to consult the Ministry first, and the Minister—"

He waved his hand and burst out into laughter.

"The Minister who appointed me, the devil knows where he is, and he will feel honored in being able to welcome me when I return. The present one, I don't even think of him, and the devil take him too! The one that relieves him will find himself in so many difficulties with his new duties that he won't be able to fool with trifles. I, my dear sir, have nothing over me but my conscience, I act according to my conscience, and my conscience is satisfied, so I don't care a straw for the opinions of this one and that. My conscience, my dear sir, my conscience!"

"Yes, General, but the country—"

"Tut, tut, tut, tut! The country—what have I to do Avith the country? Have I perhaps contracted any obligations to it? Do I owe my office to it? Was it the country that elected me?"

A brief pause ensued, during which the high official stood with bowed head. Then, as if reaching a decision, he raised it to stare fixedly at the General. Pale and trembling, he said with repressed energy: "That doesn't matter, General, that doesn't matter at all!

Your Excellency has not been chosen by the Filipino people, but by Spain, all the more reason why you should treat the Filipinos well so that they may not be able to reproach Spain. The greater reason, General, the greater reason! Your Excellency, by coming here, has contracted the obligation to govern justly, to seek the welfare—"

"Am I not doing it?" interrupted his Excellency in exasperation, taking a step forward. "Haven't I told you that I am getting from the good of one the good of all? Are you now going to give me lessons? If you don't understand my actions, how am I to blame? Do I compel you to share my responsibility?"

"Certainly not," replied the high official, drawing himself up proudly. "Your Excellency does not compel me, your Excellency cannot compel me, *me*, to share *your* responsibility. I understand mine in quite another way, and because I have it, I'm going to speak—I've held my peace a long time. Oh, your Excellency needn't make those gestures, because the fact that I've come here in this or that capacity doesn't mean that I have given up my rights, that I have been reduced to the part of a slave, without voice or dignity.

"I don't want Spain to lose this beautiful empire, these eight millions of patient and submissive subjects, who live on hopes and delusions, but neither do I wish to soil my hands in their barbarous exploitation. I don't wish it ever to be said that, the slave-trade abolished, Spain has continued to cloak it with her banner and perfect it under a wealth of specious institutions. No, to be great Spain does not have to be a tyrant, Spain is sufficient unto herself, Spain was greater when she had only her own territory, wrested from the clutches of the Moor. I too am a Spaniard, but before being a Spaniard I am a man, and before Spain and above Spain is her honor, the lofty principles of morality, the eternal principles of immutable justice! Ah, you are surprised that I think thus, because you have no idea of the grandeur of the Spanish name, no, you haven't any idea of it, you identify it with persons and interests. To you the Spaniard may be a pirate, he may be a murderer, a hypocrite, a cheat, anything, just so he keep what he has—but to me the Spaniard should lose everything, empire, power, wealth, everything, before his honor! Ah, my dear sir, we protest when we read that might is placed before right, yet we applaud when in practise we see might play the hypocrite in not only perverting right but even in using it as a tool in order to gain control. For the very reason that I love Spain, I'm speaking now, and I defy your frown!

"I don't wish that the coming ages accuse Spain of being the stepmother of the nations, the vampire of races, the tyrant of small islands, since it would be a horrible mockery of the noble principles of our ancient kings. How are we carrying out their sacred legacy? They promised to these islands protection and justice, and we are playing with the lives and liberties of the inhabitants; they promised civilization, and^we are curtailing it, fearful that they may aspire to a nobler existence; they promised them light, and we cover their eyes that they may not witness our orgies; they promised to teach them virtue and we are encouraging their vice. Instead of peace, wealth, and justice, confusion reigns, commerce languishes, and skepticism is fostered among the masses.

"Let us put ourselves in the place of the Filipinos and ask ourselves what we would do in their place. Ah, in your silence I read their right to rebel, and if matters do not mend they will rebel some day, and justice will be on their side, with them will go the sympathy of all honest men, of every patriot in the world! When a people is denied light, home, liberty, and justice—things that are essential to life, and therefore man's patrimony—that people has the right to treat him who so despoils it as we would the robber who intercepts us on the highway. There are no distinctions, there are no exceptions, nothing but a fact, a right, an aggression, and every honest man who does not place himself on the side of the wronged makes himself an accomplice and stains his conscience.

"True, I am not a soldier, and the years are cooling the little fire in my blood, but just as I would risk being torn to pieces to defend the integrity of Spain against any foreign invader or against an unjustified disloyalty in her provinces, so I also assure you that I would place myself beside the oppressed Filipinos, because I would prefer to fall in the cause of the outraged rights of humanity to triumphing with the selfish interests of a nation, even when that nation be called as it is called—Spain!"

"Do you know when the mail-boat leaves?" inquired his Excellency coldly, when the high official had finished speaking.

The latter stared at him fixedly, then dropped his head and silently left the palace.

Outside he found his carriage awaiting him. "Some day when you declare yourselves independent," he said somewhat abstractedly to the native lackey who opened the carriage-door for him, "remember that there were not lacking in Spain hearts that beat for you and struggled for your rights!"

"Where, sir?" asked the lackey, who had understood nothing of this and was inquiring whither they should go.

Two hours later the high official handed in his resignation and announced his intention of returning to Spain by the next mail-steamer.

---

1   "Hawk-Eye."—Tr.

EFFECT OF THE PASQUINADES

As a result of the events narrated, many mothers ordered their sons immediately to leave off their studies and devote themselves to idleness or to agriculture. When the examinations came, suspensions were plentiful, and he was a rare exception who finished the course, if he had belonged to the famous association, to which no one paid any more attention. Pecson, Tadeo, and Juanito Pelaez were all alike suspended—the first receiving his dismissal with his foolish grin and declaring his intention of becoming an officer in some court, while Tadeo, with his eternal holiday realized at last, paid for an illumination and made a bonfire of his books. Nor did the others get off much better, and at length they too had to abandon their studies, to the great satisfaction of their mothers, who always fancy their sons hanged if they should come to understand what the books teach. Juanito Pelaez alone took the blow ill, since it forced him to leave school for his father's store, with whom he was thenceforward to be associated in the business: the rascal found the store much less entertaining, but after some time his friends again noticed his hump appear, a symptom that his good humor was returning. The rich Makaraig, in view of the catastrophe, took good care not to expose himself, and having secured a passport by means of money set out in haste for Europe. It was said that his Excellency, the Captain-General, in his desire to do good by good means, and careful of the interests of the Filipinos, hindered the departure of every one who could not first prove substantially that he had the money to spend and could live in idleness in European cities. Among our acquaintances those who got off best were Isagani and Sandoval: the former passed in the subject he studied under Padre Fernandez and was suspended in the others, while the latter was able to confuse the examining-board with his oratory.

Basilio was the only one who did not pass in any subject, who was not suspended, and who did not go to Europe, for he remained in Bilibid prison, subjected every three days to examinations, almost always the same in principle, without other variation than a change of inquisitors, since it seemed that in the presence of such great guilt all gave up or fell away in horror. And while the documents moldered or were shifted about, while the stamped papers increased like the plasters of an ignorant physician on the body of a hypochondriac, Basilio became informed of all the details of what had happened in Tiani, of the death of Juli and the disappearance of Tandang Selo. Sinong, the abused cochero, who had driven him to San Diego, happened to be in Manila at that time and called to give him all the news.

Meanwhile, Simoun had recovered his health, or so at least the newspapers said. Ben-Zayb rendered thanks to "the Omnipotent who watches over such a precious life," and manifested the hope that the Highest would some day reveal the malefactor, whose crime remained unpunished, thanks to the charity of the victim, who was too closely following the words of the Great Martyr: *Father, forgive them, for they know not what they do.* These and other things Ben-Zayb said in print, while by mouth he was inquiring whether there was any truth in the rumor that the opulent jeweler was going to give a grand fiesta, a banquet such as had never before been seen, in part to celebrate his recovery and in part as a farewell to the country in which he had increased his fortune. It was whispered as certain that Simoun, who would have to leave with the Captain-General, whose command expired in May, was making every effort to secure from Madrid an extension, and that he was advising his Excellency to start a campaign in order to have an excuse for remaining, but it was further reported that for the first time his Excellency had disregarded the advice of his favorite, making it a point of honor not to retain for a single additional day the power that had been conferred upon him, a rumor which encouraged belief that the fiesta announced would take place; very soon. For the rest, Simoun remained unfathomable, since he had become very uncommunicative, showed himself seldom, and smiled mysteriously when the rumored fiesta was mentioned.

"Come, Señor Sindbad," Ben-Zayb had once rallied him, "dazzle us with something Yankee! You owe something to this country."

"Doubtless!" was Simoun's response, with a dry smile.

"You'll throw the house wide open, eh?"

"Maybe, but as I have no house—"

"You ought to have secured Capitan Tiago's, which Señor Pelaez got for nothing."

Simoun became silent, and from that time on he was often seen in the store of Don Timoteo Pelaez, with whom it was said he had entered into partnership. Some weeks afterward, in the month of April, it was rumored that Juanito Pelaez, Don Timoteo's son, was going to marry Paulita Gomez, the girl coveted by Spaniards and foreigners.

"Some men are lucky!" exclaimed other envious merchants. "To buy a house for nothing, sell his consignment of galvanized iron well, get into partnership with a Simoun, and marry his son to a rich heiress—just say if those aren't strokes of luck that all honorable men don't have!"

"If you only knew whence came that luck of Señor Pelaez's!" another responded, in a tone which indicated that the speaker did know. "It's also assured that there'll be a fiesta and on a grand scale," was added with mystery.

It was really true that Paulita was going to marry Juanito Pelaez. Her love for Isagani had gradually waned, like all first loves based on poetry and sentiment. The events of the pasquinades and the imprisonment of the youth had shorn him of all his charms. To whom would it have occurred to seek danger, to desire to share the fate of his comrades, to surrender himself, when every one was hiding and denying any complicity in the affair? It was quixotic, it was madness that no sensible person in Manila could pardon, and Juanito was quite right in ridiculing him, representing what a sorry figure he cut when he went to the Civil Government. Naturally, the brilliant Paulita could no longer love a young man who so erroneously understood social matters and whom all condemned. Then she began to reflect. Juanito was clever, capable, gay, shrewd, the son of a rich merchant of Manila, and a Spanish mestizo besides—if Don Timoteo was to be believed, a full-blooded Spaniard. On the other hand, Isagani was a provincial native who dreamed of forests infested with leeches, he was of doubtful family, with a priest for an uncle, who would perhaps be an enemy to luxury and balls, of which she was very fond. One beautiful morning therefore it occurred to her that she had been a downright fool to prefer him to his rival, and from that time on Pelaez's hump steadily increased. Unconsciously, yet rigorously, Paulita was obeying the law discovered by Darwin, that the female surrenders herself to the fittest male, to him who knows how to adapt himself to the medium in which he lives, and to live in Manila there was no other like Pelaez, who from his infancy had had chicanery at his finger-tips. Lent passed with its Holy Week, its array of processions and pompous displays, without other novelty than a mysterious mutiny among the artillerymen, the cause of which was never disclosed. The houses of light materials were torn down in the presence of a troop of cavalry, ready to fall upon the owners in case they should offer resistance. There was a great deal of weeping and many lamentations, but the affair did not get beyond that. The curious, among them Simoun, went to see those who were left homeless, walking about indifferently and assuring each other that thenceforward they could sleep in peace.

Towards the end of April, all the fears being now forgotten, Manila was engrossed with one topic: the fiesta that Don Timoteo Pelaez was going to celebrate at the wedding of his son, for which the General had graciously and condescendingly agreed to be the patron. Simoun was reported to have arranged the matter. The ceremony would be solemnized two days before the departure of the General, who would honor the house and make a present to the bridegroom. It was whispered that the jeweler would pour out cascades of diamonds and throw away handfuls of pearls in honor of his partner's son, thus, since he could hold no fiesta of his own, as he was a bachelor and had no house, improving the opportunity to dazzle the Filipino people with a memorable farewell. All Manila prepared to be invited, and never did uneasiness take stronger hold of the mind than in view of the thought of not being among those bidden. Friendship with Simoun became a matter of dispute, and many husbands were forced by their wives to purchase bars of steel and sheets of galvanized iron in order to make friends with Don Timoteo Pelaez.

LA ULTIMA RAZÓN

At last the great day arrived. During the morning Simoun had not left his house, busied as he was in packing his arms and his jewels. His fabulous wealth was already locked up in the big steel chest with its canvas cover, there remaining only a few cases containing bracelets and pins, doubtless gifts that he meant to make. He was going to leave with the Captain-General, who cared in no way to lengthen his stay, fearful of what people would say. Malicious ones insinuated that Simoun did not dare remain alone, since without the General's support he did not care to expose himself to the vengeance of the many wretches he had exploited, all the more reason for which was the fact that the General who was coming was reported to be a model of rectitude and might make him disgorge his gains. The superstitious Indians, on the other hand, believed that Simoun was the devil who did not wish to separate himself from his prey. The pessimists winked maliciously and said, "The field laid waste, the locust leaves for other parts!" Only a few, a very few, smiled and said nothing.

In the afternoon Simoun had given orders to his servant that if there appeared a young man calling himself Basilio he should be admitted at once. Then he shut himself up in his room and seemed to become lost in deep thought. Since his illness the jeweler's countenance had become harder and gloomier, while the wrinkles between his eyebrows had deepened greatly. He did not hold himself so erect as formerly, and his head was bowed.

So absorbed was he in his meditations that he did not hear a knock at the door, and it had to be repeated. He shuddered and called out, "Come in!"

It was Basilio, but how altered! If the change that had taken place in Simoun during those two months was great, in the young student it was frightful. His cheeks were hollow, his hair unkempt, his clothing disordered. The tender melancholy had disappeared from his eyes, and in its place glittered a dark light, so that it might be said that he had died and his corpse had revived, horrified with what it had seen in eternity. If not crime, then the shadow of crime, had fixed itself upon his whole appearance. Simoun himself was startled and felt pity for the wretch.

Without any greeting Basilio slowly advanced into the room, and in a voice that made the jeweler shudder said to him, "Señor Simoun, I've been a wicked son and a bad brother—I've overlooked the murder of one and the tortures of the other, and God has chastised me! Now there remains to me only one desire, and it is to return evil for evil, crime for crime, violence for violence!"

Simoun listened in silence, while Basilio continued; "Four months ago you talked to me about your plans. I refused to take part in them, but I did wrong, you have been right. Three months and a half ago the revolution was on the point of breaking out, but I did not then care to participate in it, and the movement failed. In payment for my conduct I've been arrested and owe my liberty to your efforts only. You are right and now I've come to say to you: put a weapon in my hand and let the revolution come! I am ready to serve you, along with all the rest of the unfortunates."

The cloud that had darkened Simoun's brow suddenly disappeared, a ray of triumph darted from his eyes, and like one who has found what he sought he exclaimed: "I'm right, yes, I'm right! Right and Justice are on my side, because my cause is that of the persecuted. Thanks, young man, thanks! You've come to clear away my doubts, to end my hesitation."

He had risen and his face was beaming. The zeal that had animated him when four months before he had explained his plans to Basilio in the wood of his ancestors reappeared in his countenance like a red sunset after a cloudy day.

"Yes," he resumed, "the movement failed and many have deserted me because they saw me disheartened and wavering at the supreme moment. I still cherished something in my heart, I was not the master of all my feelings, I still loved! Now everything is dead in me, no longer is there even a corpse sacred enough for me to respect its sleep. No longer will there be any vacillation, for you yourself, an idealistic youth, a gentle dove, understand the necessity and come to spur me to action. Somewhat late you have opened your eyes, for between you and me together we might have executed marvelous plans, I above in the higher circles spreading death amid perfume and gold, brutalizing the vicious and corrupting or paralyzing the few good, and you below among the people, among the young men, stirring them to life amid blood and tears. Our task, instead of being bloody and barbarous, would have been holy, perfect, artistic, and surely success would have crowned our efforts. But no intelligence would support me, I encountered fear or effeminacy among the enlightened classes, selfishness among the rich, simplicity among the youth, and only in the mountains, in the waste places, among the outcasts, have I found my men. But no matter now! If we can't get a finished statue, rounded out in all its details, of the rough block we work upon let those to come take charge!"

Seizing the arm of Basilio, who was listening without comprehending all he said, he led him to the laboratory where he kept his chemical mixtures. Upon the table was placed a large case made of dark shagreen, similar to those that hold the silver plate exchanged as gifts among the rich and powerful. Opening this, Simoun revealed to sight, upon a bottom of red satin, a lamp of very peculiar shape, Its body was in the form of a pomegranate as large as a man's head, with fissures in it exposing to view the seeds inside, which were fashioned of enormous carnelians. The covering was of oxidized gold in exact imitation of the wrinkles on the fruit.

Simoun took it out with great care and, removing the burner, exposed to view the interior of the tank, which was lined with steel two centimeters in thickness and which had a capacity of over a liter. Basilio questioned him with his eyes, for as yet he comprehended nothing. Without entering upon explanations, Simoun carefully took from a cabinet a flask and showed the young man the formula written upon it.

"Nitro-glycerin!" murmured Basilio, stepping backward and instinctively thrusting his hands behind him. "Nitro-glycerin! Dynamite!" Beginning now to understand, he felt his hair stand on end.

"Yes, nitro-glycerin!" repeated Simoun slowly, with his cold smile and a look of delight at the glass flask. "It's also something more than nitro-glycerin—it's concentrated tears, repressed hatred, wrongs, injustice, outrage. It's the last resort of the weak, force against force, violence against violence. A moment ago I was hesitating, but you have come and decided me. This night the most dangerous tyrants will be blown to pieces, the irresponsible rulers that hide themselves behind God and the State, whose abuses remain unpunished because no one can bring them to justice. This night the Philippines will hear the explosion that will convert into rubbish the formless monument whose decay I have fostered."

Basilio was so terrified that his lips worked without producing any sound, his tongue was paralyzed, his throat parched. For the first time he was looking at the powerful liquid which he had heard talked of as a thing distilled in gloom by gloomy men, in open war against society. Now he had it before him, transparent and slightly yellowish, poured with great caution into the artistic pomegranate. Simoun looked to him like the jinnee of the *Arabian Nights* that sprang from the sea, he took on gigantic proportions, his head touched the sky, he made the house tremble and shook the whole city with a shrug of his shoulders. The pomegranate assumed the form of a colossal sphere, the fissures became hellish grins whence escaped names and glowing cinders. For the first time in his life Basilio was overcome with fright and completely lost his composure.

Simoun, meanwhile, screwed on solidly a curious and complicated mechanism, put in place a glass chimney, then the bomb, and crowned the whole with an elegant shade. Then he moved away some distance to contemplate the effect, inclining his head now to one side, now to the other, thus better to appreciate its magnificent appearance.

Noticing that Basilio was watching him with questioning and suspicious eyes, he said, "Tonight there will be a fiesta and this lamp will be placed in a little dining-kiosk that I've had constructed for the purpose. The lamp will give a brilliant light, bright enough to suffice for the illumination of the whole place by itself, but at the end of twenty minutes the light will fade, and then when some one tries to turn up the wick a cap of fulminate of mercury will explode, the pomegranate will blow up and with it the dining-room, in the roof and floor of which I have concealed sacks of powder, so that no one shall escape."

There wras a moment's silence, while Simoun stared at his mechanism and Basilio scarcely breathed.

"So my assistance is not needed," observed the young man.

"No, you have another mission to fulfill," replied Simoun thoughtfully. "At nine the mechanism will have exploded and the report will have been heard in the country round, in the mountains, in the caves. The uprising that I had arranged with the artillerymen was a failure from lack of plan and timeliness, but this time it won't be so. Upon hearing the explosion, the wretched and the oppressed, those who wander about pursued by force, will sally forth armed to join Cabesang Tales in Santa Mesa, whence they will fall upon the city,[2] while the soldiers, whom I have made to believe that the General is shamming an insurrection in order to remain, will issue from their barracks ready to fire upon whomsoever I may designate. Meanwhile, the cowed populace, thinking that the hour of massacre has come, will rush out prepared to kill or be killed, and as they have neither arms nor organization, you with some others will put yourself at their head and direct them to the warehouses of Quiroga, where I keep my rifles. Cabesang Tales and I will join one another in the city and take possession of it, while you in the suburbs will seize the bridges and throw up barricades, and then be ready to come to our aid to butcher not only those opposing the revolution but also every man who refuses to take up arms and join us."

"All?" stammered Basilio in a choking voice.

"All!" repeated Simoun in a sinister tone. "All—Indians, mestizos, Chinese, Spaniards, all who are found to be without courage, without energy. The race must be renewed! Cowardly fathers will only breed slavish sons, and it wouldn't be worth while to destroy and then try to rebuild with rotten materials. What, do you shudder? Do you tremble, do you fear to scatter death? What is death? What does a hecatomb of twenty thousand wretches signify? Twenty thousand miseries less, and millions of wretches saved from birth! The most timid ruler does not hesitate to dictate a law that produces misery and lingering death for thousands and thousands of prosperous and industrious subjects, happy perchance, merely to satisfy a caprice, a whim, his pride, and yet you shudder because in one night are to be ended forever the mental tortures of many helots, because a vitiated and paralytic people has to die to give place to another, young, active, full of energy!

"What is death? Nothingness, or a dream? Can its specters be compared to the reality of the agonies of a whole miserable generation? The needful thing is to destroy the evil, to kill the dragon and bathe the new people in the blood, in order to make it strong and invulnerable. What else is the inexorable law of Nature, the law of strife in which the weak has to succumb so that the vitiated species be not perpetuated and creation thus travel backwards? Away then with effeminate scruples! Fulfill the eternal laws, foster them, and then the earth will be so much the more fecund the more it is fertilized with blood, and the thrones the more solid the more they rest upon crimes and corpses. Let there be no hesitation, no doubtings! What is the pain of death? A momentary sensation, perhaps confused, perhaps agreeable, like the transition from waking to sleep. What is it that is being destroyed? Evil, suffering—feeble weeds, in order to set in their place luxuriant plants. Do you call that destruction? I should call it creating, producing, nourishing, vivifying!"

Such bloody sophisms, uttered with conviction and coolness, overwhelmed the youth, weakened as he was by more than three months in prison and blinded by his passion for revenge, so he was not in a mood to analyze the moral basis of the matter. Instead of replying that the worst and cowardliest of men is always something more than a plant, because he has a soul and an intelligence, which, however vitiated and brutalized they may be, can be redeemed; instead of replying that man has no right to dispose of one life for the benefit of another, that the right to life is inherent in every individual like the right to liberty and to light; instead of replying that if it is an abuse on the part of governments to punish in a culprit the faults and crimes to which they have driven him by their own negligence or stupidity, how much more so would it be in a man, however great and however unfortunate he might be, to punish in a wretched people the faults of its governments and its ancestors; instead of declaring that God alone can use such methods, that God can destroy because He can create, God who holds in His hands recompense, eternity, and the future, to justify His acts, and man never; instead of these reflections, Basilio merely interposed a cant reflection.

"What will the world say at the sight of such butchery?"

"The world will applaud, as usual, conceding the right of the strongest, the most violent!" replied Simoun with his cruel smile. "Europe applauded when the western nations sacrificed millions of Indians in America, and not by any means to found nations much more moral or more pacific: there is the North with its egotistic liberty, its lynch-law, its political frauds—the South with its turbulent republics, its barbarous revolutions, civil wars, pronunciamientos, as in its mother Spain! Europe applauded when the powerful Portugal despoiled the Moluccas, it applauds while England is destroying the primitive races in the Pacific to make room for its emigrants. Europe will applaud as the end of a drama, the close of a tragedy, is applauded, for the vulgar do not fix their attention on principles, they look only at results. Commit the crime well, and you will be admired and have more partizans than if you had carried out virtuous actions with modesty and timidity."

"Exactly," rejoined the youth, "what does it matter to me, after all, whether they praise or censure, when this world takes no care of the oppressed, of the poor, and of weak womankind? What obligations have I to recognize toward society when it has recognized none toward me?"

"That's what I like to hear," declared the tempter triumphantly. He took a revolver from a case and gave it to Basilio, saying, "At ten o'clock wait for me in front of the church of St. Sebastian to receive my final instructions. Ah, at nine you must be far, very far from Calle Anloague."

Basilio examined the weapon, loaded it, and placed it in the inside pocket of his coat, then took his leave with a curt, "I'll see you later."

---

1   Ultima Razón de Reyes: the last argument of kings—force. (Expression attributed to Calderon de la Barca, the great Spanish dramatist.)—Tr.

2   Curiously enough, and by what must have been more than a mere coincidence, this route through Santa Mesa from San Juan del Monte was the one taken by an armed party in their attempt to enter the city at the outbreak of the Katipunan rebellion on the morning of August 30, 1896. (Foreman's *The Philippine Islands*, Chap. XXVI.)

It was also on the bridge connecting these two places that the first shot in the insurrection against American sovereignty was fired on the night of February 4, 1899.—Tr.

THE WEDDING

Once in the street, Basilio began to consider how he might spend the time until the fatal hour arrived, for it was then not later than seven o'clock. It was the vacation period and all the students were back in their towns, Isagani being the only one who had not cared to leave, but he had disappeared that morning and no one knew his whereabouts—so Basilio had been informed when after leaving the prison he had gone to visit his friend and ask him for lodging. The young man did not know where to go, for he had no money, nothing but the revolver. The memory of the lamp filled his imagination, the great catastrophe that would occur within two hours. Pondering over this, he seemed to see the men who passed before his eyes walking without heads, and he felt a thrill of ferocious joy in telling himself that, hungry and destitute, he that night was going to be dreaded, that from a poor student and servant, perhaps the sun would see him transformed into some one terrible and sinister, standing upon pyramids of corpses, dictating laws to all those who were passing before his gaze now in magnificent carriages. He laughed like one condemned to death and patted the butt of the revolver. The boxes of cartridges were also in his pockets.

A question suddenly occurred to him—where would the drama begin? In his bewilderment he had not thought of asking Simoun, but the latter had warned him to keep away from Calle Anloague. Then came a suspicion: that afternoon, upon leaving the prison, he had proceeded to the former house of Capitan Tiago to get his few personal effects and had found it transformed, prepared for a fiesta—the wedding of Juanito Pelaez! Simoun had spoken of a fiesta.

At this moment he noticed passing in front of him a long line of carriages filled with ladies and gentlemen, conversing in a lively manner, and he even thought he could make out big bouquets of flowers, but he gave the detail no thought. The carriages were going toward Calle Rosario and in meeting those that came down off the Bridge of Spain had to move along slowly and stop frequently. In one he saw Juanito Pelaez at the side of a woman dressed in white with a transparent veil, in whom he recognized Paulita Gomez.

"Paulita!" he ejaculated in surprise, realizing that it was indeed she, in a bridal gown, along with Juanito Pelaez, as though they were just coming from the church. "Poor Isagani!" he murmured, "what can have become of him?"

He thought for a while about his friend, a great and generous soul, and mentally asked himself if it would not be well to tell him about the plan, then answered himself that Isagani would never take part in such a butchery. They had not treated Isagani as they had him.

Then he thought that had there been no imprisonment, he would have been betrothed, or a husband, at this time, a licentiate in medicine, living and working in some corner of his province. The ghost of Juli, crushed in her fall, crossed his mind, and dark flames of hatred lighted his eyes; again he caressed the butt of the revolver, regretting that the terrible hour had not yet come. Just then he saw Simoun come out of the door of his house, carrying in his hands the case containing the lamp, carefully wrapped up, and enter a carriage, which then followed those bearing the bridal party. In order not to lose track of Simoun, Basilio took a good look at the cochero and with astonishment recognized in him the wretch who had driven him to San Diego, Sinong, the fellow maltreated by the Civil Guard, the same who had come to the prison to tell him about the occurrences in Tiani.

Conjecturing that Calle Anloague was to be the scene of action, thither the youth directed his steps, hurrying forward and getting ahead of the carriages, which were, in fact, all moving toward the former house of Capitan Tiago—there they were assembling in search of a ball, but actually to dance in the air! Basilio smiled when he noticed the pairs of civil-guards who formed the escort, and from their number he could guess the importance of the fiesta and the guests. The house overflowed with people and poured floods of light from its windows, the entrance was carpeted and strewn with flowers. Upstairs there, perhaps in his former solitary room, an orchestra was playing lively airs, which did not completely drown the confused tumult of talk and laughter.

Don Timoteo Pelaez was reaching the pinnacle of fortune, and the reality surpassed his dreams. He was, at last, marrying his son to the rich Gomez heiress, and, thanks to the money Simoun had lent him, he had royally furnished that big house, purchased for half its value, and was giving in it a splendid fiesta, with the foremost divinities of the Manila Olympus for his guests, to gild him with the light of their prestige. Since that morning there had been recurring to him, with the persistence of a popular song, some vague phrases that he had read in the communion service. "Now has the fortunate hour come! Now draws nigh the happy moment! Soon there will be fulfilled in you the admirable words of Simoun—'I live, and yet not I alone, but the Captain-General liveth in me.'" The Captain-General the patron of his son! True, he had not attended the ceremony, where Don Custodio had represented him, but he would come to dine, he would bring a wedding-gift, a lamp which not even Aladdin's—between you and me, Simoun was presenting the lamp. Timoteo, what more could you desire?

The transformation that Capitan Tiago's house had undergone was considerable—it had been richly repapered, while the smoke and the smell of opium had been completely eradicated. The immense sala, widened still more by the colossal mirrors that infinitely multiplied the lights of the chandeliers, was carpeted throughout, for the salons of Europe had carpets, and even though the floor was of wide boards brilliantly polished, a carpet it must have too, since nothing should be lacking. The rich furniture of Capitan Tiago had disappeared and in its place was to be seen another kind, in the style of Louis XV. Heavy curtains of red velvet, trimmed with gold, with the initials of the bridal couple worked on them, and upheld by garlands of artificial orange-blossoms, hung as portières and swept the floor with their wide fringes, likewise of gold. In the corners appeared enormous Japanese vases, alternating with those of Sèvres of a clear dark-blue, placed upon square pedestals of carved wood.

The only decorations not in good taste were the screaming chromos which Don Timoteo had substituted for the old drawings and pictures of saints of Capitan Tiago. Simoun had been unable to dissuade him, for the merchant did not want oil-paintings—some one might ascribe them to Filipino artists! He, a patron of Filipino artists, never! On that point depended his peace of mind and perhaps his life, and he knew how to get along in the Philippines! It is true that he had heard foreign painters mentioned—Raphael, Murillo, Velasquez—but he did not know their addresses, and then they might prove to be somewhat seditious. With the chromos he ran no risk, as the Filipinos did not make them, they came cheaper, the effect was the same, if not better, the colors brighter and the execution very fine. Don't say that Don Timoteo did not know how to comport himself in the Philippines!

The large hallway was decorated with flowers, having been converted into a dining-room, with a long table for thirty persons in the center, and around the sides, pushed against the walls, other smaller ones for two or three persons each. Bouquets of flowers, pyramids of fruits among ribbons and lights, covered their centers. The groom's place was designated by a bunch of roses and the bride's by another of orange-blossoms and tuberoses. In the presence of so much finery and flowers one could imagine that nymphs in gauzy garments and Cupids with iridescent wings were going to serve nectar and ambrosia to aerial guests, to the sound of lyres and Aeolian harps.

But the table for the greater gods was not there, being placed yonder in the middle of the wide azotea within a magnificent kiosk constructed especially for the occasion. A lattice of gilded wood over which clambered fragrant vines screened the interior from the eyes of the vulgar without impeding the free circulation of air to preserve the coolness necessary at that season. A raised platform lifted the table above the level of the others at which the ordinary mortals were going to dine and an arch decorated by the best artists would protect the august heads from the jealous gaze of the stars.

On this table were laid only seven plates. The dishes were of solid silver, the cloth and napkins of the finest linen, the wines the most costly and exquisite. Don Timoteo had sought the most rare and expensive in everything, nor would he have hesitated at crime had he been assured that the Captain-General liked to eat human flesh.

THE FIESTA

"Danzar sobre un volcán."

By seven in the evening the guests had begun to arrive: first, the lesser divinities, petty government officials, clerks, and merchants, with the most ceremonious greetings and the gravest airs at the start, as if they were parvenus, for so much light, so many decorations, and so much glassware had some effect. Afterwards, they began to be more at ease, shaking their fists playfully, with pats on the shoulders, and even familiar slaps on the back. Some, it is true, adopted a rather disdainful air, to let it be seen that they were accustomed to better things—of course they were! There was one goddess who yawned, for she found everything vulgar and even remarked that she was ravenously hungry, while another quarreled with her god, threatening to box his ears.

Don Timoteo bowed here and bowed there, scattered his best smiles, tightened his belt, stepped backward, turned halfway round, then completely around, and so on again and again, until one goddess could not refrain from remarking to her neighbor, under cover of her fan: "My dear, how important the old man is! Doesn't he look like a jumping-jack?"

Later came the bridal couple, escorted by Doña Victorina and the rest of the party. Congratulations, hand-shakings, patronizing pats for the groom: for the bride, insistent stares and anatomical observations on the part of the men, with analyses of her gown, her toilette, speculations as to her health and strength on the part of the women.

"Cupid and Psyche appearing on Olympus," thought Ben-Zayb, making a mental note of the comparison to spring it at some better opportunity. The groom had in fact the mischievous features of the god of love, and with a little good-will his hump, which the severity of his frock coat did not altogether conceal, could be taken for a quiver.

Don Timoteo began to feel his belt squeezing him, the corns on his feet began to ache, his neck became tired, but still the General had not come. The greater gods, among them Padre Irene and Padre Salvi, had already arrived, it was true, but the chief thunderer was still lacking. The poor man became uneasy, nervous; his heart beat violently, but still he had to bow and smile; he sat down, he arose, failed to hear what was said to him, did not say what he meant. In the meantime, an amateur god made remarks to him about his chromos, criticizing them with the statement that they spoiled the walls.

"Spoil the walls!" repeated Don Timoteo, with a smile and a desire to choke him. "But they were made in Europe and are the most costly I could get in Manila! Spoil the walls!" Don Timoteo swore to himself that on the very next day he would present for payment all the chits that the critic had signed in his store.

Whistles resounded, the galloping of horses was heard—at last! "The General! The Captain-General!"

Pale with emotion, Don Timoteo, dissembling the pain of his corns and accompanied by his son and some of the greater gods, descended to receive the Mighty Jove. The pain at his belt vanished before the doubts that now assailed him: should he frame a smile or affect gravity; should he extend his hand or wait for the General to offer his? *Carambas!* Why had nothing of this occurred to him before, so that he might have consulted his good friend Simoun?

To conceal his agitation, he whispered to his son in a low, shaky voice, "Have you a speech prepared?"

"Speeches are no longer in vogue, papa, especially on such an occasion as this."

Jupiter arrived in the company of Juno, who was converted into a tower of artificial lights—with diamonds in her hair, diamonds around her neck, on her arms, on her shoulders, she was literally covered with diamonds. She was arrayed in a magnificent silk gown having a long train decorated with embossed flowers.

His Excellency literally took possession of the house, as Don Timoteo stammeringly begged him to do. The orchestra played the royal march while the divine couple majestically ascended the carpeted stairway.

Nor was his Excellency's gravity altogether affected. Perhaps for the first time since his arrival in the islands he felt sad, a strain of melancholy tinged his thoughts. This was the last triumph of his three years of government, and within two days he would descend forever from such an exalted height. What was he leaving behind? His Excellency did not care to turn his head backwards, but preferred to look ahead, to gaze into the future. Although he was carrying away a fortune, large sums to his credit were awaiting him in European banks, and he had residences, yet he had injured many, he had made enemies at the Court, the high official was waiting for him there. Other Generals had enriched themselves as rapidly as he, and now they were ruined. Why not stay longer, as Simoun had advised him to do? No, good taste before everything else. The bows, moreover, were not now so profound as before, he noticed insistent stares and even looks of dislike, but still he replied affably and even attempted to smile.

"It's plain that the sun is setting," observed Padre Irene in Ben-Zayb's ear. "Many now stare him in the face."

The devil with the curate—that was just what he was going to remark!

"My dear," murmured into the ear of a neighbor the lady who had referred to Don Timoteo as a jumping-jack, "did you ever see such a skirt?"

"Ugh, the curtains from the Palace!"

"You don't say! But it's true! They're carrying everything away. You'll see how they make wraps out of the carpets."

"That only goes to show that she has talent and taste," observed her husband, reproving her with a look. "Women should be economical." This poor god was still suffering from the dressmaker's bill.

"My dear, give me curtains at twelve pesos a yard, and you'll see if I put on these rags!" retorted the goddess in pique. "Heavens! You can talk when you have done something fine like that to give you the right!"

Meanwhile, Basilio stood before the house, lost in the throng of curious spectators, counting those who alighted from their carriages. When he looked upon so many persons, happy and confident, when he saw the bride and groom followed by their train of fresh and innocent little girls, and reflected that they were going to meet there a horrible death, he was sorry and felt his hatred waning within him. He wanted to save so many innocents, he thought of notifying the police, but a carriage drove up to set down Padre Salvi and Padre Irene, both beaming with content, and like a passing cloud his good intentions vanished. "What does it matter to me?" he asked himself. "Let the righteous suffer with the sinners."

Then he added, to silence his scruples: "I'm not an informer, I mustn't abuse the confidence he has placed in me. I owe him, *him* more than I do *them*: he dug my mother's grave, they killed her! What have I to do with them? I did everything possible to be good and useful, I tried to forgive and forget, I suffered every imposition, and only asked that they leave me in peace. I got in no one's way. What have they done to me? Let their mangled limbs fly through the air! We've suffered enough."

Then he saw Simoun alight with the terrible lamp in his hands, saw him cross the entrance with bowed head, as though deep in thought. Basilio felt his heart beat fainter, his feet and hands turn cold, while the black silhouette of the jeweler assumed fantastic shapes enveloped in flames. There at the foot of the stairway Simoun checked his steps, as if in doubt, and Basilio held his breath. But the hesitation was transient—Simoun raised his head, resolutely ascended the stairway, and disappeared.

It then seemed to the student that the house was going to blow up at any moment, and that walls, lamps, guests, roof, windows, orchestra, would be hurtling through the air like a handful of coals in the midst of an infernal explosion. He gazed about him and fancied that he saw corpses in place of idle spectators, he saw them torn to shreds, it seemed to him that the air was filled with flames, but his calmer self triumphed over this transient hallucination, which was due somewhat to his hunger.

"Until he comes out, there's no danger," he said to himself. "The Captain-General hasn't arrived yet."

He tried to appear calm and control the convulsive trembling in his limbs, endeavoring to divert his thoughts to other things. Something within was ridiculing him, saying, "If you tremble now, before the supreme moment, how will you conduct yourself when you see blood flowing, houses burning, and bullets whistling?"

His Excellency arrived, but the young man paid no attention to him. He was watching the face of Simoun, who was among those that descended to receive him, and he read in that implacable countenance the sentence of death for all those men, so that fresh terror seized upon him. He felt cold, he leaned against the wall, and, with his eyes fixed on the windows and his ears cocked, tried to guess what might be happening. In the sala he saw the crowd surround Simoun to look at the lamp, he heard congratulations and exclamations of admiration—the words "dining-room," "novelty," were repeated many times—he saw the General smile and conjectured that the novelty was to be exhibited that very night, by the jeweler's arrangement, on the table whereat his Excellency was to dine. Simoun disappeared, followed by a crowd of admirers.

At that supreme moment his good angel triumphed, he forgot his hatreds, he forgot Juli, he wanted to save the innocent. Come what might, he would cross the street and try to enter. But Basilio had forgotten that he was miserably dressed. The porter stopped him and accosted him roughly, and finally, upon his insisting, threatened to call the police.

Just then Simoun came down, slightly pale, and the porter turned from Basilio to salute the jeweler as though he had been a saint passing. Basilio realized from the expression of Simoun's face that he was leaving the fated house forever, that the lamp was lighted. *Alea jacta est!* Seized by the instinct of self-preservation, he thought then of saving himself. It might occur to any of the guests through curiosity to tamper with the wick and then would come the explosion to overwhelm them all. Still he heard Simoun say to the cochero, "The Escolta, hurry!"

Terrified, dreading that he might at any moment hear the awful explosion, Basilio hurried as fast as his legs would carry him to get away from the accursed spot, but his legs seemed to lack the necessary agility, his feet slipped on the sidewalk as though they were moving but not advancing. The people he met blocked the way, and before he had gone twenty steps he thought that at least five minutes had elapsed.

Some distance away he stumbled against a young man who was standing with his head thrown back, gazing fixedly at the house, and in him he recognized Isagani. "What are you doing here?" he demanded. "Come away!"

Isagani stared at him vaguely, smiled sadly, and again turned his gaze toward the open balconies, across which was revealed the ethereal silhouette of the bride clinging to the groom's arm as they moved slowly out of sight.

"Come, Isagani, let's get away from that house. Come!" Basilio urged in a hoarse voice, catching his friend by the arm.

Isagani gently shook himself free and continued to stare with the same sad smile upon his lips.

"For God's sake, let's get away from here!"

"Why should I go away? Tomorrow it will not be she."

There was so much sorrow in those words that Basilio for a moment forgot his own terror. "Do you want to die?" he demanded.

Isagani shrugged his shoulders and continued to gaze toward the house.

Basilio again tried to drag him away. "Isagani, Isagani, listen to me! Let's not waste any time! That house is mined, it's going to blow up at any moment, by the least imprudent act, the least curiosity! Isagani, all will perish in its ruins."

"In its ruins?" echoed Isagani, as if trying to understand, but without removing his gaze from the window.

"Yes, in its ruins, yes, Isagani! For God's sake, come! I'll explain afterwards. Come! One who has been more unfortunate than either you or I has doomed them all. Do you see that white, clear light, like an electric lamp, shining from the azotea? It's the light of death! A lamp charged with dynamite, in a mined dining-room, will burst and not a rat will escape alive. Come!"

"No," answered Isagani, shaking his head sadly. "I want to stay here, I want to see her for the last time. Tomorrow, you see, she will be something different."

"Let fate have its way!" Basilio then exclaimed, hurrying away.

Isagani watched his friend rush away with a precipitation that indicated real terror, but continued to stare toward the charmed window, like the cavalier of Toggenburg waiting for his sweetheart to appear, as Schiller tells. Now the sala was deserted, all having repaired to the dining-rooms, and it occurred to Isagani that Basilio's fears may have been well-founded. He recalled the terrified countenance of him who was always so calm and composed, and it set him to thinking.

Suddenly an idea appeared clear in his imagination—the house was going to blow up and Paulita was there, Paulita was going to die a frightful death. In the presence of this idea everything was forgotten: jealousy, suffering, mental torture, and the generous youth thought only of his love. Without reflecting, without hesitation, he ran toward the house, and thanks to his stylish clothes and determined mien, easily secured admittance.

While these short scenes were occurring in the street, in the dining-kiosk of the greater gods there was passed from hand to hand a piece of parchment on which were written in red ink these fateful words:

Mene, Tekel, Phares[2]
Juan Crisostomo Ibarra

"Juan Crisostomo Ibarra? Who is he?" asked his Excellency, handing the paper to his neighbor.

"A joke in very bad taste!" exclaimed Don Custodio. "To sign the name of a filibuster dead more than ten years!"

"A filibuster!"

"It's a seditious joke!"

"There being ladies present—"

Padre Irene looked around for the joker and saw Padre Salvi, who was seated at the right of the Countess, turn as white as his napkin, while he stared at the mysterious words with bulging eyes. The scene of the sphinx recurred to him.

"What's the matter, Padre Salvi?" he asked. "Do you recognize your friend's signature?"

Padre Salvi did not reply. He made an effort to speak and without being conscious of what he was doing wiped his forehead with his napkin.

"What has happened to your Reverence?"

"It is his very handwriting!" was the whispered reply in a scarcely perceptible voice. "It's the very handwriting of Ibarra." Leaning against the back of his chair, he let his arms fall as though all strength had deserted him.

Uneasiness became converted into fright, they all stared at one another without uttering a single word. His Excellency started to rise, but apprehending that such a move would be ascribed to fear, controlled himself and looked about him. There were no soldiers present, even the waiters were unknown to him.

"Let's go on eating, gentlemen," he exclaimed, "and pay no attention to the joke." But his voice, instead of reassuring, increased the general uneasiness, for it trembled.

"I don't suppose that that *Mene, Tekel, Phares*, means that we're to be assassinated tonight?" speculated Don Custodio.

All remained motionless, but when he added, "Yet they might poison us," they leaped up from their chairs.

The light, meanwhile, had begun slowly to fade. "The lamp is going out," observed the General uneasily. "Will you turn up the wick, Padre Irene?"

But at that instant, with the swiftness of a flash of lightning, a figure rushed in, overturning a chair and knocking a servant down, and in the midst of the general surprise seized the lamp, rushed to the azotea, and threw it into the river. The whole thing happened in a second and the dining-kiosk was left in darkness.

The lamp had already struck the water before the servants could cry out, "Thief, thief!" and rush toward the azotea. "A revolver!" cried one of them. "A revolver, quick! After the thief!"

But the figure, more agile than they, had already mounted the balustrade and before a light could be brought, precipitated itself into the river, striking the water with a loud splash.

---

1   Spanish etiquette requires a host to welcome his guest with the conventional phrase: "The house belongs to you."—Tr.

2   The handwriting on the wall at Belshazzar's feast, foretelling the destruction of Babylon. Daniel, v, 25–28.—Tr.

BEN-ZAYB'S AFFLICTIONS

Immediately upon hearing of the incident, after lights had been brought and the scarcely dignified attitudes of the startled gods revealed, Ben-Zayb, filled with holy indignation, and with the approval of the press-censor secured beforehand, hastened home—an entresol where he lived in a mess with others—to write an article that would be the sublimest ever penned under the skies of the Philippines. The Captain-General would leave disconsolate if he did not first enjoy his dithyrambs, and this Ben-Zayb, in his kindness of heart, could not allow. Hence he sacrificed the dinner and ball, nor did he sleep that night.

Sonorous exclamations of horror, of indignation, to fancy that the world was smashing to pieces and the stars, the eternal stars, were clashing together! Then a mysterious introduction, filled with allusions, veiled hints, then an account of the affair, and the final peroration. He multiplied the flourishes and exhausted all his euphemisms in describing the drooping shoulders and the tardy baptism of salad his Excellency had received on his Olympian brow, he eulogized the agility with which the General had recovered a vertical position, placing his head where his legs had been, and vice versa, then intoned a hymn to Providence for having so solicitously guarded those sacred bones. The paragraph turned out to be so perfect that his Excellency appeared as a hero, and fell higher, as Victor Hugo said.

He wrote, erased, added, and polished, so that, without wanting in veracity—this was his special merit as a journalist—the whole would be an epic, grand for the seven gods, cowardly and base for the unknown thief, "who had executed himself, terror-stricken, and in the very act convinced of the enormity of his crime."

He explained Padre Irene's act of plunging under the table as "an impulse of innate valor, which the habit of a God of peace and gentleness, worn throughout a whole life, had been unable to extinguish," for Padre Irene had tried to hurl himself upon the thief and had taken a straight course along the submensal route. In passing, he spoke of submarine passages, mentioned a project of Don Custodio's, called attention to the liberal education and wide travels of the priest. Padre Salvi's swoon was the excessive sorrow that took possession of the virtuous Franciscan to see the little fruit borne among the Indians by his pious sermons, while the immobility and fright of the other guests, among them the Countess, who "sustained" Padre Salvi (she grabbed him), were the serenity and sang-froid of heroes, inured to danger in the performance of their duties, beside whom the Roman senators surprised by the Gallic invaders were nervous schoolgirls frightened at painted cockroaches.

Afterwards, to form a contrast, the picture of the thief: fear, madness, confusion, the fierce look, the distorted features, and—force of moral superiority in the race—his religious awe to see assembled there such august personages! Here came in opportunely a long imprecation, a harangue, a diatribe against the perversion of good customs, hence the necessity of a permanent military tribunal, "a declaration of martial law within the limits already so declared, special legislation, energetic and repressive, because it is in every way needful, it is of imperative importance to impress upon the malefactors and criminals that if the heart is generous and paternal for those who are submissive and obedient to the law, the hand is strong, firm, inexorable, hard, and severe for those who against all reason fail to respect it and who insult the sacred institutions of the fatherland. Yes, gentlemen, this is demanded not only for the welfare of these islands, not only for the welfare of all mankind, but also in the name of Spain, the honor of the Spanish name, the prestige of the Iberian people, because before all things else Spaniards we are, and the flag of Spain," etc.

He terminated the article with this farewell: "Go in peace, gallant warrior, you who with expert hand have guided the destinies of this country in such calamitous times! Go in peace to breathe the balmy breezes of Manzanares! We shall remain here like faithful sentinels to venerate your memory, to admire your wise dispositions, to avenge the infamous attempt upon your splendid gift, which we will recover even if we have to dry up the seas! Such a precious relic will be for this country an eternal monument to your splendor, your presence of mind, your gallantry!"

In this rather confused way he concluded the article and before dawn sent it to the printing-office, of course with the censor's permit. Then he went to sleep like Napoleon, after he had arranged the plan for the battle of Jena.

But at dawn he was awakened to have the sheets of copy returned with a note from the editor saying that his Excellency had positively and severely forbidden any mention of the affair, and had further ordered the denial of any versions and comments that might get abroad, discrediting them as exaggerated rumors.

To Ben-Zayb this blow was the murder of a beautiful and sturdy child, born and nurtured with such great pain and fatigue. Where now hurl the Catilinarian pride, the splendid exhibition of warlike crime-avenging materials? And to think that within a month or two he was going to leave the Philippines, and the article could not be published in Spain, since how could he say those things about the criminals of Madrid, where other ideas prevailed, where extenuating circumstances were sought, where facts were weighed, where there were juries, and so on? Articles such as his were like certain poisonous rums that are manufactured in Europe, good enough to be sold among the negroes, *good for negroes,* with the difference that if the negroes did not drink them they would not be destroyed, while Ben-Zayb's articles, whether the Filipinos read them or not, had their effect.

"If only some other crime might be committed today or tomorrow," he mused.

With the thought of that child dead before seeing the light, those frozen buds, and feeling his eyes fill with tears, he dressed himself to call upon the editor. But the editor shrugged his shoulders; his Excellency had forbidden it because if it should be divulged that seven of the greater gods had let themselves be surprised and robbed by a nobody, while they brandished knives and forks, that would endanger the integrity of the fatherland! So he had ordered that no search be made for the lamp or the thief, and had recommended to his successors that they should not run the risk of dining in any private house, without being surrounded by halberdiers and guards. As those who knew anything about the events that night in Don Timoteo's house were for the most part military officials and government employees, it was not difficult to suppress the affair in public, for it concerned the integrity of the fatherland. Before this name Ben-Zayb bowed his head heroically, thinking about Abraham, Guzman El Bueno,' or at least, Brutus and other heroes of antiquity.

Such a sacrifice could not remain unrewarded, the gods of journalism being pleased with Abraham Ben-Zayb. Almost upon the hour came the reporting angel bearing the sacrificial lamb in the shape of an assault committed at a country-house on the Pasig, where certain friars were spending the heated season. Here was his opportunity and Ben-Zayb praised his gods.

"The robbers got over two thousand pesos, leaving badly wounded one friar and two servants. The curate defended himself as well as he could behind a chair, which was smashed in his hands."

"Wait, wait!" said Ben-Zayb, taking notes. "Forty or fifty outlaws traitorously—revolvers, bolos, shotguns, pistols—lion at bay—chair—splinters flying—barbarously wounded—ten thousand pesos!"

So great was his enthusiasm that he was not content with mere reports, but proceeded in person to the scene of the crime, composing on the road a Homeric description of the fight. A harangue in the mouth of the leader? A scornful defiance on the part of the priest? All the metaphors and similes applied to his Excellency, Padre Irene, and Padre Salvi would exactly fit the wounded friar and the description of the thief would serve for each of the outlaws. The imprecation could be expanded, since he could talk of religion, of the faith, of charity, of the ringing of bells, of what the Indians owed to the friars, he could get sentimental and melt into Castelarian' epigrams and lyric periods. The señoritas of the city would read the article and murmur, "Ben-Zayb, bold as a lion and tender as a lamb!"

But when he reached the scene, to his great astonishment he learned that the wounded friar was no other than Padre Camorra, sentenced by his Provincial to expiate in the pleasant country-house on the banks of the Pasig his pranks in Tiani. He had a slight scratch on his hand and a bruise on his head received from flattening himself out on the floor. The robbers numbered three or four, armed only with bolos, the sum stolen fifty pesos!

"It won't do!" exclaimed Ben-Zayb. "Shut up! You don't know what you're talking about."

"How don't I know, *puñales?*"

"Don't be a fool—the robbers must have numbered more."

"You ink-slinger—"

So they had quite an altercation. What chiefly concerned Ben-Zayb was not to throw away the article, to give importance to the affair, so that he could use the peroration.

But a fearful rumor cut short their dispute. The robbers caught had made some important revelations. One of the outlaws under *Matanglawin* (Cabesang Tales) had made an appointment with them to join his band in Santa Mesa, thence to sack the conventos and houses of the wealthy. They would be guided by a Spaniard, tall and sunburnt, with white hair, who said that he was acting under the orders of the General, whose great friend he was, and they had been further assured that the artillery and various regiments would join them, wherefore they were to entertain no fear at all. The tulisanes would be pardoned and have a third part of the booty assigned to them. The signal was to have been a cannon-shot, but having waited for it in vain the tulisanes, thinking themselves deceived, separated, some going back to their homes, some returning to the mountains vowing vengeance on the Spaniard, who had thus failed twice to keep his word. Then they, the robbers caught, had decided to do something on their own account, attacking the country-house that they found closest at hand, resolving religiously to give two-thirds of the booty to the Spaniard with white hair, if perchance he should call upon them for it.

The description being recognized as that of Simoun, the declaration was received as an absurdity and the robber subjected to all kinds of tortures, including the electric machine, for his impious blasphemy. But news of the disappearance of the jeweler having attracted the attention of the whole Escolta, and the sacks of powder and great quantities of cartridges having been discovered in his house, the story began to wear an appearance of truth. Mystery began to enwrap the affair, enveloping it in clouds; there were whispered conversations, coughs, suspicious looks, suggestive comments, and trite second-hand remarks. Those who were on the inside were unable to get over their astonishment, they put on long faces, turned pale, and but little was wanting for many persons to lose their minds in realizing certain things that had before passed unnoticed.

"We've had a narrow escape! Who would have said—"

In the afternoon Ben-Zayb, his pockets filled with revolvers and cartridges, went to see Don Custodio, whom he found hard at work over a project against American jewelers. In a hushed voice he whispered between the palms of his hands into the journalist's ear mysterious words.

"Really?" questioned Ben-Zayb, slapping his hand on his pocket and paling visibly.

"Wherever he may be found—" The sentence was completed with an expressive pantomime. Don Custodio raised both arms to the height of his face, with the right more bent than the left, turned the palms of his hands toward the floor, closed one eye, and made two movements in advance. "Ssh! Ssh!" he hissed.

"And the diamonds?" inquired Ben-Zayb.

"If they find him—" He went through another pantomime with the fingers of his right hand, spreading them out and clenching them together like the closing of a fan, clutching out with them somewhat in the manner of the wings of a wind-mill sweeping imaginary objects toward itself with practised skill. Ben-Zayb responded with another pantomime, opening his eyes wide, arching his eyebrows and sucking in his breath eagerly as though nutritious air had just been discovered.

"Sssh!"

---

1   A town in Ciudad Real province, Spain.—Tr.
2   The italicized words are in English in the original.—Tr.
3   A Spanish hero, whose chief exploit was the capture of Gibraltar from the Moors in 1308.—Tr.
4   Emilio Castelar (1832–1899), generally regarded as the greatest of Spanish orators.—Tr.

THE MYSTERY

Todo se sabe

Notwithstanding so many precautions, rumors reached the public, even though quite changed and mutilated. On the following night they were the theme of comment in the house of Orenda, a rich jewel merchant in the industrious district of Santa Cruz, and the numerous friends of the family gave attention to nothing else. They were not indulging in cards, or playing the piano, while little Tinay, the youngest of the girls, became bored playing *chongka* by herself, without being able to understand the interest awakened by assaults, conspiracies, and sacks of powder, when there were in the seven holes so many beautiful cowries that seemed to be winking at her in unison and smiled with their tiny mouths half-opened, begging to be carried up to the *home*. Even Isagani, who, when he came, always used to play with her and allow himself to be beautifully cheated, did not come at her call, for Isagani was gloomily and silently listening to something Chichoy the silversmith was relating. Momoy, the betrothed of Sensia, the eldest of the daughters—a pretty and vivacious girl, rather given to joking—had left the window where he was accustomed to spend his evenings in amorous discourse, and this action seemed to be very annoying to the lory whose cage hung from the eaves there, the lory endeared to the house from its ability to greet everybody in the morning with marvelous phrases of love. Capitana Loleng, the energetic and intelligent Capitana Loleng, had her account-book open before her, but she neither read nor wrote in it, nor was her attention fixed on the trays of loose pearls, nor on the diamonds—she had completely forgotten herself and was all ears. Her husband himself, the great Capitan Toringoy,—a transformation of the name Domingo,—the happiest man in the district, without other occupation than to dress well, eat, loaf, and gossip, while his whole family worked and toiled, had not gone to join his coterie, but was listening between fear and emotion to the hair-raising news of the lank Chichoy.

Nor was reason for all this lacking. Chichoy had gone to deliver some work for Don Timoteo Pelaez, a pair of earrings for the bride, at the very time when they were tearing down the kiosk that on the previous night had served as a dining-room for the foremost officials. Here Chichoy turned pale and his hair stood on end.

"*Nakú!*" he exclaimed, "sacks and sacks of powder, sacks of powder under the floor, in the roof, under the table, under the chairs, everywhere! It's lucky none of the workmen were smoking."

"Who put those sacks of powder there?" asked Capitana Loleng, who was brave and did not turn pale, as did the enamored Momoy. But Momoy had attended the wedding, so his posthumous emotion can be appreciated: he had been near the kiosk.

"That's what no one can explain," replied Chichoy. "Who would have any interest in breaking up the fiesta? There couldn't have been more than one, as the celebrated lawyer Señor Pasta who was there on a visit declared—either an enemy of Don Timoteo's or a rival of Juanito's."

The Orenda girls turned instinctively toward Isagani, who smiled silently.

"Hide yourself," Capitana Loleng advised him. "They may accuse you. Hide!"

Again Isagani smiled but said nothing.

"Don Timoteo," continued Chichoy, "did not know to whom to attribute the deed. He himself superintended the work, he and his friend Simoun, and nobody else. The house was thrown into an uproar, the lieutenant of the guard came, and after enjoining secrecy upon everybody, they sent me away. But—"

"But—but—" stammered the trembling Momoy.

"*Nakú!*" ejaculated Sensia, gazing at her fiancé and trembling sympathetically to remember that he had been at the fiesta. "This young man—If the house had blown up—" She stared at her sweetheart passionately and admired his courage.

"If it had blown up—"

"No one in the whole of Calle Anloague would have been left alive," concluded Capitan Toringoy, feigning valor and indifference in the presence of his family.

"I left in consternation," resumed Chichoy, "thinking about how, if a mere spark, a cigarette had fallen, if a lamp had been overturned, at the present moment we should have neither a General, nor an Archbishop, nor any one, not even a government clerk! All who were at the fiesta last night—annihilated!"

"*Virgen Santísima!* This young man—"

"*'Susmariosep!*" exclaimed Capitana Loleng. "All our debtors were there, *'Susmariosep!* And we have a house near there! Who could it have been?"

"Now you may know about it," added Chichoy in a whisper, "but you must keep it a secret. This afternoon I met a friend, a clerk in an office, and in talking about the affair, he gave me the clue to the mystery—he had it from some government employees. Who do you suppose put the sacks of powder there?"

Many shrugged their shoulders, while Capitan Toringoy merely looked askance at Isagani.

"The friars?"

"Quiroga the Chinaman?"

"Some student?"

"Makaraig?"

Capitan Toringoy coughed and glanced at Isagani, while Chichoy shook his head and smiled.

"The jeweler Simoun."

"Simoun!!"

The profound silence of amazement followed these words. Simoun, the evil genius of the Captain-General, the rich trader to whose house they had gone to buy unset gems, Simoun, who had received the Orenda girls with great courtesy and had paid them fine compliments! For the very reason that the story seemed absurd it was believed. "*Credo quia absurdum,*" said St. Augustine.

"But wasn't Simoun at the fiesta last night?" asked Sensia.

"Yes," said Momoy. "But now I remember! He left the house just as we were sitting down to the dinner. He went to get his wedding-gift."

"But wasn't he a friend of the General's? Wasn't he a partner of Don Timoteo's?"

"Yes, he made himself a partner in order to strike the blow and kill all the Spaniards."

"Aha!" cried Sensia. "Now I understand!"

"What?"

"You didn't want to believe Aunt Tentay. Simoun is the devil and he has bought up the souls of all the Spaniards. Aunt Tentay said so!"

Capitana Loleng crossed herself and looked uneasily toward the jewels, fearing to see them turn into live coals, while Capitan Toringoy took off the ring which had come from Simoun.

"Simoun has disappeared without leaving any traces," added Chichoy. "The Civil Guard is searching for him."

"Yes," observed Sensia, crossing herself, "searching for the devil."

Now many things were explained: Simoun's fabulous wealth and the peculiar smell in his house, the smell of sulphur. Binday, another of the daughters, a frank and lovely girl, remembered having seen blue flames in the jeweler's house one afternoon when she and her mother had gone there to buy jewels. Isagani listened attentively, but said nothing.

"So, last night—" ventured Momoy.

"Last night?" echoed Sensia, between curiosity and fear.

Momoy hesitated, but the face Sensia put on banished his fear. "Last night, while we were eating, there was a disturbance, the light in the General's dining-room went out. They say that some unknown person stole the lamp that was presented by Simoun."

"A thief? One of the Black Hand?"

Isagani arose to walk back and forth.

"Didn't they catch him?"

"He jumped into the river before anybody recognized him. Some say he was a Spaniard, some a Chinaman, and others an Indian."

"It's believed that with the lamp," added Chichoy, "he was going to set fire to the house, then the powder—"

Momoy again shuddered but noticing that Sensia was watching him tried to control himself. "What a pity!" he exclaimed with an effort. "How wickedly the thief acted. Everybody would have been killed."

Sensia stared at him in fright, the women crossed themselves, while Capitan Toringoy, who was afraid of politics, made a move to go away.

Momoy turned to Isagani, who observed with an enigmatic smile: "It's always wicked to take what doesn't belong to you. If that thief had known what it was all about and had been able to reflect, surely he wouldn't have done as he did."

Then, after a pause, he added, "For nothing in the world would I want to be in his place!"

So they continued their comments and conjectures until an hour later, when Isagani bade the family farewell, to return forever to his uncle's side.

FATALITY

Matanglawin was the terror of Luzon. His band had as lief appear in one province where it was least expected as make a descent upon another that was preparing to resist it. It burned a sugar-mill in Batangas and destroyed the crops, on the following day it murdered the Justice of the Peace of Tiani, and on the next took possession of the town of Cavite, carrying off the arms from the town hall. The central provinces, from Tayabas to Pangasinan, suffered from his depredations, and his bloody name extended from Albay in the south to Kagayan in the north. The towns, disarmed through mistrust on the part of a weak government, fell easy prey into his hands—at his approach the fields were abandoned by the farmers, the herds were scattered, while a trail of blood and fire marked his passage. *Matanglawin* laughed at the severe measures ordered by the government against the tulisanes, since from them only the people in the outlying villages suffered, being captured and maltreated if they resisted the band, and if they made peace with it being flogged and deported by the government, provided they completed the journey and did not meet with a fatal accident on the way. Thanks to these terrible alternatives many of the country folk decided to enlist under his command.

As a result of this reign of terror, trade among the towns, already languishing, died out completely. The rich dared not travel, and the poor feared to be arrested by the Civil Guard, which, being under obligation to pursue the tulisanes, often seized the first person encountered and subjected him to unspeakable tortures. In its impotence, the government put on a show of energy toward the persons whom it suspected, in order that by force of cruelty the people should not realize its weakness—the fear that prompted such measures.

A string of these hapless suspects, some six or seven, with their arms tied behind them, bound together like a bunch of human meat, was one afternoon marching through the excessive heat along a road that skirted a mountain, escorted by ten or twelve guards armed with rifles. Their bayonets gleamed in the sun, the barrels of their rifles became hot, and even the sage-leaves in their helmets scarcely served to temper the effect of the deadly May sun.

Deprived of the use of their arms and pressed close against one another to save rope, the prisoners moved along almost uncovered and unshod, he being the best off who had a handkerchief twisted around his head. Panting, suffering, covered with dust which perspiration converted into mud, they felt their brains melting, they saw lights dancing before them, red spots floating in the air. Exhaustion and dejection were pictured in their faces, desperation, wrath, something indescribable, the look of one who dies cursing, of a man who is weary of life, who hates himself, who blasphemes against God. The strongest lowered their heads to rub their faces against the dusky backs of those in front of them and thus wipe away the sweat that was blinding them. Many were limping, but if any one of them happened to fall and thus delay the march he would hear a curse as a soldier ran up brandishing a branch torn from a tree and forced him to rise by striking about in all directions. The string then started to run, dragging, rolling in the dust, the fallen one, who howled and begged to be killed; but perchance he succeeded in getting on his feet and then went along crying like a child and cursing the hour he was born.

The human cluster halted at times while the guards drank, and then the prisoners continued on their way with parched mouths, darkened brains, and hearts full of curses. Thirst was for these wretches the least of their troubles.

"Move on, you sons of—!" cried a soldier, again refreshed, hurling the insult common among the lower classes of Filipinos.

The branch whistled and fell on any shoulder whatsoever, the nearest one, or at times upon a face to leave a welt at first white, then red, and later dirty with the dust of the road.

"Move on, you cowards!" at times a voice yelled in Spanish, deepening its tone.

"Cowards!" repeated the mountain echoes.

Then the cowards quickened their pace under a sky of red-hot iron, over a burning road, lashed by the knotty branch which was worn into shreds on their livid skins. A Siberian winter would perhaps be tenderer than the May sun of the Philippines.

Yet, among the soldiers there was one who looked with disapproving eyes upon so much wanton cruelty, as he marched along silently with his brows knit in disgust. At length, seeing that the guard, not satisfied with the branch, was kicking the prisoners that fell, he could no longer restrain himself but cried out impatiently, "Here, Mautang, let them alone!"

Mautang turned toward him in surprise. "What's it to you, Carolino?" he asked.

"To me, nothing, but it hurts me," replied Carolino. "They're men like ourselves."

"It's plain that you're new to the business!" retorted Mautang with a compassionate smile. "How did you treat the prisoners in the war?"

"With more consideration, surely!" answered Carolino.

Mautang remained silent for a moment and then, apparently having discovered the reason, calmly rejoined, "Ah, it's because they are enemies and fight us, while these—these are our own countrymen."

Then drawing nearer to Carolino he whispered, "How stupid you are! They're treated so in order that they may attempt to resist or to escape, and then—bang!"

Carolino made no reply.

One of the prisoners then begged that they let him stop for a moment.

"This is a dangerous place," answered the corporal, gazing uneasily toward the mountain. "Move on!"

"Move on!" echoed Mautang and his lash whistled.

The prisoner twisted himself around to stare at him with reproachful eyes. "You are more cruel than the Spaniard himself," he said.

Mautang replied with more blows, when suddenly a bullet whistled, followed by a loud report. Mautang dropped his rifle, uttered an oath, and clutching at his breast with both hands fell spinning into a heap. The prisoner saw him writhing in the dust with blood spurting from his mouth.

312

"Halt!" called the corporal, suddenly turning pale.

The soldiers stopped and stared about them. A wisp of smoke rose from a thicket on the height above. Another bullet sang to its accompanying report and the corporal, wounded in the thigh, doubled over vomiting curses. The column was attacked by men hidden among the rocks above.

Sullen with rage the corporal motioned toward the string of prisoners and laconically ordered, "Fire!"

The wretches fell upon their knees, filled with consternation. As they could not lift their hands, they begged for mercy by kissing the dust or bowing their heads—one talked of his children, another of his mother who would be left unprotected, one promised money, another called upon God—but the muzzles were quickly lowered and a hideous volley silenced them all.

Then began the sharpshooting against those who were behind the rocks above, over which a light cloud of smoke began to hover. To judge from the scarcity of their shots, the invisible enemies could not have more than three rifles. As they advanced firing, the guards sought cover behind tree-trunks or crouched down as they attempted to scale the height. Splintered rocks leaped up, broken twigs fell from trees, patches of earth were torn up, and the first guard who attempted the ascent rolled back with a bullet through his shoulder.

The hidden enemy had the advantage of position, but the valiant guards, who did not know how to flee, were on the point of retiring, for they had paused, unwilling to advance; that fight against the invisible unnerved them. Smoke and rocks alone could be seen—not a voice was heard, not a shadow appeared; they seemed to be fighting with the mountain.

"Shoot, Carolino! What are you aiming at?" called the corporal.

At that instant a man appeared upon a rock, making signs with his rifle.

"Shoot him!" ordered the corporal with a foul oath.

Three guards obeyed the order, but the man continued standing there, calling out at the top of his voice something unintelligible.

Carolino paused, thinking that he recognized something familiar about that figure, which stood out plainly in the sunlight. But the corporal threatened to tie him up if he did not fire, so

Carolino took aim and the report of his rifle was heard. The man on the rock spun around and disappeared with a cry that left Carolino horror-stricken.

Then followed a rustling in the bushes, indicating that those within were scattering in all directions, so the soldiers boldly advanced, now that there was no more resistance. Another man appeared upon the rock, waving a spear, and they fired at him. He sank down slowly, catching at the branch of a tree, but with another volley fell face downwards on the rock.

The guards climbed on nimbly, with bayonets fixed ready for a hand-to-hand fight. Carolino alone moved forward reluctantly, with a wandering, gloomy look, the cry of the man struck by his bullet still ringing in his ears. The first to reach the spot found an old man dying, stretched out on the rock. He plunged his bayonet into the body, but the old man did not even wink, his eyes being fixed on Carolino with an indescribable gaze, while with his bony hand he pointed to something behind the rock.

The soldiers turned to see Caroline frightfully pale, his mouth hanging open, with a look in which glimmered the last spark of reason, for Carolino, who was no other than Tano, Cabesang Tales' son, and who had just returned from the Carolines, recognized in the dying man his grandfather, Tandang Selo. No longer able to speak, the old man's dying eyes uttered a whole poem of grief— and then a corpse, he still continued to point to something behind the rock.

CONCLUSION

In his solitary retreat on the shore of the sea, whose mobile surface was visible through the open, windows, extending outward until it mingled with the horizon, Padre Florentino was relieving the monotony by playing on his harmonium sad and melancholy tunes, to which the sonorous roar of the surf and the sighing of the treetops of the neighboring wood served as accompaniments. Notes long, full, mournful as a prayer, yet still vigorous, escaped from the old instrument. Padre Florentino, who was an accomplished musician, was improvising, and, as he was alone, gave free rein to the sadness in his heart.

For the truth was that the old man was very sad. His good friend, Don Tiburcio de Espadaña, had just left him, fleeing from the persecution of his wife. That morning he had received a note from the lieutenant of the Civil Guard, which ran thus:

> MY DEAR CHAPLAIN,—I have just received from the commandant a telegram that says, "Spaniard hidden house Padre Florentino capture forward alive dead." As the telegram is quite explicit, warn your friend not to be there when I come to arrest him at eight tonight.
>
> > Affectionately,
> > PEREZ

Burn this note.

"T-that V-victorina!" Don Tiburcio had stammered. "S-she's c-capable of having me s-shot!"

Padre Florentino was unable to reassure him. Vainly he pointed out to him that the word *cojera* should have read *cogerá*,[1] and that the hidden Spaniard could not be Don Tiburcio, but the jeweler Simoun, who two days before had arrived, wounded and a fugitive, begging for shelter. But Don Tiburcio would not be convinced—*cojera* was his own lameness, his personal description, and it was an intrigue of Victorina's to get him back alive or dead, as Isagani had written from Manila. So the poor Ulysses had left the priest's house to conceal himself in the hut of a woodcutter.

No doubt was entertained by Padre Florentino that the Spaniard wanted was the jeweler Simoun, who had arrived mysteriously, himself carrying the jewel-chest, bleeding, morose, and exhausted. With the free and cordial Filipino hospitality, the priest had taken him in, without asking indiscreet questions, and as news of the events in Manila had not yet reached his ears he was unable to understand the situation clearly. The only conjecture that occurred to him was that the General, the jeweler's friend and protector, being gone, probably his enemies, the victims of wrong and abuse, were now rising and calling for vengeance, and that the acting Governor was pursuing him to make him disgorge the wealth he had accumulated—hence his flight. But whence came his wounds? Had he tried to commit suicide? Were they the result of personal revenge? Or were they merely caused by an accident, as Simoun claimed? Had they been received in escaping from the force that was pursuing him?

This last conjecture was the one that seemed to have the greatest appearance of probability, being further strengthened by the telegram received and Simoun's decided unwillingness from the start to be treated by the doctor from the capital. The jeweler submitted only to the ministrations of Don Tiburcio, and even to them with marked distrust. In this situation Padre Florentino was asking himself what line of conduct he should pursue when the Civil Guard came to arrest Simoun. His condition would not permit his removal, much less a long journey—but the telegram said alive or dead.

Padre Florentine ceased playing and approached the window to gaze out at the sea, whose desolate surface was without a ship, without a sail—it gave him no suggestion. A solitary islet outlined in the distance spoke only of solitude and made the space more lonely. Infinity is at times despairingly mute.

The old man was trying to analyze the sad and ironical smile with which Simoun had received the news that he was to be arrested. What did that smile mean? And that other smile, still sadder and more ironical, with which he received the news that they would not come before eight at night? What did all this mystery signify? Why did Simoun refuse to hide? There came into his mind the celebrated saying of St. John Chrysostom when he was defending the eunuch Eutropius: "Never was a better time than this to say—Vanity of vanities and all is vanity!"

Yes, that Simoun, so rich, so powerful, so feared a week ago, and now more unfortunate than Eutropius, was seeking refuge, not at the altars of a church, but in the miserable house of a poor native priest, hidden in the forest, on the solitary seashore! Vanity of vanities and all is vanity! That man would within a few hours be a prisoner, dragged from the bed where he lay, without respect for his condition, without consideration for his wounds—dead or alive his enemies demanded him! How could he save him? Where could he find the moving accents of the bishop of Constantinople? What weight would his weak words have, the words of a native priest, whose own humiliation this same Simoun had in his better days seemed to applaud and encourage?

But Padre Florentine no longer recalled the indifferent reception that two months before the jeweler had accorded to him when he had tried to interest him in favor of Isagani, then a prisoner on account of his imprudent chivalry; he forgot the activity Simoun had displayed in urging Paulita's marriage, which had plunged Isagani into the fearful misanthropy that was worrying his uncle. He forgot all these things and thought only of the sick man's plight and his own obligations as a host, until his senses reeled. Where must he hide him to avoid his falling into the clutches of the authorities? But the person chiefly concerned was not worrying, he was smiling.

While he was pondering over these things, the old man was approached by a servant who said that the sick man wished to speak with him, so he went into the next room, a clean and well-ventilated apartment with a floor of wide boards smoothed and polished, and simply furnished with big, heavy armchairs of ancient design, without varnish or paint. At one end there was a large kamagon bed with its four posts to support the canopy, and beside it a table covered with bottles, lint, and bandages. A praying-desk at the feet of a Christ and a scanty library led to the suspicion that it was the priest's own bedroom, given up to his guest according to the Filipino custom of offering to the stranger the best table, the best room, and the best bed in the house. Upon seeing the windows opened wide to admit freely the healthful sea-breeze and the echoes of its eternal lament, no one in the Philippines would have said that a sick person was to be found there, since it is the custom to close all the windows and stop up all the cracks just as soon as any one catches a cold or gets an insignificant headache.

Padre Florentine looked toward the bed and was astonished to see that the sick man's face had lost its tranquil and ironical expression. Hidden grief seemed to knit his brows, anxiety was depicted in his looks, his lips were curled in a smile of pain.

"Are you suffering, Señor Simoun?" asked the priest solicitously, going to his side.

"Some! But in a little while I shall cease to suffer," he replied with a shake of his head.

Padre Florentine clasped his hands in fright, suspecting that he understood the terrible truth. "My God, what have you done? What have you taken?" He reached toward the bottles.

"It's useless now! There's no remedy at all!" answered Simoun with a pained smile. "What did you expect me to do? Before the clock strikes eight—alive or dead—dead, yes, but alive, no!"

"My God, what have you done?"

"Be calm!" urged the sick man with a wave of his hand. "What's done is done. I must not fall into anybody's hands—my secret would be torn from me. Don't get excited, don't lose your head, it's useless! Listen—the night is coming on 'and there's no time to be lost. I must tell you my secret, and intrust to you my last request, I must lay my life open before you. At the supreme moment I want to lighten myself of a load, I want to clear up a doubt of mine. You who believe so firmly in God—I want you to tell me if there is a God!"

"But an antidote, Señor Simoun! I have ether, chloroform—"

The priest began to search for a flask, until Simoun cried impatiently, "Useless, it's useless! Don't waste time! I'll go away with my secret!"

The bewildered priest fell down at his desk and prayed at the feet of the Christ, hiding his face in his hands. Then he arose serious and grave, as if he had received from his God all the force, all the dignity, all the authority of the Judge of consciences. Moving a chair to the head of the bed he prepared to listen.

At the first words Simoun murmured, when he told his real name, the old priest started back and gazed at him in terror, whereat the sick man smiled bitterly. Taken by surprise, the priest was not master of himself, but he soon recovered, and covering his face with a handkerchief again bent over to listen.

Simoun related his sorrowful story: how, thirteen years before, he had returned from Europe filled with hopes and smiling illusions, having come back to marry a girl whom he loved, disposed to do good and forgive all who had wronged him, just so they would let him live in peace. But it was not so. A mysterious hand involved him in the confusion of an uprising planned by his enemies. Name, fortune, love, future, liberty, all were lost, and he escaped only through the heroism of a friend. Then he swore vengeance. With the wealth of his family, which had been buried in a wood, he had fled, had gone to foreign lands and engaged in trade. He took part in the war in Cuba, aiding first one side and then another, but always profiting. There he made the acquaintance of the General, then a major, whose good-will he won first by loans of money, and afterwards he made a friend of him by the knowledge of criminal secrets. With his money he had been able to secure the General's appointment and, once in the Philippines, he had used him as a blind tool and incited him to all kinds of injustice, availing himself of his insatiable lust for gold.

The confession was long and tedious, but during the whole of it the confessor made no further sign of surprise and rarely interrupted the sick man. It was night when Padre Florentino, wiping the perspiration from his face, arose and began to meditate. Mysterious darkness flooded the room, so that the moonbeams entering through the window filled it with vague lights and vaporous reflections.

Into the midst of the silence the priest's voice broke sad and deliberate, but consoling: "God will forgive you, Señor—Simoun," he said. "He knows that we are fallible, He has seen that you have suffered, and in ordaining that the chastisement for your faults should come as death from the very ones you have instigated to crime, we can see His infinite mercy. He has frustrated your plans one by one, the best conceived, first by the death of Maria Clara, then by a lack of preparation, then in some mysterious way. Let us bow to His will and render Him thanks!"

"According to you, then," feebly responded the sick man, "His will is that these islands—"

"Should continue in the condition in which they suffer?" finished the priest, seeing that the other hesitated. "I don't know, sir, I can't read the thought of the Inscrutable. I know that He has not abandoned those peoples who in their supreme moments have trusted in Him and made Him the Judge of their cause, I know that His arm has never failed when, justice long trampled upon and every recourse gone, the oppressed have taken up the sword to fight for home and wife and children, for their inalienable rights, which, as the German poet says, shine ever there above, unextinguished and inextinguishable, like the eternal stars themselves. No, God is justice, He cannot abandon His cause, the cause of liberty, without which no justice is possible."

"Why then has He denied me His aid?" asked the sick man in a voice charged with bitter complaint.

"Because you chose means that He could not sanction," was the severe reply. "The glory of saving a country is not for him who has contributed to its ruin. You have believed that what crime and iniquity have defiled and deformed, another crime and another iniquity can purify and redeem. Wrong! Hate never produces anything but monsters and crime criminals! Love alone realizes wonderful works, virtue alone can save! No, if our country has ever to be free, it will not be through vice and crime, it will not be so by corrupting its sons, deceiving some and bribing others, no! Redemption presupposes virtue, virtue sacrifice, and sacrifice love!"

"Well, I accept your explanation," rejoined the sick man, after a pause. "I have been mistaken, but, because I have been mistaken, will that God deny liberty to a people and yet save many who are much worse criminals than I am? What is my mistake compared to the crimes of our rulers? Why has that God to give more heed to my iniquity than to the cries of so many innocents? Why has He not stricken me down and then made the people triumph? Why does

He let so many worthy and just ones suffer and look complacently upon their tortures?"

"The just and the worthy must suffer in order that their ideas may be known and extended! You must shake or shatter the vase to spread its perfume, you must smite the rock to get the spark! There is something providential in the persecutions of tyrants, Señor Simoun!"

"I knew it," murmured the sick man, "and therefore I encouraged the tyranny."

"Yes, my friend, but more corrupt influences than anything else were spread. You fostered the social rottenness without sowing an idea. From this fermentation of vices loathing alone could spring, and if anything were born overnight it would be at best a mushroom, for mushrooms only can spring spontaneously from filth. True it is that the vices of the government are fatal to it, they cause its death, but they kill also the society in whose bosom they are developed. An immoral government presupposes a demoralized people, a conscienceless administration, greedy and servile citizens in the settled parts, outlaws and brigands in the mountains. Like master, like slave! Like government, like country!"

A brief pause ensued, broken at length by the sick man's voice. "Then, what can be done?"

"Suffer and work!"

"Suffer—work!" echoed the sick man bitterly. "Ah, it's easy to say that, when you are not suffering, when the work is rewarded. If your God demands such great sacrifices from man, man who can scarcely count upon the present and doubts the future, if you had seen what I have, the miserable, the wretched, suffering unspeakable tortures for crimes they have not committed, murdered to cover up the faults and incapacity of others, poor fathers of families torn from their homes to work to no purpose upon highways that are destroyed each day and seem only to serve for sinking families into want. Ah, to suffer, to work, is the will of God! Convince them that their murder is their salvation, that their work is the prosperity of the home! To suffer, to work! What God is that?"

"A very just God, Señor Simoun," replied the priest. "A God who chastises our lack of faith, our vices, the little esteem in which we hold dignity and the civic virtues. We tolerate vice, we make ourselves its accomplices, at times we applaud it, and it is just, very just that we suffer the consequences, that our children suffer them. It is the God of liberty, Señor Simoun, who obliges us to love it, by making the yoke heavy for us—a God of mercy, of equity, who while He chastises us, betters us and only grants prosperity to him who has merited it through his efforts. The school of suffering tempers, the arena of combat strengthens the soul.

"I do not mean to say that our liberty will be secured at the sword's point, for the sword plays but little part in modern affairs, but that we must secure it by making ourselves worthy of it, by exalting the intelligence and the dignity of the individual, by loving justice, right, and greatness, even to the extent of dying for them,— and when a people reaches that height God will provide a weapon, the idols will be shattered, the tyranny will crumble like a house of cards and liberty will shine out like the first dawn.

"Our ills we owe to ourselves alone, so let us blame no one. If Spain should see that we were less complaisant with tyranny and more disposed to struggle and suffer for our rights, Spain would be the first to grant us liberty, because when the fruit of the womb reaches maturity woe unto the mother who would stifle it! So, while the Filipino people has not sufficient energy to proclaim, with head erect and bosom bared, its rights to social life, and to guarantee it with its sacrifices, with its own blood; while we see our countrymen in private life ashamed within themselves, hear the voice of conscience roar in rebellion and protest, yet in public life keep silence or even echo the words of him who abuses them in order to mock the abused; while we see them wrap themselves up in their egotism and with a forced smile praise the most iniquitous actions, begging with their eyes a portion of the booty—why grant them liberty? With Spain or without Spain they would always be the same, and perhaps worse! Why independence, if the slaves of today will be the tyrants of tomorrow? And that they will be such is not to be doubted, for he who submits to tyranny loves it.

"Señor Simoun, when our people is unprepared, when it enters the fight through fraud and force, without a clear understanding of what it is doing, the wisest attempts will fail, and better that they do fail, since why commit the wife to the husband if he does not sufficiently love her, if he is not ready to die for her?"

Padre Florentino felt the sick man catch and press his hand, so he became silent, hoping that the other might speak, but he merely felt a stronger pressure of the hand, heard a sigh, and then profound silence reigned in the room. Only the sea, whose waves were rippled by the night breeze, as though awaking from the heat of the day, sent its hoarse roar, its eternal chant, as it rolled against the jagged rocks. The moon, now free from the sun's rivalry, peacefully commanded the sky, and the trees of the forest bent down toward one another, telling their ancient legends in mysterious murmurs borne on the wings of the wind.

The sick man said nothing, so Padre Florentino, deeply thoughtful, murmured: "Where are the youth who will consecrate their golden hours, their illusions, and their enthusiasm to the welfare of their native land? Where are the youth who will generously pour out their blood to wash away so much shame, so much crime, so much abomination? Pure and spotless must the victim be that the sacrifice may be acceptable! Where are you, youth, who will embody in yourselves the vigor of life that has left our veins, the purity of ideas that has been contaminated in our brains, the fire of enthusiasm that has been quenched in our hearts? We await you, O youth! Come, for we await you!"

Feeling his eyes moisten he withdrew his hand from that of the sick man, arose, and went to the window to gaze out upon the wide surface of the sea. He was drawn from his meditation by gentle raps at the door. It was the servant asking if he should bring a light.

When the priest returned to the sick man and looked at him in the light of the lamp, motionless, his eyes closed, the hand that had pressed his lying open and extended along the edge of the bed, he thought for a moment that he was sleeping, but noticing that he was not breathing touched him gently, and then realized that he was dead. His body had already commenced to turn cold. The priest fell upon his knees and prayed.

When he arose and contemplated the corpse, in whose features were depicted the deepest grief, the tragedy of a whole wasted life which he was carrying over there beyond death, the old man shuddered and murmured, "God have mercy on those who turned him from the straight path!"

While the servants summoned by him fell upon their knees and prayed for the dead man, curious and bewildered as they gazed toward the bed, reciting requiem after requiem, Padre Florentino took from a cabinet the celebrated steel chest that contained Simoun's fabulous wealth. He hesitated for a moment, then resolutely descended the stairs and made his way to the cliff where Isagani was accustomed to sit and gaze into the depths of the sea.

Padre Florentino looked down at his feet. There below he saw the dark billows of the Pacific beating into the hollows of the cliff, producing sonorous thunder, at the same time that, smitten by the moonbeams, the waves and foam glittered like sparks of fire, like handfuls of diamonds hurled into the air by some jinnee of the abyss. He gazed about him. He was alone. The solitary coast was lost in the distance amid the dim cloud that the moonbeams played through, until it mingled with the horizon. The forest murmured unintelligible sounds.

Then the old man, with an effort of his herculean arms, hurled the chest into space, throwing it toward the sea. It whirled over and over several times and descended rapidly in a slight curve, reflecting the moonlight on its polished surface. The old man saw the drops of water fly and heard a loud splash as the abyss closed over and swallowed up the treasure. He waited for a few moments to see if the depths would restore anything, but the wave rolled on as mysteriously as before, without adding a fold to its rippling surface, as though into the immensity of the sea a pebble only had been dropped.

"May Nature guard you in her deep abysses among the pearls and corals of her eternal seas," then said the priest, solemnly extending his hands. "When for some holy and sublime purpose man may need you, God will in his wisdom draw you from the bosom of the waves. Meanwhile, there you will not work woe, you will not distort justice, you will not foment avarice!"

---

1   In the original the message reads: "Español escondido casa Padre Florentino cojera remitirá vivo muerto." Don Tiburcio understands *cojera* as referring to himself; there is a play upon the Spanish words *cojera*, lameness, and *cogerá*, a form of the verb *coger*, to seize or capture—*j* and *g* in these two words having the same sound, that of the English *h*.—Tr.

GLOSSARY

abá: A Tagalog exclamation of wonder, surprise, etc., often used to introduce or emphasize a contradictory statement.

alcalde: Governor of a province or district, with both executive and judicial authority.

Ayuntamiento: A city corporation or council, and by extension the building in which it has its offices; specifically, in Manila, the capitol.

balete: The Philippine banyan, a tree sacred in Malay folk-lore.

banka: A dugout canoe with bamboo supports or outriggers.

batalan: The platform of split bamboo attached to a nipa house.

batikúlin: A variety of easily-turned wood, used in carving.

bibinka: A sweetmeat made of sugar or molasses and rice-flour, commonly sold in the small shops.

buyera: A woman who prepares and sells the buyo.

buyo: The masticatory prepared by wrapping a piece of areca-nut with a little shell-lime in a betel-leaf—the pan of British India.

cabesang: Title of a cabeza de barangay; given by courtesy to his wife also.

cabeza de barangay: Headman and tax-collector for a group of about fifty families, for whose "tribute" he was personally responsible.

calesa: A two-wheeled chaise with folding top.

calle: Street (Spanish).

camisa: 1. A loose, collarless shirt of transparent material worn by men outside the trousers. 2. A thin, transparent waist with flowing sleeves, worn by women.

capitan: "Captain," a title used in addressing or referring to a gobernadorcillo, or a former occupant of that office.

carambas: A Spanish exclamation denoting surprise or displeasure.

carbineer: Internal-revenue guard.

carromata: A small two-wheeled vehicle with a fixed top.

casco: A flat-bottomed freight barge.

cayman: The Philippine crocodile.

cedula: Certificate of registration and receipt for poll-tax.

chongka: A child's game played with pebbles or cowry-shells.

cigarrera: A woman working in a cigar or cigarette factory.

Civil Guard: Internal quasi-military police force of Spanish officers and native soldiers.

cochero: Carriage driver, coachman.

cuarto: A copper coin, one hundred and sixty of which were equal in value to a silver peso.

filibuster: A native of the Philippines who was accused of advocating their separation from Spain.

filibusterism: See filibuster.

gobernadorcillo: "Petty governor," the principal municipal official—also, in Manila, the head of a commercial guild.

gumamela: The hibiscus, common as a garden shrub in the Philippines.

Indian: The Spanish designation for the Christianized Malay of the Philippines was indio (Indian), a term used rather contemptuously, the name Filipino being generally applied in a restricted sense to the children of Spaniards born in the Islands.

kalan: The small, portable, open, clay fireplace commonly used in cooking.

kalikut: A short section of bamboo for preparing the buyo; a primitive betel-box.

kamagon: A tree of the ebony family, from which fine cabinet-wood is obtained. Its fruit is the mabolo, or date-plum.

lanete: A variety of timber used in carving.

linintikan: A Tagalog exclamation of disgust or contempt—"thunder!"

Malacañang: The palace of the Captain-General: from the vernacular name of the place where it stands, "fishermen's resort."

Malecon: A drive along the bay shore of Manila, opposite the Walled City.

Mestizo: A person of mixed Filipino and Spanish blood; sometimes applied also to a person of mixed Filipino and Chinese blood.

nakú: A Tagalog exclamation of surprise, wonder, etc.

narra: The Philippine mahogany.

nipa: Swamp palm, with the imbricated leaves of which the roofs and sides of the common native houses are constructed.

novena: A devotion consisting of prayers recited for nine consecutive days, asking for some special favor; also, a booklet of these prayers.

panguingui: A complicated card-game, generally for small stakes, played with a monte deck.

panguinguera: A woman addicted to panguingui, this being chiefly a feminine diversion in the Philippines.

pansit: A soup made of Chinese vermicelli.

pansitería: A shop where pansit is prepared and sold.

pañuelo: A starched neckerchief folded stiffly over the shoulders, fastened in front and falling in a point behind: the most distinctive portion of the customary dress of Filipino women.

peso: A silver coin, either the Spanish peso or the Mexican dollar, about the size of an American dollar and of approximately half its value.

petate: Sleeping-mat woven from palm leaves.

piña: Fine cloth made from pineapple-leaf fibers.

Provincial: The head of a religious order in the Philippines.

puñales: "Daggers!"

querida: A paramour, mistress: from the Spanish "beloved."

real: One-eighth of a peso, twenty cuartos.

sala: The principal room in the more pretentious Philippine houses.

salakot: Wide hat of palm or bamboo, distinctively Filipino.

sampaguita: The Arabian jasmine: a small, white, very fragrant flower, extensively cultivated, and worn in chaplets and rosaries by women and girls—the typical Philippine flower.

sipa: A game played with a hollow ball of plaited bamboo or rattan, by boys standing in a circle, who by kicking it with their heels endeavor to keep it from striking the ground.

soltada: A bout between fighting-cocks.

'Susmariosep: A common exclamation: contraction of the Spanish, Jesús, María, y José, the Holy Family.

tabi: The cry used by carriage drivers to warn pedestrians.

tabú: A utensil fashioned from half of a coconut shell.

tajú: A thick beverage prepared from bean-meal and syrup.

tampipi: A telescopic basket of woven palm, bamboo, or rattan.

Tandang: A title of respect for an old man: from the Tagalog term for "old."

tapis: A piece of dark cloth or lace, often richly worked or embroidered, worn at the waist somewhat in the fashion of an apron; a distinctive portion of the native women's attire, especially among the Tagalogs.

tatakut: The Tagalog term for "fear."

teniente-mayor: "Senior lieutenant," the senior member of the town council and substitute for the gobernadorcillo.

tertiary sister: A member of a lay society affiliated with a regular monastic order.

tienda: A shop or stall for the sale of merchandise.

tikbalang: An evil spirit, capable of assuming various forms, but said to appear usually as a tall black man with disproportionately long legs: the "bogey man" of Tagalog children.

tulisan: Outlaw, bandit. Under the old régime in the Philippines the tulisanes were those who, on account of real or fancied grievances against the authorities, or from fear of punishment for crime, or from an instinctive desire to return to primitive simplicity, foreswore life in the towns "under the bell," and made their homes in the mountains or other remote places. Gathered in small bands with such arms as they could secure, they sustained themselves by highway robbery and the levying of black-mail from the country folk.

BIBLIOBAZAAR

The essential book market!

Did you know that you can get any of our titles in large print?

Did you know that we have an ever-growing collection of books in many languages?

Order online:
www.bibliobazaar.com

Find all of your favorite classic books!

Stay up to date with the latest government reports!

At BiblioBazaar, we aim to make knowledge more accessible by making thousands of titles available to you- *quickly and affordably*.

Contact us:
BiblioBazaar
PO Box 21206
Charleston, SC 29413

7559

LaVergne, TN USA
13 November 2009
164090LV00001B/10/A